EX ON THE BEACH

EX ON THE BEACH

Kim Law

Montlake
Romance

Text copyright © 2013 Kim Law
Originally released as a Kindle Serial, January 2013

Published by Montlake Romance
PO Box 400818
Las Vegas, NV 89140

ISBN-13: 9781477805282
ISBN-10: 1477805281
Library of Congress Control Number: 2013931723

To Kelli. You made working on this book *so much fun!*
You're a true highlight in this crazy
(but fun-and-I-wouldn't-trade-it-for-the-world) business.
Thank you for being you!

EPISODE ONE

CHAPTER ONE

A ndie Shayne bounded up the steps to the wide porch and hurried around to the sliding doors leading to the kitchen. The sound of waves greeted her, stopping her only long enough to glance out at the ocean and smile. High tide was licking at the dunes. She sighed. Turtle Island was the best.

She stepped inside the large, comfortable room and bounced up on the balls of her feet. "I did it," she practically shouted.

Aunt Ginny and Kayla Morgan, Seaglass Celebrations' event director, both looked up from the papers spread across the granite countertop. "You did what?" Aunt Ginny asked.

A grin bloomed across Andie's face as she held the magazine up in front of her with both hands. She'd worked very hard for this.

"I got us in *Today's Brides*. A two-page spread, coming out next month. We'll be the featured business for Georgia."

Both Ginny and Kayla squealed at the news and then hurried over for a round of hugs.

"The photographer had originally wanted to come out in September and run the article in October, but when I mentioned the Jordan wedding, he rearranged his plans." Andie did a little arm-pumping, fist-squeezing wiggle dance. "He'll now be here for the wedding."

More squealing filled the air.

After everyone calmed down, Kayla moved back to the counter and began stacking the loose papers and putting them in a folder. Kayla handled the day-to-day details of coordinating the events, while Andie oversaw the business as a whole. Ginny pitched in wherever was needed. "Ginny and I were just reviewing the names of the wedding party. The first round should start arriving anytime now."

Andie glanced at her watch. She hadn't realized it was after noon already. She'd been running last-minute errands on the mainland and had then spent additional time on the ferry after it docked. She'd still been on the phone to New York, getting everything worked out for the article.

Seaglass Celebrations had been featured in a few smaller bridal magazines over the last couple of years, but this was a big step. They were finally becoming a player. And winning the contract for Penelope Jordan's wedding had gone a long way to getting them there.

They'd gotten a last-minute call only a month before from the Jordans, whose previous plans for their daughter's wedding had been thwarted due to a fire. They'd been looking for a destination site that could handle a full two weeks of pre-wedding activities. Because of a last-minute cancellation on their end, Seaglass had the inn and all eight bungalows available for the full two weeks in question. It was as if the fates in which Aunt Ginny put so much of her trust had been smiling down on them.

The Jordans expected nothing less than a top-of-the-line production, and Andie intended to give it to them.

She scooted in beside Kayla and began scanning over the notes. They had to pull this event off perfectly. A very fat bonus was riding on it. And if they didn't get that bonus, it wouldn't matter what *Today's Brides* said about them. They wouldn't be in business long enough to care.

"Have you—" she started, turning to Kayla.

"I have," Kayla answered, not letting her ask her question. Not even looking up.

"What about—"

"That, too."

"Come on, I just want to make sure—"

"Trust me, Andie," the thirty-year-old began, looking at her boss now. "I've done it. Whatever it is, I swear I've done it. We're going to pull this wedding off with such beautiful precision that no one will be able to guess we only had a month to do it in."

Andie nodded, moistening her lips, forcing herself to relax. "I know. Really, I do." And she knew she'd already asked her most-valued employee to double- and triple-check the details too many times to count. They were ready to go. "I'm just nervous with this one. It's a big deal."

A very big deal. Failing could mean losing her aunt's property. And she had a very bad habit of failing when it counted most.

"I know, darling. Just try to relax. Everything will be okay." Kayla pushed the folder over to Andie and shot her a questioning look. "Anything else before I go? I need to head out front to greet our guests as they arrive."

KIM LAW

Andie shook her head and forced air deep into her lungs. They were going to do this and everything was going to be fine. "I think we're good. We're ready to go."

"Okay, then. Let's get this party started." Kayla stood and moved past the twelve-person table, heading for the door. She glanced back over her shoulder. "You coming out?"

As official hostess, Andie should go, but right then the thought of greeting a happy June bride did nothing for her. She'd rather head over to the bar and spend some quality time behind the counter. Being there always reminded her of her earlier graduate days, those evenings when she'd only been looking forward to the stress of real life, instead of being smack-dab in the middle of it. Probably why she'd bought the bar when she'd had the opportunity.

"I think I'll skip it this time. I want to help over at Gin's for a while. I'll make sure everything is set up and ready to go for the dinner tonight. I'll welcome both families then."

The wedding party would be arriving throughout the afternoon, with activities planned for every day leading up to the big event. Seaglass would handle everything. What they didn't provide themselves, they made off-site arrangements for, and would play host at many of the events. The goal was to make everyone feel as if they were the only priority. Personalized attention was the backbone of the business, and though it was at times exhausting, Andie was proud of what they'd accomplished. All the guests were expected to do was show up, settle in to a comfortable room in either the main inn—the building she was in now—or one of the bungalows, and then proceed to take part in the wedding of the bride and groom's dreams.

4

Kayla poked her head back inside the kitchen. "By the way, you're buying me the biggest drink you can make at the end of these two weeks, you know? While we celebrate that monster bonus you'll be depositing."

Andie forced her lips to form a smile. That check would never even land in their bank account. "You bet I will."

Kayla disappeared and Aunt Ginny gave Andie a quick hug. "You did good, child. That magazine article is going to put us on the map."

"I hope so, Aunt Ginny. I'm doing everything I can think of to make this work."

"I know you are," Ginny said. "We wouldn't be anything but a big ole empty house if it weren't for you. James would have loved seeing what you've turned this place into."

Whitmore Mansion and the surrounding fifteen acres, which included a private beach, had belonged to Aunt Ginny's husband. James had died when Ginny was only thirty-five, the same year Andie had been born. Whitmore had been in his family for generations, and though distant relatives had laid claim on it, it had rightfully belonged to Ginny. She'd lived there since his death, inviting Andie to visit every summer as she'd been growing up. It had been Andie's haven during her childhood.

And when she'd needed a place to recoup a few years earlier? She'd come straight back.

"I hope I didn't talk you into biting off more than we can chew, Aunt Ginny. Some days I worry that it's all going to come crashing down on us."

"You know what I always say."

Andie nodded. She did, though she wasn't sure she believed it herself. "It's all up to the fates."

"That's right, sweet girl. Whatever happens is meant to happen." Ginny reached over and tapped a finger on the closed folder. "And that means with this wedding, too." She gave a little nod, the natural twinkle in her eyes dimming to serious. "I'm going out front with Kayla. Why don't you familiarize yourself with our impending company?"

"I will, Aunt Ginny. Thanks." That had been next on her list of tasks. Given the time crunch, Kayla had handled the details with the families and wedding party while Andie had lined up food and locked down times and dates for the activities Kayla had mapped out.

She leaned over and gave her aunt a peck on the cheek, thankful she'd always had her to turn to. "The fates or not," Andie whispered. "We have a lot riding on this wedding." Aunt Ginny knew of the upcoming payment to the bank, but didn't realize how bad a toll the unprecedented season had taken on their finances. Early hurricanes and last-minute catastrophes had pulled too many of their big moneymakers.

"And a lot will come out of it." With a wink, Ginny twirled in her best guest-greeting dress, the purple and orange panels of the skirt winking out, and headed out of the kitchen. Andie slid the folder over in front of her, but instead of opening it, she sat worrying over the days to come. There was no reason to believe the wedding would be anything but a success—they'd made a good habit out of doing just that. But the elder Jordan had also made it very clear; he demanded perfection. Don't deliver, don't get the bonus.

And don't have the funds for the balloon payment due at the end of the month.

It had been her doing to push the business further into debt. She'd insisted the bungalows would set them apart. And it had. Only maybe they should have moved slower. But because they'd done it all at once, they'd had to put the house up as collateral. And now it could be lost in the blink of an eye. Andie had a call in to the bank requesting a six-month extension. If they could get that, they'd been fine. If not...

She shook her head, not wanting to think about "if not." Risking losing her aunt's inheritance and home? What had she been thinking? She should have been happy with the wedding packages they'd already offered and left well enough alone.

Enough worrying, she silently chided herself. What was done was done. Right now, she needed to concentrate on the wedding ahead.

She had a list of guests to memorize. Though she'd scanned over the main players during the last weeks, she hadn't focused on the full list. And it would never do for the hostess not to be able to greet each member of the wedding party by name.

Thanks to Kayla, every detail was in perfect order. Andie poured herself a cup of chamomile tea and settled in to review the information on the bride's family. They were high-society Chicago, owners of an extensive line of upscale shopping centers. And though most had expected a big Chicago bash for the family's only daughter, the bride had insisted on having her wedding at a private beachfront location instead. She wanted the romance of a beach and the ocean—but was making sure not to leave her girls behind. There would be a total of ten wedding attendants, five on each side.

Seaglass Celebrations wasn't as well-known as the outfit the Jordans had originally picked, but Andie was determined to make it clear it was the better choice. The family and wedding party would be hosted on the Whitmore grounds, and wedding guests would stay in the five-star accommodations at the island's historic hotel.

Andie turned her attention back to the folder to find the groom's information, but before she could flip past the header page for that section, she paused on the last name. *Masterson.* She'd known another Masterson once. That one had been from Boston. And he'd been an ass. But he would be the exact kind of man who'd kill to marry into the Jordan family.

A turn of the page showed her the details on the Mastersons, including a photo of the groom, and she clunked down her mug of tea. The hot liquid splashed out onto her hand.

"Ow," she muttered, grabbing a towel to wipe away the liquid as she glared at the paper. Robert Masterson. The guy who'd been best man at her wedding.

Which meant he was probably also bringing—

Shit.

Her heart constricted, limiting the air being pulled into her lungs, as she couldn't help but bounce to that day four years ago. It had been a June wedding then, too.

She shoved the memories from her mind, and scanned over the sheet for more details. *Joseph* Robert Masterson. Well, dang. The man's first name was Joseph. And, of course, since she hadn't been the one doing the invites or place cards, the first names and the total number of guests were all she'd paid attention to.

She got her breathing back under control, then quickly ran through the rest of the document, skipping over a majority of the groom's information, but noting that he worked at a prestigious law firm in Chicago. She silently pleaded that he and Mark were no longer the big buds they'd been four years earlier. But she knew differently. They'd been friends since elementary school. Their families were friends. Heck, they'd all vacationed together for the last thirty years.

Robert had also likely served as best man in the wedding she'd seen announced in the Sunday Styles section of the *New York Times* last fall—that of Mark Kavanaugh and Elizabeth Ryan, a woman from an even more blue-blood, old-Boston family than Mark's.

Nope, there was no way that Mark wouldn't be involved in this event.

But a girl could surely hope.

Only, hoping was futile. There it was in black and white—Best Man: Mark Kavanaugh. A recent picture accompanied the info, and she couldn't help but linger over it.

He looked good. Damned good.

If he wasn't such a pig for dumping her the way he had, she'd be hard-pressed not to be turned on by the simple image of him.

She glanced toward the door that Ginny had disappeared through, realizing that her aunt would be aware that Mark was scheduled to arrive today. How long she'd known? But then, it didn't matter. This was a wedding they had to do. Andie wouldn't lose Aunt Ginny's house because she didn't want to face her louse of an ex.

The phone rang and she reached over to answer it, shoving Mark's picture aside to peruse the remainder of list.

"Ms. Shayne, please," said a male voice on the other end of the line.

"This is Andie. How may I help you?"

"Oh Andie, hello. This is Dan Stapleton from the bank."

Her pulse spiked. News on the loan. "Hello, Mr. Stapleton. I sure hope you have good news for me."

The uncomfortable silence that met her words turned her stomach sour.

"I'm afraid, Ms. Shayne, that I don't."

Andie closed her eyes. The bonus from this wedding would cover the loan, but just barely. If anything at all were to go wrong…

"I'm sorry to say that the committee has reviewed your request for an extension, but we cannot grant one at this time."

She couldn't breathe. "The whole amount? But there have been extenuating circumstances. Natural disasters."

"Yes, ma'am. We did take that into consideration."

"Any way we could pay half this month and half the next?" She wasn't even sure that would be doable, but it was better than all of it now.

"I'm afraid not, Ms. Shayne. The full amount of the payment will be due as stated in the original terms of the agreement; payable the last day of this month."

The sound of laughter hit her ears as she heard the first of the guests arriving in the other room. Looked like the time had come. Prove she was the businesswoman her Harvard MBA declared her to be, or…

She shook her head. There was no "or."

"I understand. Thank you for trying, sir."

After hanging up, Andie sat staring out at the waves of the Atlantic, wondering how in the world she was going to tell Aunt Ginny that they were within a hair's breadth of losing this place.

And how she would live with herself if she let it happen.

～

Mark Kavanaugh stood in the parking lot of Gin's, the beachfront bar and café, and stared up at the sign depicting the caricature with the bright red curls. There was no doubt it was meant to be Andie's aunt, Genevieve Whitmore. And it was fabulous. One look at that face and customers would know they were entering a place with life.

He'd only met Ginny the one time, but she'd made a lasting impression.

"I've heard good things about this place."

"Yeah?" Mark glanced at the man standing to his right. Grayson McTavish had gone to law school with him and Rob, and was also in the wedding party. The two of them had caught the same flight out of Boston—though Mark still didn't understand why they had to come down two weeks before the wedding. How many pre-wedding activities could one couple have? "You research it before coming down?"

Gray had a spreadsheet for everything. Restaurant ratings were a favorite.

"Bite me, Kavanaugh. At least you know you'll be eating well when you travel with me."

Mark lifted a hand and shot him the bird. "There are three restaurants on the island, moron. We'll eat what we get."

But Mark had read the same thing about Gin's when he'd been scouring the Internet for information on Andie. It was top-of-the-line. Andie owned the bar, she'd named it after her aunt, and apparently she'd wooed a top Chicago chef down south. It had a stellar rating. He'd like to say he was at Gin's for the reputation—instead of at the inn where he was supposed to be meeting up with Rob, and where he'd almost definitely run into Andie—but that would be a lie. He was there because he was stalling. It had been four years since he'd seen Andie.

He wasn't quite sure he was ready to see her now.

He'd ended things poorly, and the guilt hadn't let him forget it. This trip wasn't just about standing up for his friend. It was about finally moving on. Closure. He wanted to settle down. He wanted what his mom and dad had. And he wanted Andie's face to quit flashing through his mind every damn time he thought about it.

It was the guilt, he was certain. He still believed he'd made the right choice; he wouldn't have wanted the marriage he'd been heading into. Though the childish way in which he'd called it off had been beneath him. And his mother had let him know it.

Genevieve Whitmore had also let him know it.

But he'd never gotten to apologize to Andie. No matter what, she hadn't deserved to be left standing at the altar.

Now was his chance to make sure she was okay, and in doing so, get himself there, as well.

He took in the cream-colored plank siding of the building, with the cheery yellow, blue, and pink trim, and couldn't help but smile. It looked like Andie.

The covered patio facing the ocean struck him as exactly the kind of place she'd love to sit and read a book. She'd always wanted to go off to the beach for weekends when they'd lived together in Boston. Summer or winter, if she could sit and listen to the ocean, she was a happy woman.

From what he'd been able to find out, she'd had plenty of time to do just that since they'd broken up. Turtle Island had been the last place he'd expected to find her—what with the way she'd been going after a career as an investment banker—but it seemed she'd taken her drive for success and zeroed in on building a growing destination wedding business, instead.

He hoped she was happy.

"Check out the kids." Gray nodded toward the beach where a family of five was making their way toward the boardwalk. "They remind me of me and my brother."

Two dark-haired boys, probably ages five or six, punched each other and rolled around in the sand in front of their mother, who was carrying an enormous bag with all manner of toys sticking out of it and wrestling a squirming baby wearing a tiny hat and some sort of pink contraption. Dad pulled up the rear, both arms full of chairs, an umbrella, and a rolling cooler that wasn't doing much rolling. It was only midafternoon, but by the pink shine on the man's shoulders, they'd already waited too long before calling it a day.

"Add in a couple more boys and it could be my family," Mark muttered. "Minus the baby. Hang on a sec."

He left Gray where he stood and jogged down the walkway to the family, catching mom as she hit the stairs. The boys were now lagging behind, covered from head to toe in sand.

"Let me help you with that." Mark reached for the bag, eyeing the baby as he did. She was a cute thing. Two teeth winked at him as she opened her mouth in a slobbery grin.

"Oh," mom said. A tired smile broke out across her face as she gratefully handed over the bag. "Thank you." She motioned toward the blue minivan he'd passed on his way down. "Just drop it at the back door if you don't mind."

"Sure thing." Mark turned to go, but the boys caught his attention. They had run circles around their dad and were now racing toward the stairs, sand spraying up behind them with each step. Mom was safely out of the way, but the boys had picked up speed and were shoving at each other as they ran. The steps would be slick with sand if taken too fast.

Before Mark could say anything, one of the boys hit the bottom plank and lunged upward for the next, and just as Mark had feared, the kid's leg went flying out behind him, bringing him face-first down toward the step.

"Watch out!" Mark lunged past mom, certain there would be a broken nose at the least. But the second brother merely yanked the first down and climbed over him, leaving the kid who'd face-planted laughing and throwing a handful of sand in his wake.

"You must not be a father," the mom said. She shook her head in a sympathetic, understanding way. "I'm sure you were just as rowdy for your mother, at one point in your life."

No doubt he had been. And no wonder his mother had been coloring her hair since her thirties.

Mark watched the two kids continue to wrestle as they made their way past him, no broken nose, not even a nosebleed, only a token glance tossed his way, accompanied by an eye roll that suggested he was the biggest dork in the world for worrying. And he guessed he was.

They were just playing. No different from what he and his own brothers had done throughout their childhood. No different from any kid, he supposed.

He shook his head at his own naïveté, grabbed an armload of chairs from the dad, and then walked with the two adults back to their car.

"You here with your family?" dad asked.

"Ah." Mark paused, glanced at the boys again, then at the baby who was watching his every move. A single band of pressure tightened around his chest. "No. No family."

"You want one?" Mom jostled the chubby-cheeked kid in her arms as she took the two steps from the wooden path to the parking lot. She nodded toward the boys now shooting each other with pretend guns, each kid ducking and hiding on either side of the van. "I might be willing to set you up with a couple kids to start you off."

She chuckled at her own teasing tone, and shot Mark a grin.

"Maybe someday," he said. He gave the boys one last look, unable to keep from imagining a couple of his own on a similar family outing, and gave a slight nod. "Yeah. Maybe someday. That would be nice. But I think you'd better keep these two yourself."

He gave mom a wink, and she let out a long, overly dramatic sigh. "I suppose if I must."

Mark chuckled and deposited his load at the back bumper of the van. Nice family. Two of his brothers had that in their lives already. He liked to imagine he'd eventually follow suit.

He tossed a wave at their thanks, and made his way back to the bar where Gray was leaning against the wall beside the door, his arms folded across his chest.

"Ever the Good Samaritan, I see," Gray teased.

"Wouldn't hurt you to help."

"Never have to. You always have it under control."

Mark brushed his hands over the slacks of the suit he still wore from that morning's meetings, knocking sand from his legs. Aside from rushing forward and swooping the boys up to keep them from acting like normal boys, he supposed there hadn't been anything else to be done. He didn't speak, merely grunted in acknowledgment.

The door to the building opened and a couple emerged, laughing as they made their exit. Behind them, he could hear what sounded like a baseball game being broadcast inside. He punched his buddy in the gut and pushed past him. Might as well enjoy a late lunch before he went in search of the woman he most dreaded. And most looked forward to seeing.

It was dark and cool inside, and it took his eyes a moment to adjust. Once he could see, he scanned the area noting only two people at the bar itself, each sitting on a round-topped stool, leaning in, laughing quietly with the other.

A few other people were scattered throughout the room, talking or watching one of several TVs hanging on the walls. There were small tables for two with fancy little chairs that looked as if they belonged on the patio of someone several decades older than himself, larger tables and normal seating for bigger crowds, and a couple of cushioned loveseats tucked into one corner with a glass-topped coffee table positioned in front.

In the other corner was a piano with a microphone standing beside it. And all around the walls were shelves full of an interesting mix of metal bowls, candlesticks, shells, and what looked to be blown-glass ornaments. And that was just what he could see from a quick glance. Given the number of shelves and amount of stuff, he suspected additional items could easily be uncovered.

Beyond sheer, billowing curtains, he made out a handful of women sitting out on the patio, all wearing floppy hats and sipping girly-looking drinks. The outside space was casual and overlooked the beach, but judging by the subtle decor and tasteful lighting dotting the perimeter, he suspected that come nighttime it would be transformed into elegance.

The whole place screamed nice. Comfortable. Classy. It was Andie.

"Table for two?"

Mark looked down to find a hostess smiling up at him. Short black hair puffed out around her face, and something about the simpleness in her khaki shorts and pullover, contrasted with the stiff suit he still wore, made him feel ancient. She appeared to be in her early- to mid-twenties, and though he was only thirty-one himself, he felt a lifetime older.

Working sixty-hour weeks at your family's law firm did that to a person.

Taking a vacation, only to bring the job with you, did that to a person, as well.

Gray was eyeing the pixie of a woman, and from what Mark could tell, was enjoying the view.

"We'll just grab a seat at the bar, if that's okay," Mark said. Normally both of them would come to a place like this with a handful of buddies and take up a spot in front of the biggest TV. For this afternoon, the bar would do.

"Sure thing," the hostess replied. She motioned for them to go ahead and choose a seat and then shot Mark another quick look with a slight squint of her eyes. She scanned over his attire, scrutinizing his face closely enough to make him uncomfortable. The corners of her mouth turned down. "The bartender should be back any minute. She stepped away to take a call. Are you with the Jordan wedding?"

"That's right." Given that Rob and Penelope were pretty much taking over the property and that his own Boston accent easily stuck out, he wasn't surprised that she'd put it together. "Thought we'd grab some lunch before meeting up with everyone else."

Her demeanor suddenly changed and she thrust menus at them. "Sounds like a plan. Might want a grab a drink, too. Weddings tend to bring out the worst in people." She angled her head toward the bar. "You go on over. I'll let Andie know you're here. I'm sure she'll be right out to serve you."

Mark had half turned away, but froze in his tracks. He glanced back. "Andie is the bartender? Andie Shayne?"

It had to be her. Bartending had been what put her through Harvard Business. That and scholarships.

"Yep," the hostess stated flatly. She turned away, making it clear she was finished speaking.

From the corner of his eye, Mark caught Grayson raise his brows. Mark wasn't sure if he recognized Andie's name, or was showing his thoughts on the hostess's snub, but one thing hit home in a nauseating wave. Mark wasn't ready to see Andie.

The idea of just walking up to her after all this time and starting a conversation was far more nerve-racking than standing in front of a hostile courtroom with none of the odds in his favor. But what was he going to do? Turn and leave like a coward?

He headed to the bar without another word and parked himself on the opposite end from the couple, hoping to get a good look at Andie before she saw him. And wondering if he should be the coward he felt inside and hightail it back out the door he'd just entered.

Gray slung a leg over the stool beside him. "The ex, huh?"

Mark nodded. The ex. Though Gray had spent a couple years working in San Francisco after they'd graduated, he likely remembered Andie from their evenings hanging out at the bar where she'd worked. And then he'd been invited to the wedding.

Mark tapped a thumb against the counter, noticing that underneath the veneer were buttons of all sizes, many looking like they'd been plucked off old polyester suits.

"You knew she was here, then?" Gray asked.

Couldn't pull anything over on a good lawyer. "I knew she was here."

Gray flipped open his menu with a wide grin on his face, looking for all the world as if he was settling in to witness what was soon likely to be a very uncomfortable situation. "I think I'll have that beer the cutie suggested. Things could get interesting up in here."

Yes, things could get interesting. Mark suspected they would.

And how wonderful for him that he'd have an audience.

CHAPTER TWO

A soft grunt escaped as Andie lifted the rack of glasses from the dishwasher and headed toward the bar. She'd verified that the Mastersons were settling in, and the limo was en route to pick up the first round of Jordans. Now she needed to get everything stocked and ready for the evening crowd and the wedding party dinner out on the patio.

She also had to make sure she was mentally prepared. Seeing Mark wasn't going to be a picnic, but it had been four years. She could handle this. And she'd do it by making sure he realized he hadn't broken her.

"Andie, I need to talk to you." Roni, one of her two oldest friends, and the person currently playing the role of hostess, rushed up to her before Andie made it back to the bar. Roni had once been a concert pianist. She'd up and quit, landing on Turtle Island and changing her life almost as abruptly as Andie's had taken a turn.

"Let me put these up first. This is heavy." Andie tried to push past her, but Roni stood in her way. She reached out for the rack, taking part of the weight in her own hands.

"It can't wait," Roni whispered. "You need to know—"

The sound of a handful of men entering the bar cut Roni off midsentence. Andie shot her friend a quizzical look as she moved around her to shout out a greeting to the newcomers. It was a crowd of college-aged guys. She slid the tray of glasses in the space behind the bar, caught a glimpse of a couple new faces at the far end of the counter—their heads bent over menus—then subtly motioned Roni to get back out front and seat the new customers.

Before Andie could move to the end of the bar to take orders, the woman in front of her caught her attention. "Can I get another glass of wine, please?"

The woman's name was Janice. She and her friend, George, had been on the island for several days now and had been lingering in the bar since lunch. Janice had explained that today was their last day on the island, and neither wanted to return to the real world.

Andie could understand that. She'd sought out Aunt Ginny's home four years ago, not wanting to return to the real world herself. She'd been prepared to, however. Only, her boss had let her know there was no need.

Stood up at the altar and fired, all within days. It had not been one of her better weeks.

She drained the bottle of Moscato into Janice's glass. "That one's on me."

"Awww, thanks!" Janice's voice was an octave too high, and she followed it up with a round of giggles. "I think I've had a bit too much this afternoon."

Out of the corner of her eye, Andie caught the men down the bar turning their heads in her direction. She patted Janice's hand. "Better go easy or you and George will be spending your last evening sleeping one off."

Sending George a wink, Andie caught another strange look from Roni as she turned to the other customers. As she reached out to put away the empty bottle, she realized who sat at the far end of her bar.

The bottle slipped, tagged the corner of the stainless steel cooler, and shattered on the tile floor.

"I'll get a broom," Roni tossed out, before hurrying to the back.

Andie ignored her, not taking her eyes off Mark.

Slightly windblown hair, still as dark as she remembered, an expensive suit that looked completely out of character in a place like this, yet somehow seemed like the only thing she would expect to find him in, and those steady, penetrating eyes taking her in.

He sat, elbows propped on the polished bar as if he'd been patiently waiting for her for days, and raised his eyebrows when her gaze met his.

Her body grew warm with anger. Four years was apparently not long enough.

"Let me get it." Roni spoke softly, sliding in behind the counter.

"I've got it." Andie snatched the broom and dustpan out of Roni's hands, needing a reason to break contact with Mark. What was he doing at the bar? He was supposed to be at the house with the others.

She shot a quick glance at the other man, recognizing him from years ago, as well as from the picture she'd seen clipped to Kayla's folder earlier in the day. Grayson McTavish had been a good guy from what Andie had been able to tell, and at the moment, she wished that good guy would drag Mark out of her bar.

"Could you see what he…" Angie motioned to the men, not looking at them again. "What *they* want?"

From the rigidity of Roni's jaw, Andie knew that her friend had recognized Mark, as well. They'd met at dinner the night before the wedding that didn't happen. Then it occurred to her that *this* had been what Roni had been trying to warn her about. Andie started sweeping the broom against the glass in haphazard strokes, but was unable to concentrate fully on the task.

"They apparently want lunch," Roni stated without going over to the men. She leaned in to whisper. "Did you know he would be here?"

Andie didn't pause in her movements. "Just read it on the list today. It's Robert Masterson's wedding. He was Mark's best man."

Roni nodded. "That explains it."

But it didn't explain how out of all the places in the world, Rob's wedding had landed on her island.

Andie glanced Mark's way again, then swiveled around to Janice and George, wondering if they could tell something was wrong. When they looked from her to Mark and Grayson and then back to Roni, she had her answer. She noticed the gaggle of men that had just entered taking in the activity at the bar, as well.

Good grief, she did not want to cause more of a scene than she already had.

She fought the urge to drop everything to the floor and just walk away. She could hide in her room for the next two weeks, and she knew Kayla and Aunt Ginny would expertly handle everything. Truth be told, they'd probably do a better job without her. But it had been her idea to start this business to begin with. And she was a professional. She would not let this man run her off. Not again.

Shoving her feelings aside—and furious to realize she still had any toward him, even if it was only anger—she gave Roni a tight smile. "Never mind, I'll handle it."

She pushed the broom back at Roni and turned to the bar. With nothing left to do but face him, Andie picked up a towel to keep her hands busy and made her way to the far end of the counter. To Mark.

"Grayson," she muttered, wiping down the bar in front of him. "Mark." She did not want to see him, did not want to deal with him. And she certainly didn't want to see him and his perfect wife together. And that's when she realized, she was as jealous as she was angry. He'd tossed her aside and chosen someone who fit the mold he'd been looking for.

"It's good to see you, Andie," Mark said. Grayson nodded a greeting then leaned back in his seat.

She eyed Mark. It was good to see her? That was his opening statement? You'd think a lawyer could come up with something better than that. She did give him credit for the deep, rich sound of his voice, though. It had always felt like a warm, fuzzy blanket wrapping around her.

But he was a jerk and she hated him. She had to keep that foremost in her mind.

"I'm afraid I can't say the same." She met him head-on. His eyes had always changed with his moods or the color of his clothes; right now they were dark, a deep greenish brown. So dark there was practically no definition from the iris to the outside rim.

He had the grace to glance away at her words, possibly embarrassed, but she couldn't imagine a Kavanaugh being embarrassed.

"What are you doing in here, Mark?" She didn't wait for him to say anything else, her fury suddenly taking over all other emotions churning through her. It was four years ago, and she was standing there in front of a church of two hundred, and every last one of them was looking at poor, pitiful Andie Shayne. "Shouldn't you be at the house with your buddy?"

She hated Mark almost as much as she did Robert. And yes, she knew it wasn't nice to hate people. Her good Kentucky upbringing had taught her that, but some people didn't deserve any better.

"I'm heading over soon. Thought we'd get a bite to eat and…"

He paused and she mimicked his earlier action, raising her eyebrows, while inside she was trembling. "And what? Start the wedding out by making sure to let me know you're here? Don't worry. I'm aware of who's in this wedding. It's my job to know."

She was proud of how steady her voice was coming out.

"That's not it. I didn't even know you were here."

That stopped her, because he had a point. They hadn't been in contact at all. Had he not known she lived here now? Maybe he was as shocked to see her as she was him. "You weren't aware—"

He held up a hand and cut her off. "I knew you were *here*, on the island. I knew this was your place. It's why I recommended it. But I didn't know you were here at the bar."

She straightened, pulling herself away from the counter, and blinked. He'd recommended them? She glanced at Grayson then back to Mark. For some reason that stung. She didn't need his pity to make her business a success.

Or heck, maybe she did since she was going to lose everything if she didn't get that bonus.

Andie stared at him, wanting to reach over the counter and slap him across the face while simultaneously wanting to turn the clock back four years and ask him why he'd done that to her. Couldn't he have just figured out that she wasn't the woman he wanted *before* the morning of their wedding? Maybe faced her and talked to her himself? And why in the world had he made her be the one to address their guests all alone?

She'd never figured out what had been so bad about her that she wasn't afforded that simple courtesy from the man she'd loved. But maybe that had been the problem. Had he not really loved her? Clearly not as much as she'd once believed, otherwise she wouldn't have been left with a five-tier wedding cake to eat all by herself.

Which made her think about the woman he *had* married, and the fact that they would have shared their wedding cake together. Their wedding was probably how he'd learned about her and Aunt Ginny's business. The announcement she'd seen last year had stated that he and his fiancée planned private, out-of-town nuptials in early spring. Possibly Seaglass Celebrations had been one of the places they'd run across in their planning. Any small amount of research would have turned up her picture connected to the company.

Relief gushed through her at the realization that the two of them could have ended up there for their wedding, but thankfully had not. Talk about a nightmare. That was one job she would have vehemently turned down, no matter how the business might have suffered.

Speaking of which…she looked around, wondering where the little woman was. From the picture she'd seen, she was blonde and petite and perfect. Unlike her. Andie glanced down at herself. Average height, freckles, nothing-special hair, and too many curves. She looked nice enough, but she'd never felt quite put together around Mark and his family. Not to mention, she wasn't the stay-at-home, perfect-housewife type.

"Can you just bring me whatever you have on tap and a cheeseburger?" Mark sighed, pushing the menu away. "I didn't come here to argue with you. I'm exhausted. I just want a decent meal and a beer before I have to deal with this wedding."

"Sure thing." She ground her teeth together as she spoke, then keyed in the order, taking Grayson's, as well.

Mark had a good point; there was no need to argue. They'd done enough of that the last six months they'd been together. As far as she was concerned, she had nothing whatsoever left to say to him.

She drew their beers and slid them over, then placed the bill upside down on the counter. "Roni will bring out your food when it's ready. She can also get you anything else you need."

Before she escaped back into kitchen, Mark raised his voice loud enough for the whole bar to hear. "Wait."

And for some reason she did. She peered back at him, unspeaking. Because honestly, she had no idea if she could say anything else without breaking down. She needed to get away to deal with the returning emotions she'd thought were long gone.

"Could we…" He shrugged, lowering his voice to a more normal volume. "Talk?"

She shook her head. "I've got nothing to say to you."

She caught Grayson's grimace out of the corner of her eye.

"Fine." Mark's voice was hard. "Then I'll talk. You listen."

Andie glanced over to where Roni stood with the broom, then at George and Janice. She scanned the dining area. A waitress had taken orders and left, but every last person in the bar was fixated on her and Mark. *Great.* Nothing like making a spectacle of yourself.

She stepped back to him and spoke very softly, "I can't imagine there's anything you could say that I'd want to hear. Eat your lunch and go. We'll avoid each other over the next several days, and then you'll go back to Boston. But while you're here, just leave me alone."

A muscle in his jaw did an odd little spasm thing, and she almost smiled, knowing it irritated him when he didn't get his way.

"We're having a conversation, Andie. You might as well deal with it."

"I don't have time to—"

"Then make time. It's four years past due, as it is. We're having a conversation."

Her chest rose and fell with her breath. She'd really thought it didn't matter anymore. That she was over it. *Hmph!* What a ball of baloney. She was just as upset today as she'd been the day he hadn't shown up at their sham of a wedding.

She set her jaw to keep it from trembling and looked away from him, almost wishing his wife would show up at that moment so she'd have something else to focus on.

When she finally felt she was under control enough to face him, she decided to use that exact point to back him off. "And what would your wife think, Mark?" she whispered. "Would she be okay with you hunting up your ex to 'have a talk'? To hash out old hurts?" She shook her head, ignoring the shock in his eyes. He hadn't guessed she'd known about his marriage, then.

"I doubt it," she continued. "Most women wouldn't go for that. In fact, you might want to consider not even letting her in on the fact that you suggested Seaglass in the first place. I'm assuming the two of you are still in your 'honeymoon' phase. Knowing you brought everyone down here so you could have a chat with your ex might put a damper on things. Now I'm finished with you. Eat your lunch and go away."

Without another word, she whirled around and marched through the kitchen, ignoring the faces of her employees as she made her way to the back office. Thank goodness the manager wasn't in so Andie had the room to herself.

The sound of the broom and dustpan being put away outside the office pulled her attention. "I'm so sorry, Roni. I had no idea…"

But it wasn't Roni. It was Mark. She couldn't believe her friend had allowed him back there.

"I didn't get a chance to reply, so I told her I'd bring this stuff back." He stepped into the room, and without asking or even seeming to consider it a question, closed the door.

When he took a long step toward her, her breath hitched, and he pulled himself up short.

"Well hell, Andie. I'm not going to hurt you."

"I didn't think you were," she spat out. Her breath had caught purely at the idea of having him that close, but she wasn't about to tell him that. He was a big man, over six feet, and it looked as if he hadn't lost any of the taut muscles she'd once become so familiar with. Finding herself face-to-face with him was much different from having a bar and a few feet between them.

And furious with him or not, there was still a pull she'd never been able to ignore. Being in a small, confined room with only the two of them snarling at each other did nothing to dim it.

Plus, he was seriously hot when he was angry. Always had been.

A flash of some of the best angry sex she'd ever had popped through her mind, and she felt her cheeks begin to heat. This time, *not* because of her anger.

His eyes sharpened as he watched her. They lingered on her warm cheeks then flicked quickly over her body as if aware of exactly what she was remembering. When he returned, his gaze landed directly on hers.

"Say whatever it is and leave, Mark. I'm too busy for games." And far too busy for the testosterone in the room.

He crossed his arms over his chest and his jaw did that spasming thing again. "Good, because I'm not here to play games."

She edged her chin up, not feeling nearly as in control as she'd like him to believe. "Then what are you here for?"

The phone rang. They both glanced at it, but she ignored it. Roni or one of the employees would get it when she didn't. She made a rolling motion with her hand for him to get to it. She didn't have all day.

He took a half step closer and lowered his hands to his side. His tone warmed. "Are you doing okay, Andie? I mean, really okay?"

She glared at him. Seriously?

He sighed. "Fine. I just…" He lifted his hands palms up. "I was worried about you at first. Afraid you would think…" He shook his head instead of finishing the sentence. "And then you wouldn't even talk to me."

She couldn't help herself. She pressed her hands to the desk in front of her and leaned in, putting herself much closer to him than was smart. "What?" Her tone was not pretty. "Afraid I would think that there was something wrong with *me* because you sent your friend to our wedding instead of coming yourself? Nah…nothing to worry about there. Every girl gets left at the altar at least once in her life, didn't you know? It's pretty much a ritual. We learn about it in the sixth grade."

Man, she wanted him out of there. If he didn't leave, she feared she would step around the desk and get right up in his face. That had always been the point where she could make him snap. Once there, he was as likely to kiss her as yell at her. And for some reason, she had the feeling that either one might do it for her at the moment.

What the hell was wrong with her? She hadn't seen this man since he *hadn't* shown up at their wedding, and she was practically ready to jump his bones. And he was married!

"I'm…" he paused again, then put his hands on his hips and took a step back. He slowly pulled in a long breath then let it out. When he opened his mouth, he came out with the last thing she expected to hear.

"I'm not married."

EPISODE TWO

CHAPTER THREE

Not married?" Andie choked out a laugh. That was bull. "Come off it. I saw the announcement. You two were perfect for each other."

Mark nodded, his jaw working back and forth. "Yeah, perfect. But then…" He looked away and snapped his teeth together. He was still running on fumes. "Doesn't matter. We didn't get married." He licked his lips and gave an unconcerned shrug. "She dumped me."

That was not what she'd been expecting to hear. Nor was the rapid kick start in her chest something she'd ever wanted to feel in the vicinity of him ever again. "Good," she muttered. "A taste of your own medicine. Hope she left you at the altar, too."

He laughed, a weary chuckle that she felt all the way to her toes, and dragged his hand down over his face. "No, actually. Not at the altar. But yes, it did give me a taste of my own medicine."

The anger in the room suddenly evaporated, and they stood there quietly staring at each other. Andie had no idea what he was thinking, but she was fighting the very real urge to cry. She had once loved him so very much.

The outer corners of his hazel eyes drooped slightly with his long sigh, and a sad look came over his face. "Andie, I really am—"

The door burst open. "Andie, we need you at the house."

Kayla stood at the door, with Roni on her tiptoes behind her peeking over her shoulder.

"I'm sorry," Roni mouthed. "She wouldn't wait."

Kayla's eyes widened at the sight of Mark in the room. "I apologize for interrupting, Ms. Shayne. Mr. Kavanaugh." She gave a quick nod to Mark, apparently recognizing him from the photo in her files, then looked back at Andie. "You're needed at the house."

Escape! Though Kayla wouldn't have sought her out if it wasn't important.

"I'm sorry, Mr. Kavanaugh, but since we were finished anyway…" Andie rose. "Your meal should be coming up any minute. If you'll return to the bar, Roni will take care of you and Mr. McTavish." She eyed Roni, making it clear that she had some explaining to do for letting Mark in the back of the restaurant in the first place.

Before Mark could stop her, Andie walked out of the room and didn't look back. Only then did she notice that her hands were shaking.

She so had not been ready for him. And certainly not for an apology after all this time. She had little doubt that was what the man had been about to do, though. The sudden look of shame he'd sported had been a good indication.

Of course, he should be ashamed, but after four years, she would've guessed his past actions never crossed his mind.

And the fact that he wasn't married? A shiver wracked her body. She certainly hadn't expected that. Him being married was what she'd been counting on since she'd read his name on the list that morning—to not let it matter. To not let *him* matter. She'd put that tidbit of information at the forefront of her mind, and it was supposed to keep her from thinking about anything concerning "them." Because she did not need to think about "them."

Heck, she didn't need to think about him.

But as she hurried along the path to the inn, little else crossed her mind. He had looked really good.

And he'd smelled even better.

She closed her eyes with the memory but almost tripped, so opened them again and glanced at Kayla. "What's the problem at the house?"

Kayla averted her gaze. "Mr. and Mrs. Jordan had barely checked in when their bathroom floor flooded. The toilet ran over."

Oh geez, what a way to start the event that had to be perfect.

"The plumber is tied up with another emergency on the other side of the island. It'll be late evening before he can get here. Possibly morning."

"Well then, call someone else. But first, get the Jordans taken care of. Put them in Mr. Kavanaugh's room." She didn't want Mark under the same roof as her, anyway. "We'll move him to the hotel."

She worried that would look suspicious since she'd just been caught fuming at the guy, but she couldn't care less. The more steps she put between them, the more she remembered what it had been like when they were together.

How hot it could get in an instant. And she knew he remembered it too. She'd seen it in his eyes when he'd looked her up and down.

All Andie could think about was how four years of celibacy—on her part—and two people who had combustible pasts could turn into nothing but wrong. Especially when she was stressed to an intolerable level, and everyone knew how good sex was for stress.

~

"I can't get over the fact that Andie's running this gig." Rob Masterson cracked open a crab leg and waved it in the air as he ranted about how shocked he'd been to find her running the place. He then described how pathetic it was that Mark had suggested the wedding be there in the first place. "I mean, clearly you knew she was here. You're still hung up on her. When are you going to move on, man?"

"I have moved on," Mark uttered. "Years ago."

Gray coughed something into his hand that sounded suspiciously like, *Bullshit.*

"Shut up, Gray."

"But you knew this was her business, right?" Rob added. "That's too big of a coincidence."

Mark studied his buddy in the waning daylight, wishing Rob hadn't left Penelope's side to come over and catch up. He was not in the mood for his friend that night. "Yes," he finally answered, knowing Rob wouldn't shut up until he admitted it. Also knowing Gray would out him if he didn't do it himself. It wasn't like he could deny it after the earlier conversation with Andie. "I knew it was her place."

Rob dipped the crabmeat in butter, his attention now on his meal, giving Mark the mistaken hope that their conversation was over. He eyed Gray, who scanned the area as if looking for someone.

"Looking for Roni?" Mark asked.

"Who?" His friend might pull off a poker face for jurors, but Mark knew Gray well. He was hot for Andie's friend.

"The hostess that was here earlier. Her name is Roni." Mark tilted his beer at Gray. "You're hoping to hook up."

Gray shrugged, not denying it, and Rob interrupted, lifting his eyes from his plate to catch Mark head-on. "You and Beth come across it before she dumped you?"

Clearly, he wanted to understand how they'd ended up there. But some things were none of his business.

"Something like that, yeah."

Rob tossed the next crab leg onto his plate and turned to Mark, wiping his mouth on the cloth napkin. "Is that why she dumped you? Because you're still hung up on this one?"

Gray didn't say anything, merely smiled wide.

"No," Mark answered. "That is not why she dumped me."

"Because if so, that's even worse than I thought. Andie's a nobody, bro. Though finding out her aunt owns the place..." He whistled softly through his teeth. "That was a surprise. But still, she's Kentucky hicksville."

"Shut up, Rob," Mark and Gray said at the same time.

Mark really needed Rob to lay off Andie. They hadn't thrown punches in years, but one more crack, and now might be a good time to renew an old hobby.

Mark had never thought of Andie the way Rob did. It'd only been Rob's snotty opinion that she wasn't good enough.

Though that had been one of the arguments he and Andie often had.

He couldn't help who his family was or what their history had been. And he couldn't help that some people— *not his family*—looked down their noses at those who hadn't been born into the same kind of lineage. But Mark's home life had never been anything but normal. His father worked hard, his mother took care of his brothers and him, and everyone had eaten dinner together most nights. His dad's occasional business dinners and his mother's charity events sometimes interfered, but they'd all made it a priority to be home by seven as many nights as possible. Even when the boys had been teenagers.

Mark had never understood why Andie had seen his family as anything different from hers or why she'd worried she wasn't good enough. Of course, he also hadn't realized until the end that she'd wanted to be a part of what she saw as "better," as opposed to just wanting to be a part of him.

"Maybe you two need to go at it while you're here," Rob tossed out. "Get her out of your system once and for all. Nothing wrong with dallying with her—she's got a great bod. Just don't tie yourself to her and life will be good."

Mark stared at the man he'd known since elementary school. "You're an ass, Rob." Gray nodded in agreement. But Mark was no better because he'd been thinking the same thing. Why not an affair to get her out of his system? Walking away sure hadn't done it.

"Yeah, but an ass with the right kind of wife." Rob's smile was more smirk.

They'd been best friends for years. They'd gone to Harvard Law together. Their fathers had been childhood friends. But they'd drifted apart since Rob had been in Chicago. Hearing the words coming out of Rob's mouth now, Mark wondered what had held them together for so long.

Or had Rob simply changed that much over the years?

A sickening thought rolled through Mark's gut. Had *he* once been like that himself? Surely not.

But if so…maybe Andie's long-ago argument had held water. Had he treated her like she was beneath him?

No. He pulled in a breath, refusing to believe he'd ever been that much of a jerk. "Give it a break," he said. He was tired of this conversation, especially since they'd had it more than once back when he'd been dating Andie. "There's nothing wrong with her and never has been."

He rose and tossed down a tip then headed for the walkway that led to the beach. He was done socializing for the evening. And he wasn't even going to delve into what had put him in such a foul mood—even before Rob had sat down.

Mark stopped at the end of the boardwalk and lowered to the top step. He didn't care about sand on the backside of his chinos, but he wasn't fond of the idea of going farther and risking ruining the loafers he'd picked up in Italy the year before.

The sun was just thinking about setting on the west side of the island as he gazed out over the early evening horizon. He could see what Andie always loved about the beach. It was calming. Relaxing.

And Turtle Island was apparently her place of solace.

Andie had only hinted at that fact when they'd been together—telling him very little about her home life in Kentucky, and briefly mentioning her times with Ginny—but after the tongue-lashing he'd gotten from her aunt, and then finding out that Andie had been on the island all this time, he had to assume that to be the case. This was her oasis. He was just glad she had one.

"Not much of a coincidence you ending up here, is it?"

Mark glanced up to find one of the women he'd just been thinking about. Genevieve Whitmore.

Her red curls had been tamed tonight, into a sophisticated style back behind her head, and though her dress looked like the last thing someone would want to get sand out of, she motioned for him to scoot over and plopped right down next to him.

"You mean sitting here staring at the ocean? Or…"

She harrumphed like any good southern woman and then gave him that evil eye she'd no doubt perfected early in life. "You're not stupid, Mark. Don't pretend I am either."

"Yes, ma'am," he muttered. It had been four years, but she still had him instantly treading on fear. "And no, not a coincidence. I suggested Seaglass to the Jordans."

"That's what Andie said. She was fit to be tied over it, too. Not a word out of you in years, and then you show up, bringing a whole crew with you?"

"I was impressed by what I saw online." And he had been, but that had zilch to do with suggesting Seaglass as the wedding site. He rubbed the palms of his hands together and gazed off into the distance. "She's been all right, then? All this time?"

He didn't see them, but he felt those deep green eyes studying him. Finally, she spoke. "She's a fighter. She'll get up and keep going no matter what."

"Yeah," he said. "I remember." She'd hit a couple bumps at her job in Boston early on, but they hadn't deterred her. He glanced over at Ginny. "But how has she been? Really?"

"That would be something you'll have to ask her yourself, young man. I don't presume to speak for my niece, even when it eats at me not to." Her lips took on a slight curve, and for the first time since he'd taken the ferry over to the island, Mark's shoulders lost a little of their tension.

He propped his elbows on his knees, his head turned toward her. "She didn't seem too thrilled at the idea of talking to me earlier today."

"That's because she'd learned you were coming here just an hour before."

He widened his gaze. "And I take it you knew before then?"

"I don't miss much."

No, she didn't. The day she'd shown up in Boston to pack Andie's things, she'd given him an earful. And what he'd gotten from that lecture had been that first, she wanted to rip his balls off and feed them to the nearest snake, but also that she knew the breakup was for the best. "It was fate," she'd said. According to her, fate knew the right time for two people to get together. And it apparently hadn't been their time.

Which had left him wondering if she thought another time would be right for them.

"I never quit worrying about her," he said. That was something he hadn't admitted to anyone. Not even to his own mother. But he suspected Ginny needed to hear it to know that no matter how he'd treated Andie at the end, he had cared about her. A lot.

"And I imagine she never quit wondering what she'd done wrong."

"But Rob told her…"

He drifted off. Rob was supposed to have told her that Mark had overheard her the morning of their wedding. She'd been on a call with a client, hastily pulling out clothes for an apparent, last-minute business meeting before the wedding. And it had been clear from the snippet of conversation he'd overheard, that she was not shy about throwing around the Kavanaugh name. She was marrying him for his last name. He wouldn't have believed it if he hadn't heard it with his own ears. The impending wedding probably hadn't even registered with her, other than to invite the client over to meet his parents during the reception.

As he'd stood there that day, faced with the reality that not only had she repeatedly put work ahead of him, but that she hadn't really wanted *him* at all, Mark had refused to go into a marriage with the balance so unevenly distributed. He'd wanted Andie, and he'd wanted her forever, but he wouldn't come home to someone, day after day, who only remembered he existed when she needed something from him.

Yet knowing Rob, he'd probably told her another story entirely. Something that would have hurt her even more than the fact that Mark didn't bother to show up and have the conversation himself.

Which made Mark a grade-A jerk for sending Rob to begin with. Which he'd been aware of at the time.

Ginny nodded as if reading his mind.

"What did he tell her?"

She merely watched him with steady eyes. "Another good conversation for you and Andie to have, my dear."

"If she'll hang around long enough to talk to me."

Earlier, after greeting the wedding party at the beginning of dinner, she'd disappeared without another word, leaving Ginny and the wedding coordinator in charge.

"The way I see it," Ginny began, chuckling a little with her words, "is that you can sit around moping for a couple weeks, whining about how Andie won't talk to you. Or you can hunt her up and make sure she does. She's always liked the beach in the evenings, you know? Maybe this is fate telling you it's finally time."

"It doesn't sound like fate to me, Ginny. It sounds like manipulation of the moment."

Ginny sat quietly for a good thirty seconds before she placed a hand on his knee. Her touch was gentle, and as he looked down at her arm, he couldn't help but notice the contrast of the outrageously colored bracelets she wore to the more sedate, beige dress she had on. It reminded him Andie. Though she'd dressed conservatively in appropriate situations, she'd often paired her attire with a bit of flair. Either a unique ring, an eccentric clip in her hair, or maybe just hot undergarments that were totally opposite the clothes she wore on the outside.

"When did you find out she was here?" Ginny's tone was soft, but probing.

Odd question. "Last winter." When he'd been supposed to be helping Beth find a location for them to get married. Instead he'd been Googling his old girlfriend. "Why?"

"Why not before then?"

"I don't know. It just…" he paused. He hadn't let himself look before then. Hadn't been sure he wouldn't hunt her up.

"Fate," she said. "Everything happens when it's supposed to. You were meant to find her last year. At least, locate her last year. But you still had some issues to work through, didn't you? You weren't yet ready to face her again."

"I had no intention of facing her at all. I was—" He cut himself off. He didn't want to tell her he was supposed to be marrying someone else. How would that make him look?

"I know about Ms. Ryan. You and she should have been married already. Yet you're not."

He narrowed his eyes at her. "How do you know all this?"

The wrinkles on the woman's face weren't extensive, but were enough to indicate she was no wallflower when it came to living. "The man who shattered my only niece's heart is scheduled to come to my home. What would you expect me to do? Let that happen without looking into the facts myself?"

Of course she'd looked into his life. He would have done the same thing. "And if you'd found that Beth and I had gotten married?"

"Then Mr. Masterson and Ms. Jordan would have found another venue for their wedding." With those words, she rose, reaching around to swipe at the sand on her backside. "People may think I've done nothing my last thirty years but hang out on the beach and play bridge with my friends, but I also protect what's mine. And that girl, she needed me. She doesn't so much anymore; she's done a lot of growing. But I'm still taking care of her just the same. And just like the last time you and I talked, I'll say it again. You do not go near her without making sure you don't hurt her again."

"I didn't come here to hurt her." Mark had risen with her, but didn't know what to do next. He wanted to head down the beach and search for Andie. Instead, he caught Ginny's eye. "I swear I didn't," he stated passionately.

She nodded. "I believe that. And I believe it was time for you to finally seek her out. Fate and all. But it doesn't mean hurting her can't happen. You may both need closure, but you take very good care, son, to make sure it happens in a way that doesn't leave that child brokenhearted over you ever again."

With her words, she turned and marched back the way she'd come. Mark watched her go. What he wanted to do was shout after her that it had been he who'd been left brokenhearted. Andie might have been upset when she'd quit her job to get away from him, but it hadn't been the loss of him that had destroyed her.

He, on the other hand, had been a ridiculous mess. In a way he didn't care to ever be again. Which had been part of his and Beth's final discussion.

He only wished he knew what to do about Andie now. He had two weeks, and he'd be a fool not to use them wisely. But he'd be damned if he knew what the wise path was.

Not to mention that the thought of seeking her out scared him to death. Just seeing her for the brief moments he had earlier that day had made one thing clear. There was still something between them. She'd felt it too.

Which did not bode well for closing that door and moving on with his life.

Andie pulled her arm back and released the Frisbee, watching it sail through the air before a small arm reached up high to snag it. The little girl who'd caught it laughed and bounced up and down.

"You're the best Frisbee thrower in the world, Andie," little Maggie Walker shouted as she pulled in the disc and readied to send it back across the beach.

"Me! Me!" Roni Templeman and Ginger Atkinson, Andie's best friends since she'd met them on the very same beach over twenty years ago, both shouted and jumped up and down just like the kids they were playing with.

Maggie giggled and slung out her arm, sending the Frisbee in a crooked arc heading straight for the ocean.

"Geez, Maggie," said Hunter, her twelve-year-old brother. "You've got to use your wrist."

Hunter clomped into the water since the Frisbee had landed nearest him, shaking his head at his little sister's poor aim. Andie made a habit of playing with several of the local kids on the evenings when there wasn't an event she had to attend. She looked forward to this time of the day. It was relaxing, fun, and just pure pleasure.

And far better than sticking around some party where one of the main attendees had been shooting her dirty looks, and another had been silently watching. She hadn't wanted to give either Rob or Mark the opportunity to corner her, so she'd talked Aunt Ginny into fulfilling the hostess duties for the evening.

Hunter flicked his wrist like a pro and sent the green circle flying, and Roni ran for it.

"So..." Ginger started, both of them watching Roni as she splashed along the edge of the water. She made quite a picture in the fading light with her short bob and cut-off jeans. She could almost pass for a teenager instead of twenty-eight. "Mark, huh?"

Ginger had lived on the island her whole life, and had taken over the ferry business when her dad passed away. She'd been working hard at growing the business ever since, adding boats for dinner cruises and dolphin watches. And she'd been Andie's other maid of honor at the wedding that didn't happen. Given the three of them were such good friends, Andie knew that Roni would have spent the afternoon filling Ginger in on everything that had happened at the bar earlier that day.

Andie nodded, knowing they had to have the conversation, but regretting the stress she could already feel returning to her shoulders at the thought of it. "Yep," she said. "Mark."

Roni squealed, and Maggie clapped when Roni's toss went sailing perfectly to Hunter.

"Roni said he showed up at Gin's today, unaware you were there."

"But not unaware she was here on the island, apparently," Roni tacked on as she jogged back to the group.

Andie shot her friend a hard look. "And someone just let him waltz back through the restaurant to search for me. Come on, Roni, what was that about? You had to know I didn't want to talk to him."

The Frisbee whizzed past, close to Ginger's head, and Andie smiled at Maggie as she fell to her knees in a giggling fit.

"Did you do that, Maggie Moo?" Andie asked.

"No!" The girl giggled harder and pointed to Hunter. "It was him."

Hunter shrugged his slim shoulders. "Y'all weren't paying attention. I was just making sure you didn't forget that we're playing here."

"I see." Andie grabbed the Frisbee and shot both kids an evil grin. "Then you'd better beware! Because I have it now."

Maggie giggled louder and Hunter's eyes went wide. He held up his hands in a sign of surrender. "I'm sorry." He laughed.

"Too late for that, kid." Andie pulled back and sent it sailing well over his head so he'd have to run hard to catch it. He had a wide competitive streak. Not going after it was not an option.

Maggie took off after him, arms flailing and laughter ringing out, and Andie turned back to her friends. She really did enjoy playing with the kids. Few moments in her life were this laid-back. She loved it.

"Roni?" she asked. "What was that about? You know how I feel about Mark. Why would you let him come back there?"

Roni twisted up her mouth as she stood in front of her friend, then eyed Ginger as if looking for help. When none was forthcoming, she finally blurted out, "Because I'm not sure I do know how you feel about him."

"How can you not? He left me at the altar. How do you think I feel? I hate him!"

"Yeah," Roni started. "But that was four years ago. And Andie, you haven't dated anyone since."

"So what?"

Ginger nodded, catching the Frisbee as it came back and sending it sailing once again. "She has a good point."

"What point?" Andie asked. "I haven't heard a point."

47

"That you should be dating by now. You should be over Mark," Roni added.

"I am!"

"Then why won't you date? You've had plenty of guys ask you out. And why did you look so shaken when you saw him today?"

Andie clenched her fists at her sides as she glared at her friends, ignoring the disc that flew over their heads. She forced herself to lower her voice to keep from screaming in frustration. "I don't date because I have a business to run, and I looked shaken because I was not expecting him to show up in my bar."

"But you looked..." Roni paused, once again turning to Ginger. "Help me out here. Tell her how she looks right now, just from talking about him."

Ginger shot Andie an apologetic look and nodded. "I see what she's talking about. You look kind of...uh..."

"What? Upset? Because the man left me to explain to everyone that the wedding they'd come to see was not going to happen. Why wouldn't I be upset about that?"

"Yes, we understand that, but it's—"

"You think that since it's been four years I should be past it and welcome him with open arms?"

"No! Of course not. We're not saying you shouldn't still be upset. We're just saying..." Ginger flapped her arms in Andie's general direction and then dropped them to her sides, all the fight gone out of her. "Your eyes, Andie. Your eyes are your weakness, sweetheart. They tell everything."

Andie stood unmoving, barely noticing when Hunter mumbled something at them as he ran past to get the Frisbee. She looked from one friend to the other, then followed Roni's gaze toward the boardwalk in the distance. Mark was standing there watching them, the sky, purple and pink from the setting sun, outlining his broad frame.

She faced her friends and pinned them with a hard look. "And what do you two think my eyes are telling you?"

"That it's not over," they said in unison.

Andie turned from them without another word and motioned with her hand to Hunter, forcing the movement to look normal. "Sorry, kiddo. Toss it here. I promise to pay attention."

And she would not pay attention to her friends. Because they were wrong.

"We're not saying you need to do anything other than get some closure, Andie," Ginger said, her voice soft and urging.

"I had closure on my wedding day." Andie said through gritted teeth. "My fiancé chose *not* to marry me, and I moved on. And I am over it. Completely." She swung back to her friends. "And how could you not support me on this? You're my friends. You're supposed to be there for me when I need you."

They both nodded. "We are here for you," Roni said. She made a move with her hand that let Andie know that Mark was now heading in their direction. "And we'll destroy him if he hurts you again—trust me, I'll be first in line for that—but we think you need a chance to finish this once and for all. Face-to-face."

She did not want to finish anything with him. "He finished it years ago."

"Then why is he back now?" Ginger asked.

The same question had been running through Andie's mind all afternoon.

Mark stepped up beside her and Roni sent him a hard look, making it clear she would have her eye on him, then dragged Ginger off to fetch the kids.

What worthless friends.

Andie did not turn to Mark. Instead, she stood there in the disappearing light, watching Roni and Ginger walk Hunter and Maggie over the dunes, where they would deposit them home safe and sound. And she wanted to cry. She wanted someone to make her feel safe and sound. And she did not want to finish anything with Mark. Because she honestly had no idea what that would even entail.

"Are you going to at least acknowledge that I'm here?" he finally asked, his voice as hard as she wanted hers to be.

She merely shook her head. No. She was not.

She started walking slowly down the beach in the direction her friends had gone, fighting the tears that begged to be released.

CHAPTER FOUR

Mark remained where he was, his shoes in hand and his pant legs rolled up above his ankles, taking in the slow, carefully modulated movements of Andie's stride. At least she wasn't running from him.

He figured he could either walk away and forget why he'd come—which would definitely be the easiest thing to do—and thus spend the remainder of his time on the island avoiding her, or he could go after her and force the conversation they needed to have. But the decision had to be made right then. Whatever he did, it would impact the remainder of the trip.

If he walked away, it would be over. For good. No more conversations, no more Andie.

That thought jabbed a pinprick of pain at the base of his chest.

But if they talked…

He watched her, studied her stiff posture as she moved. If he forced a conversation, she would fight it. She wouldn't want him to see her pain, but he knew it was there. Of course he knew. He'd caused it. He'd caused his own in return. And then he'd reopened everything by showing up on Turtle Island.

He nodded to himself. They had to talk, though chances were good nothing was truly fixable at this point.

And then there was the other issue.

The one where he wanted to beg her forgiveness and ask for another chance. And how ridiculous was that? But as he'd watched her laugh and have fun out here on the beach, he'd been reminded of those early days, of the dreams he'd made with her. She'd once been that happy with him. She'd danced every night whether music was playing or not. And he'd built his world around dreams of the two of them growing old together. Raising a family together. He'd even planned to have a weekend home on the beach, just for her.

And he'd given it all up in the blink of an eye.

He'd never really doubted his decision until tonight, but as he'd stood watching her, his insides had howled at the injustice of it all. Had he given up too easily?

Was it too late to find out?

Was he a moron for even having the thought?

Yes.

"Andie," he called out. Maybe it was too late for them, but she did deserve an apology.

She didn't turn, but she did stop walking. It was so dark now that she was merely one of the shadows, but he could see her well enough. She was soft and curvy, standing there with the loose skirt of her dress billowing around her knees and her bare feet digging in the sand. She had the ankle bracelet on, too. The one she'd always worn. Something about it had always added to the need he'd felt to protect her.

Even without another conversation, he already knew that she hadn't changed that much. She was still sweet and gentle on the inside. It was the way she'd been made. But the woman could get riled. And he suspected she was very much that way at the moment.

Not only had he sought her out when she'd clearly been avoiding him, but her friends had also deserted her. Only, not before the short one had shot him the I'll-kill-you-in-an-instant-if-you-hurt-her look. That had come from Roni. She'd been at Gin's earlier. He'd finally recognized her from the rehearsal dinner from years ago. No wonder she'd gone cold on him at the bar.

He had a feeling that either she or Ginger—the other friend who'd been both on the sand with them and in Boston at the wedding—would gladly skin him alive if he hurt Andie again, but he couldn't walk away just yet. He'd found himself physically unable to not seek her out.

He moved closer, unsure where to start. Before he had a chance to figure it out, the moon peeked out from behind a cloud, and Andie rotated in his direction. It was only a half moon, but enough to illuminate her features. Her face appeared as smooth as carved rock, and her long, reddish-brown hair blew out behind her, the loose curls catching in the breeze.

"You're beautiful, Andie."

A sardonic slash angled across her mouth. "Don't try to sweet-talk me, Mark. I'm immune to you now."

"I wasn't," he said. He wanted to reach out and touch her but valued his limb. "But it's the truth. You were beautiful before, but here in the moonlight, on the beach, you're stunning. You look like you belong."

She nodded. "I do. I should thank you for that, I suppose."

Though she didn't look very thankful at the moment. When no other words came to him, he said the only thing running through his mind. "I'm sorry," he whispered.

The clouds shifted, obscuring the moonlight so that he couldn't see her eyes, but he got a good sense of her thoughts from the stiffness in her body. He swallowed against the lump in his throat.

"Is that it?" she asked. "All you wanted to say?"

"No."

She crossed her arms over her chest. "Then say it and let's call this done, shall we?"

Her attitude suddenly irritated the hell out of him. He wasn't used to people not backing down. Stepping closer, he put his face down in front of hers. "Lose the attitude, Andie, we both made mistakes back then."

"Yet only one of us was left at the altar."

"You left me little choice."

Her eyes widened for a second before her right hand rose and slapped him hard across the face. The sound rang out in the night.

"I did *nothing* to deserve being left like that," she said.

Except plan to marry him for name only.

Working his jaw back and forth, wishing it didn't sting like a mother, he shifted his shoes into his right hand, preparing to use his left to catch any additional hits if they came. He may let her get away with that one, but it would be the only one. "That make you feel better?" he asked.

"It didn't make me feel worse."

"Then how about this?" He clamped his arm around her waist and jerked her body to his, lowering his mouth to hers before she could utter a complaint.

And he nearly lost his mind in the taste of her.

He hadn't intended to kiss her, but he also couldn't say the idea hadn't played out in his fantasies over the last twelve hours, either. Nor over the last six months.

Kissing Andie once more was worth the frustration of having to see her again and know she wasn't his.

When she didn't immediately push him away, he loosened his stance and took the kiss deeper, groaning when she opened her mouth and let him in. She softened against him and made little noises that dragged way too many memories from the trenches of his mind. They had never had a problem with this.

Her tongue stroked his, and he dropped the shoes he was holding to bring both hands up to grip the sides of her face, devouring her. God, he'd missed this.

He'd missed her.

It was his Andie, in his arms again. Kissing him as wildly as she ever had.

And then kneeing him in the crotch.

He bent over at the waist, coughing and clutching at his balls. "Dammit!" The woman had landed a direct hit. "*Sonof-abitch*," he growled out. "Did you have to do that?"

Shit. He was going to lose his dinner.

"Seemed like the thing to do at the moment," she answered, her voice strangely flat. "I was feeling attacked."

He turned his back to her, fighting the urge to puke and trying to ignore the whistling that rushed through his head. His eyes watered like a baby's. He supposed he might have deserved that. If it had been anyone else grabbing and kissing her without invitation, he would have encouraged the move. But the knowledge certainly didn't make the throbbing any less.

When he could finally pull in enough air to breathe without making a panting sound, he slowly straightened and turned back to her, his chest rising and falling with the adrenaline now coursing through him. The moonlight was showcasing Andie's face once more, and he could make out the concern for him in her eyes, even though her body language read differently.

She stood there with his shoes, one in each hand, hands locked at her waist. "Are you about finished?"

He looked skyward as if something there would help make her understand. "You kneed me in the balls, Andie. Did you think it wouldn't hurt?"

And stupidly, he wanted to kiss her again.

"I'd hoped it would hurt. A lot. But to tell you the truth, I've never done that before. Didn't know if I did it hard enough or not."

"You did it just fine, sweetheart." He would laugh if he could. Instead, he took a step closer, only to watch her take one away. So he stopped and held up his hands. "Fine. I won't touch you again." He paused, unsure why he wanted to push her buttons instead of simply give her the apology he'd come to deliver. "If you'll admit you liked it."

Her mouth dropped open. "Of course I didn't like it. I was faking it, you idiot. Softening you up before I backed you off."

"And you did a good job of the backing off part, but I also caught a little moan of pleasure in there. It didn't sound fake, Andie."

"Well, it was."

He took that step closer. "Prove it."

This time her chin came up, but she didn't move away. "I will do no such thing. Didn't you come here to give me some sort of lame apology or something?"

"That was before you attempted to make me infertile." One more step and he was back within touching distance.

They stood there staring at each other, and he watched her thoughts run through her eyes. She was as intrigued as he by the chemistry still between them, yet she wasn't ready to give in to it. She was also still furious with him. And he could see the hurt. It was hiding way in the back, but it was there. Which put his testosterone level back where it belonged and reminded him that yes, he had come to apologize for his past behavior.

He held out his hands in a sign of surrender and eased back out of her space. "You're right, I'm sorry. Tonight isn't the time or place to explore what's still there between us. Hand over my shoes, and I'll give you your apology."

Her hands came off her waist to pass over the shoes, but then she stopped, her head tilting at an angle to study him. She shot him a look; the same one that had first captured his attention at Harvard. It was half mischievous, and a lot bold. And it made his blood once again begin to heat.

Before he could figure out what it meant, she'd whirled and sent one of his thousand dollar Italian loafers out into the rolling waves.

"What are you doing?" he shouted. He took off after the shoe, splashing into the water, but the wave quickly rose to his knees, almost pulling him down in the shifting sand. He turned back to her. The water lapped at her ankles now, but she didn't move away from it. "What in the world, Andie?"

She merely shrugged. "Figured it would serve you right for kissing me."

"The knee to the groin was punishment for kissing you." He continued walking through the now receding water, dragging his feet around, hoping to find his shoe.

"No, the knee to the groin was for embarrassing me in front of both of our families four years ago."

He looked back at her, his shoe forgotten, aware of how she'd stated the facts. "Not for hurting you, then? Just for the embarrassment?"

That thought disturbed him more than it should have after all this time. He'd wanted to believe that she had really loved him, even though evidence had suggested otherwise.

She nibbled on her lip but didn't immediately answer, so he headed back in her direction. He wanted to hear it. That yes, embarrassment had been his worst crime that day, not breaking her heart. Not as Ginny had implied. He wanted her to admit it. Then he would quit feeling bad for ending it the way he had. He'd deserved to maintain some amount of integrity, after all. And if the woman hadn't loved him, he figured she'd deserved to be left at the altar for breaking his heart in two.

"The knee was for the embarrassment, yes," she began, meeting his gaze as he stopped near her, the water now tickling their shins. She turned so that her face was once again thrown into shadows, and her voice grew soft. "I haven't figured out yet what to do for the pain."

And just that fast his heart cracked, and he couldn't have kept his distance if he'd wanted to. And he didn't want to.

"Aw, babe." He reached for her, cupping her lightly by the arms. "I really am sorry. I was the lowest kind of jerk that day."

She nodded, suddenly seeming fragile in his hands. "You were. But why? Was I really so bad? Did your mother talk you out of it? Did Rob?"

"No," he stated emphatically. "No to all of it. Why would my mother talk me out of it? She loved you."

Andie's shoulders lifted with a shrug. "I overheard her one day saying she didn't think you should marry me."

"What?" Without meaning to, he stepped back in shock. In doing so, his hands slipped from her arms. He immediately reached out to touch her again, but she pulled away. He lowered his hands. "I can't imagine why she would have said that. She thought you were terrific."

"Rob then?"

He shook his head. Rob had not liked her from the day they'd met, and Andie had returned the sentiment. "Rob was there when I made my decision." He'd been waiting in the car as Mark had run into the apartment. "But he had nothing to do with it."

"Yet he was only too happy to deliver the news."

Mark started to protest, but then realized that she was right. Rob had been thrilled to tell her. In fact, he'd been the one to suggest he go to the church instead of Mark.

Having just overheard Andie on her call, Mark had not wanted to talk to her. He was furious that he'd let himself fall so hard, when she'd clearly been after something else entirely. "I can't say that Rob was *unhappy* to deliver the news. He has a sick sense of humor like that."

Dark eyes studied him until Mark began to shift from foot to foot. He wanted to know what she was thinking.

Suddenly, her arm shot up and his other loafer hit the ocean.

"What was that for?" he asked, incredulity lining his voice. Not that he could have worn just one shoe, but it seemed sacrilegious to toss both of them in the water.

"For sending Rob instead of having the guts to come yourself."

He nodded, suddenly sober with the hurt he'd caused. Maybe she hadn't loved him as much as he'd wanted her to, but it wasn't as if nothing had been between them. Their kiss of only a few moments ago had shown that there had once been something there. Heck, there was still something there. She may claim she'd been faking it, but he'd felt her body tremble against his.

"I came by the apartment that morning. Did Rob tell you that?"

Wide eyes blinked up at him, confused. "When?"

Right. Of course Rob hadn't told her that.

Mark had spent the night before at his parents' home, as he and Andie had planned to follow tradition and not see each other until she walked down the aisle. Only he'd had a gift for her. Something that would've made the day even more special. And he'd wanted to give it to her with no one else around.

But seeing the bride before the wedding had definitely brought bad luck.

"The morning of the wedding. You were on a conference call when I came in."

She looked briefly stunned, and then nodded. It hadn't taken her long to remember who she'd been talking to. "Why didn't you say something?"

"Because you were picking out an outfit to wear to the office."

She lowered her gaze. They'd had many arguments about how much she'd been working. The fact that his mother had planned the majority of their wedding instead of her had been a testament to her long hours.

"It was an important account," she said, almost too softly to hear.

"I gathered that."

At some point, they'd begun walking side by side through the rising tide, and he could now make out another couple far off in the distance. He hoped they were enjoying themselves instead of ripping their hearts open like they were.

Andie stopped and faced him. "Is that why? Because I was going into the office that morning? I told you I was at a critical point in my job. But I wouldn't have been late for my own wedding."

"Andie, you'd barely had anything to do with the wedding for months. All you thought about was the job. We still made love,"—they'd come together in the middle of the night as explosively as they ever had—"but other than that, I never saw you. We never talked."

"But my job was important. I'd told you that."

He nodded. "And having a wife who thought of me on occasion was important, too."

"Thought of you, as in quit her job and stayed home to raise the kids. Right? Like your mom? We'd talked about that so much."

"Argued about it."

"Yes, argued. Because you wanted me to be something I wasn't. Did you really not realize until that morning that I wasn't going to be that kind of wife? That it wasn't what I wanted?"

"No. That wasn't it. I meant it every single time I told you I didn't mind if you worked." And he had, even though he would still argue that the job she'd had wasn't the right one for her. His father had called in a favor because she'd wanted it so bad, but it had never felt like a good fit for her. "But what I didn't realize until that morning, and what sealed the deal for me, was that you were more interested in marrying me for my name than because you wanted *me.*"

Shock registered on her face. "I was not—"

"I heard you on the phone. You were not casual in the way you tossed around the Kavanaugh name. And you invited your client to the wedding so you could introduce them to my parents. Come on, babe. What else was I supposed to think?"

The guilt on her face made it plain. He'd come to the correct conclusion.

"It wasn't like that," she started.

A small, regret-filled smile was all he had left. "It was exactly like that. You were more interested in a career and my name than in being my wife."

She was quiet for a long time, as they once again began moving down the beach. They passed behind Whitmore Inn, and he couldn't help but take in the mansion with the triple layer decks running the length of the house. In the eighteen months that they'd dated, sixteen of them engaged and living together, she'd never told him that her aunt owned a place like this. He'd barely even known her aunt existed. It made him wonder what else about her he hadn't been aware of. And why he hadn't pushed for more.

It wasn't like he'd kept his life from her.

He paused in his thoughts as he admitted that yes, actually, there had been one part he'd kept from her. But that part hadn't mattered. It had been buried long ago.

Finally she stopped walking and turned to him, and he wanted to wrap his arms around her and take them back to before she'd finished school, before she got her job. They'd been happy then.

"I might have had my priorities screwed up, but you were more to me than a name," she whispered. Lifting her hands, she stroked her fingers along his cheeks, as if seeing them through her touch. Her face was a study in thought. It caused him physical pain to stand there and let her touch him like that, but he was helpless to stop the movements. "Way more," she said.

She lifted to her tiptoes and put her lips to his, and he forced himself not to press for more than the good-bye that he could feel behind the gesture. He'd come here for this.

He'd thought it had been good-bye four years ago, but this nearly destroyed him.

When she pulled back, she swiped a thumb over his bottom lip, then lowered her hand. "I loved you, Mark. I swear I did. I just didn't know how to do that and the job, too, I guess."

And he'd tossed it all aside without trying to make it work.

Frustration had him clenching his jaw, but the soft look in her eyes made him think of another way to say good-bye. Maybe it was too late for them, but that didn't mean they had to finish it her way.

That light kiss had not been enough. They'd once been so much more to each other. And she was here now. Right in front of him. And he'd already figured out that she wasn't immune to him as she'd claimed.

Without giving it further thought, he scooped her up against him and settled his mouth to hers, giving her only the briefest chance to tell him to stop. But instead of calling a halt, she opened her lips and released the sweetest, softest sigh he hadn't heard in four years. And he was a goner.

EPISODE THREE

CHAPTER FIVE

Andie got lost in the feel of Mark's mouth. It was a bad idea, a really bad one. But she didn't care. She'd just found out that she'd lost him over a job she'd hated. A job she'd gotten fired from because she hadn't been able to win the account he'd mentioned.

Life sure had a way of laughing in your face sometimes.

So right now she was laughing back. She and Mark may still be from different worlds, but he was there now, and his kiss made her think of roasted marshmallows. He was warm and tough on the outside, but inside he was gooey and delicious and she couldn't get enough. She wanted to dip her tongue in and lap him up.

A wave crashed against them, plastering her dress to her legs, and she had the momentary thought that they needed to stop. This wasn't going anywhere—*they* weren't going anywhere. And anyway, she was pretty sure she was still mad at him. At least a little.

And she knew she'd just given him a good-bye kiss.

They should not be doing this.

Another wave slammed, and he grunted and slid his hands down to her butt, pulling her tighter against him. While trying to keep her eyes from rolling back in her head with the pure pleasure of his kiss, she sidled closer, gliding her arms up his chest to wrap tight around his neck. Her breasts pressed against his chest.

"Andie," he moaned. His mouth traced along her jaw until he reached her ear. He nipped, and shivers flew down her spine, pulling another one of those moans he'd mentioned out of her.

"This isn't a good idea," she whispered. She had to keep her sanity about her. Somebody had to, and she was pretty sure he wasn't heading down a sane path.

His lips landed on the curve of her neck, and her breasts raised their nipples for attention. *Me, please*, they seemed to be saying, and she couldn't help but laugh at the joy of it. Mark was kissing her. Stupid idea or not, she loved it. It had been far too long.

"I don't care if it's the worst idea in the world," he returned. He lifted his head to stare down at her. "It's brilliant."

His hands nudged her rear again, bringing her more into alignment with his parts, and she lifted her legs to wrap around him. His answering groan let her know that's what he'd had in mind. Then his hand came around to the front of her to stroke a hot finger down into the vee of her dress. He pulled one edge to the side so he could lick his way over the top curve of her breast, and she was pretty sure she'd died and gone home to heaven.

She loosened her grip and leaned back, thrusting up toward him, wanting his mouth on her. Ready to plead for it to be there. His mouth and her breast were meant to spend some quality time together.

A far-off sound penetrated the buzzing in her head as she worked through options for getting her hands under his shirt while not removing herself from his body. When the sound came again, she paused, twisting her head around at the same time as Mark, and that's when she realized what it was. Laughter.

They both squinted in the direction of the only other couple they could make out on the private beach. They were quite a ways up the coast. She wasn't sure if the sound was drifting down from them or not, but it reminded her that they were not alone—and this was not the time to be forgetting her priorities.

She had a job to do and a business to run, and if she spent her evenings frolicking with the guests—with Mark— she might lose focus and let something go wrong.

"We—"

She stopped talking as another wave slammed into them, splashing salt water into her mouth and knocking them both to the ground. Mark let go of her and they crawled on all fours until the water receded, then she rolled over and propped herself up on her elbows, sputtering water from her face. The tide had risen more than she'd realized. They were now both lying in water.

Helping each other to their feet, they made their way up the beach until they hit dry land, then plopped down, not touching, to sit facing the water. She pressed her fingertips to her lips.

Christ, it was still hot between them.

She looked at him. "We can't do this, Mark."

He sat there, knees raised and arms propped across them, wet hair pushed back off his face, and water dripping from his chin. And he watched her. His dark eyes stared into her soul and she wanted to crawl over in front of him and kiss him again. The man oozed potency.

"We can't," she reiterated, needing him to agree so she wouldn't be tempted to change her mind. "It's a horrible idea."

"Funny, it didn't feel like a horrible idea." His voice was low and deep, and she closed her eyes at the sound of it, turning away so he couldn't see what it did to her.

"But it is," she whispered. "And we both know it." She would have stood up if she hadn't still been out of breath from dragging herself from the water. Getting her thoughts under control, she peered back at him. "That kiss was good-bye, Mark. I never got it before, and I think maybe I needed it. But it's good-bye."

He nodded, not arguing but not looking particularly convinced, either. "Pretty hot good-bye, babe. You sure we shouldn't go with it? Could make for an interesting couple of weeks."

Light laughter lifted out of her and she dropped back to the sand to stare up at the dark sky, knowing she was a miserable mess, both inside and out. "Would definitely make for an interesting couple of weeks, but no. This wedding is important to me. I've got to focus all my attention on getting it right."

He went silent and she realized she'd just done what he'd always accused her of, putting the job before him. But she had to. The job was her life. He was not.

She peeked over at him from beneath her lashes, wishing the moment could be as romantic as the dark, warm night suggested. "I can't let a good time interfere with what could impact the rest of my life."

"Yeah," he bit out. "I know." He rose to his feet and held a hand down to her. "I wasn't thinking straight. I brought work with me, too. Dad's retiring in a couple months and I'm trying to get ahead of my own workload before I take on half of his."

She slid her cool hand into his warmer, much larger one and let him pull her up. "Jonathan still there?"

There were four Kavanaugh boys—Mark being the baby—and from what she'd learned before, they were all equally ambitious. Jonathan was the oldest, and had already been at the Kavanaugh firm when she and Mark had first gotten together.

"Yes. It'll soon be just me and him unless we bring in a partner. Ryan is still in New York, happy as a fireman, and Eddie never came back to Boston once he left for college. He should be down for the wedding, though. I'm looking forward to seeing him."

She stared up at the man Mark had matured into, and couldn't stop the shiver that wracked her body. He was hard and big and seemed unstoppable. She couldn't imagine sitting on the opposite side of a courtroom from him. Yet he was the gentlest person in the world when it came to his family. He deserved someone who could be like his mother and stay home to raise his babies.

The thought made her wonder what had gone wrong between him and Ms. Ryan, but that was one question she was not going to ask.

"We'll make sure not to kiss anymore so we'll both be able to think straight," Andie said. "That way both of us can get our jobs done."

Hooded eyes studied her mouth before slowly lifting to her eyes. Her thighs tingled, signaling they knew what he'd been thinking as he'd looked at her. "Sure," he said. "That's exactly what we'll do." He motioned with his head to the house behind them. "Go on inside. I'll wait to see you in before I head back to the bar for my car."

Because he had to drive over to the hotel instead of simply going inside with her. Which made her feel guilty. Granted, it was a very nice hotel. The oldest on the island, and it came with a five-star rating. It also had a grand ballroom that Seaglass used for receptions when couples wanted something more opulent than an open-air, tented reception area.

But still, until the remainder of the guests arrived, Mark was the only one from the group staying at the hotel. Even though the plumber had actually made it to the house earlier to take care of the problem in one of the rooms, she hadn't told Kayla to move Mark over. It felt safer knowing he wasn't just a few doors down from her.

"Thanks, Mark." She wasn't really sure what she was thanking him for. Maybe the apology, maybe the good-bye kiss. And maybe just for seeking her out. She accepted now that she had needed to have a conversation with him, had needed closure, just as her friends had thought.

They began walking toward the boardwalk that led to the back of the inn, and she almost smiled as she remembered tossing his shoes in the ocean. That had certainly made her feel better. Maybe she was thanking him for not losing his mind when she'd done that. Those shoes had to have cost a fortune.

"I'll see you in the morning," she said. They reached the steps and she smiled up at him, giving him the polite expression she'd give anyone. This was where they'd part. "Breakfast will be in the main dining room here between seven and nine, and the trolley will be out front at ten."

The group would be taking a tour of the historic section of the island tomorrow.

"I think I'll sit this one out," he said. "That work I mentioned. I'll catch up with everyone tomorrow night."

"Oh. Okay." She nodded. "That's probably a good idea."

She might have no more plans for kissing him, but knowing she wouldn't even get to see him tomorrow made her stomach feel funny. Once they returned from the tour, there was downtime, and then the group had reservations at a local restaurant.

"Okay then." She nodded again, knowing she looked silly just standing there gawking at him. Time to go in. "Then...yeah...thanks."

She headed to the house before she could utter another *okay* or *thanks*, and didn't let herself look back as she walked. She and Mark were now officially, finally over. She could report in to Roni and Ginger that they had gotten their closure. And she was fine.

When she reached the house, she let herself peek back toward the ocean, and when Mark lifted his hand in a brief wave, she was shocked to find tears fill her eyes. Ducking inside the lower level, she went to the outside shower stall and stood under the warm spray, salt water–logged clothes and all, washing the sand off. And pretending she wasn't crying.

~

Oversleeping was not the norm for Andie, but after a night of tossing and turning while thinking about kisses and one wet, hot man—and wanting more of both—she was more than a little late coming downstairs the next morning. And she was not in the best of moods.

Slipping into the kitchen, she grabbed a banana and a pear, and shoved them into her purse, hoping she'd get a minute to eat them since she'd missed out on breakfast. She then went to the fridge in search of string cheese for some protein.

"Where have you been?" Aunt Ginny asked, coming in from the main living area and laughing from something that had just been said outside the kitchen. She was wearing white gaucho pants, strappy turquoise-jeweled sandals, and a lime-green top. She looked adorable, as always.

"What's so funny?" Andie asked. She was grumpy from lack of sleep and now wished she'd dug through Aunt Ginny's closet instead of her own. Her yellow pencil skirt and cap-sleeved top weren't nearly as cute as Ginny's attire. She rubbed her thumb over the large ring on her first finger. At least her jeweled butterfly ring was cute. "And I overslept, that's all."

Aunt Ginny's eyebrows lifted half an inch but stopped when Andie made a face at her. She'd been giving Andie "the look" all her life, but Andie was not in the mood for it this morning.

"Save it," Andie growled out. "I'm fully aware I should have been up and down here at least two hours ago. But I had a rough night."

"Anything to do with an after-hours walk on the beach?"

"What?" Andie shot her a wide-eyed look. "How do you *always* know what I do?"

Ginny just shook her head, as if disappointed in Andie for coming off the information so easily.

Andie sighed and collapsed into a chair. She pulled the banana from her purse and began to peel it. "How do you do that, Aunt Ginny? You had no hard evidence I'd been out on the beach with him last night, did you?"

Andie didn't even pretend her beach romp had been with anyone but Mark. Ginny knew her too well. Heck, knowing her aunt, she'd probably told Mark where to find her. And then declared it fate.

"Simple deducing on my part, child." Ginny went to the sink to wash her hands, turning in Andie's direction as she dried them on a paper towel. "I knew you'd snuck off to play with the kids last night, and then I saw Mark when I went up to my room later. He was walking back toward the bar. Only he appeared to be soaking wet." She studied Andie with a look of confusion. "I wasn't sure if you'd been out there with him or if he'd decided to drown his sorrows and plunged his worthless self into the ocean."

Andie narrowed her eyes on her aunt. "It would spit him back out if he did. So you set me up to find out? You could have just asked."

"I know, but teasing you is much more fun." Aunt Ginny sat down across from Andie at the kitchen island, her expression going serious. "What happened? Did you talk at least? Did you push him in the water?"

Kayla made a quick pass through the room, the model of efficiency, and tossed a look at the two women. "Ten minutes, Andie. The trolley is already out front."

"Got it." Andie rose, thinking she'd leave Ginny hanging. No need to tell the woman everything. She'd likely find it out on her own, anyway. Plus, there was a tour to chaperone.

"Hold on, young lady." Aunt Ginny reached out and wrapped her fingers around Andie's wrist. "At least tell me if you're okay? Did you talk?"

Sadness suddenly filled the space behind Andie's ribs. She nodded. "Yes, we talked. And if you're the one who sent him, I should kick your butt, but I'll thank you instead. It was closure. Finally." She reached over and squeezed her aunt's forearm. "I hadn't realized I was stalled, Aunt Ginny, but I can move on now. It's what I needed."

She only wished she could move on without remembering how she'd wanted to rip Mark's clothes from his body as they'd stood in the middle of the ocean.

Aunt Ginny studied her for a few seconds, then gave a small nod and leaned over to plant a kiss firmly on Andie's cheek. "Good girl," she whispered. "I'm happy for you. Now tell me how he got all wet."

A smile bloomed on Andie's face. She was not going to admit they'd rolled around in the water and she'd given serious consideration to having a hot two-week fling, but she'd share one morsel she knew her aunt would love. She put her hand on the door, ready to slip outside, but shot Aunt Ginny a quick wink before she went. "I threw his very expensive shoes about thirty feet out in the water. And the waves weren't gentle."

She grinned wider at the sound of her aunt's boisterous laughter.

"That's my girl," Aunt Ginny said, giving Andie a fist pump.

Andie waved good-bye and hurried outside, finishing the banana as she made her way to the island trolley—and loving Aunt Ginny's ability to always brighten her mood.

It was a large group, with twenty-seven people joining the tour—not counting the groom's grandparents, who hadn't arrived yet, and Mark, who she was glad wasn't coming. Really. Because she needed to be the perfect, gracious hostess. And having Mark there would make her nervous. Or give her something to stare at that she shouldn't even be looking at. Geez, that man had only grown hotter since she'd known him.

Before she made it to the road, Mr. Jordan fell into step beside her. "Good morning, Ms. Shayne."

"Mr. Jordan." She flashed her best smile. "How are you today? I hope you slept well? The room you're in is fine?"

"Yes, yes. Perfect. In fact, we like it better than the first we'd been placed in."

"Terrific." The first room had more space, but the deck had been on the side of the house and with a smaller area to directly enjoy the ocean. It had also been on the second floor instead of the third. The third floor had more privacy and a separate shared living area for guests staying on that level.

"It has a great view," Mr. Jordan added.

Andie looked up at him from the corner of one eye, picking up from his tone that he was heading somewhere with the conversation but unsure where that might be. "Yes. You should have a fully unobstructed view of the beach from there. I glanced out myself before I went to bed last night, and the moon was hitting the water just beautifully. I hope you got a chance to take it in…"

Oh, hell. That's where the conversation was going. She and Mark had been directly behind the house. Mr. Jordan must have seen them. She wet her lips and opened her mouth to finish her sentence, but Mr. Jordan spoke first.

"That's correct, Ms. Shayne. It does have a perfect view of the beach. And though the sun sets on the other side of the island, Marilynn and I like to sit outside and take in the ending of the day when we have the chance. I thought this trip would be a good time for such an opportunity."

Andie lowered her gaze, searching for something to say to make the idea of her and Mark having a romp on the beach seem okay.

"I trust I won't see the same sight again throughout the rest of my visit, Ms. Shayne?"

She nodded, feeling like a small child who'd been caught eating Santa's cookies off the platter. "That's correct, sir. I can't speak for our guests, but I can speak for myself. You will not be subjected to...such behavior again. And I do apologize you had to witness it last night."

He patted her on the shoulder as they neared the trolley. "Good to hear," he said, then boarded to sit beside his waiting wife. Andie stepped back from the trolley and shifted her gaze, unable to meet Mrs. Jordan's look. No doubt it would be as censorious as her husband's tone.

The Jordans had been at Whitmore Mansion less than twenty-four hours, and already their toilet had overflowed and they'd had to watch her and Mark going at each other like starved animals. Thank goodness it hadn't gone any farther than kissing.

The bonus clause in the contract stipulated the wedding had to go off without a hitch. Not that there couldn't be small hiccups along the way. Though knowing that did little to settle her nerves. Nor did she consider almost getting naked on the beach with her ex a mere hiccup.

She spent the next few minutes greeting guests as they made their way to the trolley, and asking if everything about their stay met their expectations. Everyone seemed completely happy, with the exception of Wendy, one of the bridesmaids.

She had a bungalow along the north perimeter of the property. The downside was that she was within hearing distance of the bungalow that housed one of the groomsmen, who was there with his wife and their two children. Apparently the kids were loud, and Wendy was offended at having to listen to such.

"Starting tonight we'll have activities for the children, if the parents wish them to participate," Andie shared with her. "We'll do our best to tire out the young ones so they'll be less disruptive. How about that?"

Wendy rolled her eyes. "If that's the best you can do."

What a total wench. Andie pasted on her smile. "I'd be glad to have Kayla shift you over to the hotel, if you'd prefer. The accommodations there are superior."

"Are they beachfront?"

"I'm afraid not." Andie did her best to look as if she cared. The reality was that this was not her favorite part of the job. She didn't care to deal with overly picky guests, but she had yet to figure out how to escape doing so.

As her reward for dealing with people like Wendy on a regular basis, she allowed herself one day a week to volunteer at the senior center. Old people made her laugh. They were generally more easygoing than the rest of the world, and rarely took anything too seriously. They were as much fun to hang out with as kids.

"Should I make the arrangements?" Andie asked.

Wendy let out an unladylike huff. "No. I want the beachfront view. I guess I'll be fine where I am if you have nothing else."

"I'm so sorry, but everything else is full. The hotel would be the only other option." There was the room at the house that the Jordans had originally been assigned to. The proper thing to do would be to bring Mark back there since the house was typically reserved for family, the bride and groom—each with a separate room so as not to be presumptuous—as well as the maid of honor and best man.

Andie could make an exception this one time and let the bridesmaid in, but she wasn't sure she wanted her underfoot more than she already was. Something told her that if Wendy were in the main house, the woman would not only be a nuisance but also would make sure the other bridesmaids knew she was getting preferential treatment.

Which was why bridesmaids never had different accommodations from one another.

Nope, she would not break the rules this time, and she wouldn't bring Mark over, either. It would cost her money out of pocket for the additional hotel room, but it was money well spent as far as she was concerned. After their unspoken "truce" the night before, she was fairly certain it would be best to keep her distance from him for the remainder of the time he was there.

Wendy finally went to her seat, pouting, and Andie saw Robert and Penelope heading for the trolley. They were the last to exit the house. Robert stopped to talk with someone as he passed one of the middle seats and Penelope headed on toward Andie, dressed in a lovely pink sundress. The decorations for the wedding were a mix of shades of pink, with pale green and cream as accents. But it had been clear that they were to use loads of pink. Apparently it was a favorite color of the bride's.

"Good morning, Ms. Jordan," Andie greeted Penelope. "Your seat is saved up front."

"Terrific!" Penelope bunched up her shoulders as she spoke, practically bouncing in place. She was a gorgeous young woman, with beautiful honey-hued skin and long blonde hair, and Andie couldn't help but think that she was far too good for the likes of Robert Masterson.

She and Penelope had chatted for only a few minutes the evening before, but it had been long enough to make her wonder what Penelope—who was a few years younger than Robert and no doubt had the ability to get any man she wanted—saw in him. But then, Robert could be a charmer. Andie had seen that in action, herself. He'd been a regular at the bar she'd worked at during graduate school, and had taken every chance he'd gotten to practice his skills.

"I hope you enjoyed your evening," Andie said. "How was breakfast this morning?"

Penelope laughed gaily. "Everything is simply amazing. I'm thrilled we ended up here." Her eyes widened slightly. "Not that I'm glad the first place had the fire, of course."

"Of course not." Andie laughed with her. "But we're glad you're here, too. We intend to make it the wedding of your dreams."

"Well, it has certainly started out that way. And I'm so excited about this tour. I found out after we made the reservations that we had a distant family member who owned a house here on the island at one point." She named the cottage that had once belonged in her family, and Andie assured her that it was one of the homes on the tour.

"Terrific. I was hoping it would be." A bright smile spread across her face again, and Andie had the fleeting thought that she'd never smiled that big in the days leading up to her own wedding.

But she had loved Mark and had been very happy to be marrying him.

Any lack of excitement was simply due to the fact that she'd been too busy. That had to be it. She'd been trying to save her job, and the thrill of preparing for her own wedding had gotten lost in the mix.

Robert headed their way, and Andie stood a little straighter. Not wanting to be forced to make small talk, she excused herself and moved toward her seat at the back of the vehicle. Only, she didn't quite make it past Robert without him making a snide comment as she passed.

"Have fun in the water last night?"

She stopped. "Excuse me?"

He had seen them, too? Geez, had everyone?

He wiggled his eyebrows in a tawdry manner that made her skin crawl and leaned in so close that no one else would be able to hear him. "I told Mark he should go for it, you know. You may be nothing to him now, but you've still got a kickin' bod. No need letting that go to waste when he already knows how to maneuver the landscape."

Ugh.

Before she could come up with an appropriate reply—and aware she had to word any comment very carefully, as she didn't think it beneath Robert to convince the new daddy-in-law not to hand over the bonus—she realized almost everyone in the group was watching, waiting for them to board so the tour could begin.

So she mustered up her professionalism, imagining steel running the length of her spine, and didn't give Robert the benefit of looking him in the eyes. She'd gotten more than enough of this man four years ago. He could not bother her anymore.

She nodded to the driver and tour guide. "Looks like we have everyone here. Shall we go?"

CHAPTER SIX

The sun greeted Mark as he hopped out of his four-door rental and loped up the steps of Whitmore Mansion. It was going on noon, so the group should be well on its way with the tour, which meant Andie would be out of the house.

Mark had been at his desk since daylight, yet he'd found that no matter how hard he'd tried he'd been unable to concentrate on the work he needed to get done.

He was blaming the situation on lack of food.

Sure, the hotel had a perfectly nice restaurant and even room service, if that was what he wanted. But it wasn't. What he wanted was to see Andie again.

Since he'd made sure that wasn't going to happen, he'd take the next best thing. Aunt Ginny. And possibly he could talk her into lunch. He'd overheard her at dinner the night before, mentioning that she was making her famous chicken salad for lunch. For the people who'd gone on the tour. But surely she had leftovers.

The front doors to the house were wide and welcoming, with dark wood trim and clear glass panels, but when he stepped inside, the massive foyer and its attached living room were silent. Walking through the space, he admired the soft hues and the overall comfortable feeling. There were two sitting areas in the living room. One in a semicircle with four cushioned chairs and a small round coffee table. The other was more spread out, with a couple couches and additional chairs grouped around a marble fireplace. Both areas were set up to afford a view through the massive back panel of windows that stretched from one end of the room to the other. The area was inviting and relaxed, yet elegant enough to entertain the top level of guest.

Mark let the view beyond the wraparound deck wash over him. The ocean gleaming in the sun was almost magical. It looked like rippled glass, waiting patiently for some action to disrupt it.

Sounds from the kitchen caught his attention, so he headed that way. He'd checked out the first floor the day before and had gotten the lay of the place. Before he'd been kicked out and sent over to the hotel.

Not that he minded staying over there. He had a lot of work to do, so the added privacy would allow it to happen.

Should allow it to happen, anyway. This morning notwithstanding.

But what Mark wanted was to be *here*. In the middle of everything. And under the same roof as Andie.

And how stupid was that? She'd made it more than clear last night that she didn't have time for him. Not that he would expect her to drop everything and play it's-been-a-long-time-and-we-sure-do-know-how-to-heat-up-the-sheets, or that he would shortchange a major project himself for a night or two with her.

Liar. He'd go without sleep for a week for a night or two with her.

And talk about stupid.

But that's what he'd learned about himself last night as he'd sat in the sand looking out over the ocean and listening to Andie catch her breath. He wanted her back in his bed, if only for two weeks. Hell, if only for a night. But she'd wanted a good-bye kiss. And that was all.

Bullshit.

She wanted a hell of a lot more than that. She had been no more immune to the situation than he had been. She simply had more sense than him and wasn't planning to do anything about it. He should learn a thing or two from her.

The last thing he needed to come from this trip was to return home with his head even more screwed up because of her. But sweet Jesus, she tasted good. And she felt good. And she'd wrapped her legs around him like she'd been waiting to do that for years.

Good Lord, he was going to make himself hard just thinking about her.

"Morning, Mark."

He jerked to a stop and lifted his head, not realizing he'd landed in the kitchen. Ginny stood on the other side of the counter at the sink, her back to him, her face peeking back over one shoulder. Her green eyes watched him carefully.

She held her curls back out of her face with a long blue-and-yellow scarf. It was tied like a headband around the top of her head, with the ends floating out beneath the hair in back, and something about the simple, understated smile she gave him made him think of Andie. Ginny was only her aunt, but if he didn't know better he'd swear she was her mother. They had many of the same mannerisms and, from what he'd seen, the same gentle nature—both with a hint of fire underneath.

"Morning, Genevieve. How are you?" He went for his best courtroom voice, knowing the woman likely still wanted to string him up by his balls.

She shot him a squinty-eyed look, letting him know that she was already on to him. He was clearly up to no good.

And wasn't *that* the truth?

He wanted her niece hot and naked underneath him, and he feared that if someone didn't knock some sense into him soon, he was going to make a play for exactly that. Didn't matter that her job was still more important than him—he didn't care. He only wanted her for sex.

Which made the fact that he was still angry that she'd been planning to marry him for name only inconsequential. He wasn't planning to propose marriage, anyway. Simply a couple weeks of fun.

Ginny reached into a bowl on the counter beside her, picked up an apple, and tossed it to him. He caught it, eyeing the bowl it had come from. It was a woven pattern, made from what appeared to be some kind of vine. And if he were to guess, it was handmade. Very nice.

"Thanks, G.," he said. Her eyes widened at the shortened use of her name, but he just smiled at her, giving her his best innocent expression. When she didn't chunk another apple at him, this time at his head, he continued. "Any chance I might talk you out of some of that chicken salad you had us all salivating over last night?"

She made a *hmph* sound but headed to the refrigerator, wiping her hands on her apron. He grinned wide behind her. He liked her. Mostly because she hadn't castrated him four years ago, but also because he could see Andie in her. It was kind of like seeing what Andie would be like in thirty years.

85

"Don't smile like you think you've gotten away with something, boy."

He arrowed his gaze at the back of her head—how did she know he was smiling?—and wiped the grin from his face. When he didn't say anything, she turned, a heavy bowl in hand, and shot him "the look." He ducked his head and mumbled, "Sorry."

Damn, how did she manage to make him feel about twelve every time she spoke to him?

"Some reason you skipped out on the tour today?" she asked.

He lifted a shoulder. "Had work to do."

"Yet here you sit. You bring it over with you?"

"No." He shot her a look of his own. "I decided to take a break for lunch. If that's okay with you." Geez, could he not take a simple break?

"They don't have lunch at the hotel?" She plopped a plate down on the counter before him, and his mouth watered at the sight of the buttery croissant with the thick, moist chicken squishing out the sides. A pickle spear rested on the plate alongside it, along with cut strawberries and thick kettle chips. His stomach growled in anticipation.

She slid him a soft drink and pointed to a bar stool. He sat. "Something tells me I couldn't have gotten anything at the hotel that would be near as good as this is going to be."

"Well, at least you have half a brain."

He bit into the sandwich, ignoring her jab, then moaned out loud at the crisp mix of flavors hitting his taste buds. "Genevieve, you sure do know your stuff."

"*Hmph,*" she muttered again, then went back to washing the vegetables piled beside the sink. She had her back to him, so he almost missed it when she said, "I hear Andie had her closure last night. She's ready to move on. About time."

A bite of chicken stuck in his throat. After several seconds of choking—during which Ginny made not the slightest effort to help—he picked up the soda, his eyes watering, and took several gulps. When he had cleared his airway, he wiped off his mouth with the back of his hand and looked over at her. She'd finished with the vegetables and was facing him.

"She tell you about last night?" he asked. Hoping Andie hadn't mentioned that he'd had his tongue down her throat and his hand quickly heading to heaven.

She arched her brows. "Told me you talked. Something else you want to share?"

"No." The word came out too fast. "Just that we talked. And then she threw my shoes in the ocean."

Laughter rang from Ginny as the stern expression she'd been going for vanished. Her eyes brightened and her face creased with slight lines. It was a sight to see. But when she bent over at the waist, holding her stomach and still guffawing, he decided it hadn't been that damned funny. He muttered, "They cost me a thousand dollars," which only made her laugh louder.

With nothing to do but wait for her to calm down, he returned to his sandwich. Cooking was one thing Andie hadn't picked up from her aunt. She could barely scoop store-bought chicken salad onto a piece of bread and make it edible. Maybe she'd gotten that "ability" from her mother.

Not that he had any real idea. She'd never said much more than the basics about either her mother or her step-father. He hadn't realized this until after they were engaged, because they'd moved so fast and run so hot. And by the time he'd begun to push for more details, they were already arguing about other things.

Such as her working so many hours.

He still didn't understand why she'd suddenly turned into a crazed workaholic. She'd been fairly normal the first six months of the job. Stressed occasionally, yes, and working the occasional late night. But not putting the job before everything else in her life.

But something had changed her. She'd gone from the happy, gentle girl with the sneaky, mischievous eyes—the girl who'd liked to snuggle with him in the moonlight and dance in the snow—to a singly focused workaholic who barely remembered that he existed. And he'd never been able to get her back. It still hurt that they'd lost what they'd once had, but it had been better to figure that out before it was too late.

Saved each of them from having to hurt the other even worse down the road.

Ginny finally straightened up and swiped fat, dripping tears from her eyes. The smile covering her face pulled at him, and he chuckled lightly along with her, shaking his head at how funny things must look from her point of view.

"She told you about that, too, didn't she?" he asked. "I could see it in your eyes the instant I blurted it out."

He couldn't read her as easily as he could Andie, but easy enough.

Ginny nodded. "She told me that she'd done it, but I don't know more than that. I feel like I should offer some restitution for her misbehavior, maybe offer to pay for them, but I'm not going to."

Mark gave her a droll look. "And I wouldn't let you even if you tried. I probably deserved it, anyway."

"Yeah," she agreed. "You probably did." She pulled out several jars, some oil, and a mix of spices, then set to work tossing together what looked to be a marinade. "She didn't say how it came about, though. Did you make a move on her? Is that what happened?"

A blush he hadn't anticipated swept over him and her eyes grew wide.

"Don't you dare laugh at me," he ground out. He could see that she was about to. The danged woman should be mad he'd put the moves on her niece, and instead she was going to laugh in his face. "She..."

He stopped, unsure what to say, and let out a frustrated sigh. He couldn't very well tell the woman that Andie drove him insane with hunger while at the same time making him want to shake some sense into her.

"She still gets to you, doesn't she?"

The potato chip he'd put in his mouth lay salty against his tongue as he eyed her. He slowly chewed until the chip was nothing but mush, then swallowed. This was what he remembered about Ginny from her trip to his apartment. It had been only days after the wedding, and he'd been hoping that Andie would eventually show up so he could apologize. Instead, Ginny had knocked on his door, there to collect Andie's things.

She had been furious with him, ready to rip him a new one. Yet before she'd left she'd also looked at him as if she'd understood that he was hurting as bad as Andie. Maybe worse. There had been no victorious gleam from her over this fact, merely acknowledgment and acceptance.

He hadn't walked away from Andie easily, and Ginny had known it.

He nodded, not saying a word. Hell yes, Andie still got to him. And how could that be?

It had been four years! He'd had numerous women since. He'd been engaged to be married.

But one look at Andie standing on the beach last night, anger radiating off her at the same time he made out the tender vulnerability he'd always known she held in check, and he'd wanted to wrap her up in his arms and never let her go.

"I don't know what I'm doing here, Ginny. I shouldn't have come."

"Oh, I don't know." She dumped the vegetables in a bag with the marinade and shook the whole mess. "I think you might figure it out if you let yourself."

He thought he might go insane via a slow burn. He should have moved on years ago, but he found he wanted Andie as much today as the first night he'd gone home with her.

And she wanted closure.

These next couple weeks were going to be heavy on frustration.

Kayla came in through the outside door carrying a large empty box, and Ginny patted Mark's hand.

"Did you get it there in time?" Ginny asked, heading over to take the box from Kayla.

"Barely." She let out a long breath. "They were just about to sit down for lunch, and Andie was in a near panic. I showed up at the perfect time and made it look as if it had been the plan all along."

She turned then and headed to the middle of the kitchen, where Mark was perched, but stopped, giving him a small smile when she caught sight of him. "Mr. Kavanaugh.

Did you wish to pick up with the group in the middle of the tour? I can take you to meet them."

"No, thanks. I'm good." He held up the apple he was now working his way through. "Just stopped by for some lunch. G. fixed me up."

Ginny gave him one of her evil-eye looks. He just smiled.

"I have more work to do this afternoon, anyway." He crunched into the apple, not in any hurry to leave. He liked it there. He felt more relaxed than he had in years.

"Oh." Kayla nodded, her eyes questioning Ginny's as if asking why one of the guests was in the kitchen instead of following along with the laid-out plans. "Okay."

If Kayla had been the one to organize the wedding expeditions, he had to give her credit. She had quite the two weeks laid out for them, and she hadn't seemed to miss any details. Even, apparently, saving Andie's rear when they'd somehow managed not to get lunch delivered as planned.

Ginny put the box away in a back pantry, then returned, eyeing him. "You're good in the hotel, then?" she asked.

"Sure." He shrugged. "It doesn't have the view of this place, but the bed is nice."

Kayla jumped as if she'd been shot. "Wait. We have a room for you here now. We got it fixed." She nodded and smiled at him, then did the same to Ginny. "Right? Shouldn't I put him back in the house?"

The look on Ginny's face was total innocence, but Mark knew exactly what she was thinking. She wanted him back under the same roof as Andie. But why?

And how did he feel about her wanting him there?

Because he knew how he felt about being there. Very damned good.

CHAPTER SEVEN

The sound of the waves pounding into the shore eased the tension from Andie's shoulders as she slid down lower in the swing, her back curving at an angle no doctor would approve of. She snuggled in deeper as she held her e-reader up. She was in her spot, and though it was nearing midnight, she did not want to leave.

She'd had a long couple of days. Today nothing had gone wrong, at least, but yesterday on the tour they'd gotten to the midpoint, where they had an arrangement with the historical society to use the grounds for lunch, and she'd realized that because she'd overslept—because she'd been thinking about Mark, and about kissing Mark—she'd forgotten to run lunch over to the storage cooler before the tour had begun.

Thank goodness Kayla had realized this and showed up just in time. Sometimes Andie wondered what in the world she was doing. Kayla should be running things instead of her. But it was her and Aunt Ginny's business, and she was determined to do a good job.

Another wave broke and she peered up at the sky. All the stars were gone. The sea had been growing rougher over the past hour, a good indication that the weathermen had been correct. A storm was heading their way.

She just hoped it moved out before morning so they didn't end up with a house full of guests looking to be entertained. She needed to spend some quality time working before she headed to her weekly class at the senior center. The business had gotten a lot of calls over the last couple of days, both from excited brides as well as inquiring magazines.

Word was getting out: Seaglass Celebrations was making waves. She suspected it had a lot to do with Penelope Jordan. The girl was sweet, and Andie was pretty sure she'd been calling everybody who would listen and letting them know how the trip was going. It was far more than Andie could have asked.

The sky lit with a flash of lightning, and she let out a sigh and rose from her seat. She'd had the swing installed a couple of years ago. The area was separated from the house enough that she could disappear in the evenings if she wanted to, and rarely did any guests find their way to it. There were walking paths nearby, just down the slight hill, and an area with a waterfall and benches. There was little reason for anyone to look beyond that.

She could sit hidden in her cocoon for hours and no one would notice.

But right now, she was about to get soaked.

She gathered her pillow and set out for the house. It wasn't a straight shot, and in the silent darkness the stroll was almost eerie, but she enjoyed it. She loved being out there by herself after everyone else was in bed.

And from all accounts that's where they now were. The chartered bus they'd hired for the daytrip to Savannah had pulled up a couple hours ago. She'd heard the noise as everyone had made their way either into the house or back to their bungalows. They were a fun group, but she would be glad for them to be gone.

Avoiding Mark hadn't been too hard yet—she hadn't seen him since two nights ago on the beach—but she knew she couldn't escape him for long. He was a part of things, and her newly acquired talent for hiding out from the group couldn't last for much longer. Phillip Jordan's watchful eye would make certain of that.

The clock ticked on the mantel as she let herself in through the back door and pulled off her sandals. She didn't want to wake anyone. When she reached the second floor, she turned right. She had the large corner room on the end, directly below where Phillip and Marilyn Jordan now slept. It was a nice room, and though she'd offered to move to a smaller one when she and Aunt Ginny had decided to open to guests, Aunt Ginny wouldn't hear of it.

It had been the room Andie had slept in since she'd been a little girl, and it would remain her room. She hadn't argued. She hadn't wanted to turn those memories over to strangers, anyway. It *was* her room. And chances were good it would be her room for a long time. Possibly forever.

A breath whispered past her lips as she stepped inside without turning on any lights. Was that how her life was really going to play out? Alone? Forever? She was only twenty-nine, for crying out loud. It didn't make sense to throw in the towel yet. But then, she'd likely have to quit working so hard if she wanted anything more. Possibly quit working altogether if she wanted kids.

She leaned back against the wall, thumping her head softly in the dark as the thought rolled through her.

It wasn't realistic in this day and age that in order to raise kids she'd have to be a stay-at-home mom, but what floored her was the fact that the idea didn't upset her as it once had. When she'd been with Mark before, that had been one of their many arguments. He'd claimed he didn't mind if she worked, yet something had bothered him about the idea of her not being there for any kids they might have. He'd never admitted it out loud, but she'd always felt it. Since his mother hadn't worked, she'd assumed he'd expected the same from his wife.

Yet honestly, that had never felt quite right, either. Something had just been "off" when it came to him and talking about kids. Not that he didn't want them. He did. But something odd, which she'd never quite been able to put her finger on, had lingered in any such discussion they'd had.

She shook her head, clearing it from the past, and from thoughts of giving up her life to raise kids. That wasn't who she was. She was a career woman. Just like her mother.

She was also very much like her aunt, who had been alone and happy since she was thirty-five. So it wasn't out of the question that Andie might follow suit.

But she wanted sex.

She thumped her head against the wall again.

Her inner voice had recently developed the silly notion that there was more to life than going home alone every night and burning up the occasional battery-powered device. It wanted hard-core, full-body-contact extracurricular activities.

And right now, it wanted that with Mark.

Ridiculous, but ever since that scorcher of a kiss, her insides had been lit up like a Christmas tree. Her libido suddenly remembered what sex was and it wanted it.

But with Mark? Really? She couldn't have grown and evolved over the years?

Why did he have to be the one who still set her on fire?

She plopped down on her bed, making a face in the dark, and wondered what it was about him that made it near impossible to put him out of her mind.

It was all the abstinence, she decided. Her friends had been right. She should have started dating again a long time ago. Then the first sighting of Mark wouldn't have made her remember with clarity how good he was with his hands. And other parts of his body.

Go out with a few men, kiss a few. Surely someone would wake her up like Mark did.

She rose and went to the sliding doors to push them open, wanting to hear the night. Seeing the slow, straight rain coming down, she tossed her e-reader on the nightstand and went to the mini refrigerator she kept in the room. It was the perfect night for a glass of wine and a quiet, introspective sit on the deck. She'd think about the men she knew from the island, and figure out who she would be inviting out on her first date.

No need to wait for them, she decided. If she wanted to do something about the situation, she needed to make the first move.

And making sure she didn't get caught wanting to wrap her legs around Mark again was priority number one.

So she needed a date.

She poured herself a glass of Riesling and took a sip as she slipped out of the shorts and T-shirt she'd been wearing. The ankle bracelet caught the light shining in through her balcony doors, and she paused to lift her leg, wondering why she still wore it.

It had been her mother's, though she'd never seen her mother wear it. Andie had found it in her jewelry box when she'd been young and asked about it. Cassie had merely taken it from her and put it back, telling her not to bother it again. It wasn't something anyone needed to wear.

Years later, Andie had taken it when she'd gone away to college. She had no idea why, but she'd wanted it. Something about the delicacy of the chain combined with the single crescent moon charm had always called to her. Also, if she were to be honest, the jewelry had made her feel closer to her mother.

Granted, it hadn't done a thing to improve their actual relationship. Her mother had still worked sixty hours a week, all for the purpose of looking forward to vacations— with her husband. And she did not worry about Andie. Yet Andie continued to wear that chain.

Some things didn't make sense. Not worth thinking about tonight, though.

Nor was it worth wondering what had happened to the sea turtle charm Mark had once given her to go on it. It hadn't been there when she'd dug the anklet out of her jewelry box after Aunt Ginny had returned from Boston. Andie had sent her to pack up her belongings. She'd known Mark wouldn't be there since he and Rob had apparently headed off to Vegas after bailing on the wedding, but she hadn't even wanted to step foot in the place again. It had been too raw. Too painful.

The loss of the charm had at first made her sad, but she'd used Ginny's logic and scratched that one up to fate. She hadn't needed that reminder of Mark for all these years, anyway. Just as she didn't need to be reminded of anything about him now, either.

She tossed down another gulp of wine, then topped off her glass, pulled on her pajamas, and slipped out into the night.

The breeze hit her first and then the smell of honeysuckle from below. She leaned against the railing and inhaled, staring out over the pool and on to the ocean, watching the slow rain dance upon the water. Occasionally the sky lit as if a massive flashlight beam arced briefly across it, followed by the distant rumble of thunder. Maybe Mark leaving her and her subsequent firing had been the best things to happen to her.

And maybe she wouldn't screw up and lose this place next.

Ugh.

She had no idea why she'd let herself go there. She just wanted to relax. Tomorrow would come soon enough, and she'd go back to worrying then. Tonight she wanted to get more than a little lit and think about all the good-looking men she wanted to date.

She settled into a lounge chair that was pushed up near the exterior wall of her room. With the rain falling as it was, and the third-floor deck shielding her, she could easily sit there without getting wet. She tilted her head back and tossed down more wine, searching for the light-headedness that would soon come. She wanted to float in a major relaxed state, and not worry about one single thing.

When over half the glass of wine was gone, she smiled, slumped low in her chair, and closed her eyes to think of men.

"You've been avoiding me, Andie."

Andie shot up in her seat, spilling the remainder of the wine across the legs of her pajamas, and whirled around to stare at the man standing quietly in the shadows, about fifteen feet from her.

Mark was propped against the stucco wall beside the open balcony doors of the room next to hers, his arms crossed over his chest. His bare chest. Of course. And he looked as tasty as a forbidden snack. Good enough to sneak a nibble.

She'd never regretted not installing partitions to separate the deck space until tonight.

"What in the devil are you doing over there?" she whispered. Her pulse pounded in her throat. The man had nearly scared her to death. That room was supposed to be empty until the elder Mastersons arrived next week. She glanced past him to ensure no one else was out on the deck.

"Kayla invited me back over. Said there was no need to stay at the hotel when there was a perfectly good room right here in the house."

Andie blinked, wishing futilely that she hadn't guzzled the wine so fast.

"Well, that room isn't it." Stinking, efficient Kayla. "You'll need to move your stuff. You belong at the other end of the hall." The room on the side of the house that *didn't* have a deck connected to hers.

She heard a shuffling noise and squinted in hopes of seeing more clearly. He was heading her way. She started to get up, but he lowered himself to another lounger before she could get her feet under her. He was still on his side of the deck, but now within a couple feet of her.

Forcing herself to relax, she leaned back in her chair. Hadn't she promised herself that she wouldn't allow him to run her off anymore? So she had to stay. And she couldn't help it if she checked him out. Any woman would.

His bare feet stretched out before him, strong and sturdy, looking for all the world as if they would run over hot coals to save his woman if they needed to. Soft, faded jeans covered his legs. She was pretty sure those were jeans he wouldn't wear out in public, as they caressed him a little too snugly in places. He might be built as if he didn't work behind a desk and demand hundreds of dollars per hour in front of a judge, but that didn't mean he'd show up in public underdressed. And as already noted, above the waist…he wore nothing.

The moon was nowhere to be found, so she couldn't enjoy the view to the fullest, but it wasn't as if she'd ever forgotten what he looked like without a shirt. Nor what he'd felt like.

She'd gotten reminded of that a couple nights ago as she'd clung to him in the water.

He was hard. Ripped. Everywhere.

And she suddenly wanted another drink.

"I spilled my wine," she murmured, straddling the chair on her way to standing up. She was not quite steady on her feet but not what she'd call shaky, either. "I'm getting some more." She stepped just inside her room before pausing. "You want a glass?"

They'd once sat together on the small deck of their Boston apartment in the evenings, drinking wine and enjoying the end of the day. Only they'd always drunk from the same glass.

"No, thanks," he said.

She disappeared into the room without another word, quickly shedding her wet pajamas and tugging back on the shorts and T-shirt she'd recently discarded. She glanced down at her obvious lack of a bra but decided she didn't care. It was after midnight, and she didn't want to be bound. A woman had a right to sit on her own deck however she wanted.

She topped off her wine and headed back outside. When he saw that she'd changed, his glance lingered on her chest before he lifted his eyes to hers.

"You made me spill my wine on my bottoms," she said. "I couldn't very well sit out here like that."

He nodded and she slipped back into her seat. What was she doing? She should run him off, or better yet, run back into her own room. She should not be sitting out there like she was. It was too personal. Too much like the old days. Yet sitting there was exactly what she wanted to be doing, so she stayed. Because she was a glutton for punishment.

He finally spoke. "Thought we could talk a little."

"Probably it would be better to just sit. And then you'll need to go find your room."

"This is my room."

"No, it's not." She scooted her chair around so she could see him better, then curled over onto her side. She took another sip before resting her head against the vinyl strips of the chair. The sound of the rain soothed her. "Mr. and Mrs. Masterson will be in that room when they arrive."

They were a couple in their eighties who were unlikely to do anything at all to cause her any distress.

"The other room is bigger," Mark said. He rested his hands in his lap, clasping them together, his thumbs tapping out a slow rhythm against each other. Her gaze locked on the movement. "And there are two of them," he continued. "Me taking this room makes more sense."

"That's a load of crap," she said, her voice a soft whisper. "You took it just to screw with me." She did not need him on the other side of her wall.

He turned his head, his eyes laughing, then reached out and took her wine. "Screw with you, huh? When did you develop such a potty mouth?"

She shrugged. A little wine and Mark in close proximity, and there was no telling what she might come out with next.

A couple drinks later he handed back her glass. "You should have brought out the bottle."

"I should have brought you your own glass."

The broad slash of his mouth turned up in a curve and Andie realized it was the first time she'd seen him smile since he'd arrived. And of course, her temperature shot off toward the sun.

"Would it upset you if I told you that your aunt Ginny was the one who let me move into this room?"

She most definitely should be upset. But the wine was doing its job. She was more relaxed than anything. And she couldn't say that she was surprised, either. Ginny had been sufficiently mad on her behalf when the wedding hadn't happened, but Andie had always sensed that she'd understood something about Mark that she'd never shared. Though who knew what that might be. "Why would she do that? She should be busy hating you like I do."

"*Awww.*" He blew her a kiss before stealing her wine again. "You don't hate me, sunshine. And neither does Ginny."

"I do too hate you." She squinted again, as if that would help her brain focus. "And why'd you just call me sunshine?"

He shifted in his chair until he was lying on his side, mimicking her position. "Because for some reason the days have seemed brighter this week. I credit that with you."

With the soft rain and the dark night surrounding them, it felt as if they were tucked away in a cave.

"That makes no sense," she said. She took back the glass, but it was empty, so she shot him a frown. "Really? You show up uninvited and drink all my wine? Rude."

Before she could rise to go for a refill, he took the glass from her and walked straight into her room. He didn't flip on any lights—as if he'd been there a hundred times before and knew his way around—and she busied herself with watching his butt move under the denim. Appeared to still be in nice shape. And firm. Then she rolled her eyes. *Sheesh!* She really should not be out there with him. Wine and dirty thoughts were doing nothing but telling her libido that it was winning this round.

When he returned he handed her the glass and set the bottle on the ground beside her. "And for the record, you don't hate me, either. Your kiss the other night said otherwise."

"That was a good-bye kiss." She kept her eyes on him until he was back in his seat, half-afraid he was going to push the point and try to kiss her again. Between her hormones and the wine, she suspected she would let him. And if those abs didn't quit catching her attention, she might even start it. "Did you forget that?"

"I didn't forget." He turned to her, his strong face clear in the darkness, with the smallest glimmer of humor coloring his features. "I just didn't buy it."

"Well, you might as well get on board, because this train is leaving without you." She closed her eyes and thunked the side of her head against the chair. What in the hell had that meant? She rolled to her back and let out a long, weary sigh while Mark chuckled beside her.

"Can't hold your wine these days, babe?"

"I can hold it fine. I just skipped dinner."

"Ah." With that he reached over and took the glass from her once again. "Maybe I should finish it for you, then."

"No. Give it back." She reached out, intent on not letting her good buzz go anywhere, but he caught her wrist with one hand and held it up high in the air. The playfulness disappeared from his gaze.

"I've done a lot of thinking these last couple of days," he said. "I suspect you have, too."

"Have you?" She wiggled her fingers in the direction of the glass, wanting desperately to break the mood he was trying to create. And no way was she going to admit that she'd done a lot of thinking, too. "About how to steal a woman's wine and get away with it?"

He brought the glass to her mouth then, her hand still caught in his, and she quit moving. He tilted it so she could take a drink, and she watched him over the rim as the clear, cool liquid slid down her throat. His eyes never left her lips.

When he pulled the glass back, he took another sip, licked his lips, then set it on the ground between them. He lowered her hand to his lap and caressed his thumb along the center of her palm.

Finally he admitted, "It scares me. This thing between us. I'd rather it was gone for good."

She nodded. Her, too. Since it wasn't, there was the constant fear she'd screw up and get her heart broken again. And that had been no fun at all the first time around.

"But it is there," he said. "Whatever it is. And I came to a decision about it earlier today."

She caught the intent in his eyes and quickly shook her head, panic flaring to life inside her. She did not want to hear that decision.

When he only smiled in reply, she shook her head again. More deliberate this time. "No," she whispered. It came out like a plea.

He chuckled and ran a finger down her cheek. "Yes."

She closed her eyes, then shivered as she felt the heat of him hover near her.

He whispered directly into her ear. "I don't think it should be good-bye yet."

EPISODE FOUR

CHAPTER EIGHT

*F*_{*uck*}," Andie murmured, and Mark laughed out loud.

"Shhh," she whispered, pointing to the deck above them. "Mr. Jordan already saw us out in the water the other night. Don't you dare let him realize you're down here with me right now."

He looked up. "He saw us?"

She nodded, not looking pleased, but Mark couldn't help the smile.

"Bet he liked it." Who wouldn't like seeing Andie all wet?

"No, he did not. And I'm pretty sure his wife isn't speaking to me."

He laughed again, but at her stern look covered his mouth with his hand. When he did, their eyes met and they both seemed to return to his statement about their kiss not being good-bye.

The tight, annoyed look on her face would be funny, except it wasn't. They had some kind of ridiculous chemistry between them.

"It's too late," she said. "It was good-bye, Mark. Really."

"It didn't feel like it."

The way she'd clung to his body had felt like the sweetest woman he'd ever known, coming darn close to falling apart in his arms. And it had felt amazing.

She remained silent, so he reached out and grabbed her lounge chair, yanking it over to his. He shot her an apologetic grimace when the move knocked over the glass between their two chairs, followed by the unmistakable sound of glass shattering. He owed her a wineglass. Probably should throw in a bottle of wine while he was at it. Leaning in, he got close enough to smell the alcohol on her breath.

"You going to tell me it honestly felt like good-bye to you, Andie?" He stroked along her neck, dipping his thumb to the pulse at the base of her throat. It was not beating slowly. "Because if so, I'd be willing to wager that you'd take another good-bye right now."

"What it felt like was two people who once knew how to kiss each other, who…" She paused, and he felt her throat rise and fall with a swallow. She twisted her hand, which still rested in his, and freed herself but didn't pull back. "Who… apparently needed to kiss and get it out of their system. And they needed to kiss *good-bye*."

He grinned. He'd always been able to fluster her. The wine seemed to be helping, too. Plus, she was cute when she drank. "Then how about we kiss good-bye for the next two weeks?"

"No." Her eyes rounded. "Why would we do that?"

He pushed an errant strand of hair back behind her ear, and knowing she wasn't wearing a bra, forced himself not to lower his gaze to her T-shirt. But he couldn't keep from leaning in and whispering in her ear, "Because it would be…*So. Much. Fun.*"

She shoved him, and he allowed her to put space between them but didn't let her get up and walk away. He wanted to discuss this. It could be exactly what they both needed.

"Okay, serious," he said. "Here it is. From what I'm guessing we're both unattached?"

He left it as a question, and as he sat there waiting, she finally looked away from him and made a face but gave a little nod.

"Good." He nodded, too, then turned her back to him. "And I suspect we both could stand a break from working so hard. I'm here, you're here—we both know how good it could be between us." He shrugged, hoping she was buying his casual tone. "No strings attached. Why not?"

Those eyes that still had a way of getting to him—even today—blinked, and then scanned slowly down over him as if she were trying to determine if he was worth spending her free time with. She'd already checked him out once when she'd first realized he was on the deck with her, but this time was different. This time it was as if she was viewing him as a potential bed partner. As he watched her gaze inch down his body, the jeans he wore became tight.

Maybe a two-week, no-strings affair was just what he needed to push her from his mind and finally move on. Because he couldn't go back to Boston still thinking about her.

Finally, she opened her mouth and shocked him with the words that came out. "Because you already know how to maneuver the landscape?"

He cringed. "Where did that come from?"

She turned away and crossed her arms over her chest. "Rob told me he suggested you *maneuver my landscape* while you're here."

"Awww, that's just wrong. You should know I never listen to Rob when it comes to women. The guy has the couth of a caveman." He reached out and nudged her face back around to his. "No, sunshine," he whispered, shocked at the amount of feeling in the words. "This has nothing to do with Rob. It's just between you and me. And I think we need to let this play out."

She nibbled on her bottom lip, her nervousness clear on her face.

He tried reminding himself that she'd only wanted him for his name. That she'd worked so much she'd barely even remembered he was there. But none of it mattered.

He wanted her naked, and he wanted her in his bed.

And he was pretty sure he wasn't going to stop until he got her there.

"I came out here tonight to make a list of all the men I'm going to ask out over the next few weeks," Andie admitted.

That caught him off guard. He jerked himself back, putting distance between them. A hot flare of an emotion he didn't want to acknowledge lit inside him. Though she'd likely dated plenty of men since they'd been together, the thought of her going out with someone else suddenly irritated the hell out of him.

"Or you could just date me for the next two weeks." Desperate much?

A smart man wouldn't go down this path, but he admitted to himself that he wasn't so sure he was smart. She was cute and hot and sweet, and all he could focus on was wanting her naked and writhing in his arms.

As she thought through her options, he grabbed her hand and slipped his fingers between hers, tugging her closer. He'd always enjoyed spending quiet time with her like this, and tonight was no different

"You about finished thinking it over?" he asked.

"No." She lowered her gaze to the broken glass on the concrete between them and snuck her free hand out behind her to find the open bottle. When she tilted it up to her mouth and finished off the wine, he couldn't help but laugh out loud again, unconcerned whether Phillip Jordan heard them or not.

"Encouragement in a bottle, babe?"

She swiped her mouth on the back of her hand, the neck of the bottle still in her grip, and grinned. And he fell a little harder. "More like hoping it'll make me so drowsy I fall asleep before answering you."

Oh. He had her. He just had to wait for her to come around.

"Come on." He stood up and took the empty bottle from her. "I'm going to put you to bed."

When she began to protest, he stressed, "Alone," and pulled her to her feet.

"I'm giving you a day to think about it," he finished. "One day."

She let him tug her along behind him to her open door. "Leave the door open when you leave," she murmured. She was practically asleep on her feet. "I like to hear it rain."

Before he crossed into her room, he stopped and looked back at her. The tips of her hair floated in the wind, dancing around her face, and she swayed sleepily on her feet. Her eyes were already closed. He scooped her up and tucked her in tight against his chest. "You're going to fall flat on your face before I get you to bed," he murmured.

Instead of answering—or complaining that he'd picked her up—she burrowed her cheek against his chest, her hot breath puffing across his bare skin and sending vibrations skittering over every inch his body. He stood unmoving, fighting the urge to return to the past. They had been really good at one point.

When her arm slipped over his shoulder to hook around his neck, he stiffly turned to her darkened room and forced himself to put one foot in front of the other. He was tucking her into bed to sleep tonight. *Sleep*, he reminded himself. He pulled in a deep breath. *That's all.*

He glanced down at the gentle curve of her face—her eyes closed, her mouth soft and relaxed—and felt his own lips curve involuntarily. She was exquisite.

As he moved through her room, he checked it out with more than the cursory glance he'd given it when he'd gone in for the wine. The layout very similar to his room, though hers was larger and much more frilly. There were pillows everywhere, a set of shelves that held an assortment of knickknacks, baskets, photos, and books. There were also what appeared to be a handful of decorative boxes stacked under the small bedside table.

Who kept boxes for no reason other than they looked pretty? He supposed there could be something useful in them, but he would lay money down, based on the way they were stacked in such a precise pattern, that they were for aesthetic purposes only.

Stopping beside her bed, he tossed pillows to the floor and tugged back the ruffled bedspread—and only then did he allow himself to look back down at her. She was watching him.

"You sleeping in the shorts?" he asked. His windpipe had narrowed, and the words came out as a strangled whisper. "Or should I help you into pajamas?"

Her gaze lowered to her clothes long enough to let him know that she was considering door number two. Oh, hell no. He quickly settled her on the mattress, almost dropping her in his haste, and yanked the covers up to her neck.

"Never mind," he said, his voice as tight as his skin suddenly felt. "It'll have to be the shorts tonight. Or you can change after I'm gone. But this is me being a gentleman, sunshine. So I beg of you, do not take those shorts off in front of me."

A light note of laughter floated up from the bed, and he wanted to lean down and hug her to him. At one point in their lives he'd been the person who made her laugh every day.

He couldn't resist pressing his lips to her forehead, though. And he lingered there against her warm skin. "Get a good night's, sleep," he whispered.

Thick eyelashes rested against her cheeks, and the sight flipped something over in his chest. He needed to keep this light. Fun. Otherwise at least one of them was going to get hurt.

And one just might not get over it. Again.

∾

The next afternoon, four-foot-ten-inch Viola Bean, otherwise known to her friends as "Vanilla" Bean, scooted in beside Andie at the senior center, and peered over her bifocals at the basket Andie was making.

"Show me how you do that again," Mrs. Bean said.

Andie smiled and put her basket down, helping the older woman by wrapping her hands over Mrs. Bean's more frail ones and showing her in slow motion how to twist the vines into the weaving pattern they had learned that day.

"It's the same moves, over and over again," Andie said. "For the next sixteen rows."

Mrs. Bean nodded, her head bobbing with its fringe of white hair tinged in blue. She scrunched up her face in concentration, taking another stab at it while Andie moved around the room to ensure no one else needed help. All were diligently focused on their projects except Chester Brownbomb, who was spending more time watching Vanilla Bean than working on his own basket.

Both of them had spouses who'd passed, and if Andie were to guess, she'd say Chester had his eye on Vanilla for his next conquest. The man thought he was the Don Juan of the senior center. And apparently most of the women there thought so, too. They lined up for his attention.

She shook her head at the romantic madness running rampant through the group but grinned when Chester caught her watching him. He gave her a big wink. She loved coming there. It was zero pressure, she was doing something she loved, and she was helping make people happy. It was good all around.

"I got it!" Vanilla squealed, and Andie laughed with true happiness. "My daughter is going to love this basket."

"You're not keeping it for yourself?" Andie crossed back to Mrs. Bean.

"No. Her birthday is next month. She likes it when I give her handmade gifts."

Andie suspected the daughter probably also liked knowing that her mother was taking part in activities she enjoyed. Being fulfilled in life was a nice reward for surviving it.

When Andie was assured that everyone was sufficiently engrossed in their tasks, she headed to the other side of the room to sit beside Roni and Ginger. Her friends made a habit of dropping in on her weekly classes. It was a fun way to spend a couple hours together. But since the class was for seniors only, Andie put them to work whenever she needed extra hands.

Not that Ginger was much help, nor was Roni patient enough to do much more than damage, but both would do in a pinch.

Now the two of them smiled at her expectantly, and Andie let out a groan, knowing what was coming.

"Is this going to be about Mark, or about me dating? Because I have news on both fronts," she said.

Roni raised her shapely brows. She was the cultured one of their group, and as such she would be taking the women in the wedding party on a shopping expedition on Saturday. At the same time, Ginger would entertain the men with a deep-sea fishing trip several miles off the coast. It was a pretty good deal, having friends who could help with wedding activities.

Ginger poked at her lopsided basket with a finger, then frowned when it sagged inward where she'd touched it. "How do you get it tight enough not to do that?" she asked. When Andie started to answer, Ginger waved her off, shaking her head. "Never mind. I don't want to talk about baskets—I want to talk about you. And Mark. Tell us what's happened since Sunday night."

"You mean since you both deserted me on the beach with the man who'd once crushed my heart?"

Roni nodded, unmoved by the play for guilt. "Exactly. What happened? Have you talked?"

"Have you kissed?" Ginger added.

Andie's jaw dropped open. "What would make you think we've kissed? Wasn't I supposed to get closure?"

"Well, yeah," Ginger agreed. "But that doesn't mean closure wouldn't involve kissing."

"Really?" Andie eyed her friend, shocked by the words coming out of her mouth, then turned to the other side of the table to study Roni. Roni's annoyed expression said she wasn't as gung ho for the kissing thing, but she didn't voice the words *don't go for it,* either.

Which made no sense. Had Andie been a betting woman, she would have laid odds that not kissing Mark would be near the top of their list of priorities.

"What would make it okay to kiss the man who once left me at the altar?" She asked the question as if she were not guilty of that very act. She would eventually have to confess but not quite yet.

Ginger's light green eyes went a little hazy. "Because he looks like a Greek god."

Roni shrugged, a sign that she agreed—he looked like a Greek god—and Andie shook her head at both of them.

"That's it?" she asked. "Because he's hot? So...what? Should I sleep with him, too?" Because *oh,* she wanted to.

Ginger sucked in a quick breath but offered no additional thoughts.

"What about him breaking my heart again?" Andie asked.

"How could he do that?" Roni's voice was the portrait of incredulity. "You know what he's like now. So yeah, if you wanted to use him for a little R&R while he's here, seems to me you'd have the upper hand this time. Not that I'm suggesting it—I'm merely pointing out the facts."

"I'm suggesting it," Ginger plugged in.

Andie sputtered in indignation. "I cannot believe you said that."

Before anyone could say anything more, Andie detected an issue brewing across the room. She narrowed her eyes in Chester's direction. He'd moved over to Ms. Sherman's table and was openly flirting, while Vanilla Bean eyed the two of them and was clearly getting her feathers ruffled.

Andie went to break up the blue-haired catfight before it erupted, and sent Roni and Ginger to help two other ladies who needed more vines for their bowls.

"Chester!" Andie was determined to sound stern as she approached. He wore an instant look of a devil, his eyes sparkling with mischief. She would have laughed, but doing so might have hurt one—if not both—of the women's feelings. "Why don't you work on your own basket for a while?"

"How about I come sit with you and the two cuties and work on it?" Chester said, waggling his bushy eyebrows at her.

Andie furrowed her brow and pointed a finger at his seat. "Your basket, Chester. There are no rewards for bad behavior in my class."

"Well, you're no fun at all." His grumble was good-natured, and she couldn't contain her laughter any longer.

Instead of returning to her seat, she settled down beside Chester and worked with him until she was sure that he had the pattern down—and that he wasn't intent on stirring up more trouble.

She made another sweep through the room, stopping at each table to chat with different people, helping if they needed it. They all liked to talk, and sharing a few moments in their worlds was one of her favorite parts of the day. She enjoyed hearing their stories, seeing life through their eyes. The conversations made her wish she could be as unconcerned with trivial things as most of them seemed to be.

Maybe someday.

Today she had a business to run.

And a house to save.

Finally, Roni and Ginger headed to the table the three of them had occupied, and Andie made her way in the same direction. They had a conversation to finish.

And she had to figure out what to do about Mark. He'd said he'd give her one day to think about his suggestion. That meant he'd seek her out that night. Her girl parts tingled at the very thought. Which wasn't a good indication that she was going to say no.

If she agreed to an affair, would it start tonight?

She bit the inside of her lip to keep from smiling as she had the thought: *it had better.*

Once seated, Andie turned her gaze to Roni's. "So?" she asked, picking the conversation back up where they'd left off. "What do you *really* think? Should I consider doing the wild thing with Mark while he's here?"

Roni held her hands out in front of her, palms turned up. "It's been a long, dry spell for you, sweetie. If you want a summer fling, I'd say he'd give you one. I saw the way he looked at you the other day. There are memories there. Naked ones."

Yeah, she had some of her own, too. Especially after he'd carried her to her bed the night before. But did she really want to go there? She'd just gotten closure. Was it worth risking it for a few nights of fun?

She let her eyelids drift shut. She had to tell her friends about last night.

Lowering her face into her hands, she hid behind her fingers and muttered, "He actually suggested a fling last night."

A soft gasp came from Andie's right, but Andie once again focused her attention on Roni. She was the practical one.

"So you think I should go for it? Date him while he's here?" Andie asked.

"God, no," Roni stated emphatically. "Don't *date* him. Just do him. If you want to. Geez, I'm thinking of doing his friend myself. Did you catch how hot Gray is?"

And Roni would. She was more worldly than Andie or Ginger. She could easily do the carefree summer fling.

Andie wasn't yet so sure she could.

Or *should.*

"Wait," Roni said, holding up a hand. "Last night...you talked about this last night? You didn't do it already, did you?"

"Of course not!"

Ginger shoved the dilapidated basket she had worked on earlier to the side and leaned in with both elbows on the table. "But do you want to?" she whispered.

And wasn't that the million-dollar question?

Andie looked at both friends—Roni, with her cool, casual, do-him-and-don't-look-back attitude, and Ginger, with her romantic streak a mile wide—and while she was glad to have both women in her corner, they were turning out to be of little help. They hadn't convinced her of anything that she hadn't already talked herself into.

Because yeah, she wanted to do it. She was a grown-up. Why shouldn't she be able to handle a little affair? They were talking less than two weeks.

What could go wrong?

Other than getting her heart broken again.

"I have to admit something," she said.

Both of them looked at her with anticipation, and Andie felt her face heat.

"We did kiss Sunday night," she admitted. "In the ocean—with our clothes on, of all things."

"Oh my God." Ginger's eyes went wide.

Andie nodded. "But it was closure. It was a good-bye kiss."

Roni silently studied her before asking, "So you're ready to date, then?" At Andie's nod, she added, "Someone *other* than Mark?"

Andie nodded again.

"Good. I'll set you up."

"No, no setups. I'm going to make a list. I'll ask someone out myself." She shifted her gaze away from her friends and mumbled, "But maybe I'll wait until this wedding is over."

Both of them went silent for several seconds before Ginger whispered heatedly, "You're going to sleep with him."

Andie fought to deny it, but in the end she lost. She nodded. "Probably."

"And you'll really be okay if you do?" Roni asked. "Can you keep emotions out of it?"

Andie lifted her shoulders in a shrug. She sure hoped she could, but honestly she had no idea. All she knew was that Mark's proposition seemed like the best thing she'd heard in years. Four, to be exact.

"Maybe it's not such a good idea after all," Ginger offered.

"Two minutes ago both of you were for it, telling me to use him and don't look back. What's different now?" Andie asked.

"You have that look." Gingers fingers closed around hers. "Like it's already more than sex."

"No, it's not." Andie shook her head, trying to convince herself as well as her friends.

"Do not go to bed with him if you're ultimately just going to get hurt," Roni stated. Wise words. And a wise woman would heed them. Certainly someone responsible and always working hard to prove herself would not do something so stupid as to risk getting her heart entangled *again* with the man who'd already broken it once.

But Andie was kind of tired of proving herself. She wanted orgasms, and she wanted Mark to give them to her.

And she wanted to pretend that was all it was going to be.

CHAPTER NINE

The strains of music filled the air at Gin's on Thursday afternoon as Andie went about cleaning the shelves lining the walls. Roni was at the piano, playing something classical—Mozart maybe. It was three in the afternoon on a bright, beautiful day, and the only customers were a couple of ladies on the patio who seemed to be enjoying the music as much as Andie.

On slow days, Roni often spent time at the piano. Though she'd given up playing as a career, it wasn't as if she could give it up for life. It was a part of her. When she'd moved to the island, she'd brought the piano with her, installed it at the bar, and declared herself Andie's newest hostess/entertainer.

Andie hadn't minded. In fact, she'd thought it an ideal situation. A piano was exactly what the bar had needed. And someone to play it on occasion was even better. And though Roni was playing classical at the moment, she often pulled out jazz or contemporary pieces in the evening. Sometimes old show tunes. Whatever the selection, the patrons seemed to enjoy it.

Classical was her go-to, though, and if the place wasn't filled with men watching ballgames, it was usually what she played.

As the tempo picked up, so did the swipes Andie took with the duster. The regular bartender had called in sick, so she had rearranged her schedule to help out for the afternoon. It wasn't as if she had to get to some hot affair or anything.

She gritted her teeth at the thought—as she'd pretty much been doing since she'd come in from the deck the night before. Where she'd stupidly been waiting for Mark to show up and have that promised conversation.

Instead, he hadn't returned to the house until after midnight.

As Andie had waited for him alone on the deck, she'd finished off an opened bottle of wine by herself, made her list of men to date, and then had gone in to bed when she'd caught sight of him, Rob, Penelope, and the rest of the wedding party staggering across the beach.

They'd obviously gone to Gin's after dinner, but what had gotten to her wasn't that he'd forgotten the conversation the two of them were supposed to have but that Mark had his arm draped around Wendy's shoulders. The bridesmaid-from-hell Wendy.

Andie had watched them part ways at the back of the house. He'd headed inside with Rob and Penelope and the maid of honor while Wendy had trudged back to the bungalows with the remainder of the group. But even after seeing them go their separate ways, Andie's irritation hadn't subsided. Though she supposed she should have been grateful.

Not that she was jealous.

Or that she'd answered the soft knock at her door only moments later.

She figured he must think he could play with both Wendy and her, and that would be okay.

Not in her lifetime. Andie may be willing to try a casual summer fling, but she wasn't going to share while she did so.

He could just forget it. She didn't need the complications from getting involved with him, anyway. And she didn't *need* sex.

She sighed. She just wished her libido was in sync with that last part.

One of the ladies on the patio signaled for Andie's attention, so she headed past the gauzy curtains separating the bar area from the patio to see what they needed. A server was working the afternoon shift, but given how slow business was just then, Andie had suggested she take her break. She and Roni could handle the front for the time being.

"Can I get you something else?" Andie asked.

The two women looked to be in their twenties. They wore sunglasses and bikinis with near-sheer cover-ups, and they'd been enjoying cocktails on the patio for the past hour.

The one who'd called her out giggled, and the other didn't pull her gaze from the beach. Andie followed her line of sight, discovering that the Jordan party had made its way to the volleyball net not too far from where she stood. It was a beach day for the group, with a formal dinner slated for evening, but this was the first she'd seen of any of them since they'd headed out earlier that morning.

Before leaving, Mark had tried catching her alone, but she'd made sure to stay busy. She'd also refused to acknowledge to herself how delicious he'd looked in his navy swim trunks and tight T-shirt. With his hair unkempt and a relaxed smile on his face, he'd seemed more at ease than she'd seen him since he'd arrived.

Apparently spending time with Wendy had been good for him.

She gritted her teeth again.

"I'd like a Sex-on-the-Beach, please," the lady watching the action said. Her tone was somewhat dreamy, and her intention clear. There was something—er, *someone*—in the good-looking beach group she'd like to do more with than just watch play volleyball.

Andie empathized.

Mark had pulled his shirt off, and even from this distance, she could make out the firm muscles that sculpted his chest. And his shoulders. Oh geez, she would love to run her hands over those bare shoulders.

And down his back.

And over his rear.

Another giggle jerked her attention back from the beach to the women before her. She blushed when it became apparent from their pointed looks that she'd been caught staring. "Sorry about that," she said.

"Oh, we understand," the first woman replied. "Though there's a nice breeze out here, the temperature has definitely soared since they arrived."

Andie had to agree. Every man in the group could be on the cover of a magazine. Even Rob, who now chased a runaway ball with Wendy. Andie glanced at the bride on the other side of the net, noticing her arms crossed tight over her chest. Rob was a jerk for not taking every opportunity this week to make his bride-to-be feel special. Penelope definitely deserved better.

"Look at the one in red trunks," Sex-on-the-Beach said. "*Ohmygod*, he's heading this way!"

Andie pulled her attention from Mark—where it had once again drifted—and noticed Gray making a direct path to the bar. He looked like a man on a mission. When he caught sight of the three of them watching him, he shot them a wide, bright grin and tossed out a wave.

Andie waved back.

"You know him?" Sex whispered.

"I know all of them, actually."

"Even the tall one on the far side?" the first one asked. "The one in blue."

That would be Mark. Who was now chatting up Wendy. That girl sure got loads of attention.

"Um...yep." Andie nodded. She wanted to say that he was her ex, in hopes of keeping the women at bay, but kept her mouth shut. Who he did or did not hook up with was none of her business. As long as he didn't think he could toss her into the mix, too.

She shifted her focus back to the woman. "Can I get you something else to drink?"

"I'll take another pomegranate martini. A strong one." The woman watched Mark a little longer, and as if he sensed the attention, he turned his head in their direction. All three of them held their breaths.

Though it was impossible to tell for certain who he was focused on, with the three of them lumped together, the back of Andie's neck tingled. She had a very strong suspicion of just who he was looking at. And she had the sense he was telling her that she wouldn't avoid him another night.

"Hey, Andie!" Gray called out as he crossed the sand and entered through the patio gate.

The two women tittered in their seats, as if their very own man-Popsicle was being hand delivered.

"Hey, Gray. Tired of the game?"

His gaze strayed to the curtains behind her, where the music was roaring to a crescendo in the bar. "Just thought I'd take a quick break." He nodded toward the ogling women, then looked back at the curtains. "Roni happen to be inside?"

Andie smiled. Looked like Roni wasn't the only one interested in a little summer fun. "That's her playing the piano."

"Oh." His tone was one of surprise. No doubt the music had drifted down to the beach, reeling him in like a siren's song.

"Go on in," Andie suggested.

"You don't think she'll mind being interrupted?"

She put her hand on Gray's arm, and when he looked at her, she said conspiratorially, "I think she might like it."

One side of his mouth hitched up in the cutest smile, and she couldn't help returning the look. Roni was about to be one very lucky girl. It made Andie wonder...if Gray didn't have his sights set on her friend, could she get past her infatuation with Mark by spending time with someone like him?

Interesting question. Not that it mattered. She still had a business to run.

She was still smiling as Gray headed into the bar, which is when she glanced back at Mark. He was standing in the middle of the players, ignoring the volleyball as it bounced around him, and this time there was no doubt about who he had his gaze on.

Her pulse spun out of control. Even from a distance, the man had the ability to bring her to her knees. Which only proved that even if someone else was interested in her, it wouldn't make an impact. She had Mark right smack in the middle of her head.

Forcing herself to look away, she turned back to the women who were still watching Gray, and murmured that she would be right back with their drinks.

Likely, she'd find the server and send her out. Because she certainly didn't want Mark to see her again, and get the idea to follow Gray up to the bar.

∾

Andie collapsed back against the sofa, laughing at the two children still under her care. She'd had four to watch tonight, a ten-month-old baby girl, a three-year-old girl, and these two, Max and Anna, who were brother and sister. Max was seven and Anna six.

Seaglass Celebrations provided onsite child-care services for some events, so tonight while the grown-ups had gone to an exclusive seaside restaurant on the mainland, she'd volunteered to relieve the regular babysitter. She'd been playing charades with these two since the others had been picked up a little over thirty minutes ago, and Andie had to admit she was not good at the game.

"I can't believe you couldn't get that movie," Max said. "Everyone knows *Brave*."

Except her, apparently.

"I really am bad at this game, aren't I?" She'd thought putting them on a team against her would be fair. Big mistake.

The outer door opened and Andie looked up, expecting to find the kids' parents, but instead it was Celeste

Kavanaugh, Mark's mother. She and Wayne hadn't arrived on the island until a few hours ago, and since they were staying at the hotel, Andie hadn't yet had a chance to say hello.

She stood and headed toward the woman with her arms outstretched. Celeste was dressed to the nines in a tea-length pale pink dress that set off her short black hair. A gorgeous diamond bracelet circled her left wrist, and a matching necklace glittered from her neck.

"Mrs. Kavanaugh," Andie greeted her warmly, squeezing her hands. "It's so good to see you again."

She'd once loved being around Mark's mother. Had enjoyed hanging out and talking with her, helping her with her charity work. She was so much more relaxed than Andie's own mother.

"Andie," Mrs. Kavanaugh said. "It hasn't been so long that you don't remember my name, surely. Please, call me Celeste."

Celeste held Andie's arms out at her sides, taking her in. Then without warning, she wrapped her in a warm hug. "It's so good to see you, dear," Celeste whispered. "I was so sad about…" she paused, then leaned back and gave Andie a sad smile, stroking a hand down her face. "About everything. I hope you're doing well."

Andie nodded, refusing to let herself get teary at the memories that seeing Celeste stirred up. She'd been so ready to be a part of the Kavanaughs. "I'm doing great, Celeste. And I'm so happy to see you. I was hoping you and Wayne would be able to make it down before the wedding."

"Oh, sweetheart…" she started, letting go of Andie and glancing around to take in the two children who sat watching them. "I had to drag that man out of the office this morning. Since he's retiring soon, he kept insisting he couldn't take a vacation. But it's little Rob's wedding—we've known him since he was a baby. We had to be here." She stopped and tilted her head as she looked at Andie. "Maybe you weren't aware Wayne's retiring? I'm going to get that trip around the world he's always promised me."

Andie laughed, enjoying the moment. It was good to see Celeste again, even though Andie knew Mark calling off the wedding four years ago had probably pleased the family more than Celeste would ever admit. Andie would love to know the reason Celeste had thought they shouldn't get married. Had it been lineage, as she'd assumed, or something else? "I had heard, actually. About the retirement. Mark told me."

An interested expression crossed Celeste's face. "I see. So you two are...talking?"

"Yes." Andie nodded. Talking. And not having a hot affair. "We've cleared the air a bit. It was good. We needed to talk."

Celeste patted Andie on the cheek. "That's terrific, sweetheart. I know it couldn't have been easy. But I want you to know, I gave him a piece of my mind for the way he ended things. That was no way to treat a lady."

"Did you?" The conversation was moving into an area Andie preferred it didn't go. Maybe she and Mark had moved on, but it didn't mean she enjoyed talking about it. "Well, I do appreciate that. I suspect it turned out for the best, though."

And the funny thing was, she really was starting to believe it had. She'd been angry for so long, she hadn't realized that maybe they hadn't been ready to get married.

She wasn't sure when she'd started thinking that way, but it felt right. She'd been wrapped up in work, and he'd been... she couldn't quite put her finger on it, but she felt as if calling off the wedding might have been a relief to him. He'd started as many arguments as she had in their last few months, and it made her wonder now if he'd been looking for things to pick at. Had he been hoping for an excuse to end it?

She returned to her seat and motioned for Celeste to follow, telling herself she'd chase that train of thought later. Right now she wanted to spend time with Mark's mother. "Tell me about this trip you'll be taking," she said. "When will you be heading out?"

"As soon as I can drag him off." Celeste chuckled as she spoke. She sat and they continued talking, the two of them catching up like old friends. They soon formed a team against the kids. They still lost, though Celeste was better at charades than she was.

"I guess my grandchildren keep me more in tune with what kids know these days than I realized," Celeste said.

Andie's heart squeezed at the thought of the Kavanaugh clan. She'd loved spending time with them. She'd first met them all at Christmas Mass the night after she and Mark had first gotten together.

Being with them at the holidays was one thing she'd truly missed over the years. They were a close family. She liked that. But she had Aunt Ginny, and Ginger and Roni, of course. Though Roni returned home for Christmas each year, she, Aunt Ginny, Ginger, and Ginger's mother often ended up spending the holiday together. Andie no longer went home to Kentucky for holidays, though her mother and stepfather were always invited down to Aunt Ginny's. They just never came.

"How many grandchildren do you have now, Celeste?"

Celeste's laughter rang out with unadulterated happiness. "Five. Jonathan has three and Ryan just had his second. They'll all be down next weekend. I can't wait for you to see them."

The back of Andie's nose suddenly burned as if she were about to cry. She'd seen her life going in such a different direction at one point. But it *would* be terrific to see everyone again. They had all done their part to make her feel welcome.

The door opened again and this time, instead of the kids' parents, Mark stood there. Andie's breath caught. The man knew how to wear a suit. She'd seen him in one plenty of times before, of course, but he carried himself a bit differently now than he once had. More mature, assured. Sexy.

He wore no tie tonight, but a black shirt with a deep blue suit. He looked dark and dangerous. She gave thanks for the fine work of whatever tailor he used. From his broad shoulders all the way down to his black wingtips, everything fit him to a tee.

So perfect, in fact, that she wanted to take it all off of him.

"I hope you don't intend to treat these shoes to the same behavior as the ones the other night?" His rough baritone jerked her attention away from where it had landed, on his feet, and she couldn't help the flush that rose.

She glanced at Celeste before looking back to Mark. "Hopefully, I won't have cause to toss this pair in the ocean."

"Oh." The soft sound came from Mark's mother as she rose from the sofa. "That's a story I do want to hear, but I'm afraid I'll have to beg another time."

"Please don't leave, Celeste." Andie, too, stood from the sofa. She wanted to reach out and stop Celeste for fear she was about to be left alone with Mark. Because Andie already felt her resolve weakening. She just might find herself naked and horizontal if he so much as looked at her the right way. "No need to run off."

"Yeah," piped up Max. "Don't leave yet. You were better than Miss Andie."

Andie shot the child a look. "Hey," she said. "Be careful who you're making fun of, mister. You might have to put up with me again while you're here."

Anna giggled and Max merely rolled his eyes. He glanced over at Mark. "Will you play? I could use another guy in the room. It's been only me and *girls* all night long."

The way the kid said *girls* made it sound as if he'd been forced to play dress-up and wear pink all evening.

Celeste gave Mark a light kiss on the cheek and turned back to Andie. "I do need to go—Wayne is waiting on me. We're taking a romantic stroll along the beach. But I hope we'll have time to catch up more while I'm here? I wanted to drop in tonight just to say hello."

"Absolutely." Andie nodded. "There should be plenty of time."

The elder Kavanaugh disappeared through the doors, and Mark was left standing there, watching Andie, and she suddenly felt underdressed in her simple summer dress.

"Will you play?" Max asked again.

Before she could point out that Mark surely had more important things to do, he'd planted himself where his mother had been sitting. "Absolutely. What are we playing?"

"Charades!" Anna squealed. "We're beating Miss Andie a lot."

"Is that so?" His eyes were blue and calm tonight as he sat peering up at her. It made her feel not so calm. "I'm pretty good at charades," he said. "I hope you two are ready."

When Andie didn't move to sit back down, Mark patted the seat beside him. "Come on, Miss Andie. We have a game to play."

She looked at the chair perpendicular to him, but he quickly stretched out a leg and scooted it out of the way. He then patted the spot on the sofa again.

With an ungrateful attitude and an unladylike noise, she returned to her seat. She'd very much enjoyed her evening—first dinner with the kids, then Chutes and Ladders, and now charades. Somehow she didn't think she'd enjoy it the same way with Mark there.

But she was wrong.

Forty-five minutes later, the kids' parents showed up—the mom clearly having had a glass of wine or three and the dad wearing the kind of smile a man wears when he's just gotten what he wants from a woman. And Andie had to admit that she'd had a really good time with Mark. Plus, he'd managed to pull them back to within a respectable point range of Max and Anna.

"I'm sorry we're so late," the mother hurried to say. "We…uh…took a walk on the beach when we got back. It's such a lovely night."

"No problem at all," Andie assured them. "We've had a wonderful evening. And that's why we offer child care for those special occasions. So the parents can make some memories of their own."

Andie watched the dad, who looked at his wife with so much love that Andie wanted to turn to Mark and point out that he'd never looked at her like that. But when she glanced at him, she remembered the past with clarity. He *had* looked at her like that. Many times.

He'd loved her. She'd always thought so until he hadn't shown up for their wedding.

Maybe his not coming to the church had been as difficult for him as it had been for her? Especially if he really believed she'd been using him for his name.

When he'd accused her of that other night, she'd felt the shame of it on her face. Yes, she'd been tossing around the Kavanaugh name to her potential client, but only because she'd been desperate. If she didn't win the contract, she was out. She'd made too many mistakes before having that deal come to the table. It had been her last chance. And having learned how much power the Kavanaugh name wielded around Boston, she'd lowered her standards and used it.

She was pretty sure simply marrying Mark would have gotten her the deal. But the wedding didn't happen, her clients didn't meet any Kavanaughs, and her boss had had enough. She was done. After moping around Aunt Ginny's for a couple weeks, she'd realized she was thrilled not to have to go back to Boston. She'd hated every second of that job.

Mark rose from the sofa and spoke with the father. He was one of the groomsmen in the wedding. In fact, this was the couple whose children apparently made too much noise for bridesmaid Wendy. Andie had come to the opinion that the children couldn't have been better behaved. Just as she'd thought, Wendy was merely high maintenance and wanted to cause trouble. There was always at least one like that in the mix.

With the family of four heading out the door, Mark turned to her and she instantly looked for something to do.

"Thanks for helping entertain them," she hurried to say. "I'll see you later. I've got to clean up the kitchen."

She shot off in the direction of the other room, knowing she was being rude, but it was either that or risk falling under his spell again. And it had taken her too long to crawl out from under it four years ago.

But instead of taking her blatant hint, he followed her into the spotless kitchen. Where there was nothing whatsoever to clean up.

When she looked at him, he merely raised his eyebrows.

"Fine." Her shoulders sagged, as she admitted, "I was lying. I just wanted to get away from you. Does hearing that make you feel better?"

It was nearing eleven, and the room was dimly lit by only a small light burning over the stove. The outside lights were off, too, as it was bad to leave them burning after dark. It confused hatching sea turtles, potentially leading them away from the sea instead of toward it.

"Come on," Mark said, holding out his hand.

She tucked her hands under her arms. "I need to go to my room. I have a long day tomorrow."

Which was another lie. Kayla would be taking the entire group on a parasailing trip, leaving Andie with the day to herself.

Mark crossed the room and untwined her arms, sliding one of his hands down to one of hers. "It's time to talk."

"We can talk in here."

"No. I found the perfect spot outside. Come on." He tugged and she took one step before pulling back.

"I can't get caught out there kissing you again, Mark. Mr. Jordan already looked down his nose at me as if I were nothing but white trash. This is my business. I have to act businesslike." Not to mention, she could still picture him with his arm around Wendy.

That mouth that she liked so well curled up again, and the lower half of her body turned to melted butter. "I wasn't planning on kissing you at the moment, Andie. I just want to talk." He tugged again, and pulled her within a couple inches of him. "But I'll be glad to kiss if that's what you'd prefer."

She huffed out a breath. He could kiss Wendy. "You know you were thinking about kissing. We never have been able to be near each other without kissing."

"And more," he said, his deep voice tickling her panties. "Yes, I was thinking about kissing you. I've done little else for…" He shrugged. "Too long."

What did he mean? He'd been thinking about kissing her before showing up there?

"Then see? We can't go out there. You want to kiss me."

"And you want to kiss me, too, sunshine, but that's not what this is about. Right now I just want to be with you. I want to talk to you. Hold your hand if you'll let me."

She looked down to where their fingers remained linked. "You're already holding my hand."

He smiled. "Seems I am." He tugged again, and this time headed toward the door. "Come on, babe. I promise not to bite."

She made a face behind him but followed along anyway. Maybe she wanted to be bitten. Maybe it had been far too long since she'd been bitten.

And maybe she'd lost every last brain cell, because not only was she following him out into the dark of the night, but she wanted to go with him—whether he'd been kissing Wendy or not. And she wanted that no-strings thing he'd talked about. She wanted that a lot.

CHAPTER TEN

M ark kept hold of Andie's hand until he had her beyond the walking paths, and up the slight hill where there was a fantastic view of the ocean. He'd found a swing there earlier, and he wanted to sit in it with her. If anyone had claimed it before he could get her out there, he would hand over all the money in his wallet to get whoever it was to leave. Immediately.

He'd done a lot of thinking over the past few days, about both the present and the past. And he needed to figure out a few things. Like if what he was feeling was purely lust. He had the sneaking suspicion it wasn't. No matter how bad he wanted it to be.

Because like Ginny had guessed, Andie got to him.

"Have a seat," he said when they reached the spot, which was, blessedly, empty.

The swing sat on a small ridge overlooking the ocean but was also completely hidden from the house by massive live oaks draped with Spanish moss. Instead of sitting, Andie looked up at him in the darkness, a small smile playing around her lips.

"Do I need to beg?" he asked.

"No." She shook her head and then did as he'd asked.

She waited for him to join her before pushing off with her feet to set the swing in motion. After a few minutes of silence, as he sat wondering just how they'd gotten there, she pointed out a light in the distance. "That's Ginger's dinner cruise boat."

"Ginger? Your other maid of honor?"

She went still and he realized that had probably been a bad way to put it. Bring up the past immediately. Way to go, Kavanaugh.

"So you remember who Ginger and Roni are?"

"Yeah. I only met them the once, but the cold shoulder I got from Roni at the bar was a good clue. The follow-up that night when her look threatened to do me bodily harm sealed the deal." He reached for her hand and held it, palm up. "Have they both always lived here?"

"Only Ginger. Her father owned the ferry when we were growing up."

He shifted on the swing to bring one knee up, keeping her hand in his. He wanted to see her face as they talked. It was too dark to get a good read from her eyes, but he'd once been good at knowing the facial expressions that went along with her thoughts. "I know you'd told me before that you visited Ginny here as a kid, but I never had the impression it was that often. Yet you two seem really close."

At her questioning glance, he squeezed her hand. She'd never been overly forthcoming with personal information.

"Must have been more than the occasional trip?" he prodded.

She glanced toward the water instead of focusing on him and finally answered. "Yeah, every year since I was eight. I spent summers here. About ten weeks each year."

"Why did I never know that?"

Her gaze shifted to his. "Did you want to know it?"

"Babe, I wanted to know everything about you. I only realized recently how much I didn't know."

"Hmmm," she answered, and he could see her realizing the truth of the statement.

"What about your parents? I met them that one time at your graduation, and then again when they were in for the wedding. But you never really talked about them, either. And we didn't go visit. Why?" He couldn't understand why he'd never pushed for more details back in the day. She'd known everything about his family. Everything about him that had mattered.

She shrugged, and he could tell this was not an easy subject for her as her shoulders pulled in, making her appear even smaller than she was. He turned her hand over and traced the length of each finger with one of his. He enjoyed the smooth, silky feel of her skin.

"Tell me about them. Why did I never know much more than that they lived in Louisville?"

"There isn't that much to tell."

"Do you still see them? Are they together? Do you get along?"

A soft laugh slipped past her lips. "Okay, fine. As you do know, it's my mother and stepfather. I never even knew who my father was. I usually visit once a year but don't stay more than a couple days at a time. Their choice as much as mine. And they never come here. Oh, and yes, they're still married. Have been since I was eight. Both of them are retired now—Mom just last year—both from the same insurance company. We get along fine. Have never had what some would call a 'bad' relationship."

He studied her in the dark. "But you've never had a good one, either, or I would've known more about them. You'd see them more often."

At her silence, he pushed. "Am I right?"

Her forehead scrunched in thought and he had a memory of the first time he'd asked her out. They'd been on the Harvard campus. He'd seen her in passing several times, had even talked to her the few times he could catch up with her. She had always intrigued him, always seeming to be focused on getting somewhere, as if whatever the destination was couldn't wait. But that night, as he'd watched her, he'd been unable to let her go without asking her out. He'd wanted a shot.

She'd been sitting in the library, talking with another guy—one who'd clearly been trying to pick her up by feeding her a line of total crap—and she'd simply seemed to want to get rid of him and get back to her studying.

But what caught his attention was the bullshit meter he'd seen in her gaze. That's what had always pulled him to her, her eyes. She had the most beautifully expressive eyes, and whenever she was talking to someone, he could read her thoughts as clearly as he knew she was thinking them. And he'd loved that her thoughts were often not as sweet and gentle as she appeared on the outside.

It had been as intriguing as hell, and he'd wanted to be the one to bring out that side of her.

So when the guy got turned down and left, Mark had gone over. He'd wanted to see what her eyes said about him. Of course, he'd gotten turned down, too, but he'd liked what those blue-gray depths had been whispering: she was interested. And she wanted him to keep asking.

She hadn't agreed to go out with him until after he was out of school. He'd been a year ahead of her. It had been December twenty-third, and he was working with his father and brother at that point. He'd gone back to the bar where he knew she worked. He and Rob and other classmates had hung out there during their years on campus, but that night he'd gone because he wanted to take her a present. He'd wanted her to know that he was still thinking about her.

It had been a sea turtle charm. He hadn't seen her in months, but every time before, she'd always had on the ankle bracelet with the lonely single charm. He'd once overheard her mention sea turtles in a conversation with a customer, and he had watched her eyes light up.

He'd wanted to give her something she could add to that bracelet. And to see if her eyes would light up for him.

After she'd gotten off work that night, he'd ended up in her bed. They'd gotten engaged and moved in together two months later, which had surprised him as much as her. It had always been like that with them, though. Fast and furious.

He realized he'd drifted to the past and turned his attention back to Andie, who sat waiting, a patient smile playing around her lips. He couldn't help but laugh out loud. "I've missed you, babe. So damn much."

"I've missed you, too." Her words were soft, almost as if she hadn't meant to say them. Her bottom lip slipped between her teeth before she continued, "And yes. You're correct. I've never had what you'd call a 'good' relationship with my parents. Not anything like you have with yours, or even like *I* had with yours. But we got along fine. They were just always so busy, Mom climbing the ropes in the finance department of the insurance company where she'd worked, and John already at the top. They worked really hard, and it was very important to them." She grew pensive, staring off at the ocean again, then whispered in a soft, accepting voice. "Their careers were more important than me."

Her words shut off and he would have given anything to be able to see her eyes. Had she just realized that she'd done the same thing with him? They'd fought about her long hours so many times, but she'd never seemed to understand his issue with it. He'd wanted to be number one in her life. Just like she had been in his.

She leaned in, tightening her fingers around his, and blinked up at him. "I did that, too, didn't I?" she whispered. "I'm sorry, Mark. I didn't even realize."

He forced a smile and settled his forehead against hers. God, he'd once loved her so much. Hearing her figure that out did nothing to convince him that what he was feeling now was purely lust. Which was a problem. Knowing he shouldn't, he tilted her face up and put his mouth to hers.

She was warm and soft, and she tasted like candy. And he was suddenly ready to shuck their clothes and forget this talking thing. But he'd promised her he wasn't after kisses—just yet—so he pulled back. Slightly.

A soft sigh whispered through the night and then her lips reached for his. And he wasn't stupid. He let her find him.

Suddenly, the inches separating them were too much. He lifted her to his lap and groaned like a dying man when she crossed one leg over to straddle him, her dress now bunched up around her waist.

"Andie." It wasn't easy to talk when the heat from her burned through his pants.

"Shut up, Mark. Just shut up. I know what I'm doing. And I know why I'm doing it."

He had the thought that he'd like to know why, too, but it was fleeting. Instead, since it was what he'd been hoping for, he shut up and went with it.

Her hands worked fast, getting the buttons opened down his shirt before he could remember to put his hands on her. As her mouth went on a trail over his neck, he got busy himself. He wanted to touch her. He *needed* to touch her.

Luckily, the dress had its own set of buttons, all the way down the front. He found them and amazed himself with his speed. He soon parted the fabric, leaving her sitting atop him with her pretty lace panties and bra peeking out and nothing else. Waiting for him to take them off her.

"Just shoot me now if we're going to have to stop this." He didn't give her a chance to reply before he shoved his hands in her hair and dragged her mouth back down to his. She clung to him. Tight, as if afraid he might try to escape.

But she didn't have to worry—he wouldn't leave if the swing were on fire.

He opened his mouth wider, taking the kiss deeper, and he literally shook when that little moaning sound he loved so much came from her. He lowered his hands, smoothing them down over her back—and dying at the feel of her against his palms when he slipped his hands under her dress and settled them around her hips. He slid his fingers inside the back of her panties and gripped her ass, and she jerked forward with a groan, settling down perfectly over him.

With the unzip of his pants and the shift of her underwear, he could be inside her in seconds. He wrenched his mouth back, needing to breathe and trying to figure out what to do next. Enter her? Or take her to her room and do it right? When her hand slipped inside his belt, he didn't think he had a choice.

"There's a..." he panted out, lifting his hands because he'd decided he wanted her bra out of the way. "A condom. In my wallet."

His fingers slid across the tops of her breasts, almost reverently, and she arched forward, the stars shining down on her. He curled his fingers underneath the lace and yanked, jerking it below the perfect, heavy mounds he remembered so well.

"Oh, fuck," he whispered. And then he cupped her, holding her and silently cursing all the time he hadn't had the right to do just that.

He scraped his thumb over her hard nipple and she grew wet against him, then he looked up at her face and made himself slow down. She was watching him. Silent and hot and sexy, watching him from hooded eyes, and he could look at her like that for days. "You're beautiful, Andie. I never should have—"

"Shhh," she said. "Don't. Don't bring up the past. This is right now, that's all. It's all I want to think about."

He nodded. It was all he wanted to think about, too. That, and getting the damned condom out of his back pocket.

Before he could pull out his wallet, the sound of someone walking nearby hit his ears. Andie's eyes grew round and she flattened herself against him, her fingers working overtime to close up her dress.

"Oh, God," she whispered, her tone panicked and urgent. "Who is that? Can you tell?"

Mark wrapped his arms around her and peered over her head, scanning the area for the source of the noise. It was so dark under the trees, it was hard to make out anything but shifting shadows. Then he landed on the culprit and his erection wilted as if it had been doused with ice water.

She was not going to be happy about this.

Andie grabbed his jaw and jerked his face around to hers. "Who?" she demanded softly.

"Aw shit, Andie. It's Phillip Jordan. And it looks like Penelope with him. They're about twenty feet away on the path under the trees."

Her mouth spewed words he couldn't believe she'd ever used. He would have fastened his own clothing, but she had her face dug into his shoulder, and her body so tight against his he wasn't sure they could fit another pair of hands between them.

"It'll be all right," he started, knowing the words were lame.

"No, it won't," she whispered. "I've already had too many slipups. This wedding is supposed to be perfect. And I can't even keep my clothes on in public."

His arms tightened around her, hoping to calm her, but she had a very good point. Being caught in their current situation was not going to look good to the man paying the bills.

Her fingers finished with her clothes and turned to his, but he pushed them out of the way. "Scoot back a little and I'll do it. I can go faster."

Somehow he got everything back in place and buttoned up, and got her to the other side of the swing, without—he was pretty sure—either Phillip or Penelope noticing them.

"What are they doing?" she asked. "Is Rob with them?"

"Rob said earlier that he had a call to make tonight. Something about one of his cases." He craned his neck until he could finally make out the two of them, turning and heading along the path directly below them. As they made their way closer, Mark began to pick up their voices, suddenly realizing theirs wasn't your typical are-you-ready-to-get-married conversation.

"He'll need to spend at least two years as assistant SA before we can get him in as state's attorney," Phillip was saying. "But I got the call today. The job is his as soon as you return from your honeymoon."

"Oh, Daddy, that's terrific."

"And you're sure you can get him to do it?"

"Of course," Penelope said, but she didn't sound so sure. "Why wouldn't he?"

"Honey, he makes a load more money where he is. You might have some convincing to do to get him to leave."

"I can handle it. He loves me. He'll see this is the right move for us." She rose to her tiptoes and wrapped her arms around her father's neck. "Don't worry about it, Daddy. I'll make it happen."

The two talked about Rob's apparent career move for a few more minutes, then headed around the bend of the path, back toward the house. Mark sat immobile, shocked at what he'd heard. Rob's new father-in-law wanted him in the state's attorney's office? Why? Because it looked better for the Jordans to have a prosecutor in the family than a defense attorney?

"I need to find Rob." Mark stood up and reached back to help Andie to her feet.

"Why?"

He looked at her. Wasn't it obvious? "To tell him what we just heard. She's clearly marrying him with the intention of turning him into their pet project."

"That's not necessarily the case." Andie ran a hand over her hair, pulling the length of it together behind her neck. "And he's probably aware of it, anyway. Probably wants it himself."

"Andie, Rob moved to Chicago specifically to be at the firm he's with now. I know, Dad helped him get the job. He's a partner. No way he wants to move to the other side. I have to warn him."

He moved to head for the path that would take them back to the house, but she grabbed his arm and stopped him. When he looked at her, she pleaded with her eyes.

"You can't let this wedding get canceled, Mark. It's important to me."

"Baby, if he's walking into a trap, he has to know. I have to tell him."

"But if they pull out…" She stopped talking and began to pace, panic lining her features and her moves. "You can't let him stop the wedding. Please. You can't."

He reached out to her, turning her to him. "Why not? Would you really rather see someone get trapped in a loveless marriage?"

The irony almost made him laugh. She'd planned to marry him for a similar reason. Maybe there had been something between them, and maybe even some amount of love on her part, but her priority had been his name. And she'd been willing to marry for it. Of course she wouldn't see anything wrong with this.

When she looked away, he gripped her hands and squeezed. "Why, Andie? You've got to let me in on this. Are you not covered in your contract? Will you lose money? What?"

She turned the look on him then, the one that had always made him want to push away all the bad guys and protect her with his life. She seemed young and fragile, and it scared him how bad it affected him. "Because I'll lose Aunt Ginny's house if the wedding gets canceled."

EPISODE FIVE

CHAPTER ELEVEN

The temperature outside was heading for an early-June record, keeping the cool air inside pumping fast and hard, but Andie was having a difficult time caring about the common sense of having the windows closed. She needed fresh air. And she needed to know how the conversation was going between Rob and Mark.

Marching across the living room, she began cranking open the row of windows facing the ocean, being careful not to look at Aunt Ginny because Andie knew she was acting like a crazy woman.

"What are you doing?" Aunt Ginny calmly asked.

Andie's chest rose on a shaky breath. Nerves and stress were getting to her, and what she was doing was trying *not* to lose her mind. "I want to feel the breeze."

"Oh. Well then, I see."

Ginny's matter-of-fact tone annoyed Andie to the point that she spun around, hands on hips. "What's that supposed to mean?"

Ginny shrugged. "That I understand," she said. "You'd like fresh air."

The two of them were working on welcome bags for the guests, and Ginny currently sat on the couch in the middle of a mound of pink ribbon.

It was Friday afternoon, and guests would begin trickling in over the weekend, with all of them scheduled to arrive no later than the following Wednesday.

Not that anyone was likely to get a single bag that was being assembled.

Not if Mark got the wedding canceled.

And just when things were finally starting to go well, too.

The wedding party had headed out on a parasailing adventure early that morning, and the parents of the bride and groom, along with Penelope's grandparents, had all loaded into a limo at lunchtime to attend a mystery theater show. On his way out the door, Mr. Jordan had actually complimented the attentiveness and attention to detail that Seaglass Celebrations had so far provided.

Great. Good to know she wasn't a total screwup.

Except after Mark got finished talking with Rob, everything would be shut down—with Kayla's wonderful attention to detail being turned to contacting guests before they could catch their flights out, letting them know that there was no reason to come.

Because Mark was right. If anyone was suited to defending the guilty and making hundreds of thousands of dollars for doing it, it was Rob. She couldn't imagine him rolling over and giving up his high-powered career, playing good boy to his new father-in-law's wishes. Rob was definitely not prosecutor material.

She growled under her breath, causing Ginny to narrow her eyes. "What's wrong?"

Oh, nothing, except I'm going to lose your house for you.

Andie forced herself to sit down on the couch with her aunt, taking deep breaths to calm her nerves. She had to tell Ginny.

She picked up one of the bottles of wine Penelope had picked out for her guests and rolled it back and forth between the palms of her hands, hoping the rhythmic motion and the cool glass would help calm her. There was simply no easy way to do this. "We need to talk," she said.

Aunt Ginny nodded. She was a bright woman. She'd likely already figured out there was an issue with the wedding, maybe even figured out it had something to do with the loan. "What is it, doll? You want my opinion on you and Mark?" She nodded, her face completely sincere. "I think you should go for it."

"What?" Andie's jaw fell open. She shook her head in confusion, caught totally off guard when she'd been so deep in thought in the other matter. "No, Aunt Ginny. That wasn't what I was going to ask, but...really? Why? And shouldn't you still be mad at him on my behalf? Instead of inviting him into the room right next door to mine?"

She gave her aunt a hard glare. She hadn't yet had time to confront her about that little situation, but now seemed as good a time as any. Anything to postpone the inevitable. Plus, she needed to direct her anger somewhere.

"I've been mad on your behalf long enough," Ginny noted. "It's time to move on."

"You think?"

Her red head bobbed up and down. "I know. It's not good to hang on to hatred like that. Eats away at a person's soul. He was a moron. A big one. But I already let him have it back then. Now is now, and I think it's time for you to go for it."

Andie stared down at the woman. "Is that why you gave him the room? So he'd have easier access to 'go for it?'"

Good grief. What did Ginny know about going for it? It had been thirty years since Uncle James had died.

And then something else registered about what Ginny had just said. "Wait." Andie held a hand up, palm out. "You talked to Mark back then? When?" She hadn't realized they'd spoken other than at the rehearsal dinner. When Rob had come to the church, he'd said he and Mark were heading to Vegas for the week. Mark shouldn't have been at the apartment when Ginny had gone up there.

Aunt Ginny picked up a pink ribbon and began twining it in the pattern Andie had shown her earlier. "He was there when I went up to pack your stuff. He thought you were out on that cruise you two had planned for the honeymoon."

Andie thunked down into her seat. "He thought I'd gone on the cruise?"

"He'd assumed so. I got the impression he'd told Robert to tell you to take it."

"Well, Robert didn't. Not that I would have anyway, but no, that was not what Rob said to me."

"I didn't think so," she murmured. "But anyway, back to Mark. I ripped him a new one. His behavior was childish and selfish and he wasn't man enough to deserve you in the first place."

153

Andie leaned across the space to give her aunt a hug. She could totally see Ginny giving Mark a piece of her mind. "Then why do you think I should go for it now?" she asked. As if she hadn't already thrown caution to the wind and been heading in that exact direction without any prodding. "Are you assuming he isn't childish or selfish any longer? Or are you just telling me to have a summer fling and whatever he's like now doesn't matter?"

Steady green eyes studied her to the point that Andie began to squirm. Maybe she shouldn't have mentioned a fling so casually? She felt her shoulders drawing up as if she were a small child being chastised.

Finally, Aunt Ginny seemed to make up her mind about something and shoved the bag she was working on to the side. "Scoot over here, Andromeda. Let's talk."

"O-kay." Andie slid over, closing the distance to her aunt, and wondered what could possibly call for the use of her real name. No one ever called her Andromeda.

"I'm okay with it now," Aunt Ginny started, "because, yes, I suspect he's grown up, but also because you had no business getting married back then in the first place. It wasn't your time."

"Fate, you mean? I wasn't fated to be married four years ago?" Sometimes this fate business got old.

"No, you weren't. But that's not what I'm talking about. You simply weren't ready, child. You had no idea who you were—and Lord knows you weren't the woman trying to carry that job you had. You needed to grow, figure things out."

Like she had them figured out now. If she did, she wouldn't be on the brink of losing her uncle's legacy. Nor would she be throwing herself at Mark every chance she got. She felt a blush threaten each time she thought about how bold she'd been the night before. She couldn't get within ten feet of that man without wanting to rip her clothes off. Or wanting him to rip them off for her.

Enough thinking about that, or she'd blurt out that she'd already gone for it—only they'd gotten interrupted. "I thought that job fit me well," she said instead. "It was what I went to school for."

"Oh pooh." Aunt Ginny waved a hand in the air and shot Andie a disgusted look. "Save that crap for your mother. She's the one who might believe it. But I know you, Andromeda Rose. And that job was not you. You were going for the career you thought your mother would be proud of, choosing finance because that was her line of work. But honey…you are not your mother. And you're especially not a corporate, cubicle-walls-and-no-fresh-air kind of girl. Look at you now. It's near one hundred degrees outside and you have the windows open so you can feel a breeze. How could you have married a man and expected to be happy when you didn't even know who you were?"

Andie stared at her aunt. Why had she never said any of this to her before? "Because I loved him."

"Yes." Aunt Ginny let out a long, impatient sigh. "You loved him, but surely you know by now that's not all it's about. The physical stuff…" She paused and tilted her head at Andie with a look. "And I'm not blind, either. I see that the physical stuff is still there just fine. If you don't sleep with that boy soon, one of you is going to go up in flames."

"Aunt Ginny." Shock registered in Andie's voice.

"Oh, don't you 'Aunt Ginny' me. I know all about it. Do you really think I've been without a man all these years? And more than just Chester Brownbomb, too."

Ewww. Andie didn't need to know that her aunt had been with Chester.

"I know exactly what you're thinking every time you look at that beefcake," Aunt Ginny finished.

"Oh, man, I do not need to hear this." Andie started to rise, uncomfortable with every direction the conversation was taking, but Ginny pointed a sharp finger at the couch.

Andie sat back down.

"Now, as I was saying, you were in no position to get married, and I was actually glad he figured it out before it was too late. You certainly weren't going to. And though his actions were deplorable, in the end it saved you both a lot of heartache."

"You think marrying him would have been worse than not marrying him?" Possibly it would have. Andie was just coming to realize that herself, but she was surprised to hear it from Ginny. "Did you forget how hard it was for me to get over him?"

Ginny snorted. "Like you ever got over him. But yes, I do. Because you two would have fought more than you loved. You had something special between you. I heard it every time you talked to me on the phone. Saw it in the pictures you e-mailed me. I even saw it at the rehearsal dinner that night—though I also saw the tension sitting thick as mosquitoes in July. But special or not, it wasn't yet ready to be there, hon. And you weren't grown up enough to know how to handle it. Marrying, having that specialness, only to watch it be slowly ripped apart?" She shook her head, the sadness pulling at her face seeming to say even more than her words. "It would have broken you, sweetheart. A piece of you would have died inside."

Andie licked her suddenly dry lips, wishing she had a glass of water. Aunt Ginny's words made a strange kind of sense. "And what?" she asked. "You think it's ready to be there now?"

Aunt Ginny patted Andie's knee. "I think it's much closer today than it was then. And I think you two still have something special."

"We still have heat, Aunt Ginny. But I think that's all. He lives in Boston—he has his whole family there. I love it here. Plus, I still want a career, even if it's not the one I had back then. I'm not who he needs."

Her aunt picked up a thin strip of ribbon and tied it in a simple bow, watching her own movements as if they held the secrets to the universe. Finally she looked over at Andie. "Just don't close your mind to it, okay? Things aren't always what they seem."

Andie studied her aunt, feeling like the conversation was heading in a different direction.

"I lost James and...well, other things had happened in the year before his death. Things that I didn't know if I could survive. But then he was gone. Forever. And I thought I would die from the pain of it. It took me a long time, but I finally started living again. But it was too late for me. I'm alone now. Because I was too stubborn to get past mistakes a long time ago. I don't want that for you, sweetheart. I don't want you to grow old alone."

Andie's heart seized in a tight knot. She'd never heard her aunt talk about her husband in any way other than how much she'd loved him. How happy they'd been. It made her think about the fact that everyone has their issues, whether they're publicly exposed or not. She wondered what Ginny could have possibly gone through that had left her struggling for so long to move on.

She grabbed her aunt's hand and squeezed it. "You are not alone, Aunt Ginny. I'm here. And I'm not going anywhere."

Crap...unless they lost the house. Which was what they were supposed to be talking about.

Andie lowered her head to her hands and moaned, the sound striking her as a painful wail one might hear from an injured animal. "I have something I have to tell you," she finally whispered. "Something *really* important."

Ginny grew still beside her, and it was as if the breeze quit blowing in through the windows as well. Everything felt stuck in time. "I've always been able to read you, you know?" Ginny began, her words slow and gentle. "It's about the loan, isn't it? Something's been eating at you for days. And I know we have that payment due this month."

Andie nodded, her head still in her hands. "I think I've messed up, Aunt Ginny."

"Nonsense. Whatever it is, we can fix it."

Except Andie had no idea how to fix it.

"We need the bonus from this wedding to make the payment." She peeked out through her fingers and focused on the strength she felt in Ginny's trust—even though that trust was clearly misplaced. "And I think there's a really big chance the whole thing might get called off."

"Oh my." Shock put an instant pallor in Ginny's skin. "What's happened?"

"Mark overheard something last night. Something that didn't sound good. I begged him not to tell Rob, but he said he had to."

"Bad enough that it could hurt Rob?"

Andie nodded again. "It wasn't good."

The look Andie hated was suddenly shot her way. The one that said she should know better. "And you suggested Mark keep quiet and let a wedding happen if it shouldn't?"

"You'll lose the house if we don't get that bonus! Of course I suggested he keep quiet."

"If we lose the house, then that's just fa—"

"I know, fate. Only it won't be. It'll be me, making another mistake in a long line of many. Except this time, instead of merely getting fired or losing my fiancé, I'll lose your home. Oh my God, Aunt Ginny. I don't know how I'll live with myself if I cause that to happen."

Ginny dropped the bow to the floor and turned to Andie, taking both her hands in her own. "We aren't going to lose the house. Something will come through, don't you worry. But even if the worst did happen, it's not your fault. I'm the one who signed the house over."

"Because I talked you into it!"

"You think I don't have sense enough to think on my own?"

"I think you did it for me. Because you trusted me. And now I'm going to let you down."

Tears were falling from Andie's eyes. Tears she'd been holding back for days. Years. Everything was too much. She wanted to escape, even if for just a night.

She tugged against Ginny's hands, needing to swipe at her eyes, wanting to hide the sign of weakness, but Ginny didn't turn her loose. "The only way you can let me down is by not doing the right thing," Aunt Ginny said. "Investing in our business was the right thing. We've helped many people have the weddings they envisioned. And more. Hopefully we'll get to continue doing that. But you can't lower your standards, child. If this thing that Mark overheard is bad enough, you have to let the chips fall where they may. You and I will deal with the outcome. And just maybe, it won't be as bad as you think."

Andie yanked her hands free and stood, hearing everything Ginny was saying, but knowing her aunt didn't understand. "It's me, Aunt Ginny." The tremble in her voice infuriated her. "Don't you get it? I'm the screwup. I always have been." Her words lumped together in her throat but she kept going, forcing them out one by one. "That's probably the real reason Mark didn't want to marry me. He knew I'd bring his family down. I'm a failure. Same reason my mother never liked me."

She couldn't handle the conversation anymore. Whirling, she intended to leave, even if that meant running to her bedroom and hiding like a child. But before she could take a step, she found her mother standing in the entrance to the room, her eyes wide.

And even better, Mark stood only a few feet behind her.

Great, pour all the crap on top of her head at once. Just perfect.

Andie set her gaze back on her mother, unable to face the incredulity she read in Mark's. Cassie Winters was sixty-six, had the red hair and green eyes of her sister, but dressed as if she'd just come from a modern business woman photo shoot. Multi-hundred-dollar pumps, a small handbag over her shoulder, and a cream-and-black business suit, not a wrinkle in sight. It made Andie sick.

"Andie." Her mother's tone was a mix of surprise and... disbelief? Her gaze bounced between Ginny and Andie, as if looking for whatever else she wanted to say.

Andie shook her head. She hadn't seen her mother in over a year, and she had no desire to see her now. What in the hell was she doing there, anyway?

"No," Andie murmured. She was not having this conversation. Not now.

She lowered her gaze and ignored all of them as she hurried through the room, yanking her arm away when Mark reached for her.

"Just leave me alone," she snarled.

As she ran up the stairs, the last thing she noticed was that Aunt Ginny now looked at her sister with the same fury that Andie herself felt.

∿

He had to go after her.

That was the message that kept rolling through his mind. He had to go after her. She was upset. And whatever the issue between her and her mother—and from what he'd just caught, there was definitely an issue—he wanted to help.

Or hell, maybe he just wanted to go to her.

Even though he'd come back early because he had a load of work he should be doing.

"Cassiopeia," Ginny stated, her tone cold. Even colder, he thought, than when she'd read him the riot act four years ago. "What brings you to my house after all this time?"

He glanced at Andie's mother. *Cassiopeia?* He shook his head. He didn't have time for this.

Ignoring the two women, who both had their noses stuck high in the air, he turned to the stairs and took them two at a time. Whatever their problem, they could work it out. He had another, more pressing matter at hand.

When he reached Andie's door, he rapped softly with his knuckles. She didn't answer.

He rattled the knob, but it was locked. He heard nothing from inside.

Knowing the better thing might be to leave her alone and simply tackle the work he'd come back to do, he made the decision to step in even if she didn't think she wanted him to. He had to. She needed him.

He passed through his room and headed out to the deck. It was hot out today, but he'd lay odds she was sitting in her room with the door to the deck open, listening to the ocean.

Bingo.

It was open only a few inches, but enough to let the outside in. He stepped over and slid into the quiet room.

The moment both feet were on the carpet inside, something hit him in the face.

"Get out of my room." Andie's voice was low but held an edge. She was sitting up in the middle of her bed, tears streaming down her face. She was normally such a tough cookie. So much so that he couldn't remember having ever seen her cry. The sight broke off another chunk of his heart and handed it over to her.

Picking up the pillow she'd thrown at him, he tossed it in a chair and stopped in front of her. "I'm not leaving. Would you like to talk?"

"No, I would not like to talk. I would *like* to be alone."
Her glare was heartfelt, he'd give her that.

Choosing to ignore her request, he crossed to the sitting
area and rooted around in the small fridge for a bottle of
water. He held it up in question.

She grudgingly nodded, her gaze darting away from
him. After handing it to her then heading for the couch,
the bottle hit him square in the middle of the back.

"What the hell, Andie?" He spun around. "Quit acting
like a child."

She rose, stalking over to shove her nose in his face.
"Then get out of my room."

"I will not. You're upset. You said some things downstairs
that we need to talk about. I'm not leaving until we do."

"I didn't say anything that we need to talk about." She
poked him in the chest.

"Come on, babe." He grabbed her hand and stroked
his thumb back and forth over her clenched fingers. She
thought she was a failure? And *that* was why he hadn't married her? He reached out and rubbed a thumb across her
cheek to wipe away tears. "Your mother is here. Do you want
to talk about that?"

And the fact she'd said her mother didn't like her?

"No, I don't want to talk about that. Can you not hear? I
want to be left alone." She finished this outburst with a slight
upswing of her hand as if planning to smack him across the
face as she had the night he'd arrived.

He didn't wait to see if that was her plan.

Catching her wrist, he jerked her arm around behind
her, which pressed her chest squarely into his. At the touch
of their bodies, she sucked in a sharp breath. And he'd

swear her body began vibrating from head to toe. Her gaze dipped to his mouth.

She wanted sex? Seriously? Right then?

He would be a jerk to take it. But that didn't mean he wasn't thinking about it.

When her eyes narrowed and slowly lifted back to his, he reacted before she devised another way to provoke him. He twisted her other arm behind her back and shoved her up against the wall, his body trapping hers beneath his. Her soft panting breaths and the lushness of her curves were almost enough to make a man whimper.

They'd had some pretty good make-up sessions in the past, and he got the distinct impression she was intentionally trying to tick him off now with the hopes of heading in that same direction.

"You want sex, don't you?" he asked, his own breathing as unsteady as hers. "Right now? Right here?" He leaned in and whispered against her ear, "Up against the wall?"

She bucked against him. "Of course not." The vehemence in her voice almost convinced him. "Especially not when I know you've been out playing with Wendy the wenchy bridesmaid all day long."

"I've been out what?" He pulled back to peer down at her, having no clue what she was talking about but glad to see her tears had dried up.

The shirt she wore had buttons running down the front, and somehow the top couple had popped undone. He could see a gorgeous amount of cleavage and orange lace, and luscious round breasts. And he almost released her wrists to go after them.

EX ON THE BEACH

"Wendy," she spat out. "The woman I saw you with your arm around the other night. I'm sure you enjoyed hanging out with her all day. Bet she wore a hot little bikini too, didn't she? Probably wiggled her butt in your face every chance she got."

Oh, Wendy. How in the hell did she get into this conversation? And when had Andie seen him with his arm around her? And then he remembered. The other night when they'd all gone to Gin's. Wendy had been a little too friendly with Rob on the dance floor, so Mark had taken it upon himself to be her shadow for the remainder of the evening.

The funny thing was, Rob hadn't seemed to mind the attention.

Penelope had, though.

How had Andie seen them together? She hadn't been at the bar.

The empty wine bottle he'd found on the deck the following morning flashed through his mind. She'd been out there? Waiting for him?

The thought warmed his blood. He'd wanted to go to her when he'd come in that night, had wanted to have that talk he'd promised. But all had been quiet on the other side of the wall, so he'd spent the night hours working, instead. He wanted to be caught up so that when he got Andie to admit that she wanted an affair with him, he could lavish her with attention.

But he liked the idea of her being jealous of Wendy. It meant she cared. At least a little.

"The fact is …" he started, his gaze roaming over Andie's chest as he taunted her. She reminded him of a ripe peach.

And he liked peaches. He dipped down to nip the inside curve of one breast and smiled when he felt her catch her breath. "She did have on a bikini," he whispered against her. He flicked his tongue out to soothe over the spot he'd just tasted. "It was red. And very tiny." He nipped again. "And so *hot*."

"Of course it was," she growled out the words.

"And it was held together with itsy-bitsy little strings."

Her leg shifted, but he shoved against her before she could lift it, trapping her two legs beneath one of his. "No, no, no," he tsked. He stared down into her face. "You don't get to knee me again, sweetheart. Especially when you're just looking for a fight. That was a one-time-only deal."

"I am not looking for a fight. I'm pissed at you. You're trying to stop the wedding, you're flirting with Wendy, probably sleeping with her, and you—"

He closed his mouth over hers, swallowing her words and catching a moan. He gave one in return. Damn, she was hot. He'd always loved her riled up. It might be the wrong thing to do when she was clearly trying to avoid certain issues, but she had him so turned on he was going to take what she was offering and worry about his conscience later.

It wasn't as if they weren't going to end up in bed together anyway. They would have been there last night if they hadn't gotten interrupted.

He turned one wrist loose only long enough to bring both her hands together above her head, clasping them against the wall. He liked her stretched out in front of him like that.

"You wanna fight, babe?" he asked, holding her trapped before him, one thigh now sliding between her legs. He nibbled along her neck and nudged his leg upward until he felt her tremble. "Because I've decided I'll give you what you want. But I don't think it's a fight you're looking for."

He brought his free hand to the front of her shirt and yanked, ripping it the rest of the way open. "I think you want me. Inside you. And I think you want it right here."

"No, I don't." Her words came out breathy and he couldn't help but laugh.

"Guess I should turn you loose, then." As he said the words, his hand slipped behind her and undid her bra. Her breasts dipped with their weight, as did she. She now sagged against the hand holding her up.

"Don't stop, Mark," she whispered, all the fight gone from her, her voice breaking. Slate-colored eyes pleaded up at him, her rosy lips mesmerizing to watch. He liked that he'd put the flush on her cheeks. "Please," she begged. "Don't stop."

He wasn't planning on it.

Getting a firmer grip on her wrists, he cupped her jaw and brought her mouth to his. She met him move for move, her tongue darting out to play with his until he felt his knees go weak. When he eased his mouth back an inch, pressing his forehead to hers while trying to catch his breath, she dipped her head and put her lips to the spot just below his ear. Her teeth bit down gently and he shuddered against her.

"Hurry," she whispered. "Fast."

Oh, hell. He'd intended to do a bit more than unzip and push into her, but she was making it very hard. In more ways than one.

"Let me take you to the bed, sweetheart. Slow down and do this right."

She shook her head and put her mouth back to that spot just under his ear. "No time. I want you now."

In a matter of seconds he was sufficiently protected, had his shorts dropped to his ankles, her panties tossed across the room, and was gripping Andie's bare ass in his hands. When her legs and arms all wrapped around him, he knew she'd won.

She dug her hands into his hair, and he slammed her back against the wall. Then he was in her. They both reared back, their breaths momentarily caught as they eyed each other from under their lashes. And then he pulled out and plunged in again.

Everything about her was both hot and soft. She tasted good, she felt good. She was freaking dynamite in his arms. He couldn't focus long enough to do more than hang on and keep pounding.

"Oh God, Mark," she whimpered. "Yes."

Yes. He had to agree. *Yes.*

This was where he belonged.

Her legs squeezed tighter and her arms clenched him like a vise. She had his mouth fused to hers as if she'd never get enough. He was going to finish in a matter of seconds if they didn't slow down. But damn, she was wanton. Bucking and whimpering. She murmured his name over and over.

"Baby," he whispered. He kicked off his flip-flops and the shorts around his feet, then shifted the two of them to another wall where he could see the ocean sparkling outside the window. Focusing on it was almost enough to help him slow down, but then she tightened her inner muscles and arched herself back just enough to make their contact a little more exact, and he knew it was over. His biceps tensed, a lamp crashed to the floor, and he shoved her into the corner and braced his palms against the wall so he could drive himself home.

He wanted to make sure she was there with him, but he couldn't wait. His mind was blown. She'd pushed him over the edge.

The last thing he remembered before he threw back his head and let out a groan was seeing her do the same thing. Her breasts rose in the air, her back arched, and she ground herself into him.

They shook against each other, their orgasms seeming to go on forever. He was pretty sure his leg muscles were going to give out before he was empty, but somehow he managed to hang on. And he hung on to her at the same time. Or even better, she hung on to him.

Her hands clutched at his arms as she convulsed around him, animal noises coming from her throat. He couldn't help but smile.

This was his Andie.

The one he'd wanted to keep forever.

The one he was terrified he still wanted. Forever.

They both calmed, and he wrapped his arms around her and pressed a gentle kiss to her open mouth. She let out a tiny sighing noise in return.

She was sated. His woman. And he'd done that.

Keeping her tucked against him, he crossed to the bed and yanked back the covers, then followed her down. He'd thought he was taking advantage of her when they'd started, but he had the sudden notion that maybe she had been the one taking advantage all along.

If that were the case, would she now tell him to go? Because he wasn't ready to leave. He didn't know if he ever would be.

And how ridiculous was that? He closed his eyes, praying that he wasn't falling for her again.

CHAPTER TWELVE

Andie let out a happy groan and stretched, enjoying the feel of Mark up against her. That was one way to release some stress. "Can we do that again?" she asked. It was all she could do not to purr like a cat. Why hadn't they been doing that for the past week?

A large hand slid over her bare stomach, fingers stretching from one side to the other, and she looked over to find Mark smiling wickedly at her. His hand crawled under her skewed bra to settle around the bottom curve of her breast and he gave a little squeeze.

"We can do that as many times as you'd like. The next time should be slower, though. So I can properly touch you." His thumb slid over her nipple, making it instantly hard. "And taste you." He licked her through the lace. "Just let me catch my second wind."

Her eyes lowered to his crotch. "Is that what it's called these days? A second wind?"

"Smart-ass," he muttered. He squeezed her again, then shifted so that he could grab a tissue and dispose of the condom. Next he ripped off his shirt and propped himself up against the headboard. He then pulled her in snug beside him and turned his gaze on her with a knowing look.

It made her feel guilty. If he'd used her as she'd just done to him, the situation would not be pretty.

"I feel like I should apologize," she whispered. Embarrassment engulfed her and she tried to duck her head. He wouldn't let her. "I wouldn't have slapped you," she tacked on, her voice quiet as she glanced down at the shirt hanging off her shoulders and the jean skirt bunched up at her waist. "I only acted like it because I knew you'd stop me."

The gravity of her actions rested heavily on her, but at the same time her inner voice kept shouting: *I had sex with Mark! I had sex with Mark!*

"I see," he said. He slid a hand down her arm, then reached around front to locate her breast. It had always amazed her how much of her he could palm at one time. "And what about the kick?" he asked. "Were you going to try to kick me in the boys again? Because I'll tell you, it wouldn't have gotten you the result you were looking for."

"Not a chance." She closed her eyes as he caressed her, enjoying the slow touch. It was heating her up again, much faster than she would have thought possible. "And I have to tell you that I felt really bad about that the other night."

He chuckled, then pulled his fingers away from her skin.

"Hey." Her eyes popped open. "I was enjoying that."

"I know, too much. That's why I stopped."

"Well, that makes no sense at all."

He tilted his head down and kissed her on the nose. "I thought maybe we could talk first."

"Oh, come on. I don't want to talk." She made a move to get out of bed, but his hands wrapped around her waist and brought her back to him, this time settling her directly on his lap. She couldn't help it, she wiggled her butt on his crotch.

"Stop it," he growled. "We're going to have a grown-up talk now. Not hide things with hot sex."

The way he said it made her think he was under the impression that that's what they'd done in the past. She studied him, thinking back to heated arguments and even hotter make-up sex, and wondered if he might be on to something. Had they skirted around too many issues in the past? She'd have to give it more thought later.

"What if I did naughty things to you?" she asked. She wiggled against him again and felt him stirring beneath her. "Could we have more hot sex then?"

He shook his head at her. "You are the devil, woman." He parked her back on the bed and pointed a finger at her, strangely reminding her of Aunt Ginny. "Stay put."

He got out of bed and headed to pick up the bottle of water that she'd thrown at him, while she got busy shedding the remainder of her clothes.

"I'm sorry I hit you with the bottle of water," she said. She really was. It had connected harder than she'd intended.

He looked back at her and she smiled. She was now completely naked. Just exactly as he was.

"And that I hit you with a pillow," she added.

He turned up the bottle and drank half the water, all the while eyeing her as she sat in the middle of the bed. She did her share of eyeing, too. It had been a really long time since she'd had the chance to do that.

She wet her lips. "Looks like you still work out."

He smiled around the mouth of the bottle, and kept drinking.

Looked like he never put an ounce of anything bad in his body, actually.

How could a man have such defined abs? It made her want to suck in her own stomach, but the way he was looking at her implied he hadn't noticed their differences. Or if he had, he liked what he saw, anyway.

When he lowered the water to his side, she couldn't help but notice that he was hard again. Fully.

"Do you want a bottle?" he asked. His voice was tight.

She nodded. "Please."

He got her one and crawled back into bed with her, but when she started to scoot over next to him, he pointed back to the other side of the mattress.

"Come on, Mark. Why not?"

"Because we have things to talk about, babe. *You* have things to talk about. You said a lot downstairs."

She made a face at him and pulled the covers up, tucking them under her arms. "Then cover that thing up so I don't have to look at it."

He grinned at her—his entire face softening and looking like the man she'd once fallen head over heels for—but did as she'd asked. With both of them sufficiently hidden and once again propped up against the headboard, she let out a long breath and asked with a petulant groan, "What do you want to know?"

He laughed, the sound almost bitter. "Where to start? There are so many things."

Well, she wasn't going to start it. When she remained silent, he finally came out with a question.

"Your mother's full name is Cassiopeia?"

She jerked her gaze to his and burst out laughing. "Yes. My mother's full name is Cassiopeia. My grandmother apparently saw her as the beautiful one. My oldest aunt was Athena, the wise one. But apparently by the time Aunt Ginny came around, Grandmother had moved on to patron saints. There's no telling what a fourth child would have been named."

"And your mother continued the tradition by naming you Andromeda?"

Andie shrugged. "Apparently. The myth goes that Andromeda was Cassiopeia's daughter. I can't imagine why my mother did something so fanciful. From what I can tell, she's never had another moment's lightheartedness in her life."

Which led them to the topic of her mother. Both of them sat quietly, and Andie knew that he was waiting for her to bring up the fact that her mother was there on the island. At the house. And possibly he wanted her to bring up that Andie had declared that her mother had never liked her. But how did one just bring that up?

Especially when she'd hidden it from him the whole time they'd been engaged?

Not to mention that it barely mattered because Andie had always loved Aunt Ginny more than her own mother, anyway?

A soft whimper embarrassed her as it slipped from her throat, and Mark's strong arm came around her and pulled her to his side. His embrace gave her the courage she needed. She rested her head in the curve of his shoulder and began talking.

"She was thirty-seven when she had me. You might remember that from…before, though. Anyway, she'd been married for years, and from what I can gather, the two of them never wanted kids. Then she got pregnant with me and he left her." She glanced up at Mark before continuing. "But he wasn't my father. Though I've no idea who was. I told you that before, too. Then she met John when I was seven. They dated for a year and got married. And I started coming to Aunt Ginny's the next summer."

"But you spent the remainder of each year with your mother?" he asked.

She nodded. "Better schools. She expected the best from me." Still expected the best from her.

"With a Harvard MBA, I'd say you gave it to her."

She looked away from his probing eyes. That wasn't exactly the case.

He stroked his thumb over her shoulder as if knowing that he was giving her the courage to continue, simply from his touch. That was one of the things she'd always loved about him. He knew when she needed him. His mere presence gave her the courage to step outside herself.

The night he'd shown up at the bar with the charm for her ankle, she'd just gotten off the phone with her mother, having discovered there was no need for her to fly home the next day for Christmas. Cassie and John were heading to Europe for the holidays. Andie's mother had forgotten to tell her.

Mark had shown up when she'd felt at her lowest, and though she'd ignored his advances for months when he'd been a regular in the place—mostly because he'd been friends with Rob—she'd been unable to look away from him that night. Somehow he'd known she needed someone, and there he'd been. He'd given her the gift, then had sat at the bar for hours, talking to her any chance she got.

When the bar had closed, she'd taken him home with her and they'd remained together every day that followed... until he hadn't shown up for their wedding.

She sucked in a breath and continued, "I *didn't* give it to her, actually. Not what she wanted. I was never good enough. No matter how hard I tried." She plucked at the bedspread covering her, wondering if she would ever make her mother proud. "I can't be like her," she whispered. "I can work just as hard. I *do* work just as hard. But things never turn out the same for me. I'm a screwup. A failure."

And she was tired of trying so hard. What was the point, anyway? Especially now that her mother was there to see her fail spectacularly with her own two eyes.

"Are you kidding me?" Mark's harsh tone surprised her. He stopped her fiddling with the bedspread by weaving their fingers together, and she couldn't help but look up at him, his vehemence sending a small thrill sizzling through her. "How can you even say that?" he asked. "You're far from a failure, Andie. Far from it. You—"

"Got fired from my job in Boston," she said, shutting him up. "Yep. I lost you and got fired, all within days. That was not a proud time for my mother."

"Baby," he uttered. "I..." He shook his head and then gripped her face between his hands. His arms were tense, but his touch was soft. "You got fired?" She read the shock in his gaze. His eyes were a stormy blue at the moment. "I thought you quit. To get away from me."

She laughed, but it came out as dry as she felt inside. "Funny thing is, I considered it. But that job was what I'd worked for—what was going to earn me the love of my mother. Finally. So, no, I didn't walk away. But because I didn't win that account, the client I invited to our wedding..." She paused and raised her eyebrows to make sure he understood which account. "Because I failed, they let me go."

"But that makes no sense," Mark began.

"It makes perfect sense. I'd already made several mistakes since they'd hired me. I wasn't holding up my end." She lifted a shoulder and tried to look away, but he had her face trapped. "I was on probation, Mark," she whispered in shame. "It was my last opportunity to keep the job."

His eyes softened. "You never told me you were having that kind of trouble."

"No, I didn't." She peeled his fingers from her face then crawled to the middle of the bed, taking a section of the cover with her. "I just worked around the clock instead. Trying to keep my job. I was so far out of my element with you and your family as it was. And then your dad..." She peeked at him. "He got me the job. The job I couldn't even do well enough to keep. So, no, I didn't tell you. I couldn't let you see that I was as big a misfit there as I was trying to fit into your family."

"Baby, you were never like that. My family loved you."

"And I loved them." She couldn't hide from the lost sound of her words. "Very much. But I was a girl playing pretend. I wasn't anybody. Not like you. I didn't fit in. No matter how nice your family was to me." She shook her head, refusing to look at him now, and trying her hardest not to let him see her cry again. "I never fit. Anywhere."

Except there.

With Aunt Ginny.

~

Mark stared at Andie, her words threatening to dig up long-ago memories while setting his chest on fire. Memories that felt a lifetime old. Or older.

He shoved the thoughts aside. It didn't pay to think about it.

"You are not a failure," he started, knowing he should address the way she'd felt about fitting in with him and his family, but not sure he could have that conversation while keeping his past at bay. "You've built this place, baby. Practically on your own, I'd imagine. Not a failure in the least."

"And I'm going to lose it," she stated flatly. She turned back to him, her eyes empty and hollow. "Did you forget that? If the wedding is called off, I'll lose the bonus and we'll lose the house. I did that, Mark. I talked Ginny into it. It's all on me."

She'd explained the loan to him the previous evening. Right before he'd gone off to find Rob.

"What did Rob say, anyway?" she asked. Fear flickered across her face, making her look about six years old. "Should I tell Kayla to alert the rest of the guests of a cancellation?"

He felt like a heel. "I didn't get a chance to talk to him yet. He wasn't in his room last night, and Penelope was stuck to his side the whole day today. They're going out tonight, so I'm going to talk to him on the fishing boat tomorrow."

Frustration filled him. The last thing he wanted was to be the reason for her business shutting down, but he couldn't let Rob walk into a marriage without knowing what he was up against. Without knowing what was expected of him.

"I've got to talk to him, Andie," he whispered. He reached for her, but she slipped away and stood from the bed, her body naked and glorious in the sunshine streaming in from the open door.

"You know I do," he pleaded when she didn't say anything. "But I want to cover the payment for you."

She gaped at him. "I can't take your money."

"Why not?"

The fact that she stood glaring at him while as naked as when she'd entered the world, was not lost on him. He wanted to forget the conversation and drag her back to bed. He wanted to take his time with her and explore all those places he'd only thought about over the last few years.

Instead he stood, too, and slipped on his shorts. He could already feel her putting a wall between them, and he'd be damned if he was going to sit there naked and vulnerable while she did it. Taking in his movements, she grabbed her panties off the floor and jerked them on, then pulled a T-shirt from a drawer and slipped it over her head.

"It's my problem, Mark." Her tone was steady and strong. She lifted her chin. "I can't take money from you."

"You could as a loan." As far as he was concerned, she could have the money outright, but if her pride made her need to call it a loan, he would do it that way.

She paused in thought for a moment but shook her head no, her shoulders slumping a fraction. "I need to do this," she said softly. "*I* need to make it work. Not have someone swoop in and save the day."

He *wanted* to save the day. He'd always liked taking care of her. And he wanted to be her hero now. Especially since he'd just realized that having sex with her wasn't going to give him the closure he'd been seeking.

Which royally sucked. He was ready to move on with his life. Not spend it pining over Andie.

He studied her—her flushed cheeks, her hair slightly wild as if it had been tossed around for a really good reason, and the ever-present vulnerability deep in her blue-gray eyes—and he knew that she *did* need to do this on her own. He didn't get why but understood that proving herself was important. He just wondered if she was trying to prove her competence to Ginny or to herself. Or more likely, to her mother.

"Okay." He nodded and held out a hand for her, beckoning her back to him. He wanted her in his arms. He wanted her to come to him. "If that's what you want. But the offer stands. All you have to do is say the word and the money is yours."

"Thank you." She crossed her arms over her chest, the action plumping the unencumbered curves of her breasts, and eyed his outstretched hand. When she lifted her gaze to his, he wanted to put his fist through a wall.

"We're just going to be *friends* now, I take it?" he asked. His tone wasn't polite.

She nodded, nibbling on her lower lip. "I'm pretty sure that would be best."

"Why's that?" Irritation flooded him. He should let it go, but he couldn't help himself. "I'm only good for burning off some steam?"

She cringed. He knew his comment was ugly, but she'd pissed him off. It wasn't like he was asking for a commitment.

"Mark, please," she started. "We were friends once. I don't see why we can't be again."

Because she'd been the kind of friend he'd wanted to keep forever. He shook his head. "It won't work, sweetheart. I can't be that guy for you."

Wide eyes blinked slowly at him. "Okay," she said. She nodded. "Yeah, I'm sorry. I guess we shouldn't have—"

"Just stop it." He cut her off with the slice of his hand. "We both wanted it. We did it. End of story. And you wanted it as much as me, so don't try to pretend otherwise."

"I never said I didn't." Anger flared on her face. It was better than the withdrawn look she'd been wearing. "In fact, I'm the one who started it. I'm not pretending anything else. I just don't think we should—" Her words came to an abrupt stop and she shrugged one shoulder. "You'll be leaving as soon as you tell Rob, anyway."

She was right. If the wedding was canceled, he would have no reason to stay. Except...

"I could stay. I *am* on vacation."

She sighed, a long, sad sound that lodged a rock deep in his gut. "What would be the point, Mark?"

"The point would be us having a good time," he urged. And maybe more. He didn't voice his second thought, but had the feeling she'd felt it hanging in the air between them.

With a slight shake of her head, he heard her answer loud and clear.

They couldn't be more. Wondering "what if" would only lead to more heartache, which neither of them needed. She was right to say no.

They'd tried "more" already and it hadn't worked. Heck, they'd been engaged for over a year and he'd never even known that she thought her mother didn't like her. Or that she'd been on the verge of losing her job but was too afraid to tell him for fear of how it would make her look to him. To his family. How could he have missed all that?

Had he really been that self-involved?

But he knew the answer. He'd been working on getting his own career off the ground. A career that—if he were to be completely honest with himself—he'd probably seen as more important than hers. It was the family business, after all. What he'd spent his whole life working toward. It had been priority number one.

So, yeah, he could admit as he looked back now, he'd seen her career as not nearly as important as his. He was the man, after all. The provider. The protector. He was the one who would take care of her.

He'd loved her, yes, but he hadn't seen her as his equal.

The thought disgusted him. Maybe he had been as big a jerk as Rob.

Their issues hadn't begun or ended with his warped perspective, though. They'd jumped into everything way too fast, which he could also take credit for. He'd pushed for more early on, for fear that she'd leave Boston, and thus him, before they had time to figure it all out and do it right. He'd been terrified she'd graduate and head off to find a job. So he'd pushed. He'd asked her to marry her, moved her in, and—it seemed—they'd both promptly forgotten to keep learning even the most basic things about each other.

Not the way a relationship was supposed to go.

Mark's brow furrowed as another thought smacked him in the face. She'd said her job in Boston was supposed to earn her the love of her mother. That was why she'd worked such long hours?

That put a whole different spin on many of their arguments.

He'd always assumed the job more important than him. But maybe what had been more important was her winning her mother over. And though he had no similar experience to relate to, he couldn't blame her. He wouldn't be the person he was if he hadn't had the loving support of his mother.

"You need to talk to your mom," Mark said. His voice came out gruffer than he'd intended, but it didn't seem to faze her.

She nodded and the vulnerability he often saw in her increased tenfold. "I know. She'll be disappointed that I've kept her waiting so long, as it is."

He couldn't help it. He took the two steps to close the distance between them and wrapped her in his arms, breathing in her light fragrance as he did so. His lungs expanded with the sweet smell of her.

As her arms closed around him, his life flashed before his eyes: he'd let one girl down a long time ago and was about to do the same to another now. Ruining Andie's business wasn't the same as what he'd done to Tiffany—*thank goodness*—but it did make him wonder what kind of future lay before him. Was he doomed to never have the family he longed for because he couldn't protect the women he loved?

Was he doomed to always do nothing but harm?

EPISODE SIX

CHAPTER THIRTEEN

Andie handed her car keys to the valet and paused, looking past the wide steps in front of her to the entrance of the historic Turtle Island Hotel. With its three sets of double doors spanning the entryway—all arched in a curve along the tops and with muted lights glowing through the glass panels—she was immediately transported back in time. The lighting, coming from inside and from under the awning, reminded her of the warm tones from old-timey kerosene lanterns. The building held the air of money, class, and 1900s turn-of-the-century style. It was glorious.

And her mother was inside. Waiting for her.

Andie started slowly up the stairs, dread pulling at her every step.

Earlier that day, when she'd come downstairs at the house, she'd been embarrassed because she suspected Aunt Ginny would be fully aware of what she'd been doing upstairs with Mark. She'd been equally mortified at the thought that her mother might guess, too. Not that there had been anything wrong with what she and Mark had been doing. They were both grown adults. They could do whatever they wanted.

But still, in the same house as her mother and aunt? And in the middle of the afternoon?

She blushed merely thinking about it.

But she'd been worried for nothing. When she'd returned to the living room, neither her mother nor her aunt had been anywhere to be found. The gift bags and assorted paraphernalia to assemble them had disappeared from the room, and the house had been totally silent. The only indication that anything was amiss had been the note Andie had found pinned under a bowl of fruit on the kitchen counter:

Andie, I'm at the hotel. I have reservations for a late dinner at 8:00. Please join me.

It hadn't been signed, but then, it didn't need to be. The message was in her mother's precise handwriting, with her typical short-and-to-the-point style. After twenty-nine years of her mother's abrupt mannerisms, Andie would recognize it anywhere.

Having several hours between finding the note and the time she was summoned to arrive for dinner, she'd decided to spend the time working at the bar. Instead of going back upstairs to Mark's bed.

Because *OHMYGOD*, she couldn't believe she'd just done that!

And that she wanted to do it again. And again.

And again.

But as she'd made clear, what was the point? He would be leaving after he talked to Rob the next day, and she would go into cleanup mode—while also trying to figure out how to save Aunt Ginny's house. There were two weeks left in the month, and she would not go down without a fight. Even if that meant doing something as drastic as selling the bar to make the loan payment.

"Ma'am." The doorman tipped his head as Andie approached, opening the overlarge door for her. She glanced up immediately upon entering and took in the ceiling covered in original artwork. The island historic foundation had helped fund a project a couple years earlier to restore the rice-paper artwork on the ceiling. It had taken most of the year, but what had been cracked and showing its age now looked as good as new. There was little chance of further damage happening anytime soon.

Andie lowered her gaze to admire the gleaming wood paneling that reached up along the walls and columns throughout the space, as well as the plush gold-and-burgundy rugs covering the floor. Everything shone to a bright polish and signaled quiet dignity. If she hadn't gone into business with Aunt Ginny, she might have considered applying for a job here. She liked being in this space.

With a smile for the familiar faces she passed, she headed through the room. The concierge and staff knew her well, as Seaglass held regular events on the grounds.

She turned right down the hall to the main dining room, her heels clicking as she moved into an area with no rugs. She glanced down at the sleeveless pearl-colored dress that just brushed the tops of her knees and the modest pumps she'd changed into before coming over, making sure everything was as it should be. The restaurant wasn't formal, but it was as close to sophisticated as they got on the island.

"Good evening, Ms. Shayne." The willowy host gave her a slight nod as Andie stepped up to the lectern. "Table for one tonight?"

"No, I'm..." Andie did a quick scan of the area, hoping to find her mother without having to go into detail. Cassie looked enough like Ginny that those who knew her aunt might put two and two together, and Andie wasn't in the mood to answer questions. "There," she said, forcing a smile. She made a quick motion with her hand. "I see my dining companion has already arrived, Lydia. Thanks. I can seat myself."

"Of course." Lydia nodded in acknowledgment, then greeted the guests who'd come up behind Andie.

Attempting not to draw attention to herself, Andie slid quietly into the room, face forward, and didn't stop until she got to her mother's table. She caught herself picking at the seams on the sides of her dress and silently admonished herself to stop. Nerves had her throat sticky, as if she'd spent the last week in the desert with barely enough water to survive.

"Andie." Her mother looked up, greeting her with a slight uplift of her lips, and Andie was momentarily taken aback. Her mother had aged. A lot. There were lines around her eyes and mouth that hadn't been there before—and that not only made her look older than her sixty-six years but also made her seem sad.

There appeared to be a loss of elasticity to her skin—and the texture of her neck had a scratchy look about it. The green of her eyes was downright dull.

Andie hadn't noticed any of that at the house. Probably because she'd barely glanced her mother's way as she'd run from the room.

The signs of aging made Andie feel uneasy. She'd always thought of her mother as a strong, nothing-can-bring-me-down kind of woman.

Murmuring a soft hello, Andie settled into the empty seat across from her mother. She swept her gaze over her mother's dress, noting that she'd changed as well. Gone was the businesswoman Andie had always known. Tonight her mother wore a dark green sheath, accessorized with a strand of pearls that wrapped around her neck and then dipped low over her chest.

The material of the dress shimmered in a way that made Andie think of a 1920s flapper style. There was no fringe, but the pattern hinted at it in a way that left her feeling as if the designer had very much wanted there to be fringe. The dress was gorgeous. And fun.

And not like her mother at all.

"You look lovely, Mom," Andie said. She reached over and gave her mother's hand a squeeze, and the tension from her mother's face eased. Andie suddenly felt bad for having deserted her all afternoon. "Sorry about running out at the house earlier. I…uh…"

"You were clearly upset, dear," her mom tacked on. "It seemed I'd come in on a big conversation."

Andie nodded and picked up the wine list, focusing on it instead of her mother. "You could say that," she muttered.

She bit the corner of her bottom lip to keep from asking her mother just what she'd overheard, and pointed out a German wine to their server. It was a favorite of hers. She turned back to her mother, who sat with a half-filled martini already in front of her. She'd obviously come down to the dining room a bit early.

Andie should have asked Mark how long the two of them had stood outside the living room, listening to her and Ginny's conversation, so she'd have some idea what her mother might have overheard. Instead she'd…

She blushed again. She'd done other things with Mark.

"So," her mother began. She cleared her throat. "You're about to lose the house? Did I understand that correctly?"

Perfect. Why not start with her biggest failure and work backward. Because even with the whole stood-up-at-the-altar thing, losing her aunt's house would definitely be her grand "accomplishment."

"There's a potential issue, yes," Andie said. She fiddled with the stemware on the table. "But nothing for you to worry about, Mom. Why don't you tell me instead why you're here? I'm sure Aunt Ginny was excited for you to visit."

If her mother could get right to the point, so could she. Cassie had never visited Ginny on the island—at least as far as Andie knew—so this was a momentous occasion. And the look on Ginny's face as Andie had headed upstairs…had not been one of excitement.

Which led Andie to wonder what the deal was between her aunt and mother. She'd always just assumed that Cassie didn't have time for Ginny, just as she didn't have time for her, but the look on her aunt's face had indicated there was more to the story.

A shadow passed briefly through her mother's eyes, and she once again looked older than her years. The look disappeared almost as quickly as it had arrived, and her mother put another smile on her face. This one was fake.

"Your aunt wouldn't tell me what's going on, either. Not that I'm surprised. But if the house is at risk"—her mother paused, took a sip of her martini, shrugged one slim shoulder—"I'll be glad to help."

The waiter arrived just as Andie was gaping like a schoolgirl. *I'll be glad to help* were the last words she'd ever expected to come from her mother's mouth. *I'm not surprised... What else is new?...*Or: *It was only a matter of time.* Any of *those* sentences wouldn't have surprised her.

Her mother had loved her throughout the years, Andie had no doubt. In her own, tough-love kind of way. But she'd never been one to bend over backward to help, or to be more involved than the bare minimum required to make the reluctant, expected appearance.

The waiter mutely set the glass of wine Andie had ordered on the table and retreated without taking their dinner orders, obviously understanding that they were in the midst of an intense conversation and he needed to get lost.

"You'll be 'glad to help'?" Andie asked when they were once again alone. She twisted her hands together in her lap. "What does that mean exactly?"

Another quick shoulder shrug from her mother. "I assume the problem is about money. Most things are. Therefore, I mean exactly what I said. I'll be glad to help. If you need money, let me know how much."

She was the second person who'd offered Andie money that day. And for the second time, Andie wanted to jump at the chance. But where did that leave her? She wouldn't have solved anything. She wouldn't have *fixed* anything.

She would still be the screwup. Only this time, she'd be screwing up and relying on someone else to dig her out of the mess she'd made.

She'd rather just fail.

But then, they were talking about Aunt Ginny's house. She couldn't let her own pride stand in the way until she lost it. Once more, the idea of selling the bar floated through her mind.

She loved the place. Loved the relaxed atmosphere, the people—both the ones who hung out there and the ones who worked there. And she loved the ability to disappear from her other responsibilities for an afternoon and have no more worries than what drink to fix or what order to place. But if selling the bar meant saving Ginny's house, then she would do it.

Only, she'd have to find a buyer soon. With the equity she had in the bar and the savings in her bank account, that should just about cover the payment.

First, however, she had to deal with her mom. Figure out what she was doing there.

Andie noted the faraway look in Cassie's eyes. Something wasn't right with her. The two of them may not be overly close, but she knew her mother well enough to sense that something was off. "Why, Mom?" She spoke quietly, setting the tone as serious.

Cassie lifted delicate brows in reply. "Why what, dear?"

"Why would you offer to help? You've never even visited. Why are you even here now?"

"I've been here before."

"When you were in college, maybe. But not to Aunt Ginny's house." If Andie remembered the stories correctly, her mother and aunt and their older sister, Athena, had spent the summer on the island before Athena had gone off on her flower-child/cross-country psychedelic-fueled trip with her hippie boyfriend. Athena had been twenty-two; Andie's mother, eighteen—and just about to start college; and Ginny, sixteen. Cassie and Ginny had returned to the island the following two years, and then Athena had died from an accidental overdose the next year. Cassie hadn't come back since.

Ginny had met and fallen in love with James during that last summer she and Cassie had been on the island—right after she'd graduated from high school—and they'd married here on the island the following spring. She had not gone to college like Cassie, instead choosing to be a full-time wife. Though she and James never had kids.

Andie pulled her mind back to the present. "Why would you suddenly show up and offer to help when you don't even know what the problem is about?" she asked.

"Because I can," Cassie stated matter-of-factly. "I retired last year from a Fortune five hundred company, where I had climbed to a senior vice-president position. You realize I got a hefty retirement package?"

"I'm sure you did. So why aren't you out spending it by traveling the world with John?" That's what Cassie had lived the last twenty-plus years for.

Cassie blotted her lips with her napkin, the deep red of her lipstick barely transferring to the linen, and looked around for the waiter. She motioned him over to take their dinner order. "We aren't traveling, and I have the money. End of story. I'm not going to beg you to take it, Andromeda. But if you need some, it's yours."

Andie went silent, speaking only to place her order. She then sank back into her thoughts. Something was definitely off. Her mother had never refused to part with her money—though early in Andie's life, she hadn't had a whole lot to hand out—but she sure hadn't doled it out as if she were spring cleaning and looking to unload last year's fashions on the first available taker. Cassie hadn't even paid for Andie's college years, instead encouraging her to work and apply for scholarships. Which she had done.

So, yeah, this conversation was definitely odd. And Andie hadn't missed the fact that her mother hadn't answered the question of *why* she wasn't out traveling with John.

Andie looked across the table and made eye contact with her mother, knowing deep down that something was going on. "What's wrong, mom?"

Was there a medical issue? What else would drag her mother to the island?

Instead of answering, Cassie changed the subject. "I can't believe you told your aunt I never liked you. Of course I like you. I *love* you. You're my daughter."

Oh, so her mother *had* heard that part of the conversation, too. Andie flushed.

"I didn't mean you didn't like me, Mom. Not really."

"Then what?"

"Well," Andie began, glancing out the window behind her mother and focusing on the moss hanging from an old oak tree just beyond the courtyard area. The tree was outside the ring of lights on the patio, but with the faint glow from them, she could make out the moss swinging slightly in the breeze. She loved the live oaks that covered so much of the island, but they seemed so sad to her—heavily laden with moss, all of it drooping toward the ground.

She focused again on her mother, deciding to put everything out on the table. Might as well state all the things she'd felt over the years. Wasn't as if she was going to risk ruining a good relationship by doing so.

"It's not like you ever went out of your way to see me, Mom. From the first day I left for college. Visiting me just never seemed important enough. I figured that was because I didn't meet your expectations." She looked away, unable to continue making eye contact. "Like I wasn't good enough," she whispered.

They both sat silently for a long time, each fiddling with whatever she found in front of herself, doing everything to keep from looking at the other. After several long seconds, her mother spoke in a low, heartbreakingly sad voice. "You were more than I could have ever asked for, Andie. I just wasn't a good mother."

A heaviness lodged in Andie's heart. What did she say to that? Because, no, Cassie hadn't been a good mother. But for the first time, Andie wondered if that was because of her mother's inabilities instead of her own faults. She glanced up from where her hands played with the silverware. "Why?" she asked softly.

Her mother ran a slim finger down the outside of her water glass, making a path through the condensation. "I wasn't born to be a mother."

"Maybe not, but couldn't you have at least tried?"

"John wanted to go places. It was one of the things I promised him when we got married."

"That you would travel a lot?"

Her mother nodded.

"And what? That you two would do it alone? Without me?"

"Genevieve wanted time with you, Andie. She wanted to see you."

Andie hadn't known her aunt before she'd been shipped to Turtle Island that first summer when she was eight. She'd been terrified but had quickly fallen in love with Aunt Ginny. The woman had been more of a mother to her than Cassie ever had, and Andie had cried when she'd had to return home at the end of that first summer. "Then why didn't I know her before you married John?"

"There were...extenuating circumstances. Your aunt and I...had a falling out."

"Yet she knew about me?"

Cassie nodded. "From before you were born."

Andie had a lot of questions in her mind about her aunt and her mother's relationship. Neither had ever claimed a problem, but when she'd been visiting her aunt on the island and had called home to her mother, or vice versa, she was always the one on the phone, relaying messages between the two. The sisters rarely, if ever, had spoken to each other directly.

"When was the last time you were here, Mom?"

This question seemed to catch Cassie off guard. Unconsciously, she slipped a hand to her stomach. "For James's funeral. I was seven months pregnant at the time."

"So you knew Uncle James?"

Cassie nodded. "I met him here one summer, before he and Ginny married," she said. A faraway look crossed her face, as if the memory was a nice one, and Andie wondered if her mother had secretly liked her uncle more than anyone knew.

Had that been the falling out? Ginny had married James, but Cassie had liked him, too?

"I was there for your wedding," her mother blurted out.

"Yes, but would you have been if I'd been marrying someone you didn't feel would up your standing in the world?"

An angry flush stole across her mother's face. "Really, Andie. That's just rude."

"Yet the question stands."

Green eyes narrowed on her before Cassie broke connection and took another quick sip of her drink. "The Kavanaughs have a good name, yes. But of course I would have been there, no matter who it had been. You are my daughter, after all. You were getting married."

"Only I didn't." And she'd seen even less of her mother in the years since.

"His loss." Her words shocked Andie. "He was an idiot for letting you go."

"I've come to realize it was probably the best thing for both of us. We didn't really know each other like we should have back then."

"Then you could have learned. I can't imagine you weren't the best thing that ever happened to him." Bright spots of anger flushed her mother's cheeks, and all Andie could do was pick her jaw up off the table and continue listening to the words pouring from her mother's mouth. "And just look at him now. Back here. Still mooning over you. That boy knows what he lost. You shouldn't give him the time of day."

The tirade floored Andie. She would never have guessed that her mother had any of the thoughts she'd just voiced. Andie had spent the last four years assuming Cassie thought she was the one who'd taken the loss that day.

"You really believe that?" Andie asked.

"Of course I do. I'll also join your aunt with kicking his butt if he hurts you again. He was a jerk to you before. I won't stand for that again."

Oh my God! What had happened to her mother?

"Is he trying to get you back?"

Andie almost spat out the sip of wine she'd just taken. "No, Mom. He's not trying to get me back."

"He sure went after you today like—"

"He went after me like a friend would," she interrupted, not wanting to get into what they'd done after he'd come upstairs to check on her. "We've had a couple talks since he's been here. He's apologized. Explained himself. And we're..." Andie waved her hand in the air. "Friends, I guess. We're friends now."

Except they weren't. He'd said they couldn't be.

"I don't like the way he looks at you," Cassie stated. It wasn't a question, and it didn't require a response. She simply didn't like the way Mark looked at her.

The admission made Andie smile. Who knew her mother could be protective?

She suddenly wondered what the two of them had missed out on over the years. And why they'd never been close. She wanted to understand the gap between them. And she had the idea that she just might want to try to change it.

"What was the deal with us, Mom?" Andie felt the walls she always erected between herself and her mother take a hit. It was twenty-nine years in the making, but wasn't it time to try a real relationship? "I know you never wanted kids, but couldn't you have at least pretended that you cared? Did you blame me for your first husband leaving you? Was that the problem?"

Cassie blanched at Andie's words. Before she could reply, servers arrived with salads. Dishes were placed on the table, freshly ground pepper was offered, and water glasses were topped off. Her mother ordered another martini, and Andie pointed to her mother's drink and nodded. She'd take one, too. It seemed like the night for it.

After the servers retreated, she and her mom spent the next few minutes digging into their salads, and though Andie felt a little ashamed at what she'd said, it was time to get it all out in the open. There had been a distance between the two of them their whole lives, and Andie wanted it gone.

Maybe they could form a decent relationship and maybe they couldn't, but she wanted to try. Her mother wasn't getting any younger. But could she ever accept Andie for who she was without Andie having to constantly work to prove herself?

With the salads eaten, the servers promptly exchanged the empty plates with their entrées, and at last, her mother looked across the table at her. "It was not your fault Parker left me. That was all me."

The bread Andie had just swallowed sat heavy in her stomach. Parker had left because her mother had had an affair with Andie's father. That had always been clear. Good to know her mother didn't have some misplaced blame about that.

"What, then?"

Her mother remained quiet for so long that Andie didn't think she was going to answer, but finally she peered across the white linen tablecloth, and locked her gaze on Andie's. Vulnerability unlike any Andie had ever seen from her mother shone from her eyes.

Gone were the barriers Andie had witnessed her whole life. It was just her mother, looking old and seeming to beg for some sort of forgiveness. "Talk to your aunt. She'll tell you everything."

"What does Aunt Ginny have to do with you and me?"

"I should have let you live with her year-round. She would have been a better mother than I ever was."

That was no answer. In fact, it ticked Andie off. Now her mother wished she hadn't had to put up with her at all?

Andie had had enough.

She tossed her napkin to the table. "Fine, Mother. If that's the way you want it, we'll go on as we've always been. I'll talk to Aunt Ginny. Like I always have. She's always been the one to be there for me, anyway. Not you." She glared at her mother, then sighed in resignation. She muttered, "Never you."

She rose from the table and, with shaking hands, opened her purse for money to pay the bill.

"Don't insult me by offering to pay for dinner, Andie."

Andie shot her mother a snide look. "I don't think insults matter at this point. I stupidly had hoped that you'd shown up because you wanted something from me. From…" Andie's words slowed and softened, and she let out a long breath. "…us," she finished. She dropped back to her seat and leaned across the table to whisper, "I'd hoped you might finally want a relationship with me, Mom. Seems about time we try one."

"I do." Cassie said quickly. Her words were urgent, but she neglected to make direct eye contact.

"Right." Andie wouldn't believe it until she saw proof. "That's why you send me to Aunt Ginny for answers."

"It'll be better coming from her, is all." Her mother reached out and squeezed Andie's hand. "She would have made a great mother. She'll do a better job explaining than I could."

A sudden realization hit Andie on the head. Whatever was going on, did it have something to do with the rift between her mother and her aunt? But that made no sense. Given that her mother hadn't visited in over forty years—other than for Uncle James's funeral—how could *their* issue have anything to do with Andie?

But fine, she would talk to Ginny.

And she would insist someone come clean about what the heck was going on.

She stood again, but her mother's words stopped her cold before she could walk away. "John and I are getting a divorce, Andie. That's why I'm here. I'm sixty-six, alone, and I miss my family."

The room spun with her mother's rushed words. "What?" Andie whispered. "Oh, Mom. I'm so sorry."

Her mother nodded, taking the bill from the server and signing the charge to her room. She then rose beside Andie and began walking with her out of the restaurant.

"I retired last year, and we've been around each other every day since." She took Andie's arm as they walked from the restaurant and headed to the lobby. "I discovered I don't like him."

The way her mother voiced the statement made Andie suddenly burst out laughing. She'd sounded half shocked and half disgusted.

"I'm serious, Andie. I've been married to the man for over twenty years, and I can't stand to be around him."

Andie continued to laugh but worked to rein in her giggles. "That's something I'd have thought you'd have figured out a long time ago, Mom."

"You would have thought, but we both worked such long hours that, actually, we rarely saw each other. Even working at the same company, I didn't see him until whichever one of us got home last each night."

She'd seen him enough early in her career or she never would have caught his eye. Andie had often thought that their relationship was based more on how he could help her mother rise in the company instead of honest love.

Looked like that was potentially turning out to be the case.

"So, what?" Andie asked. "You decided to hide out here?"

They reached the front doors and her mother turned to Andie. "I decided it was time to heal past wounds with my sister," Cassie admitted. She squeezed Andie's hands in hers. "And to work on a relationship with you. I miss you, Andie."

Would wonders never cease? "I didn't think you'd ever missed me, Mom."

Pain triggered by Andie's words quickly flashed across her mother's face. "I deserve that, I suppose. But it's true, nonetheless. I miss you. And I'd like to spend some time getting to know you. I plan to stay here for a while so I can do just that."

A heavy pressure pushed in against Andie's sternum. She wanted that, too. But again, she wouldn't believe it until she saw it. And sending her away to talk to Ginny instead of talking to Andie herself was not a good start.

"I'd like that too, Mother," Andie whispered, and leaned in to give her mother a brief hug.

They said their good-byes, and as she stepped through the outer door to ask a valet to fetch her car, her mother softly called out her name. Andie looked back.

"The ankle bracelet looks good on you."

Andie glanced down to see the gold chain glittering in the light. She'd forgotten to remove the jewelry. She'd never worn it around her mother before, but her arrival had come as such a shock—and then there was the sleeping with Mark thing—that it had never even crossed Andie's mind to take it off.

She wore a proper look of being caught red-handed. "I'm sorry, Mom. I just—"

"You liked it," her mother finished for her. "It always intrigued you. Called to you."

"I can return it."

"No. It's yours." Her mother put her fingers to her lips and blew her a kiss. "It always belonged more with you than with me."

The door closed between them and Andie stood there staring, wondering what in the world the entire night had been about.

She definitely had to talk to Ginny.

CHAPTER FOURTEEN

The forty-three-foot fishing boat slapped through the choppy waters, causing Mark to breathe in deep through his nose for another gulp of fresh air. He wasn't normally prone to seasickness, but after the last couple hours of the constant up and down, he was beginning to worry he wasn't immune, either.

Eyeing the rest of the men in the boat's cabin added no reassurance that he wouldn't succumb. All of them, with the exception of Rob, were some varying shade of green. Rob looked his usual self, and was busy regaling the group with stories from his and Penelope's fishing trip in Canada earlier in the spring. Rob had gone out with a group of locals for some ice fishing.

Mark loosened his fingers around the bar above his head and then closed them more securely, getting a firmer grip on the metal. He stood just outside the cabin, leaning back against the bait well they'd loaded up before daylight as they'd headed out for their all-day excursion.

The charter was owned by the same company that owned the ferries, all a part of Andie's friend Ginger's business. But what had shocked him wasn't seeing Andie board with them that morning but watching Ginger take the captain's seat.

It had to be rough on the green crowd inside to watch the two women at the helm, seemingly suffering no ill effects, and to know that the women were "tougher" than the men.

To Mark it was pretty hot, actually.

As was Andie, in general.

Mark shifted his gaze to watch her where she stood next to Ginger, her back to the front window and facing the crowd of men. She wore pressed capris in a light olive-green color and a simple white button-down shirt. She looked utilitarian yet comfortable. But the way she had her hair tied back in two low ponytails, each twisted off with a long orange ribbon, reminded him that she had that slight edge about her. She was cute yet professional. Fun. Her casual flair made him wonder what kind of underwear she wore beneath.

He'd tried to catch her alone that morning, but she'd avoided him at every turn.

But he had caught her looking more than once.

Each time her gaze found him had been like a lit match touching his skin. A sharp jab with a hot poker, then the shock of a live wire streaking through his veins. Her looks had been a mix of frustration—he assumed over the conversation he would have with Rob that day; along with undercover glances at his body—likely her remembering their activities of the afternoon before.

It wasn't as if he'd be forgetting those activities anytime soon himself.

Or knew what to do about them.

They'd had sex. Unbelievably good sex. She'd told him they shouldn't do it again. She'd turned down his offer to stay on longer and continue. And then he'd realized he was far more of an idiot than he'd ever given himself credit for.

He craved her.

He wore the desperate need to be close to her, to talk to her, and to be inside her. He wanted everything.

And yet she wanted to send him on his way.

This whole trip had backfired in a fashion he couldn't have imagined.

Rob finally seemed to catch on that no one cared to hear his stories, and he fell silent. Irritation began at the base of Mark's spine. He knew he had to tell Rob what was going on right under his nose, but his doing so would put Mark on a plane out of there. And he wasn't yet ready to go.

"Rough trip." Gray slipped from the cabin and settled in beside Mark, looking pale but not necessarily green. "She doesn't get this boat to where we're going soon, I fear the inside of that cabin is about to smell very bad very soon."

Mark chuckled. "That's the truth." He nodded toward Max, the boy he and Andie had played charades with a couple nights ago. "Kid's been holding on to his breakfast, but it can't be for much longer."

Gray's lip curled at the suggestion, then his skin lost more color as the boat hit yet another wave. This one seemed to suspend the front of the vessel in the air for several seconds before it came down, pitching to one side. A groan rose from inside the cabin, and Mark clenched his teeth as he sucked in a long breath. The boat righted itself and kept chugging right along through the water.

"Shopping with the girls is beginning to sound better than this crap," Gray muttered.

Mark would have laughed if he hadn't been focusing so hard on breathing. He even had his eyes closed. "You mean shopping or sniffing around Roni?" The other half of the wedding party was on dry land today. "And does the decision really have anything to do with the stomach-clenching ride of this trip?"

He'd watched Gray head up to Gin's during their volleyball game Thursday afternoon, and was aware his friend had not joined their dinner party that same evening. He'd also bailed on the parasailing yesterday.

At Mark's question, a half smile settled on Gray's face.

"Nothing wrong with shopping is all I'm saying."

Mark glanced back at Andie and caught her watching him. His pulse sped up.

"So you and Roni?" Mark asked. "You talked her into it, then?"

Gray lifted one shoulder. "Wasn't much talking to be done. The girl's fun. She was looking for some fun. I happened to be the lucky bastard to give it to her."

Laugher burst from Mark at the smug look on Gray's face. Gray wasn't a jerk with the ladies. Far from it. But he *was* known for having a good time. Anywhere he went.

"Someday, McTavish. Someone's going to catch you and put a stop to your ways."

"Yeah?" The boat suddenly slowed, and the rocking motions ceased. Mark lost his balance for a second before he righted his footing and stood at last without a death grip on the overhead bar. "Like Andie has caught you?" Gray asked.

The words caught Mark off guard, and he scowled. "She hasn't caught me."

"You haven't quit looking at her all morning."

"She's hot. It's either puke my guts up or focus on something that keeps my attention elsewhere."

"The blonde is cute, too."

Mark lifted an eyebrow. Yeah, Ginger was cute, too. But she wasn't Andie.

"But she's not the one who spent the night in your bed last night, is she?"

Mark jerked his gaze from where it had eased down to Andie's thighs—remembering them squeezed around him—and squared off with Gray. "No one spent the night with me last night, asshole."

"Ah." Gray clapped him on the shoulder. "That must be why the frown today." He chuckled and headed up one side of the boat, tossing a wave back over his shoulder. "Better luck next time."

Annoyance fizzed inside Mark. He'd wanted Andie in his bed last night.

The boat stopped, and the men in the cabin started to move, coming out for fresh air. Poor Max—as well as his father—ran to a railing and leaned over, retching. Mark grimaced at the noises. Looked like quite the bonding experience for father and son.

As Ginger finished up whatever she was doing at the helm, Mark was surprised to see Andie heading through the cabin. This was the first time she hadn't been glued to Ginger's side all morning.

He wanted to ask how it had gone with her mother yesterday. And why she hadn't come to him last night to talk about it.

She could have knocked on his door. He would have helped.

But she hadn't. And he hadn't gone over to her when she'd slipped quietly into her room, either.

She stepped out of the cabin and lifted her face to the sun, her nostrils flaring and her chest rising as she took in deep gulps of air. Her eyes were closed as she stood there, and as he watched, she slid one hand low over her stomach. The movement made him realize that the rolling waves had gotten to her after all. Yet she'd hidden her discomfort well. But then, she was good at keeping things close to the heart when she didn't want to share.

He suddenly wanted to push at her. Poke at her until she cracked. It annoyed the hell out of him the way he was so churned up over what had happened between them, and yet she seemed perfectly neutral.

She'd rocked his world yesterday afternoon!

Had that done nothing for her?

When she turned and went around the side of the boat, heading to the front, he followed. Most everyone else remained at the back, hanging out near the sides in case they needed to go the way of Max and his dad. Ginger had yet to come outside to issue instructions. This left Andie and him more or less alone.

"Andie." He spoke softly when she reached the bow of the boat and was surprised when she jerked around quickly, as if she hadn't known he was there. Her attention seemed to be a million miles away.

"What?" she asked.

He caught a wary look in her eyes.

"Are you okay?" He hadn't followed her to ask that question, but she looked so lost standing there by herself.

"Sure." She nodded. "Just needed some air. And wanted to be away from everyone for a bit."

She glanced back at the crowd, then plopped down on the wide bench seat that backed up to the front windows of the cabin. With a long sigh, she stretched out her legs in front of her, leaned her head back against the window, and closed her eyes. She looked exhausted.

"What's going on?" He lowered himself to the space on the bench beside her, half expecting her to pull away, but she didn't so much as move.

"I'm just tired. I had a long night."

"And that's all?"

She peeked at him from under her lids. "What else do you think it is?"

There were so many things. He lifted his brows to make a point. "Your mother did something to upset you? You're about to toss your cookies like everyone else?" The "toss your cookies" line brought a tiny smile to her lips, which made him lean in slightly. "Us?"

He spoke the last word softly, and her eyes drifted shut instead of giving him an answer.

"I heard you at my door last night, Andie."

~

Andie went immobile at Mark's words.

What was she supposed to say to that? That she'd wanted to knock, had wanted him to hold her, all because her mother was hurting? Because *she* was hurting? Because she wanted a relationship with her mother but wasn't sure she wouldn't mess it up before it even got off the ground?

Or maybe she should just blurt out that she'd wanted to knock on his door and then crawl into his bed.

And not to sleep.

"I wasn't at your door," she lied. She kept her eyes tightly closed, unwilling to look at him. Of course he knew she was lying. He wouldn't have brought it up if he hadn't heard her out there. "Plus, you left out one thing that I might be upset about."

Her tone was mulish, but she didn't care. She was exhausted from tossing and turning all night. And though it was the last thing she wanted to admit, she was sexually frustrated.

She'd spent the morning watching Mark, thinking about yesterday afternoon, and knowing that he'd been thinking about the same. She'd seen it every time he'd looked at her.

Which had been pure torture for her libido.

The two of them weren't even going to be friends. Merely acquaintances. Her girl parts needed to get on board with that!

Mark remained silent for so long that she almost gave in and opened her eyes, but finally his low voice touched her, caressing her almost as if he'd stroked the palm of his hand slowly down over her body. "What else are you upset about, sunshine?"

She curled her fingers into her palms and forced her eyes open, focusing on the horizon and thinking about the glorious colors of the sunrise they'd witnessed earlier that morning. It had felt as if they were driving right into it.

She did not think about how nice it was to have Mark there beside her as if he cared. Or how much she loved the sound of his voice when he spoke so gently to her.

"Rob," she uttered. "You're going to talk to Rob today." Mark was going to upend her life, and she had to be prepared for the upheaval.

"I am," he agreed.

"And I have to stop it."

"You can't stop it, Andie. I'm going to talk to him."

She glanced over at him then. Bluish-green eyes stared solemnly back at her, a day's worth of whiskers making him look rough. It fit with the out-to-sea fisherman look he had going. "Not you," she said. "I'm not going to stop you. I'm going to change Rob's mind after you talk to him."

"Ah." He nodded as if something finally made sense. "So that's why you're here today."

"Instead of shopping with the girls?" She smirked. "Yeah. That's why I'm here today. On zero sleep. Because I've got to do everything I can to save my business."

"Why didn't you get any sleep?"

Her gaze widened for a second. Oh, crap. She hadn't meant to say that.

"Why didn't you knock on my door last night, Andie?" He zoomed in on the crux of the situation.

She gritted her teeth.

He pushed closer into her space, and she could smell the hint of coffee mixed with mint on his breath. "I could practically hear you breathing as you stood there, you know?"

And he was so close, he was practically breathing for her now.

She rolled her lips together, wishing she hadn't come to the front of the boat alone. She'd needed some air. It had taken everything she had not to get sick through the rough twenty-five miles they'd sped across. She'd simply wanted to take a couple of deep breaths and focus before she spent the remainder of the day keeping tabs on Mark, ready to pounce the minute he'd talked with Rob.

"I…" She paused, suddenly feeling pressure behind her eyes. She was going to cry. Fury at her overwhelming emotions half blinded her.

"Ginny said you had dinner with your mother last night," Mark said. He reached for the end of one of her ponytails and flipped it back and forth between his fingers, and Andie was grateful that he'd put a few more inches of space between them. "Was that why you stopped by my door? Did you want to talk about that? Did she upset you?"

Andie shook her head.

"Were you going to ask me again not to talk to Rob?"

She shook her head again.

Then she made the mistake of looking him dead straight in the eyes, and she knew that he knew.

She'd come to his door because she'd wanted him.

She'd wanted to crawl into bed with him, and let him wrap his arms around her.

And it hadn't been purely for the physical benefits either.

CHAPTER FIFTEEN

Kavanaugh!" The shout came from the back of the boat, and both of them turned to find Rob standing there—his feet apart and his hands on his hips—glaring in their direction. At least Andie assumed he was glaring. She couldn't tell from his sunglasses, but the guy hated her, so no doubt the look was lethal.

Ginger stood behind him, eyeing the scene as well. Her look was speculative.

"You plan to fish today?" Rob asked.

Andie blinked, no longer needing to squelch the tears that had been threatening, and ducked her head when Mark turned back to her. She held her breath, hoping he didn't insist on pointing out what she knew he'd just figured out.

"We'll finish this later," Mark said.

He rose from the bench, pulled his sunglasses from where they hung on the front of his lightweight button-down shirt, and headed to the other end of the boat. Ginger passed him about halfway and ended up standing in front of Andie, her stance similar to Rob's.

"You slept with him," she quietly announced.

Andie rolled her eyes at her friend. "Like that's a shocker. You knew it would happen."

"Oh yeah. I knew. When?" They hadn't talked since they'd seen each other at the senior center three days before.

"Yesterday."

Ginger shot her a quick look. "That why you're so tired this morning?"

The sound of her mother's voice explaining that she was getting a divorce pierced Andie's thoughts. "Afraid not. We did it in the middle of afternoon." She paused just long enough to watch the surprise cross her friend's face, then added, "While Aunt Ginny and *my mother* were both downstairs."

"Andie!" Ginger's whispered response was a mix of shock, horror, and concern. She landed on concern. "Your mother is here?"

Andie nodded. "I had dinner with her last night."

"She never comes down."

"I know. Saves it for special occasions apparently."

"And what was so special about this one?"

Andie wanted to go into detail, but she wasn't in the mood for that level of discussion just yet. She would talk to Aunt Ginny first, see what that was all about, and then she'd get her girls together. After the wedding had been canceled and everyone had gone home.

If anyone could help her sort through the mess that was her life, it would be Roni and Ginger.

Andie turned to watch Mark, who stood at the edge of the boat among several men, all of them dropping their lines into the deep water. Ginger had gotten them started, then put her assistant in charge of watching over them. She rarely went out on the deep-sea trips but worked them into her schedule when she could.

However, spending time in the ocean was what she enjoyed the most. Not the actual act of fishing.

Andie shifted her gaze back to her friend, knowing she couldn't leave her hanging. She gave a small, tight smile. "Mom's getting a divorce. I don't want to talk about it today though, okay? Too much else on my mind."

Ginger lowered herself onto the seat beside Andie and reached out a hand to hers. "Oh, sweetie." She squeezed Andie's hand. "Okay, we won't talk about your mom today. Not if you don't want to." She tossed a quick nod in Mark's direction and waggled her brows. "Will you tell me about that, then? With details?"

Andie laughed, appreciating Ginger's attempt to lighten the mood. "Of course."

The last day and a half had been stressful—so, yes, she'd appreciate a little girl talk. Especially if she would be talking about how Mark had pushed her up against the wall.

Her thighs tingled just thinking about it.

"You're blushing, Andie."

She put a hand to her cheek and grinned at the warmth she felt. "Because it was really, really good," she whispered.

Ginger sucked in a little fake gasp. "You're going to do it again, aren't you?"

Andie shrugged, because yes, she'd like to, but then she forced herself to admit the truth. She shook her head and sighed, feeling her shoulders droop. "No, actually, I'm not. He'll be leaving, so-o—"

She stopped as she caught sight of Mark leading Rob over to the far side of the boat. Alone.

She had to hear that conversation.

∼

Thankful the boat wasn't filled to capacity, so there was plenty of room for a private conversation, Mark pulled Rob off to the side, determined to get the shit part of the day over. It was possible—*likely*—that when they'd finished talking, Rob would demand to go back immediately. Which would put everyone dealing with seasickness all morning for no good reason.

Mark should have had the conversation before they'd even pulled away. But Phillip Jordan had seemed to be constantly underfoot back at the dock. And then Mark had seen that Andie was going with them. And he'd selfishly wanted a chance to have some time with her.

But he couldn't put the conversation off any longer. It was tearing both him and Andie up, and they had more important matters to discuss.

Like the fact that she cared for him, too.

He knew she did. He'd read it clearly on her face only moments before.

He just had no idea how to get her to admit it, or do anything about it.

Or if they even needed to do anything about it. They had spectacularly crashed and burned once upon a time. Why should he think they'd be any different this time?

"It's been too long since we've done anything like this, bro," Rob pointed out as they made their way along the side of the boat, their rods pointed toward the blue sky as they went. There were metal holders attached to the railing of the boat every few feet so they could move around, repositioning their rods throughout the day. So far, no one but the two of them had made it to the section where they now stood.

"Too long," Mark agreed, though deep down he felt it probably hadn't been long enough. Which was not a good thing for the best man to be thinking. "What? Three years?"

Three years ago the two of them, along with several other buddies from Harvard, had taken a long weekend trip to the Caribbean. It had been a bachelor party for one of the guys. Rob had partied hard and hooked up with several women that weekend, while Mark had wondered when he'd gone off and grown up without his buddy.

"At least," Rob agreed. "We should make it a yearly thing."

Mark didn't answer. He suspected that after their conversation today, Rob might not want anything to do with him for a while.

Movement from his right caught Mark's attention, and he realized that someone had entered the cabin and was sitting practically behind them, just inside the window.

He began to move farther down the boat, before recognizing the someone was Andie.

She was eavesdropping.

The knowledge should have annoyed him, but given the guilt he felt for what he was about to do, he would let her listen in. She needed to understand that some things simply could not be changed.

Rob put his rod down and kicked back, leaning against the wall of the boat directly in front of where Andie sat. He pulled a pack of cigarettes from his shorts pocket, and held it out to Mark.

"No, thanks." Mark hadn't smoked a cigarette since he and Rob had been teenagers, trying to act cool. "And I can't believe you're still doing that. Those things are nasty."

"Yeah, but Penelope isn't here. She gets all bitchy if I smoke around her, so I take the opportunity when I get one."

Mark set up his pole and dropped his line into the water, wishing he didn't have to be the one doing this. "Phillip doesn't get on your case about it, then?"

He'd watched Rob's future father-in-law today, and the man kept an eye on Rob, that was for sure. Probably making sure his would-be state's attorney prodigy didn't do anything to embarrass the family.

"I do what I want."

"Except when Penelope is watching."

Rob tipped his hand in a touché signal as he blew out a steady stream of smoke. Before he took another drag, he gave Mark a look. "So what's up?"

It had been too many years since the two of them had held a serious conversation. The idea of doing so now suddenly didn't sit well with Mark. But it wasn't as if he could back out. Facts were still facts. Might as well put it out there and get it out of the way.

"Your fiancée and future father-in-law are setting you up."

Rob's posture went momentarily stiff before he puffed once more on the cigarette and then tossed it into the ocean. He straightened from his relaxed position and slowly exhaled, letting the thin stream of white smoke drift out to sea with the butt.

"What are you talking about?"

Mark glanced around to make sure no one—except Andie—was within hearing distance, then explained what he'd overheard.

"So it seems," Mark finished up, "Phillip has plans for you, and Penelope is going along with them."

Another cigarette appeared between Rob's fingers. "And you feel this is bad because?"

It was all Mark could do not to let his mouth hang open. "Because you're a defense attorney and have always wanted to be one."

"Sometimes people change."

"So you're telling me you knew about this?"

"I didn't *know*, but I had my suspicions."

"Then you're okay with it?"

Rob lifted a shoulder and gave the shit-eating grin he'd been using since elementary school. It didn't make Mark any more comfortable now than it had twenty years ago.

"It's one less thing I have to orchestrate," Rob finally replied.

Mark dropped back against the boat, stunned. "One less thing you have to…" He stared at Rob. "Orchestrate?"

"Yeah. Far less work for me."

"What are you talking about?"

Rob took another puff and looked around as Mark had done, stopping when his gaze landed at the front of the boat. Mark turned his head to find Phillip watching them.

"You don't think I'm marrying her for love, do you?" Rob's tone was derisive.

"Actually, I had assumed so, yes."

Rob flicked the second cigarette into the ocean. "I'm not a pansy, Mark. I have plans. I'm acting on them."

"I thought your plans focused on the firm where you are. Where you've made partner."

"And now my plans are on being a state's attorney." Rob focused his flat gray eyes on him. "Next, a US attorney. Hell, maybe someday I'll shoot for Supreme Court justice. I have the world, man. Do you know how far the Jordan name can get me? They aren't only well-respected in Chicago, you know."

Wow. The facts suddenly hit Mark in the face like a bucket of ice water. His best friend—the guy he'd always thought to be his best friend—was a complete jerk. Which suddenly made Mark wonder if they'd ever really been friends at all.

The Kavanaugh name was far bigger than Masterson in Boston. Maybe Rob had only liked him for that.

And Mark's father had pulled some strings to get Rob his Chicago job.

Mark suddenly felt sick, and it had nothing at all to do with the waves. He stepped to the side of the boat, certain he would be the next one to lose his breakfast, and heard Rob laughing beside him.

The sound echoed in his ears as if it were being piped in from a long tunnel, and Mark fought the urge to turn and punch Rob in the face, certain in the knowledge that their friendship had never been more than a means to an end.

It was the elder Kavanaugh and elder Masterson who had been true friends all these years. They were the ones who'd held Mark and Rob together.

"Son of a bitch," Mark muttered, glad when his stomach settled back down. "You're nothing but a complete ass."

Rob scratched the side of his chin and shot Mark a condemning look. "And you need to grow a pair. Quit playing with the help." Rob motioned toward the front of the boat as if Andie was still where Mark had left her. "You shouldn't have ever let Beth get away. She had the name and the prestige."

Mark saw red.

"Just because you can't get over killing your girlfriend all those years ago—"

Mark's fist jerked through the air to land on Rob's jaw before Mark was even aware he was moving. Rob went down hard. His shocked eyes stared up at Mark as other noises began to penetrate. People were hurrying to where they stood—to where Mark stood and Rob lay—with Phillip Jordan leading the pack.

Mark jabbed a finger at Rob. "You keep that out of it," he growled. "That has nothing to do with you being a bottom feeder."

He quickly reeled in his line and grabbed his pole, determined to leave Rob on the ground for someone else to clean up, then turned in the opposite direction.

As if in slow motion, he saw Andie running toward him. Gray and Ginger and several of the others were crowding behind her, pushing and trying to see around her. Then Andie was lifting her hands up in the air as if to shield her face.

The hook from his line swung out, making a perfect arc toward the outer palm of one of her hands. Mark was powerless to stop it, though he did reach out, trying desperately to catch the glittering object before it hooked her.

He missed.

The next thing he knew, Andie stood before him, her mouth agape, with the tip of his hook stuck in the flesh of her hand. Ginger gawked at the hook, and Phillip Jordan harshly shouted something from the other side of Rob.

Mark looked back to where Rob still lay on the ground. The bag of hot air wouldn't say anything else about Mark's past, he was sure of that. To do so would invite Mark to share what he'd just learned.

With a slight nod to Rob, as if to signal that they understood each other, he shoved his rod in Ginger's hand and took Andie by the wrist to lead her away, brushing Ginger off when she offered to take care of Andie.

"I've got it." His tone left no room for argument.

≈

Andie couldn't stop gaping at her hand as Mark dragged her away, assuring Ginger as they went that *he* was taking care of her. The hook wasn't in deep, and it didn't even hurt too much. The worst were the words rolling over and over in Andie's head.

"You can't get over killing your girlfriend."

"You can't get over killing your girlfriend."

What in the world did that mean?

And Rob was using the Jordans just like they were using him? Maybe more so?

Everything was crowding her brain so quickly that she almost missed the tortured look on Mark's face every time he glanced at her hand.

"It's not that bad—"

223

"I put a damn hook in your hand," he snarled. "It's bad."

He pulled her around the corner and into the cabin, then shoved her into the small restroom, following her in and slamming the door behind them. He picked her up and set her on the tiny sink, then took her hand gently in his.

The world was suddenly shut out, and it was just the two of them in the cramped compartment, Mark looking as if he'd just driven a car over her—twice—and Andie realizing what one very important part of all the drama meant.

The wedding was not being called off.

She wasn't going to lose Aunt Ginny's house.

But what did the rest of it mean? She swallowed against the lump in her throat and peered up at Mark. He was carefully poking at the skin around the hook, cringing each time he did.

"Mark," she breathed out his name, fear skating down her spine.

His stony face looked up at her in question.

"What did Rob mean?"

An eyebrow arched high. "That he's an arrogant jerk who's done nothing but use everyone he's come into contact with his whole life?"

He grabbed the first-aid kit from the shelf above the small mirror and set it in Andie's lap as he pawed through it.

"No, about…" She paused at the sight of Mark's jaw growing even more tense. "Something about a girlfriend," she finished softly.

"It was nothing." He shook his head, then mumbled, "I was a teenager. I wasn't even in the car with her."

"So somebody did die?"

He ripped open an alcohol pad and some gauze, and as he did, he made the slightest motion with his head. It was a nod. Andie's chest ached for him. What could have happened? And why had she never known about this? Seems she wasn't the only one who hadn't been good with sharing information in the past.

"You never told me," she whispered.

He stared into her eyes, his face a mask, and she felt a quick tug against her palm. They both glanced down at the hook, now in his hand, and the small bubble of blood coming from her skin. He wiped the spot with the alcohol pad.

"Mark?" She was still whispering, suddenly aware that the space was small and they could easily be heard by someone outside the room.

"What?"

"You never told me," she repeated.

"Nothing to tell."

"We were *engaged*."

Acceptance clouded his gaze when he finally looked back up at her. He knew he'd intentionally kept it from her. Just as she knew.

"Is that why you have issues with getting married?" she asked.

"What are you talking about? I don't have issues."

So many things were suddenly clear. She had no idea what had happened when he was a teen, but whatever it was had impacted his every move since. "You made up reasons to dump me. At the very last second."

"You were using me."

"I was not, and you know it. You knew it then, too. I loved you. I used your name because I was desperate in that

225

moment, but I loved you, and there's no way you didn't believe that with every fiber of your being. You were looking for an excuse to walk away, had been for months. And sending Rob to the church kept you from seeing how your decision would hurt me. It allowed you to not risk changing your mind and going through with it."

He didn't deny it, but he looked almost as shocked as she was to hear it.

"What happened with Beth?" she asked. "Did you do something lame so she would dump you? So you wouldn't have to do to her what you did to me?"

Mark's mouth snapped closed. "You don't know what you're talking about. I didn't even love her like I did—"

He bit off his words, seeming to realize what he'd just said. He hadn't loved Beth like he'd loved her. Her throat threatened to close up.

"I know you're afraid," she whispered. "You're so afraid, you were just trying to break up *someone else's* wedding."

"I was trying to help him," he growled.

"Then planning to run back to Boston as fast as you could so you didn't risk getting involved with me again."

Her hand was now patched up, and she could see Mark growing more irritated by the second. He snapped the first-aid kit closed and shoved it back on the shelf above her, then leaned in so close that his face was directly in front of hers, mere inches separating them. His hot breath bathed her skin. "I'm not the one running from it. I offered to stay."

"For a few days."

"Did you want me to stay longer? Hell, did you want to go back with me?"

The words froze both of them. How had they gotten to arguing over his leaving? Which he wouldn't be doing now since the wedding wasn't canceled. Unless he decided to skip out on the wedding altogether. He *had* just punched Rob in the face.

But what she wanted to know was when she'd begun thinking that Mark was leaving her instead of risking getting involved with her again.

Getting involved with him wasn't what she wanted.

She had a business to run. On the island.

She didn't want to go to Boston.

"Andie," he said, the anger in his voice diminished. "Did you want more?"

She shook her head. "No," she whispered. "We can't be more. We're just..." She brought one hand up but had nowhere to put it. She rested it on his chest, lowering her gaze to watch as she touched him. He was so big and strong. "It was just the one time."

"Except now I'm not leaving yet."

Her gaze slowly lifted to his. He wasn't leaving. Her throat went dry. "What does that—"

A knock sounded on the door, startling both of them, and Mark pulled slightly away.

"What?" he asked, his voice falsely calm.

"I just wanted to check on Andie." It was Ginger. Her voice came out both hesitantly questioning and determined to make sure her friend was okay.

Mark reached behind him and flipped the lock, the *click* clear from both sides of the door. "Andie is fine. Give us a minute."

Uh-oh.

Andie swallowed, trying to bring saliva back into her mouth. The look on Mark's face was no longer anger.

Heat focused on her. "I'm not leaving yet," he repeated, his intent clear.

"We can't, Mark." She shook her head as she whispered the words but couldn't help the grin that suddenly covered her face. She wiggled slightly on the edge of the sink, her skin bursting with expectation. He wasn't leaving today. They had at least until the wedding.

He gripped the backs of her knees and tugged her a slow inch closer. "We could..." he suggested.

She bit her lip and looked around the compact space, her entire body blazing at the idea of the two of them being in there together. *Not* seeing to her injured hand.

"We *shouldn't,*" she stressed. "Anybody could hear us— Rob, Mr. Jordan, Ginger."

Her voice had grown quieter the more she talked. Was she really thinking about *doing it* on the boat with everyone there?

Mark didn't seem to see it as a question. His mouth quirked up on one side, then he put his lips to her ear and whispered, "Then we'll have to be very, very quiet."

EPISODE SEVEN

CHAPTER SIXTEEN

Andie gasped at the tickle of Mark's mouth moving against her ear. The heat of his body engulfed hers, making her suddenly certain she was wearing too many clothes in a too tiny room.

She shoved against his chest, thinking she really should discourage what was about to happen, but when he pulled back, his gaze hot and intoxicating, her insides melted and she admitted that she didn't care where they were. She wanted him. And she wanted *this*.

Wrapping her hands around the back of his head, she pulled his mouth down to hers. Heat blasted between her legs as his tongue pushed past her lips.

An almost imperceptible groan sounded deep in Mark's throat, and she scooted closer, spreading her legs around his hips. With just a little tilt backward, she could...she sucked in a deep breath and shifted, angling her hips forward until his thick ridge pressed hard against her...and then she smiled against his mouth. Her "special place" was now perfectly aligned with his "*very* special place."

"I'm going to make you come, Andie." Mark's soft whisper turned her nipples to beads.

"We'll get caught."

"Not if you don't make too much noise."

He was going to give her an orgasm, and she was supposed to not make noise?

Sure. And why not just toss her into the ocean and expect her to swim the twenty-five miles back to land?

"I'm not sure I can—" She caught her breath when he slipped one hand expertly down the front of her capris, his long fingers gliding beneath the top edge of her panties.

"Shhhh," he whispered against her lips. "You can," he encouraged her.

His finger touched her where she was most sensitive, and her hips gave a reflexive jerk, lifting slightly up off the counter. Then his finger slid down through her folds and slipped inside her, and she groaned into his mouth. Chances were good she might just come on the spot.

She pushed against the counter surrounding the sink for more leverage as she pressed herself against his probing hand. Simultaneously, she arched her head back, exposing her neck to him. His lips touched a strained tendon running along the side of her neck, and her breasts ached, begging for attention.

"Mark." She barely heard the word herself, but he whispered in return, "What?"

"There are people out there. They'll be wondering what's going on in here."

He pulled his hand out of her pants and quickly parted the fabric, the zipper sounding overloud in the cramped space. "Then we should go fast," he said.

He was insane. *This* was insane. Everyone was going to know what was going on in there.

But she wasn't sure she cared.

She was so turned on that it would likely only take Mark pushing into her and she'd plunge over the edge. Wanting just that, she reached for the front of his pants, but he caught her hands in his.

"What?" Her breaths came out in shorts pants. She looked up at him. "Are we stopping?"

A devilish gleam shone back at her as he shook his head from side to side. "Definitely *not* stopping, but I had something else in mind."

He gripped the back of her capris and tugged downward. "Lift your hips," he instructed.

She did as she was told.

Two seconds later her naked rear was seated on the stainless steel of the sink, and her pants and purple lace underwear were on the floor at Mark's feet.

And then he dropped to his knees.

Oh.

She let out a rush of air at the thought of what he was about to do.

Before she could figure out if she should protest, he had his head between her legs—and all she could think about was the fact that he was about to touch her there. With his tongue. And it had been four freaking long years since anyone had touched her there with anything!

There was no way in the world she was going to put a stop to that.

He nipped a thigh, teasing her, his mouth hot, his stubble scratching against her skin, and she forgot to hold in the whimper.

"Shhhh," he reminded her. He gripped both thighs and pushed them farther apart, and her clit twitched.

Her nipples hardened to the point of being painful.

She dropped her head to the small mirror behind her.

And he nipped her other thigh.

"Please, Mark," she begged. Her body was shaking in his hands. She wanted him to touch her. *Now.*

And then his tongue stroked slowly over her and she came up off the counter.

"Ooohhh…" She breathed out the sound as stars burst behind her eyes.

Her thighs were tense, and her arms stiff where they now gripped the sides of the sink. Her upper body was at a diagonal as she pushed herself against Mark's mouth.

"You taste good," he murmured.

She whimpered at the words. He was killing her, sending shock waves through her body and flutters low in her gut.

And it was going to be over way too fast.

He stroked his tongue over her again, and she once again thrust herself closer. She groaned and bent her knees, wrapping her legs around his shoulders.

His low chuckle echoed against her parts.

"Oh God, Mark." She couldn't help the words. She bit down on her lip to keep from making another noise, but some things couldn't be helped. She wanted this. She *loved* this.

A thump sounded on the door and she froze in shock, her eyes going wide. They needed to stop.

Laughter followed the noise. Then someone said Mark's name.

Oh God, they *had* to stop! They were doing *things* right in the middle of everyone. AND THEY ALL KNEW WHAT WAS GOING ON!

Andie tried to pull back, away from Mark's seeking mouth, but his hands slid under her rear and crushed her to him. And then his mouth went on a wild journey.

And her entire body went hot.

"Crap," she whispered. She was not going to be able to do this without noise.

He nipped gently on her clit, and she almost bit through her bottom lip.

He sucked. She gasped.

He pulled, he nudged, he ground his mouth into her.

And she began to tremble.

She was going to come, right there on the boat, with fifteen other men—and her best friend—knowing exactly what was going on inside that room.

One last time, she had the thought that they should stop. She couldn't just walk out there with orgasm written all over her.

But then Mark lifted his head, and she let out an uncontrolled moan at the sudden loss. Her hips lifted up off the sink as if seeking his mouth.

She caught his eyes, burning as he looked at her, and it occurred to her that everyone was going to think naughty things had been done even if she stopped him right that very moment. The damage was done. She was free to continue.

"Get ready, babe," Mark warned. His gaze dipped, taking in her body spread wide before him. "I'm about to make you lose your mind."

And then he did.

He returned to her, plucking and pulling and sucking at her sensitive, swollen flesh. Spreading her wider with his thumbs, being relentless in his mission. And she could do nothing but hold on for the ride—and silently plead for him to never, ever stop.

She whimpered again, desperate to put her hands to her mouth to muffle the noise. But if she removed her grip from the sink, the action might change the angle between her hips and his mouth. And she wanted *nothing* to change about what was going on down there.

With one last motion, Mark closed his mouth around her, holding her tight against him, and then every square inch of her clenched from the inside out.

There was no going back. She only hoped she could hold in the scream.

The orgasm hit her like the boat had hit the waves earlier that morning—slamming into her and tilting her on her side. She crested, held suspended for a brief second, and then everything was out of her hands. She was crashing, rolling over and over, free-falling through the air. She was finding nirvana through the touch of Mark's mouth.

Arching up farther, she groaned and her thighs clamped around Mark's head, holding him tight to her. She bit down on her lip every time she made a noise, but even that wasn't enough to stop her.

She simply had no control.

So she let the feelings inflame her. Screw whoever was listening from the other side. She needed this.

And she needed Mark.

When her body was spent, she sagged against the mirror and gazed down to watch Mark. He lifted his head, a satisfied smile on his face, and she felt raw fear.

Was this only physical?

She wanted to say "yes"—to scream *"yes!"*—but deep inside she feared it wasn't.

She was falling for him again. And it had nothing at all to do with a perfect orgasm in the middle of the Atlantic.

Her chest tightened at the thought of opening her heart, only to lose him again. It had hurt four years ago, but Aunt Ginny had been right—she hadn't been ready to get married. They'd moved too fast, missed too many important steps in their relationship.

That's why she'd failed to feel the full bridal excitement she saw in the women she worked with each day. She and Mark hadn't been ready. They hadn't known nearly enough about each other.

But things were different now.

She wasn't blinded by love. But then, she feared she wouldn't be able to keep it at bay, either. Especially if they ended up spending the next week together.

"I think I'm going to take full credit for that." Mark finally spoke as he rose to his feet. His mouth and the area around it wore her sheen like a prize.

And he was right. He got full credit for that.

"I suppose now you'll want the favor returned?" She hoped the teasing would keep things light. Because she didn't need him to know that he had the power to break her.

He chuckled softly as he retrieved her panties and capris, then tugged them up her legs. "I wouldn't say no to that idea."

She lifted her hips so he could slide the material over them, then jumped from the counter to tuck in and zip up in an attempt to make herself presentable. As she began inching to the other side of him so he could wash his face, she caught a glimpse of herself in the mirror. She noticed a dribble of blood on her lip and leaned in to stare more closely at her reflection.

"I'm bleeding," she gasped. "How did I cut my lip?"

Warm eyes met hers in the glass and caressed over her face. Then they landed on her mouth. "You were trying hard not to be noisy, babe."

Embarrassment heated her cheeks as she remembered biting down on her lip in an attempt to keep the sounds in. "Did I succeed, at least?"

The slow smile he gave her was the sexiest thing she'd ever seen. "Didn't even come close."

"Oh fuck," she murmured. Mark simply laughed.

They switched places, and he splashed water on his face, catching her eye as he did. "Think I could take a rain check?" he asked.

"For?"

Oh. Her returning the favor. She blushed more deeply. He chuckled again.

"Not that I wouldn't love it now, but I suspect we should get back out there."

"I suspect you're right," she agreed wryly. It was going to be embarrassing enough to go out now, but if they stayed in there long enough to—

She lowered her gaze to his crotch, where she could see the firm outline where he was still hard, and thought about taking him in her mouth. The idea was almost enough to have her saying forget about everyone else. But he was right. Plus, how much more guilty would she feel standing in the midst of everyone, knowing she'd had him in her mouth?

"Quit looking at me like that or I'll change my mind about that rain check." The deep growl of his words set her on fire again, making her want to drop to her knees and see if *he* could keep quiet while she sent him over the edge.

"Oh, geez," she murmured. She peered back up at him. "I shouldn't even ask, especially since I suspect you're trying to get into Wendy's panties, too, but will you come to my room tonight?"

If they were going to do this, she didn't want to miss a moment. She also wanted to make sure he didn't spend any of those moments with Wendy. Andie wanted him. And she wanted an exclusive.

Mark finished washing his face, then leaned down to press a soft kiss to her cheek. The mood in the room suddenly went from sexy and hot to deep and intense. "I'll come to your room every night if you'll let me, sunshine. And I haven't done a thing more than put my arm around Wendy. In a platonic fashion."

When Andie started to suggest he was stretching the truth, he gripped her chin and lifted her face to his. "*Nothing.* Nor have I wanted to. She's a flirt. She was flirting with Rob that night at the bar. I was trying to keep Penelope from kicking a bridesmaid out of the wedding at the last minute. That's all."

What kind of bridesmaid flirted with the groom?

One like Wendy, apparently.

Andie believed Mark when he said he wasn't after Wendy. He watched out for his friends. He would have tried to keep the peace that night.

She reached up and stroked the stubble on his cheeks, appreciating the rawness of the man along with the protectiveness that he couldn't put on the back burner.

"I've got to spend some time with Ginny tonight," Andie said. She wanted to have that conversation her mother had suggested. And possibly she should hunt up her mother and spend some time with her, too. "Come over after everyone is settled. I'll be waiting for you."

Mark put his mouth to hers and left her breathless in under ten seconds. And left her wanting more.

A lot more.

"You couldn't keep me away," Mark promised.

CHAPTER SEVENTEEN

The sound of seagulls filled a hole in Andie she hadn't even known was there, comforting her and making her wish the rest of the world would disappear for a while. What a day.

It was Saturday evening and she was exhausted after the fishing trip, both emotionally and physically. It had been bad enough worrying about the wedding being canceled over the past few days, but then there was her and Mark. In the bathroom. On the boat.

And tonight he would be in her bedroom.

Was she crazy? She was pretty sure she was barreling toward caring for him again. Actually, she'd pretty much accepted that she'd passed that corner a while back. Which did not bode well for a happy ending.

Definitely not if he was still hung up on whatever had happened in his past.

He'd killed—caused to be killed?—an old girlfriend? What the hell?

She'd been unable to find out more details from him, or to get Mark to talk about what she'd accused him of— that he had issues about getting married—throughout the remainder of the fishing trip. But that didn't mean she wouldn't seek answers later.

Then there was the question of what next. Was there a next? She had accused him of *leaving* her rather than risk getting involved with her again.

Sheesh! That had come out of nowhere.

But it posed a crucial question: Did she want more than just something physical with him?

She honestly had no idea.

And she really didn't want to think about it right now. The subject tended to bring on a headache.

Andie stepped quietly from the dark kitchen onto the wraparound deck, and inhaled the night air and the breeze from the ocean. No matter what went on in the rest of her life, this was her home. She was so glad she'd ended up here.

She pushed the many unanswered questions from her mind as she found Ginny curled up on the wicker love seat out back. She was engrossed in a hardback romance novel with a small reading light attached, a peaceful aura surrounding her as she sat there in the breeze. The material of Ginny's long blue-and-green gypsy skirt lay twisted around her legs, and her red curls danced lightly at her shoulders with each whisper of the wind. Andie took a moment to look from her aunt's attire down to her own.

She'd changed when she'd gotten back to the house. After a quick shower, she'd pulled out a spaghetti-strap maxi dress with a skirt that flowed free. The cream-and-light-blue material billowed in the wind, just as she knew Ginny's would when she stood. Andie couldn't help but smile. One look at the two of them side by side, and anyone could tell that they were related.

They both even had a handful of bracelets on their left wrists. Andie's climbed higher up her arm, almost snakelike in the way they wrapped around her forearm. And she had on a couple of large rings. It was all costume jewelry, but she loved the oversized pieces.

She also wore the ankle bracelet that had been her mother's. It was clear from the conversation she'd had with her mother the night before that there was a story behind the jewelry, but she didn't know how to go about getting it out of her.

If Cassie was going to stick around for a while as she'd implied, though, Andie hoped the opportunity would arise. There were many things about her mother she'd like to know and understand. With any luck, the missing pieces would start falling into place with her aunt tonight.

"Want to go for a walk?" Andie asked, catching her aunt's attention.

Ginny looked up from the page she was reading and studied Andie for a long moment, her gaze flickering over her niece just as Andie's had flashed over her aunt only seconds before, then she flipped off the light and put her book down on the cushioned seat. Aunt Ginny nodded solemnly, as if she knew what they needed to talk about. Andie only wished *she* knew what they needed to talk about.

Something was up between Ginny and Cassie, and whatever it was somehow tied in with Andie. And she wanted answers. She would be demanding them tonight.

"I would love to go for a walk with you." Ginny stood. She patted Andie on the cheek as she crossed to her on the porch. "A good long one."

Perfect. Because they needed a good long talk. And Andie needed to figure out some things. Specifically, some of the thoughts that had run through her head throughout the afternoon on the boat.

She and Mark had emerged from the restroom, doing their best to look as if they'd only been in there bandaging up her hand, but she knew they had fooled no one. Ginger had given her a raised eyebrow. Most of the men had sent Mark nods or nudged him as if he'd triumphed over some secret guy ritual. And Phillip Jordan had scowled at her as if she wasn't worth being the dirt on the bottom of his shoe.

There was no doubt in her mind that Phillip knew what she and Mark had done. Well, the basics, anyway. Probably all of them had thought they'd had sex in the small room the "normal" way. Intercourse. Except they must have believed Mark was quiet in the act, since she'd been the only one making any noise.

But for the rest of the afternoon, she'd held her head high, pretending not to know what they were thinking about her. She and Mark had had a good time. Outrageously so. And she wasn't going to apologize for it.

Nor was she going to apologize because she wanted to do it again.

Which had led to her no longer wanting to apologize for a slew of other things.

Not being any good at the job in Boston.

Not *wanting* the job in Boston.

Not wanting a career like her mother's.

She absolutely was not going to apologize for that. She'd tried for years to please Cassie Winters, and that had gotten her nowhere. Now she would please herself.

And that thought had led her to evaluate her current job.

She was proud of the company she and Aunt Ginny had built. She couldn't be more so. And she was equally proud of the bar, her employees, and the atmosphere at both Seaglass and Gin's. She'd done all that. It had been her idea, her vision. She and Aunt Ginny worked well together.

But if she were being 100 percent truthful, the business didn't make her happy. She enjoyed giving people the weddings they'd dreamed of, yes. But all the details involved— and then dealing with everyone. Not everyone was a happy person. And even those who were happy to be getting married—or to be a part of a wedding—were sometimes just miserable to be around.

She could do without the frustration.

Though she wasn't sure she knew what *would* make her happy, either.

She loved working at the bar, loved volunteering at the senior center, and she even liked the nights she held babysitter detail for the company. So what did that make her? It felt like it made her a slacker.

But she would let no one call her that, so she wouldn't do it to herself.

She just had to figure out what in the world she wanted— and then how to get it.

First, though, she would make sure Seaglass was stable, and then she just might talk to Kayla about taking on an even bigger role. Kayla did the majority of the work already. Why not promote her and hire her some additional help?

And then what? Andie could mix drinks and talk to customers all day?

She sighed. The possibilities had sounded better in her mind when she'd been floating in the middle of the ocean earlier today.

She and Ginny headed down the raised walkway to the beach. She was glad the night wasn't too dark and they could see without need of the flashlight tucked in her pocket. Ginny linked an arm through hers, and Andie smiled over at her aunt.

"Your mother and I spent some time together today," Aunt Ginny said. The news wasn't surprising, since her mother was supposedly there on the island to spend time with both of them.

"And how did that go? Ready to run her back to Kentucky?" Andie quipped.

Ginny's laughter surprised Andie. It was light and… happy.

Andie peered at her. She had gotten the feeling that whatever was between her mother and her aunt, it was *not* light and happy. But maybe she'd been completely off base, and there wasn't a big, bad secret between them.

But then again, what was going on that her mother wouldn't talk about?

"She wants to stick around here for a while," Aunt Ginny continued, which Andie already knew. But Ginny's next words surprised her. "I invited her to stay at the house."

Andie gaped. "Where? The house is full."

"She can stay in my room."

Those words really did come as a shock. Ginny was a welcoming, open woman, but she also valued her privacy. This had been clear to Andie her whole life. "You're sure you're okay with that?" she asked. "You're not used to sharing your space."

"It'll be fine. And when the house isn't full, she can stay in another room."

Except that the house was full most of the time. "As long as you don't put her in with me," Andie muttered.

Ginny patted Andie's arm but didn't reply.

"When?" Andie let a few seconds go by before asking the question.

"Tomorrow."

Hmmm. So her mother would move in with them the next day. But since Andie wanted to work on a relationship with her anyway, that was a good thing, right?

One could always hope.

"Did she say much about the divorce?" Andie asked. Whether her mother liked John or not, after twenty years of marriage, it had to be rough to walk out on him.

"Not too much. She's sad, but I think also looking ahead to what's to come."

Which made Andie wonder exactly what was to come. The idea that they could all overcome the past and be one big happy family didn't seem possible, but that didn't mean Andie didn't wish it could happen. Cassie *had* said she missed Andie. And that she wanted to heal the wounds between herself and Aunt Ginny. So maybe she was willing to make a change.

Only time would tell.

Ginny and Andie walked to the end of the boardwalk, both stopping to remove their sandals, then continued arm in arm down the stairs and across the sand to the lapping water. Yet another way in which she was like Ginny. They both loved the ocean.

Her mother—as far as Andie knew—had no such affinity.

When they reached the water, they turned loose of each other and lifted the hems of their dresses so they wouldn't get wet. Then they turned north and headed up the beach, splashing their feet through the edge of the water. It was a ritual they'd shared many times together.

"What happened with Rob today?" Ginny asked a few steps into the walk. "Did Mark talk to him?"

Meaning, did Seaglass have a wedding to finish? Surprisingly, yes.

"He did, but it didn't go the way either of us expected," Andie replied, still reeling from what she'd heard. "He apparently *wants* to change careers. That was what we overheard the other night. Phillip is planning to get Rob into the state's attorney's office."

"And he's a defense attorney now, right?"

"Exactly. A partner in a major firm. One he worked hard to get into. But apparently he was already intending to finagle his way into state's attorney by using the Jordan name. Seems Phillip and Penelope will be doing him a favor."

Which was sad, given that Andie had also overheard him declaring that he wasn't marrying Penelope for love. What was wrong with the man? Penelope was a terrific woman. She certainly deserved better than Rob.

Andie glanced at her aunt, wondering if she should reveal that last tidbit. Would Aunt Ginny suggest she share her newfound knowledge with the bride-to-be?

If she did, the wedding might once again be on the chopping block.

But if she didn't…was she taking an active role in sending Penelope into a life of loneliness and deceit?

Aunt Ginny finally spoke again. "People do unexpected things." Her tone had drifted to a faraway place, so Andie gave herself permission not to bring up Rob's lack of love to Ginny.

However, she would need to think about it more later. Possibly, Penelope wouldn't care. Maybe she even knew. Not all marriages came together out of love. But Andie had watched Penelope over the past week, and that girl was thrilled to be marrying Rob. She had stars in her eyes, she was so head over heels for him.

Dammit, it wasn't fair that she had this knowledge.

Especially when her business was riding on the outcome.

Andie pulled the small flashlight from her pocket as they rounded an area that was darker. She preferred not using it for fear or disturbing sea turtles, but the section of beach where they were walking was not a prime nesting spot.

When she flipped on the light, she saw ghost crabs scurrying away from them. Their little white legs moved so fast, it looked like their bodies were perched on wheels.

Ginny continued to walk silently beside Andie, seemingly lost in thought, and Andie found herself reluctant to bring up whatever lay between the two sisters. Maybe they could just walk for a while longer first, enjoy the peace and the gentle sound of the waves. Relaxing in this fashion was one of Andie's favorite ways to end the day.

"So you and Mark got busy, huh?"

Andie came to an abrupt halt, nearly tripping and falling face-first into the water. Clearly, she should *not* have felt bad about bringing up her aunt and mother's issues if she and Aunt Ginny were now going to talk about *this*.

"I'm not sure I know what you mean," Andie replied. Ignorance. Always a good strategy.

Ginny grabbed Andie's hand, the one that held the flashlight, and turned it so the light shone directly on Andie's face. She squinted into the glare.

"You think I don't know what went on in your bedroom yesterday afternoon?" Ginny asked. "Neither of you is walking around as tight as a guitar string needing plucking today. I know exactly what took the pressure off, child. I'm just wondering if it was good."

Unable to hide her reaction, Andie gave her aunt a horrified look. She jerked her hand free and turned off the flashlight, pitching them into instant darkness. "Why do you insist on talking about stuff like that?"

What was wrong with discussing the weather? Maybe gossiping about some of the locals. But not chatting up her sex life!

"It's a natural part of life. Why wouldn't we talk about it?"

"Because some things should be kept private."

"Only, your room is right above mine. I hear things."

Andie's stomach rolled, and the sandwich she'd grabbed for dinner almost insisted on a reappearance. Visions of her and Mark slamming against the wall, a lamp crashing to the floor, heated Andie's face. And who knew what kind of noises they'd made during their...*escapade*. It wasn't as if keeping quiet was what they'd been thinking about.

Andie turned back the way they'd come, suddenly ready to return to the house.

She maintained the silence for only a moment before admitting to herself that she actually wanted to talk about Mark. Maybe Ginny would have some answers.

But she did *not* want to talk about what had happened in her bedroom.

Or on the boat.

Another flush spread over her face as she thought about what Ginny would say if she'd been on the fishing trip with them. Heck, she probably would have asked for a full account of the bathroom activities before they'd made it back to shore.

With her anger abating, Andie slowed her steps and reached out to take Ginny's arm in hers, pulling her close. They both still had their skirts lifted above the splashing water, and Andie now rested her head against Ginny's shoulder. Her aunt had helped her out with a lot over the years. No reason they couldn't discuss the situation now.

"I'm scared, Aunt Ginny," Andie admitted softly. "I worry I'm falling for him again."

And she worried she would end up in the same place she had last time. Brokenhearted.

"That's to be expected, child. He was your love."

"Was." She lifted her head and looked at Ginny. "Right? He *was* my love. So why do I have to let that play into it this time? I'm trying to just have a casual fling and move on. I'm settled. I'm happy." Except she knew she wasn't really. "I thought casual would be fun."

Ginny patted her cheek. "I'm not sure you're made of casual, sweetheart."

Pain settled behind the wall of Andie's chest, and she wanted to turn into her aunt's arms and cry. She wasn't sure about casual, either. But she also wasn't sure Mark could do anything else—even if she wanted him to. What she'd heard on the boat had explained so much. He had hang-ups with commitment.

Not that she had any idea if she even wanted a commitment.

But it did explain why it had seemed he'd been pushing her away in the past as much as she was now certain she herself had been pushing. Maybe he wanted marriage and a family, but she wasn't convinced he was ever going to take them on.

She just wished she understood why. What had happened to him?

"I accused Mark yesterday of wanting to leave me to go back to Boston rather than risk getting involved with me again," she admitted in the darkness. They were well away from the houses and cabins, so the only light was from the moon and what reflected off the water. "I hadn't even realized I'd had that thought, yet there it was, just blurted out like that."

"And what was his answer?"

The simple question had Andie turning loose of her aunt to stare at her face-to-face. His answer had shocked her as much as her making the statement had. "He asked if I wanted more."

Aunt Ginny's slim eyebrows lifted. "Do you?"

Andie paused, thinking about the question. Then she slowly shook her head. She did not want to be hurt again. Not that way. She'd rather give up wishing for more and live the life her aunt had instead of allowing herself to be vulnerable to Mark again. Or any man.

"I don't think I do," Andie finally answered. "It hurts too much when it falls apart."

Ginny's face wrinkled as if she were in pain, and she slowly nodded. She glanced away from Andie's gaze to stare off into the dark waters. Lines etched her mouth as it pulled down in a frown, and she suddenly appeared to have aged, just as Andie's mother had the night before.

"It does hurt when it falls apart," Ginny whispered, almost as if to no one. "Even when it's family instead of a man."

Andie held her breath. Aunt Ginny had to be talking about her and Cassie.

A beat later Ginny grabbed Andie's arm, and they once again headed slowly back toward the house.

"Your mother and I were once the best of friends, Andie." Ginny squeezed her arm. "The best."

It was hard to imagine the two totally different sisters being in the same room together, much less being best friends. "I find that a bit hard to believe."

Ginny laughed, but the sound was small. "I can understand that, child. Your mother is a different person than she was fifty years ago."

"How?"

"Well…" Ginny thought about the question for a minute and then grinned wide. "She and I once went skinny-dipping, right here on Turtle Island."

Andie turned loose of both her aunt and the skirt of her dress. It dipped into the water. "No you did not." She shook her head. "No way. My mother is all about being serious. She's worked sixty hours a week my whole life. No way did she take off her clothes and jump in the water with you."

Andie wasn't even sure that was something *she* would do.

Ginny merely nodded, her natural smile coming back. "We did. When she was nineteen. And yes, your mother has always been serious in the way of wanting to make something of herself, but she used to be a whole lot more like me than you realize."

They were walking again, Andie's wet skirt plastered to her legs, and she couldn't help but think of her and Mark in the water the night he'd arrived. She could see herself skinny-dipping with him. But her mother and her aunt?

It was too much.

They could now make out lights in the distance, and the two women slowed even more—an unspoken agreement between them not to get back too soon. They still had things to discuss.

"What happened, Aunt Ginny?" Andie asked. "What turned my mother into the woman she is today?"

"It was my fault," Ginny admitted, and the sadness in her voice broke Andie's heart.

She wanted to demand answers, ask how that could possibly be, but she sensed that Ginny needed to tell the story in her own time. So Andie remained silent, squeezing her aunt's arm lightly for encouragement.

Once again she thought of Mark. He was good at giving her the same kind of gentle encouragement.

"The first time we came to the island, your mother was about to branch out on her own. She'd just graduated from high school and was looking forward to college. Athena was older and had a boyfriend she didn't want to leave, but we talked her into coming with us. That's the only way our parents would let us all come down here together. And we had the best time. We all agreed to come back the next summer, only when it rolled around, Athena didn't show up. It was just me and your mother."

Aunt Ginny paused before continuing. "And James. We met James here that second summer."

"Your husband," Andie stated.

"Yes. But I was only seventeen then, and he was more interested in your mother than me. He was several years older than me, so I was simply the little sister of Cassiopeia." She smiled. "He loved our names. Always called both of us by our full names."

So she'd been right, Andie thought. There had been something between her mother and James. "She told me last night that she'd met him before you two got married, but she didn't say it had been anything more."

Ginny nodded. "It was. She fell in love with him that summer."

A wave slammed into Andie's legs, and she looked down. They'd drifted farther into the water, and Aunt Ginny's skirt was getting wet, too. Andie angled them back toward dry sand but squeezed her eyes shut at Ginny's next words.

"Of course, I fell in love with him that summer, too."

"Oh, Aunt Ginny," Andie whispered. She wrapped one arm around her aunt. "I'm sorry. That couldn't have been easy."

Ginny shook her head. "No, it wasn't. Nor was the next summer when we came back and once again met up with him. He spent all his time with us. With your mother. It hurt me to watch them together, yet that's what I did all summer long. And then she went back to college, and I moved here and got a job. I'd just graduated high school. Pop had passed during that year, and Mama had to focus on taking care of her mother. So I packed my bags and headed here for a job." She paused again, then admitted, "And for James."

The pieces started clicking into place. Her aunt had stolen James from her sister.

"Mom really loved him?" Andie asked.

Ginny nodded, looking so ashamed. "She did. But I wanted him. I wasn't the type to want college, and I couldn't see anything else ahead of me in life. Other than James. I knew if I could win him, I would have everything I ever wanted. A husband, kids." Her voice broke and she lifted a hand to wipe tears from her eyes. "I told him that your mother had moved on. Said she'd never really cared for him."

Ouch. It wasn't merely that he'd chosen her Ginny over her mother; Ginny really had stolen him.

"I take it Mom had done no such thing?"

"She was planning to look for a job in Jacksonville when she got out of college. It's a long drive, but within driving distance of here. She wanted to marry him."

"But you married him first." Andie didn't have to ask; she knew. Ginny had married James the spring that her mother had been a junior in college.

"She didn't come for the wedding, of course. Only Mama. Athena had passed away from an overdose a couple months before, and Grandmother wasn't healthy enough to make the drive."

They'd originally been from a small town in northeast Georgia. Andie's grandmother hadn't passed away until Andie was seven, and she and Cassie had never visited her. She seemed to remember Cassie going to the funeral, though. Alone.

"Mama couldn't forgive Cassie for not coming down for the wedding, especially after losing Athena earlier in the year. She didn't know what had transpired between us."

That made sense. So Cassie had lost the love of her life, her sister, and her mother all at the same time. Not to mention her other sister dying that same year and her father the year before. No wonder she was so hard.

They were nearing the back of Aunt Ginny's house now, so they both trudged through the sand and sat down on the wooden steps of the walkway. With their backs to the house, they stared out at the water.

Neither of them touched the other, and Andie didn't know whether to reach out and take Aunt Ginny's hand or not. It almost seemed like she was purposely drawing in on herself.

Maybe she was too embarrassed to let Andie comfort her at the moment.

"We bought those ankle bracelets that last year she was here," Ginny whispered.

Andie jerked her head around. "What?"

"The anklet you wear all the time." Ginny motioned toward Andie's ankle. "We bought them the summer I graduated high school. Hers was the moon, mine was a star. Together forever. That's what they stood for. We were so close back then."

And then Ginny had stolen her mother's man, and her mother had never worn the jewelry again.

A knot formed in Andie's throat. She felt like she should be mad on her mother's behalf, but seeing Ginny's overwhelming sadness kept her in check. Plus, it wasn't as if Cassie had been a great mother to her. Ginny had played that role more than anyone.

Andie turned to Ginny and took her hand in hers. "Why did my mother not like me, then? She implied the issue between her and me had something to do with whatever had happened between you two." Andie shook her head, unable to make sense of it. "I don't get it. That was all years before I came along. Mom had a husband, you had James. What could all that possibly have to do with me?"

Sad, weary eyes lifted to Andie's face and a cold tremor of dread started at the base of Andie's spine. She couldn't quite put her finger on the problem, but she knew the next words out of Ginny's mouth were going to be bad.

"James traveled on business. The year he died, he spent a couple days in Louisville."

Her mother had lived in Louisville.

"He called her. Invited her to his hotel for dinner."

Andie closed her eyes. She could see exactly where this was headed. "James is my father, isn't he?" she whispered.

Ginny's hand now squeezed hers, but she didn't speak. Instead, she waited for Andie to open her eyes again.

When she did, Ginny explained, "He knew he was dying. I didn't know it yet, but he did. So he went to see your mother. He wanted to know why she'd changed her mind all those years ago."

Andie ached for her aunt. "He found out she hadn't?"

Ginny nodded. "And they made you. Sixteen years we made love, and I couldn't get pregnant once. One night with your mother, and you were conceived. He came home and told me he'd found out the truth. And he told me he'd been with your mother. He felt guilty, I think. So he confessed. I was furious, yet I couldn't help but take part of the blame myself. He'd loved her first. I knew that when I married him."

"But he loved you, too, right?" Andie could see her aunt's pain, and she wanted desperately to put a stop to it. "He wouldn't have married you if he hadn't loved you, right?"

"Oh, sweetheart." Ginny chuckled. "Don't worry about me. Yes, he loved me. Very much. We were very happy together. But I don't think he ever quite got over your mother."

"He didn't plan to leave you for her, did he?" Andie gasped. "Oh my God, he didn't leave you?"

"No. He didn't leave me. Though Lord knows I was mad enough, I wanted to leave him. But instead, he told me that he had a rare cancer and had been given less than a year to live. He was dying. He would honor our vows and be my husband until the day he died, because, yes, he did love me. But he'd wanted to see your mother one last time before he passed. He said he hadn't intended to make love to her, but at the same time, he didn't regret it.

"It hurt me," Ginny continued. "Broke my heart and crushed my spirit. We'd had something that had been so special. But I couldn't leave him, either. I'd promised to stand by him, and I would. I did. Until his dying breath." She closed her eyes for a moment and then opened them. "I even called Cassie to come see him before he died, but she refused. I think she was as mad at him for believing what I'd told him as she was at me for doing it."

"But she came for his funeral?"

"And I saw she was seven months pregnant."

Andie's chest felt hollow. Seeing Cassie carry the baby Ginny had wanted all her life must have been catastrophic. "You knew the baby—that I—was his?"

"There was no doubt in my mind."

"That must have been hard."

A sardonic smile lifted Ginny's lips. "I'd thought finding out James still cared for her after all those years had been hard. But this…" She shook her head. "I'm sorry, child, but I hated you for the first few years of your life. I couldn't stand knowing you existed."

"That's understandable, Aunt Ginny." And then it made sense why as a young child she hadn't known Ginny. "But after Mom got married, again, I started coming to see you. What changed?"

"After about four years, I finally pulled myself out of my grief and anger over everything that had happened. I started believing in fate. I believed you'd been born for a reason, and that reason included me." She gave Andie a sad smile. "I called your mother. I wanted to see James's child. I deserved to see my husband's child."

"She refused," Andie guessed.

Ginny nodded. "She refused. I can't say I blamed her. I'd hurt her bad."

"But it wasn't like she was the mother of the year or anything." Andie suddenly found she was mad at her mother. "She wasn't doing a good job—she didn't even want to be a mother—and at the same time she was keeping me from *you*. Someone who did want kids. Someone who cared about me."

"Don't be mad at your mother. And never think she didn't care for you. She had gone her whole life being someone other than a mother. She'd lost James, and she felt all she had was her career. She worked hard for what she had. Then you came along, and she didn't know how to revert to being anything else. Plus, if she had, I suspect it would have brought out the hurt of everything all over again."

"She was not a good mother," Andie insisted. "She should have let me see you earlier."

"She needed to punish me, Andie. I'd hurt your mother a lot. She needed to feel like she had some control in the matter."

"Then why did she finally let me see you?" And then her mother's words came back to her: *John wanted to go places. It was one of the things I promised him when we got married.* "She only let me come when she found someone else," she accused.

"But at least she let you come here, baby. That's what counts."

Anger for the games her mother had played made her clench her hands into fists, but at the same time, she could see her mother's reasoning. She glanced at Ginny. "She knew you'd be a good mother, didn't she? She told me last night that she should have let me stay with you year-round. I thought it was because she didn't want me at all. But it was because she could tell I was happier with you."

The guilt of that had been with Andie most of her life. She liked her aunt better than her own mother.

Aunt Ginny reached out and wrapped both arms around her. "She loved you, sweetheart. She just had no idea how to be a mother with the years of anger she'd built up. And now she wants a second chance." Ginny leaned back and stroked Andie's cheek. "I hope you'll give it to her."

Andie didn't even have to think about it, and that amazed her. Of course she would give it to her. She wanted a relationship with her mother, too. She always had. She wouldn't be petty and play games as her mother had.

She stood, ready to go in so she could digest everything she'd just been told. When she looked toward the house, she could make out Mark sitting on the balcony, watching them. He was waiting for her. Just as she'd asked him to.

And she found that for the first time in her life, she wanted to go to him and bare her soul. She wanted to let him share her burdens, and help her figure out what to do next. And then she wanted to share his bed and let him hold her through the night.

But at the same time she was terrified. She cared about Mark way more than she should.

Ginny saw where Andie's line of sight had landed. "He still cares for you, you know?"

"I know." Andie was having a hard time making her feet take a step forward. "I'm beginning to wonder if he ever stopped."

"Like you never did?"

Andie looked at Ginny and nodded. "Like I never did." She turned back to Mark. "Mom says she'll help you kick his butt if he hurts me again."

Ginny laughed then, sounding more like herself than she had all night. "That sounds like a good plan to me. Your mother did know how to kick some butt in her day."

Again, Andie couldn't picture it. Her mom might break a nail and rip a brand-name business suit if she kicked someone's butt.

She peered at Ginny in the dark. "You two going to be able to fix this between you?"

Ginny nodded. "We've already started. Today was a good day."

"And between her and me?" Andie asked. "You think that's possible?"

"I've no doubt, sweetheart. You might find that you even like who she is if you give her a chance."

That might be stretching it, but Andie was willing to give a relationship a try.

"Let's go in," Andie suggested. "I want to talk to Mark."

They picked up their sandals, and Ginny slipped her arm through Andie's as she had done on the walk out. "I think you should consider going for it with him," Ginny said.

Andie eyed her aunt. "Did you forget our earlier conversation? I already did. And since you wanted to know," she added in a teasing voice, "it was off-the-charts good."

Ginny's laughter rang out into the night, and Andie smiled with her. If her aunt was ballsy enough to ask about her love life, she figured she should feel free to tell her about it.

"Good to hear it. Though from the sounds coming from your room, I assumed it had to be."

Andie felt that heat rising to her face again.

"That wasn't what I was talking about, though," Ginny confessed.

"No?"

"No." Ginny squeezed Andie's arm as they stopped, and both of them stared up at Mark. "I think you should go for love again."

This shocked Andie. "After all you went through, you can say that? Don't you have regrets? Seems life would have been easier without love."

"I have few regrets in my life, child. I regret losing your mother for all those years. And I regret that I went about things the way I did. I should have at least told her I felt the same way about James, and then let him choose. But I can't truly regret anything else, because I got sixteen good years with my husband, and I got you out of it."

Andie looked up at Mark again. "It's scary," she whispered.

"The best things are."

And she knew that she did want to go for it. She wanted love, and she wanted Mark. But she just wasn't sure she wouldn't get crushed in the deal.

"I do have one more thing to admit," Ginny said as they started forward again, heading toward the back stairs to the house.

"Oh geez, Aunt Ginny." Andie glanced sideways at her aunt. She wasn't sure could take much more. "What else?"

"Apparently James was sneakier than either your mother or I thought. He somehow knew that she was pregnant with you. After he died, his lawyer surprised us both."

"He left something for Mom?"

Aunt Ginny shook her head. "He left something for you." She motioned to the house. "The house is yours, child."

EPISODE EIGHT

CHAPTER EIGHTEEN

Mark heard Andie's bedroom door open and close from where he sat on the deck. Her lights didn't go on. Nor did she step outside.

He tapped his thumbs against each other as he waited. He was relaxed back in the same lounge chair he'd been in the first night they'd sat out there together, and he wondered if she would make him go in to her. His eyes closed as he concentrated, forcing his breathing to remain steady. It would be nice if she came to him.

She knew he was on the deck. He'd seen her catch sight of him as she'd returned to the house with Ginny. Although it was dark outside, he had no doubt that her gaze had been on him.

She and Ginny had both worn an air of stress as they'd walked, as if they'd been in deep discussion about a difficult subject. To the casual observer, the strain might not have been noticeable, but neither of them had moved as gracefully as they usually did. Their gaits had been tight, their steps short. And they'd held each other's arms as if needing the physical comfort of the other.

He assumed the issue between them had to do with Cassie. And though he could easily step inside Andie's room and offer a shoulder to lean on, he couldn't help but want her to seek him out.

That desire came with knowing that he was once again vulnerable to her.

Just like before, he was in too deep. There was no other way to go but forward, and though he knew she cared for him, he wasn't sure how much. He had no idea if they stood the chance of going anywhere, or if she could simply walk away at the end of next week.

He'd figured out his own feelings that afternoon on the boat. It had been a culmination of things. His desire to *not* talk to Rob because his doing so would hurt Andie. The fact he'd put a hook in her hand—and he'd just about shriveled up and died at the sight of it. And then her unbridled excitement when he'd locked them in the small bathroom together.

He would have opened the door if she'd preferred. Done nothing. Pushed for nothing. But the way she'd lit up in front of him had given him a power he could get addicted to.

She'd wanted him. And she hadn't cared—*too much*—what anyone else had thought.

Of course, it could have just been desire on her part and nothing else.

Not for him.

He'd looked into her eyes in that room and known he had to figure out a way to get her to see it could be more. *They* could be more.

The screen door opened and she stood there, her long dress flowing around her legs in the breeze and her hair lifting up off her shoulders. She looked at him and his heart settled into a steady thump.

"Good talk with Ginny?" he asked. He cleared his throat when his voice came out tight.

She nodded but didn't step any farther out onto the deck. Just watched him, her eyes steady and direct—but not necessarily seeing him after that first glimpse. She'd drifted a million miles away.

He waited. Something was bothering her. She'd held back a lot in the past. Either not bothered to share with him, or skated over the issues. Of course, he'd allowed it. But tonight he wanted her to see that he was there for her. He wanted her to *want* to share with him.

Finally, she sucked in a deep breath and blinked, and her gaze once again sought his. He let out the breath he'd been holding.

"This house belongs to me," she stated.

He sat up. "What?"

"This house," she murmured. She stepped across the threshold of her room and slid the screen door shut behind her, then moved across the deck and stared out at the sea. "It belongs to me—or it will."

Mark rose and went to her side. "Is that what Ginny told you tonight?"

"Some of it." She nodded. "Her husband, James, left it to me, to be signed over at my aunt's discretion. Aunt Ginny said she'd sign it over now if I want. But I said no. It's her home."

"Sounds like it's yours, too." What a shocker. "Any idea why he left it to you? He died before you were born, right?"

Andie turned to lean against the railing so that she was face-to-face with Mark. The skin between her eyes pinched as she held his gaze. Then she glanced away—looking over his shoulder. "He was apparently my father," she whispered into the night. "He and my mother had a past *before* Ginny, and then they had one night together years later. I was the result. Then he died." Her voice trembled. "Seven months later."

"Oh, babe." Mark took her hands in his, wanting to pull her close, but fearing the movement would squelch the flow of words. But he had to touch her. Had to let her know he was there for her. "You never had any idea?" he asked.

She shook her head, the slow movement signifying her bewilderment. "Mom never wanted to be a mother, and Aunt Ginny couldn't get pregnant." She turned her gaze back to his. "Fate. That's what Aunt Ginny said. I was some-how their fate?"

Confusion marred her features, but he thought he got it. Ginny saw the good side of things.

"Ginny has always loved you like a mother, hasn't she?" Mark asked.

"Since the day I met her. More than my own mother ever did."

The lost sound of Andie's words pained him. "And she wouldn't have had you to dote on if James and Cassie hadn't gotten together, right?"

Andie nodded again. "Right." She glanced down where their hands were clasped. "But fate? He cheated on her, Mark. Broke her heart, and Aunt Ginny calls it *fate.*"

Mark shrugged. "She believes that everything happens for a reason. Exactly when it should."

He was starting to wonder if that wasn't actually the case. He had Andie back in his life, after all. Maybe it simply hadn't been their time before.

"It's an interesting concept," Andie murmured. She let go of his hands and turned to the railing. She wrapped her fingers around the metal and leaned the top half of her body out over the deck, sucking in deep gulps of air. He mimicked her breathing, pulling in the scent of the flowers from below. The scent was sweet and potent, and he realized it was the same fragrance that Andie often wore.

"It smells like you out here," he said.

She turned her face to him and he smiled at her in the dark. She was still leaning over the railing, and she reminded him of a little girl—a child with her head hanging out the car window, her hair blowing in the wind.

"It's honeysuckle," she told him. "I've loved the smell since I first discovered it here as a kid. Aunt Ginny always buys me perfume as one of my Christmas gifts. She gets me honeysuckle."

Her words stopped, and he sensed she was wrangling with something else. All he could do was wait to see if she wanted to talk. In the past they wouldn't have even made it this far.

Finally, she straightened and put her back to the railing. She crossed her arms over her chest. "You know those scholarships I worked so hard for?"

He nodded. She'd earned scholarships all through her undergrad years as well as during her master's program.

"I apparently could have slacked off." She glanced at him, the look hard and angry. "It came from a trust my father set up."

Wow. "That was—"

"Underhanded," she stated, the word blunt. "Why didn't anyone ever tell me it was coming from him? Hell, why didn't anyone ever tell me who my father was?"

Anger burned brightly in front of him. She was a sweetheart, but when she got angry, she held nothing back.

"Did you ask Ginny?"

She glared at him as if he'd said the wrong thing. Before he could come up with anything else to try, she huffed out a breath and stomped back into her room. As she stepped through the doorway, she glanced over her shoulder. "Will you come in with me?"

Into her bedroom? He pushed off the rail. Oh, hell yeah.

Though he had no idea what was going to go on in there. This evening was not going in any way he'd imagined.

Andie's mood made him wonder if they'd even get to the topics that had come up on the boat earlier that day. They'd eventually need to talk about them. What Rob had said about Tiffany—he supposed Andie deserved to know how badly he could let someone down—as well as what Andie had said about him having issues with marriage. Not to mention, her accusing him of wanting to leave instead of risking getting involved with her again.

He didn't want to leave.

And he did want to get involved.

Also, he didn't have issues with marriage.

Maybe he *had* been looking for excuses to end their engagement before. He hadn't realized it at the time, but the instant the words had come out of Andie's mouth, he knew they were likely correct. Something between the two of them just hadn't been quite right. Not back then.

He'd started arguments during those last months, just as she had. He'd also jumped at the excuse that she was using him when he'd heard her on the phone the morning of their wedding.

He had known she loved him, yes. But he still maintained she'd loved her job more. That it would have eventually come between them in their marriage.

That didn't mean it had been right to send Rob to the church instead of him.

But history couldn't be changed. They could only move forward.

And he most definitely *didn't* have issues with getting married. Marriage and a family were what he wanted. Tiffany and his past played no part in anything.

Once he'd stepped inside, Andie pushed the balcony doors closed tight and then pulled the curtains over them, leaving Mark and her standing in the dark.

"You don't want to hear the ocean tonight?" he asked. And then it occurred to him. This was her house—or it would be. She could listen to the ocean for the rest of her life. He wondered vaguely how that might play into the two of them.

Heck, he didn't even know what he wanted from the two of them. But he loved her. That was a fact. So it wasn't as if he could just walk away without trying.

"I don't want to risk Aunt Ginny overhearing us talk," she said. "Or Phillip Jordan for that matter." She grumbled the last words as if the man had done something to annoy her. She turned on the corner lamp. The one they'd knocked to the floor the day before.

"Did he say anything to you today?" he asked. At Andie's glance, he added, "On the boat. After…"

Mark knew Phillip had his nose stuck in the air about catching Andie and him on the beach together that first night. After the bathroom escapade, he could only imagine what the man thought of them now. He hadn't looked Mark in the eye once all afternoon.

Of course, that could also have been because Mark had punched out his daughter's fiancé.

"He didn't say anything on the boat," Andie answered him as she clicked on another lamp. The room was cast in a warm, inviting light, showcasing that it was as pristine as ever. "Though Lord knows, he shot me enough venomous looks," she continued. "But he did catch me downstairs as I came in."

"What did he say?" Mark had the fleeting urge to go upstairs and pound a fist into Phillip's face, too. Seemed like a great way to end the evening.

"That Penelope is upset." She crossed to the bed.

"Oh?" Not what he'd expected.

"Apparently she's been humming a lot." Andie turned down the covers on the side of the bed closest to them. "Seems she does that when she's upset."

What did humming have to do with anything? And were they about to crawl into bed together like a couple? His heart picked up speed. He hoped so. He forced his mind back to the conversation. "Did he bother to ask *her* about it?" he asked.

Andie shrugged as she moved to the other side to turn down the covers over there. "Her mother did, apparently. But Penelope's not talking. However, Phillip *knows* she's upset, therefore he assumes it has something to do with the wedding." Andie gave Mark a tight, sarcastic smile. "It is now my responsibility to figure it out."

"The man wouldn't abuse a bonus clause, would he?"

"Just like he wouldn't sneak his future son-in-law into office." She shook her head as she headed to the small kitchen area that held the minifridge and a microwave. "What a piece of work. Both of them." She whirled on him, her eyes wide. "Rob *wants* to be in the state's attorney's office? Why? Is it purely the notoriety?"

"Probably. I wouldn't be surprised if he isn't serious about wanting to go all the way to the Supreme Court someday. He's got to start somewhere, I suppose."

"So he's using them as bad as they're using him."

"Probably worse." Mark was still pissed at Rob over that. Even without everything else that had been said, the guy should not be using marriage simply to slide into office. "He's made a habit of using people over the years."

Their friendship. Mark's father to get a job. No telling what else.

"Poor Penelope," Andie said softly.

Mark nodded in agreement. The girl didn't deserve the mess she was walking into.

Andie grabbed two bottles of water and a plastic-wrap-covered piece of pie from the fridge, and they met on the small couch. She handed him a bottle, and he noticed the pie was, in fact, cheesecake. His favorite.

"I feel like I should say something to her." Andie sat on the couch, one leg bent underneath her as she unwrapped the cheesecake. "If I was that madly in love with someone and he didn't love me back, I'd want to know."

Yet telling Penelope would put Andie right back where she'd started the day. With no wedding. No bonus money.

Mark wondered what she would do.

She suddenly looked up, studying him as if she were working to figure something out. "After you punched him,

I thought you'd leave, you know? If he didn't tell you to get lost first."

Mark reached out and brushed a lock of hair behind her ear, letting his fingers linger for a moment. He hadn't even considered leaving. Instead, he'd had more of a quiet celebration because he no longer had to.

"He won't kick me out," he said. "It would mess up the symmetry of the wedding party. The pictures would be off."

Andie nodded in understanding and took a bite of the cheesecake. Brides weren't known for being happy if the wedding didn't go off as planned. Rob may not love Penelope, but he respected the trouble she would make if he sent his best man home.

"And I stayed because of you," he told her.

Her eyes widened slightly, and then she reached out and fed him a bite.

The creamy filling was rich and decadent, and he had the urge to smear the rest of it all over her before licking it off.

"You stayed so we could have a fling?" she asked. Her tone was light and teasing, but he could see beyond the words. She was wondering, as much as he, where they were headed.

"I stayed because I want to be with you," he admitted. "To figure this out."

He didn't want to scare her away, so he kept the tone easy. She bit down on her bottom lip and fed him another bite.

After he swallowed, he took the plate from her and set it aside. Then he wrapped her hands in his. "You were pretty upset outside, babe. About the house. Your father. Want to talk about that some more?"

"I do," she admitted. "Just like I want to know about this ex that you supposedly killed."

Mark froze. He did *not* want to talk about that. Not tonight. He wished he could get away with never.

However, knowing Andie was ready to share things with him warmed him. That was different than the past. Even different than a day ago when her mother had shown up. They could start off slow. Build up to his past.

"Okay." He nodded, keeping hold of her hands. "Then let's talk. You go first."

She peeked up at him, her nose crinkling with a grimace. "Don't think I'm avoiding the issues, because I'm not. But everything has just been too much today. How about we finish the dessert I stole for you from downstairs, I return *the favor*, and then we talk in the morning?"

He was about to argue, thinking she was just trying to get out of a tough conversation, when his brain engaged to decipher what she'd just said. "Return the favor?" he asked. He'd heard those words earlier that day. On the boat. As he'd been pulling up her panties.

He gulped.

She grinned.

"I have to tell you, though," she spoke in a loud whisper, "you're going to need to try to be quiet. Aunt Ginny already heard us going at it up here yesterday."

Mortification had him jumping to his feet. "She heard us?"

Andie nodded. "Asked about it, too. She wanted to know if it was any good."

"I hope you told her it was none of her business." He couldn't imagine what he'd do if his mother questioned him about a similar situation. What was wrong with the woman?

Andie only smiled sweetly and stood, cheesecake in hand. "I told her it was off the charts."

She forked a bite of cake and slipped it between her lips, and he went hard.

"Take your pants off, Mark," she said after slowly chewing and swallowing the bite. She licked a spot of cream cheese off her lip. "Then climb into my bed."

No dummy, he had his pants off before she'd finished the request.

He lowered himself to her bed, stacked two pillows together, and lay down on them, legs stretched out down the middle of the mattress. Then he realized he was still wearing his shirt. He quickly sat up and shrugged out of it, tossing it to the floor.

"You shaved," she said. She made it sound as if he'd done something wrong.

"I showered after I got back." He rubbed a hand along his cheek. He hadn't shaved that morning since they'd only been going out on the boat. "Figured I should clean up."

She set the plate down momentarily, then slipped her dress off over her head. She had on white bikini panties and a white strapless bra underneath that did amazing things to her breasts. They were lifted and separated just right. With the bracelets she wore, the mix of colors and shapes circling one arm up to her elbow, she looked like a mythical goddess.

His breathing became a short pant.

"I liked the rugged look," she admitted. She picked up the plate and climbed onto the bed with him, then straddled his feet. "Did you want another bite?" she asked.

He nodded. He had no clue what he wanted at the moment, but he would say yes to anything she asked.

She forked up a mouthful and leaned forward on her knees, holding it out to him. At that angle, her breasts looked as if they were about to slip right over the edge of her bra. He was prepared to catch them, but they stayed firmly tucked away.

"You left your underwear on," she accused.

He nodded again. "Seemed forward to remove them," he explained.

"Yet I just told you that you are about to get a blow job."

His dick turned to stone, and he smiled. "Yes, ma'am."

She lifted her ass up off him and slid another bite of cheesecake between her lips. He kicked his boxer briefs past his feet.

Then he lay back, splayed out before her, his cock waving like a flagpole, and she still didn't touch him. She only scooped up another bite and made love to the damned fork.

"You're killing me down there, babe."

"I'm trying to decide how I want to start," she said. "And what will get you to make the most noise."

His eyes bugged. "I won't be uttering a sound."

"Yet everyone heard me on the boat."

"That was different." That wasn't him. And he knew it would be a sexist thing to say, so he kept his mouth shut.

She grinned wickedly. "Guess we'll just have to find out if you want to finish or not."

She set the plate aside then dipped and immediately took him into her mouth. He gasped and came up off the bed but held in the groan. The woman was naughty.

Long reddish-brown hair brushed against his stomach. He reached down to sweep it back out of her face so he could watch. She was beautiful. And he was going to lose his mind trying to stay quiet as she worked him with her mouth.

One of her hands reached out to the side and scooped cheesecake with her fingers. Then she stretched her hand up to his mouth. She lifted her heated gaze from his crotch and watched as she slid one finger at a time into his mouth. He licked the sweet dessert from her fingertips, all while she continued tugging on him with her lips.

When she lowered her gaze and once again completely focused on what she was doing, he dropped his head back against the pillow. His eyes crossed with the sweet torment of her mouth. It became a struggle to breathe.

Her fingers now sought him out, wrapping low around the base of his cock, and then she squeezed. He gritted his teeth.

He moaned—just a little—as she looked up at him again from under her lashes. She pulled back slowly, sucking the tip of him hard before popping him out of her mouth entirely and licking her lips. His moan turned to a groan.

He took in the smattering of freckles across her nose, her wickedly evil grin, and he knew he'd do whatever he could to get her back in his life. Permanently. He loved her that much.

He wanted to tell her but feared that would ruin the moment.

She reached behind her and undid her bra, and his hands suddenly burned with the desire to touch her. Everything about her was exactly what he wanted. Her insides, her heart. Her body. He just wanted *her*.

Her full breasts swayed as she once again dipped forward, letting them lightly rub against him. The softness of her contrasted starkly with the hardness of him, and he couldn't help but take her in his hands and press her around him.

He pumped a little, involuntarily—and then she lowered her head and he let out another sound as her mouth once again found him.

He shuddered. There was an overload of sensation going on, and he suddenly didn't care who heard him. It had been too long since she'd touched him like this, and he almost shouted at the joy of it. He didn't want to be without her ever again.

∾

Wednesday brought sunshine, blue skies, and the fourth day without Mark.

Before they'd gotten out of bed on Sunday morning, his cell had rung. His brother was calling from Boston. One of their longest-standing clients was in the middle of a crisis, so Mark had rushed back to help with the situation.

It had been three and a half long days since he'd left, and he wasn't supposed to be back until the following evening. To Andie it felt as if he'd been gone forever. Which was no good at all. It made her needy. Left her open to hurt.

They were having a fling here. Nothing more.

They were having a good time.

Saturday night had been spent focusing on fun. First, she'd done her best to make him be too loud in the eerily quiet house. He'd ended up holding a pillow over his head, groaning into it as she'd divested him of his strength to do anything else. Then they'd turned to each other during the night, both being as quiet as possible but giving up nothing in terms of what they'd sought from each other.

He was a good lover. Always had been. And unlike her, it seemed he'd practiced over the years. The man had some good moves.

She'd planned to spend Sunday morning talking with Mark, not intending to rouse to the outside world until noon or after. It had been her day off, so she'd been determined to make the best of it. Ginny had suggested she go for love, but she wasn't quite on board with that way of thinking. There were things she needed to know first.

Like…who had died? And why?

And how in the world had Mark been involved?

But because he'd had to tiptoe out of her room at dawn, she'd gotten no questions answered.

Until she did, she wouldn't consider anything more between them. She would not risk heartache again.

Something had held him back from marrying her four years ago. She'd let it go with his explanation about her using him, because it had been easier to do that than to hear something along the lines of "You weren't what I wanted." But she knew there was more to the story.

He'd been too quick to run. Too quick to find an excuse and abort.

And then on the boat, Rob had said he'd once killed a girlfriend.

Her instincts told her that whatever had been behind his actions before was still in place today. He might want more in his life. He might want the wife and kids and the house in the suburbs.

But she thought he might just balk before ever taking them.

And she did not want to find herself with dreams again, only to have her heart ripped open and bleeding.

Therefore she and Mark were having a fling. And that was all.

She'd simply enjoy it until it was over.

Andie hurried through the halls of the Turtle Island Hotel, where she'd spent the majority of the day, heading to the room that would hold Penelope's bridal shower.

The event had originally been planned to be held on the grounds of the hotel, but they'd gone to plan B due to the high temperatures. Everything was currently being moved from under the massive oaks to the air-conditioned space inside the hotel. Kayla had been following along throughout the whole process, fussing over every detail, as Andie had roamed between the new location and the lobby, where Ginny had planted herself, greeting arriving guests and welcoming them with gift bags.

It was midafternoon now, and Andie found Kayla in the overlarge sitting room, picking at small details. The shower would be lovely in the comfortable space. The room was pale yellow and had warm wood flooring, with white-framed floor-to-ceiling windows that opened onto a view of the lush hotel lawn.

Thanks to the tent set up just outside the sitting room doors—where guests would later mingle with drinks and hors d'oeuvres—no sunlight would stream through the many panes of glass to shine directly on any guest.

Andie stopped in the middle of the room and took in the sedate cream and pink flowers arranged throughout the area. They'd been intended as centerpieces for the round-tops that had been part of the original plan, but the shower would now be a bit more relaxed, with guests seated on sofas and casual chairs. White folding chairs had been brought in as additional seating, but overall the feeling remained elegant and sophisticated.

"They've done a wonderful job," Andie murmured to Kayla as they stepped outside into the tented area and surveyed the preparations. A large fan was stationed at each corner of the tent, keeping a nice breeze moving.

Kayla nodded and took a sip of the lemonade she'd brought outside with her. "I think I like this better, actually. The more casual seating seems to fit more with our bride."

Andie had to agree. Penelope knew how to do class, but Andie sensed that deep down she was an easy-to-get-along-with, laid-back girl. Which, once again, made her feel bad that Penelope would be marrying Rob.

She pushed the thought from her mind. It was none of her business. Seaglass had been hired to do a job, and that's what they would do. She checked her watch and saw that guests should start arriving soon, then she accepted her own lemonade from a passing server.

A table was being set up that would hold various platters of the best food the hotel served. Kayla wandered over to discuss details with a worker, and Andie took a sip of her drink as she watched the action. The tart liquid was refreshing as it slid down her throat.

"Andie, sweetheart."

Andie turned to find Celeste Kavanaugh approaching from the side walkway. She wore a pale green dress, with a flounced skirt, that was simply too cute.

"Celeste." Andie greeted the woman with a warm hug. "I've barely seen you this week. Have you and Wayne been enjoying yourselves?"

Celeste practically giggled. "Once I got him to forget work, it's been like a second honeymoon. I can't wait for our trip later in the year," she confided but then let out a tiny sigh. "I just wish I could take everyone with us."

Andie studied the glow coming from her ex-almost-mother-in-law and then leaned in to whisper, "Something tells me that isn't really true. Looks to me like you'll enjoy the time alone with your husband."

A pretty blush touched Celeste's cheeks. "I will. But I'll also miss the family. And the grandkids. We'll be gone for a couple months."

"Then you must learn to Skype."

Celeste laughed. "I definitely must learn to Skype." She accepted a proffered glass of lemonade and took a moment to look around. "It's lovely out here, Andie. You do good work."

"Kayla does most of it." Andie pointed out her event director, who was rearranging the stacked serving dishes that had been placed on the tables. "You've met Kayla, right? She's the secret behind everything Seaglass does. We'd be lost without her."

"Oh yes, I met her. Considered trying to talk her into a move to Boston." Celeste winked. "One of my charities could use a talent like hers."

"I'm afraid I'd have to hunt her up and drag her back."

They laughed together, then fell into a comfortable conversation, similar to many they'd had years before. They had been at ease with each other since the day they'd met.

Which brought to mind the question of why Celeste had once said she didn't think Mark should marry Andie. That had bothered Andie a lot. She'd struggled to feel like she fit in with the Kavanaughs since they were so high profile but had felt she was holding her own. Maybe she hadn't quite belonged, but she hadn't seen herself as an embarrassment, either.

To hear Celeste say that she didn't want her in their family had hurt. It had damaged Andie's pride.

They headed inside to the cooler air, and Andie considered bringing up the topic as she held the door open for the other woman. She didn't want to put Celeste on the spot, yet she wanted to know—what had been so wrong with her? Had it simply been the lack of money? Class?

Had Celeste thought Andie couldn't do the Kavanaugh family proud at events?

None of it felt right. Celeste had never struck her as that type of woman.

"This is simply gorgeous, Andie." Celeste breathed out the words as she got a look at the room. She crossed to admire the picture mounted above the fireplace on the far wall and ran a hand along the wood of the mantel. "Everything about this fits with what I've learned about Penelope. She's a good girl, right?" she asked, turning back to Andie.

"I've talked to her a few times this week, and she seems like someone with a level head on her shoulders."

"Yes." Andie nodded. "I think that describes her well. She's sweet and smart, and very down-to-earth."

"Exactly what Rob needs."

Andie didn't reply, as she had other thoughts about what Rob needed. A good swift kick in the crotch, for one thing. She joined Celeste by the fireplace and decided to ask about the past. There were only a couple of days left before everyone would depart. This could be her only opportunity.

If the conversation caused a strain between the two of them...well, Celeste would soon return home, and Andie wouldn't see her again.

"Can I ask you something, Celeste?"

The woman turned to her. "Absolutely. Anything, dear."

Nerves battled in Andie's stomach, but she forged ahead.

"I once overheard you saying that you didn't think Mark should marry me," she said. She held her head high, her chin out, unwilling to appear as anything but an equal. "*After* we were already engaged," she added.

Lines formed in the space between Celeste's eyes as if she were thinking, and then she murmured, "Oh dear." Embarrassment stained her cheeks. "I never realized you'd heard that."

"You remember saying it, then?"

Celeste nodded. "To my sister. She'd come out to visit one afternoon, and I remember talking about our boys. You and Mark came up."

For some reason it bothered Andie more that Celeste remembered her comment so clearly. "Can I ask *why* you said that? What it was about me that was the issue?"

"Oh, darling." Celeste reached out and took Andie's free hand. "It wasn't about you. It was about Mark."

"Mark?" Andie shook her head in confusion. "I don't understand. If you didn't want him to marry me then—"

"I would have loved having you in our family, Andie. Very much. And I could see how much you two loved each other."

Andie stared at her. The words didn't make sense.

"What then?" she whispered. "It's bothered me since I heard you say it." Andie glanced away, taking in the opulent surroundings and knowing that she still sometimes felt like a fraud, even in this world she was a part of every day. "I didn't come from prestige, but my family has done fairly well for themselves."

"Oh, sweetheart. Let's sit down." The older woman tugged Andie to a settee. They put their lemonades on a low table in front of the sofa and then sat, knees angled toward each other.

"Mark was…" Celeste began, then paused as if considering what to say. She gave Andie a hesitant smile before lifting a shoulder in apology. "I felt like he was bulldozing you. He'd always been that way. He sees what he wants, and he makes it happen."

He did. It was a trait Andie liked about him.

She never would have guessed his mother thought he was doing it to her, though. "How so?" she asked.

"You moved into his place only two months after you met him."

"Because we got engaged."

"Right." Celeste gave a little nod. "But *why* did you get engaged so fast? Was that really what you wanted?"

Andie started to say that of course it had been what she'd wanted. But then she thought back to that time.

From the moment Mark had first taken her out, she'd started falling hard for him. He had put the full-court press on her, but that had been fine. She'd loved it. She'd enjoyed being around him and his family, and had loved the devotion he'd bestowed on her.

But she had been shocked on her birthday when he'd pulled out his grandmother's ring and asked her to marry him.

She hadn't been expecting a proposal because of the short time they'd been dating. And she certainly hadn't expected him to slide the old-fashioned heirloom onto her finger. His doing so had added pressure to the whole situation.

In the end she'd said yes because they loved each other, but they'd agreed upon a long engagement. That had more to do with her job than with anything else, though. She'd first needed to *get* a job, and then she had needed to establish herself. There hadn't been time to plan a wedding.

"You don't think I was ready to be engaged?" she asked Celeste, thinking about Aunt Ginny's words of only a few days before. It made sense that if she hadn't been ready to get married, she of course wouldn't have been ready to be engaged.

"Honey, I don't think either of you were ready to be engaged. *You* hadn't spent time in the real world figuring out who you were yet. And *he* didn't want to risk losing you. He moved fast because of it. Even got his father to help get you the job there in Boston."

"But I wanted that job." And then she remembered Mark being the one to suggest that his dad could help her get it.

She'd thought it lucky at the time, but looking back, she wondered if that had been the right move. She hadn't even applied anywhere else. She'd merely taken Mark's word that Wayne could get her in. And he had.

Then she'd failed, of course. Getting fired certainly hadn't been in the plans.

But that hadn't been Mark's fault. That was all her.

Because…she studied the woman before her and pulled in a deep, lung-filling breath as she realized something for the first time. She'd failed at that job because it hadn't been right for her. It hadn't been the right *career* for her. Not necessarily because *she* had been a failure.

Wow. Talk about taking a long time to realize the obvious.

Celeste gave her a small smile, as if she understood the moment Andie had just experienced. Then she leaned in close, the scent of her light perfume wafting between them, and gave Andie a hug. She whispered, "And it pissed me off that he fussed so much about you working long hours. To succeed there, you needed to work hard."

Andie nodded. "It's a competitive field. You have to be driven to be an investment banker."

"Mark worked just as hard, too," Celeste said, sitting back and reaching for her lemonade. "Only it seemed to me that he saw *his* job as the one that was the important one in the relationship. It made me angry on your behalf, sweetheart. He was taking advantage of you because he saw himself as the more important one in the union. I'd taught him better than that."

Her last words were said with such disgust that Andie couldn't help but grin. She loved Mark's mother.

"I always thought he'd be happier if I quit," Andie admitted. "If I'd be a stay-at-home wife and mother, but he swore that wasn't what he wanted. He said he just wanted me around more."

Celeste smiled wistfully and patted Andie's hand. "Deep down he probably did want that, even if he didn't realize it. He'd grown up with that lifestyle. He was used to it."

"That's what I thought, too."

"But you wanted more," Celeste stated. It had been clear to anyone who'd known Andie back then. She'd wanted a big-time career.

She'd wanted to be like her mom.

It wasn't what she wanted now. Though she still didn't know where her true desire lay.

"You've done well here, Andie," Celeste told her. "I'm so proud for you. And I'm sorry my words hurt you before. I never meant anything negative about you. I simply didn't want you to wake up one day with regrets because my son had pushed you before you were ready. Before you figured out who you were. Have you done that now, sweetheart? Are you happy?"

Andie started to nod but paused, her gaze holding on the woman in front of her. Of course she was happy. She had her aunt, her business. Great friends. And she was doing what she wanted.

Only, she also had a hole in her heart that had become obvious since Mark had shown up.

She wanted more.

She wanted it all.

Nodding carefully, she shifted her gaze so she didn't lie to Celeste's face. "I have a great life now. I'm thrilled with it."

The lie lodged in Andie's heart.

Celeste patted her hand again and leaned closer, brushing her lips over Andie's cheek. The gentleness of the gesture almost brought Andie to tears. "Then I'm happy for you," Celeste said softly. "That's all I ever wanted. For you to be happy."

Before Andie could figure out how to respond without making the fib worse, Penelope swept into the room. She wore a broad smile and had her blonde hair swept up into a loose pile on the top of her head. And she was dressed in pink again. She wore a deep-carnation-pink-and-white striped skirt with a softer pink ruffled top. Her heels matched the shirt. Andie couldn't help but laugh at the giddy expression on the woman's face.

Andie had found Penelope a couple days before and discussed her father's concerns—that she was unhappy. That there was some issue with the wedding.

Penelope had assured her she was perfectly fine. She simply had normal bridal jitters, but there was nothing to worry about. Andie hadn't been completely convinced, but with no specific issue brought to her attention, there was little else she could do.

"I can't believe this is all for me," Penelope gushed. She turned in a circle in the middle of the floor, taking in the decorations. "And that in only three days I'll be marrying the man of my dreams."

Andie couldn't believe it either.

She rose. Seaglass Celebrations had a job to do, and she was going to make sure Penelope felt special throughout every minute of it. Even if the girl could do better for a husband.

CHAPTER NINETEEN

Late Wednesday night Andie decided it was time to confront her mother and aunt about the secrets they'd kept from her over the years.

She'd spent most of Sunday with Cassie since it had been Andie's day off and Mark had returned to Boston, and though she'd been upset about all she'd learned from Aunt Ginny the night before, she'd been reluctant to bring up the subject of her father. It had seemed a better use of time to spend the day simply getting to know her mother a bit rather than immediately laying into her about the years of secrets.

So they'd gone shopping, shared a late lunch in a quaint little café on the mainland, and then met up with Aunt Ginny later that evening. The three of them had enjoyed dinner and live music at a total dive on the south side of the island.

It had been fun. A good day.

Since then their paths had crossed in the house, they made the occasional small talk, had shared a meal or two together, and generally acted as if they were all getting along.

But Andie was pissed. At both of them. She felt lied to and betrayed. And it was time for answers.

She changed from her pajamas into shorts and a T-shirt, then stepped out of her bedroom and headed down the stairs. Her mother and aunt had gone off to Ginny's room a while ago, but she doubted either of them was asleep. Whenever she'd passed by Aunt Ginny's room late in the night this past week, she'd heard them talking or laughing softly behind the closed door.

On the one hand, she was glad they seemed to be making up for lost time. She liked seeing both of them happy. But on the other hand, why couldn't they have told her years ago who her father was? Maybe if they had she wouldn't have wasted so much time wondering why her mother didn't like her.

Maybe she would have believed there wasn't anything wrong with *her*.

Stopping outside her aunt's bedroom door, she paused, pulled in a fortifying breath, and then softly knocked.

Two seconds later the door swung open and Aunt Ginny stood there in cotton button-up pajamas, her face void of makeup.

"Andie, hon," Ginny said. "Is everything okay?"

Andie glanced past her to see her mother with her feet up on the couch, wearing a similar pair of pajamas. Jealousy caught her off guard at seeing them growing closer. She and Aunt Ginny were the ones who were supposed to have the special relationship. Not these two.

She shook off the thought as quickly as it had arrived. That wasn't fair. And she wasn't that petty. She was simply upset and looking for excuses to be more so.

"Can I talk to you both?" she asked. Her voice was clipped and hard.

"Of course," Aunt Ginny murmured. She stepped back and let Andie in.

Instead of sitting when her mother lowered her feet from the couch and offered the spot beside her, Andie began to pace. Aunt Ginny stood at the end of the bed, her hands gripped together, and Cassie sat stiffly on the couch. Both of them watched Andie guardedly.

When she didn't say anything for several paces back and forth, her mother finally spoke up. "What are you most upset about, Andie? We've been waiting for you to tell us."

Andie stopped in the middle of the room and looked from one to the other, her irritation rising, then planted her hands on her hips. "I want to know why you never told me about my father."

Identical expressions formed on the faces of both women. Eyebrows lifted, eyes widened, and the corners of their mouths turned down. With the two of them having the same red hair and green eyes, it was a striking moment.

She could suddenly see them being close, as Aunt Ginny had said they'd once been.

And though angry, she found herself glad for both of them that they were overcoming their pasts. They would have a second chance. Maybe neither of them would be alone the rest of their lives.

Her mother was the first to speak. "We felt you didn't need the confusion in your life. James was gone, so it wasn't as if you could get to know him."

"But I deserved to know." Andie pointed her finger at her mother. "And you lied to me. You always told me my father was unimportant. That he was no one who would ever matter in my life."

This had bugged Andie most over the last few days. He wasn't unimportant. The man had paid for her education. He'd left her a house. He was somebody. And she'd been unable to feel gratitude in her heart all these years because these two women had kept him from her.

She'd been unable to pay her respects.

Aunt Ginny lowered herself to sit beside her sister, her red head nodding. "You probably did deserve to know. We were selfish. We were busy being mad at each other and didn't want to deal with you knowing. But Andie, what good would it have done *you*? Then you would have been upset over the rift between your mother and me all this time. That would have affected you. We didn't want that. It was our issue. You didn't deserve to have it dumped on you."

Ginny's words resonated deeply with Andie, causing her to take a step back. Would the knowledge have impacted her? She tried to imagine being at Ginny's for the summer, knowing her mother hated her. Knowing she was there because her father had cheated on Ginny.

Then she tried to imagine being at home with her mother, calling Aunt Ginny up to talk when all the while knowing her mother hated her. And why.

Probably she wouldn't have called as often.

Or maybe she would have asked to live with Ginny instead of her mother.

And though her childhood hadn't been perfect, Andie couldn't imagine that scenario either. She loved her mother. She wouldn't have wanted to live year-round anywhere else.

Tears suddenly appeared from nowhere to pour down her cheeks, and both women rushed to her side. Four arms closed around her. The three of them stood there for several long minutes, Andie crying, both of them holding her tight.

It was unfair that she'd never known the truth. It was unfair that James had died before she'd gotten to meet him.

And it was unfair that she felt like this knowledge was now shifting the world beneath her feet.

The man had been gone for years. There was nothing that could change that. Only, for the first time in her life, she felt as if she had a parent who'd loved her unconditionally. And she hadn't even known about him so she could love him back.

"I feel betrayed," she finally said. A hiccup came out with her next sob. "And I feel like we should have done better for him."

Both women nodded against her as the three of them remained clutched together.

"We should have handled it better," Aunt Ginny said. She stroked a hand down over Andie's hair.

"We shouldn't have remained angry with each other for so long," her mother replied.

At the words, Ginny lifted her head off Andie's shoulder and peered at her sister. "I shouldn't have caused it," Ginny whispered.

Two sets of green eyes stared at each other with Andie caught in the middle watching. She'd come in to have it out with them, and in the end, it seemed she'd helped them take another step in their recovery. It was powerful to witness the connection build between them.

It made her wish she'd had a sister to be close with.

It made her wish she had a bond with someone who would stick over the years, no matter what they went through.

It made her think of Mark.

She closed her eyes and cried some more. There was a mix of grieving for the father she'd never known, happiness for her aunt and mother, and sadness that she and Mark would never be more than a couple of weeks. There might be a bond between them, but she wouldn't wait around for something that wasn't going to happen.

And then she realized what else she'd been upset about this week. Her mother was stealing her aunt from her. And Andie had to step back and let it happen.

The two sisters deserved the chance to renew their bond.

More tears fell as Andie accepted that her life was changing. Nothing would ever be the same again.

She only hoped she could eventually figure out a way to make it okay.

∼

Headlights flashed over the roadside parking lot, briefly highlighting the crowd of people waiting on the beach, then blinked out. Andie's blood began to pump. The car door opened and closed, and a tall, broad man emerged. He also appeared to be wearing a suit. It was Mark.

She let out a breath and forced herself not to hurry to his side.

She'd missed him. And she was really glad he'd gotten back in time for the sea turtle walk. Looking for nesting turtles was one of her favorite things to do in the summer. She'd wanted to share the experience with him.

The tour guides had already given their presentation, and the group was just about to head off down the beach. They'd been waiting a few more minutes to see if Mark would arrive in time.

Barefoot, sans suit jacket, and with his slacks rolled up at the ankles, he reached her side, and she grinned up at him, happier to see him than she wanted to admit. She kissed him lightly on the cheek, and then he kissed her on the mouth.

It wasn't light.

And she almost forgot they were in the middle of a crowd.

It had been a long four days.

"Good trip?" she asked when they'd finally pulled apart. There was some snickering among those in the crowd around them, but she ignored it. She and Mark had talked briefly on the phone a few times over the past few days, but that didn't compare to having him there with her. It would take the earth opening beneath her feet to get her focus off him.

"Fruitful." He snuck in one more kiss, his warm lips grazing the spot just in front of her ear, and he whispered, "I missed you."

She melted a little. "I missed you too."

The tour guides got everyone's attention, and the group took off down the dark beach, the moon hidden by clouds. Andie and Mark hung back to bring up the rear. She put enough distance between them and everyone else so they could talk without being heard, then pulled a pair of night-vision goggles out of her bag and handed them to Mark. The guides had a couple of pairs to share with others in the group, but these were her private set.

There were also turtle-safe flashlights that had been passed around to at least half the members of the party, which meant the lights had red filters over the bulbs. Red light doesn't confuse the turtles' sense of direction the way the white light does.

Mark held the goggles up to his eyes. "These are amazing," he whispered. "I feel like I'm spying on everyone."

Andie laughed lightly as she walked by his side. She wanted to wrap her arm around his waist so they were touching, but she kept reminding herself that what they had was temporary. There was no purpose in acting like it was more. "You're supposed to use them to look for turtles," she told him.

"Yeah, yeah," he mumbled. "That too, but is that your mother and aunt I see up at the front? They're walking so close together they're practically holding hands."

"They seem to be making up for lost years," Andie informed him. It was still odd, seeing the two women hitting it off so well. But after their talk the evening before, the new closeness between them was beginning to feel more natural. "I ended up spending Sunday with Mom," she said. "And then she moved into the house."

He pulled the glasses from his face and peered down at her. "She moved in?"

"Aunt Ginny invited her."

"Wow," he said. "Big strides. How did your day with her go?"

She nodded and slipped an arm through his, unable to help herself. "Really well, actually. She seems legit in saying she wants to have a relationship." She shrugged. "We're working through it. The three of us had another good talk last night."

"That's good, babe." He wrapped his arm around her waist, pulling her closer to him, and she rested her head against his shoulder. He felt so good next to her. "Having your mom in your corner will be nice," he said.

Just like Celeste had always been there for him and his brothers, Andie remembered. She'd once been so jealous of what Mark had with his family. He'd even had the fatherly support she'd never known.

She took the goggles and lifted them to her face. Instead of scanning the dunes, though, looking for a nesting logger-head, she watched the crowd, as Mark had. It was a relaxed group tonight. The men had played golf most of the day while the women had enjoyed a spa day. They would end tonight with a fire pit, s'mores, and more than likely, too much beer.

The majority of the wedding guests had arrived, but tonight was a wedding-party-only event—though a tour for other guests would follow this one. Tomorrow would con-sist of the rehearsal dinner, and then the bachelor and bachelorette parties.

And then the wedding.

There was little time left to do anything but wedding activities, but Andie would be finished with her duties for the day at the conclusion of the walk. She only hoped Mark wasn't interested in s'mores. She was itching to get him alone.

She was also upset with herself for making the decision not to mention Rob's lack of love to his soon-to-be bride.

The thought that she was the kind of a person who worried more about herself and her business than to help someone see the truth caused a weight to settle heavily in her chest, but she consoled herself with knowing that she was merely the service provider. It was not her job to counsel the couple on the intelligence of their decision to marry.

And maybe she wouldn't rot in hell for helping send a sweet girl like Penelope into a marriage with a cad like Rob.

"You okay?"

She could sense Mark looking down at her in the dark, and she pulled the glasses far enough away so she could see him. She nodded. "Just thinking about Penelope," she said. "And Rob."

Mark grunted. "He do anything else stupid while I was gone?"

"No." Though nothing would surprise her at this point.

She lifted the goggles again and focused on Rob and Penelope. They were walking hand in hand, but from what she could see, they weren't talking. Rob called out to one of his groomsmen and they talked a bit, but he said nothing to his bride.

The man was an ass. She should have maimed him years ago when he'd come on to her.

As she scanned the group, her gaze zeroed in on her mother and aunt, and she noticed something about Aunt Ginny that she hadn't before. She zoomed in on the woman's ankle and sucked in a short breath. She was wearing the matching ankle bracelet. The one that supposedly had a star to go with the moon on hers.

Apparently old wounds could heal.

She didn't know if she and her mother would ever completely get there, but knowing that the gap between her mother and aunt was being bridged did good things for her heart.

"I have a surprise for you," Mark murmured in her ear.

She glanced over and gave him a wicked smile. "Does it involve me and you and none of our clothes?"

Heat suddenly burned in his eyes, and she couldn't wait to get him alone. They might still have a tough conversation or two ahead of them—she deserved to know about his past after all they'd been through together—but talking was not the priority tonight.

She just wanted him.

He pulled her closer and heat from each of his fingers burned into her waist where he kept a tight grip on her. "That's a given, sunshine." His voice was low and throaty, and she began to tingle from the inside out. "But I actually had something else I wanted to give you first."

He reached into his pants pocket and pulled out a small Ziploc bag. "I shouldn't have it," he said as he held it out. "So I'm giving it back."

Curious, Andie exchanged the night-vision goggles for the bag, and she and Mark separated as she worked to see in the dark. There was something small and hard inside the bag. "What is it?" she asked.

She held it up, trying to make out the contents in the dark night while rubbing her thumb and fingers across the small shape. Then she realized what she was touching. It was the sea turtle charm he'd once given her. She caught her breath. The one Aunt Ginny had not returned with when she'd come back from Boston.

Andie turned to walk backward in the dark so she could see Mark. "You kept it? I thought it was lost." Then she whispered, "I thought it was fate telling me I didn't need the reminder."

He gave her an embarrassed shrug. "I didn't want to let you go. So yes, I kept it."

His words hurt. He sure had an interesting way of treating someone whom he didn't want to let go.

She faced forward again, thinking about the day he'd given it to her. It had been the beginning of their relationship. She'd taken a look at the small charm and had seen a man who "got" her. He'd asked her out a few times before that but had gracefully accepted her nos and backed off. Only that night he'd brought her something that had touched her heart.

He'd said her moon charm looked lonely, so he'd wanted to give her a new one to add to it. Then he'd looked at her as if he'd made a decision. One that meant he was in her life to stay. She'd known he wouldn't be hearing "no" that night. And that had been okay with her. She'd been so ready for him.

The fact that he'd picked the loneliest day in her life to do all this had seemed like a sign.

She'd probably fallen in love with him that very day.

Tucking the sadness from all they'd lost back inside, she gave him a tight smile. "Thanks for returning it. I always loved it."

The thought struck her that the first time he'd given her the charm, it had marked the beginning of their relationship. This time, it felt like the end. They might have a couple of days left, but that would be it.

She wouldn't do anything long-distance, and she especially wouldn't drag out a relationship that in the end would hurt her. Because whether she lied to herself or not, she knew that deep down she'd never gotten over him. She still loved him.

Her chest squeezed hard.

Life was so freaking unfair.

Mark hadn't changed…and she still wanted more out of life. Nothing was different. She would enjoy what time they had left. Then she would say good-bye.

They walked in silence a couple more minutes before Mark lifted the glasses and peered through them once again. She could tell he was people-watching instead of seeking out the elusive turtles.

"You're totally not getting the hang of what we're doing out here, you know?"

She saw his mouth curl up in a smile, and her heart thumped heavily.

Oh god, she loved him.

It already hurt.

Mark stopped walking and brought his other hand up to hold the goggles steady. Andie noticed his stance was feet shoulder-width apart, chest out, as if ready to defend against a threat. He seemed to have grown in size right before her eyes. And he looked intimidating. Before she could ask what he'd seen, he lowered the lenses and stared at her, his expression blank.

"What?" she asked, her voice a worried whisper.

He handed her the goggles and motioned with his chin. His jaw was clenched tight.

When she looked, she saw the problem immediately. Rob had separated from Penelope and was now walking alongside Wendy, several people back in the group. He kept bumping his shoulder into her as they walked, his head bent close. And Wendy was not shy with the giggles in response to whatever Rob was saying.

Andie sought out Penelope, up ahead of Rob and Wendy. She walked alone, her arms crossed over her chest, with the occasional worried look back as if trying to find Rob. Her looks coincided with the laughs bubbling from Wendy.

This did not look good at all.

EPISODE NINE

CHAPTER TWENTY

The screech of table legs scraping across the floor made Mark cringe. He then caught sight of Kayla hurrying from the back room at Gin's and shooing the man who'd made the noise out of the way.

"Pick it up," she told him. "Like this." She and a khaki-shorts-clad server hoisted the table and aligned it with two others where the bride and groom and their parents would later sit. "Pay attention to what you're doing, Owen. *Please.* We don't have time to scrub the scuff marks from the floor that scooting will cause."

Owen appeared sufficiently chastised. Poor guy. He looked to be about twenty, and as if he couldn't care less about marks on the floor. But the censure from Kayla did sting, apparently; the kid went back to work with his gaze lowered and an embarrassed glow burning from his ears.

Mark smiled. Young crushes were tough.

Kayla had to be at least ten years older than Owen, but Mark had caught him watching her every move each time she'd hurried through the room to direct the servers how to set up the dining area.

It was Friday afternoon, and Gin's had just shut down for a private event—the Masterson-Jordan rehearsal dinner.

That had to cost a pretty penny, shutting down the entire bar and restaurant. And from what he understood, the meal wasn't only for the wedding party but for all guests who'd shown up for the next day's wedding.

Which included his brothers and their families.

Mark looked at his watch. He sat at the bar, waiting for his cell to ring to let him know that the rest of his family was on the island.

He'd come over to the bar to offer help—since he'd been unable to get a minute with Andie all day due to her preparations for tomorrow's ceremony and reception. She'd been busy since the moment she'd climbed from his arms that morning, so he'd enjoyed time on the beach with the assorted wedding guests before deciding to head over to see if he could do anything here. Kayla had taken one look at him and suggested he have a seat and enjoy a beer.

Grinning, he'd done so. He liked the OCD woman. She got a lot done, and didn't mince words as she did it. Though he had yet to witness her being anything but polite. Even when she was lecturing Owen on the proper way to rearrange tables, she'd said *please*.

He leaned back against the bar and watched the action, thinking about the upcoming wedding. He'd avoided Rob since returning from Boston, and especially after seeing the man practically making moves on one of the bridesmaids last night.

There was so much wrong with what was going on with this wedding.

Rob was—had been?—his friend, but that didn't mean he felt right about not warning Penelope away. He wouldn't do it, of course. Doing so would hurt Andie. And he'd hurt her enough for a lifetime.

Now he was all about *not* hurting her—and instead, figuring out a way to do just the opposite. That meant Rob and his pathetic ways were being pushed to the side. Including the bachelor party scheduled for that night. Best man or not, Mark was skipping it.

Kayla had everything planned out anyway, including limos to take their drunk selves back and forth to wherever the party took them. Given that Mark and Rob had spoken no more than the stilted pleasantry since he'd knocked the guy on his ass, it seemed a good plan to make an excuse and sit this one out.

Plus, he intended to spend every minute he could with Andie.

They'd returned to the house the night before having seen no sign of a sea turtle. Nor had they joined the group at the fire pit for s'mores. The instant her bedroom door had closed behind them, they'd had each other's clothes off.

Then they hadn't come up for air for hours. And again, this morning. He closed his eyes as he thought about it.

They'd made love in total silence as the sun had risen, with her balcony doors thrown wide to the welcoming day. It had been one of the most intense experiences of his life.

He intended to have a similarly intense moment tonight.

He'd been moved out of the house earlier in the day, having been asked to stay in one of the bungalows for the remainder of his visit. He wasn't sure of the need for the move, but with the added privacy, he could see it only as a good thing. Given the way Andie clung to him each time they were together, he couldn't imagine not being able to persuade her to stay at the cabin with him.

They had less than two days left. He would make the most of the time.

He also intended to make sure *they* didn't end when he boarded a plane on Sunday.

Andie hadn't said anything about love yet, but he had to believe she still cared for him in that way. It came through in her every touch, her every look. And he was definitely still head over heels for her. He was pretty sure that had never changed. He'd only ignored the fact for the past four years.

That being the case, he was going for a commitment tonight. Before it was too late.

He had a moment of pause as he thought about the past with Andie, and then even further back to his teen years. Andie had accused him of having problems with marriage. Rob had reminded him he'd been responsible for Tiffany's death—as if he'd needed reminding.

Had that come into play in any way with him and Andie before?

He'd asked himself that several times over the past week. But no, it hadn't. What had happened to Tiffany was unforgivable. And it would always be there. Always be his fault. But it wasn't holding him back. He'd gotten beyond it. He'd moved on.

He and Andie would soon move on, too. They had to. He couldn't picture a world without her in it.

Maybe she wouldn't be able to follow him back to Boston immediately. She did have a business to run here, and she would need to take care of getting that in order before she could do anything else. But he wanted her with him as soon as possible. He'd missed her when he'd been gone earlier in the week. He wanted to love and protect her as he should have years ago.

It was all still there between them. He simply had to prove that he was the man for her. No matter how terribly he'd *not* proven that very thing years before.

"You planning to take up space here all afternoon?"

Mark opened his eyes to find Roni propped against the bar beside him. She had a salad in her hand and an evil eye trained on him. Her short black hair was once again exploding from her head.

"Am I in the way?" he asked. "I can get out. I was just waiting for a call." He looked at his watch and had the thought, *And wishing Andie were here with me.* He was such a sap. "Shouldn't the afternoon ferry have already arrived?"

Roni nodded and climbed onto the seat next to him. "Ten minutes ago."

That's what he'd thought. His phone should be ringing soon.

"What are you doing with Andie, Mark?" Roni leaned over the counter to grab a fork, then sat back down and dug into her salad. "Playing? Planning to break her heart?"

Mark swiveled around on his stool so they sat side by side, both facing the row of liquor bottles behind the bar. He could see her in the mirrored areas between the bottles, and watched her watching him.

"Planning to steal her away from us?" Roni asked.

"I'm not playing," Mark said, carefully choosing the words she had used. "Nor am I planning to break her heart."

Roni lifted a brow, silently asking her third question again.

He returned the look. "How would that one be any of your business?" he asked.

"You head out of here in less than forty-eight hours, right?"

Mark nodded. He did.

"Ginger and I will be left to pick up whatever pieces you scatter. I want to know what we're looking at." She chewed and swallowed another bite, then jabbed the fork toward the mirror, toward his reflection. "Plus, she's my friend, you arrogant prick. *That* makes it my business."

A smile fought to make its way out. He loved that Andie had friends like Roni. But he wasn't about to tell *her* that he was going to propose before Andie heard it herself.

He picked up the beer he'd been nursing for the last thirty minutes and took a long drink. When he set it down, he turned and faced Roni head-on. "I'm not going to hurt her," he said. "That's all you need to know."

With his words, he gave her a nod and stood. Time to find his brothers.

∼

Andie walked from the kitchen area of Gin's to stand behind the bar, where she surveyed the dining room. Kayla had done well. Cream-colored linens covered clusters of tables. Not overly elegant, but with a nice touch of class. Simple centerpieces stood with handfuls of fresh-cut flowers for each of the guests to take with them. Huge baskets of flip-flops, serving as party favors, sat by the patio doors. And candles were flickering everywhere.

As the sun set, the room, along with patio, would become an intimate setting.

On the wall behind the table where the bride and groom would be seated with their parents and grandparents, there was a family tree of photographs. The branches showcased both families separately, before coming together with Penelope and Rob mixed in among the members of the two families.

The collage made a lovely statement about two becoming one, and Andie suspected Penelope would love it. The bride's and groom's mothers had hatched the idea, then kept it a surprise from Penelope. They'd worked closely with Kayla over the past few days to create it.

If only it were for two people who were genuinely in love, it would be a treasured gift. As it was…

Andie shook her head. She would not think about seeing Rob flirt with Wendy the night before. Nor would she think about the fact she was going to do *nothing* to change the course of the upcoming events.

She had a photographer for *Today's Brides* in town—who'd arrived in time to attend the earlier rehearsal on the beach, one hundred of the couple's closest friends and relatives gathering, and nothing but beautiful weather ahead.

They were having a wedding.

And it was going to be spectacular!

Seaglass Celebrations would pull off an amazing event, and everyone would go home giddy from the happy times that had been had by all. Michael, the photographer, would extol the company's virtues to the magazine. And Seaglass's phone would soon be ringing off the hook.

And there would be no guilt for knowing that this wedding was a sham and Andie was doing nothing about it.

Well, not much guilt.

The outside door opened and the first of the guests arrived.

As the tall, good-looking blond came in, Andie was impressed. He stood straight and proud, and he had the short haircut that spoke of the military, but she couldn't remember having seen him before. Penelope stepped in behind him, bursting with excitement, and Andie got it. This was her brother. He'd been unable to make it to Georgia until now.

Andie gave Roni, who stood off to the side in a knee-length sundress and strappy wedges, a slight nod, and she headed to the piano to begin softly playing a medley of classical songs. At the same time, Andie stepped to the bartender and reminded him to go light on the alcohol.

"This bunch is going out later tonight for bachelor and bachelorettes parties," she told him. "We want at least a few of them sober by the time of the wedding tomorrow afternoon."

"Got it, boss." Kevin, the bartender, winked at her. "I might mix you up a strong one, though. You look wound a little tight."

"Don't you dare." Andie saw the photographer come through the door with the next batch of guests, and her nerves cranked up a notch. "I have too much riding on tonight."

Kevin chuckled, then turned to the first guest to approach the bar. The evening had now officially begun.

It was cocktail hour, and the family members and guests would take the time to meet and greet one another. Derrick, the chef she'd coerced from Chicago, would then serve a selection of his seafood specialties. He enjoyed the receptions because they were opportunities for him to try out new dishes. With many couples choosing buffet-style dinners, Derrick always included a unique dish or two.

Tonight would be plated dinners, however. And then a buffet of desserts, all pink—in honor of the bride.

Andie hurried to the kitchen to check on Derrick and the waiting servers. When she saw that Kayla was going over the schedule and assignments with the crew one last time, she knew all was fine. At least with this, she could take an easy breath.

She returned to the front at the exact moment that Mark walked through the door. He entered with Grayson McTavish, and though both men were striking—in their dark slacks and button-down shirts—she had eyes only for Mark.

Seemed he had the same issue.

He zoomed his gaze directly to her the moment he'd cleared the door, and she could tell from the glint in his eyes that he was not thinking about the next couple of hours. He was thinking about tonight.

They had two nights left together, and she'd had Kayla move him to a bungalow. She'd given his room to Michael.

She did not intend for him to spend his time there alone.

Mark came to her side immediately. She tossed him a quick glance and a soft smile, but then refocused on the room in front of her. So far everything was as it should be. Rob had arrived, and he and Penelope were giving the appropriate *oohs* and *ahs* over the family tree and other decorations, and had formed a receiving line of sorts to greet their guests as they arrived.

Michael was snapping pictures and jotting notes.

The wedding photographer was also there, taking his own set of photos.

"You've been busy today," Mark said, speaking softly so as not to draw attention to himself.

"I barely have time to remember to shower on the day before and day of a wedding."

"You can shower at my place," he murmured.

She couldn't help it, she turned to him. And then she got lost in the warmth of his gaze. And that's when she got it. It wasn't naughty thoughts he was thinking so much as heartfelt ones. The knowledge caused her anxiety to register another notch higher. She couldn't get swept away with promises he wouldn't keep.

"You like your new room?" she asked, returning to surveying the crowd. She didn't do a lot during these events, but was there with Kayla to oversee the details and handle any issues that might arise.

"It's spacious," Mark said. "And has a nice view of the ocean."

"You lucked out. One of the groomsmen went home sick this morning."

"Ah." He gave a small nod, which she noticed from her peripheral vision. "That explains the stand-in during rehearsal."

"The stand-in fit the tux." She laughed softly. "He's now the fourth."

Mark laughed with her and narrowed the gap between them. The heat from his body made her lean an inch closer.

She wanted to go away with him right that very moment. It was disconcerting how she couldn't seem to get enough of him.

She kept telling herself it was because she knew their time was limited.

He touched a hand to the small of her back and put his mouth to her ear. "I hope you plan to be in that space with me tonight."

She closed her eyes and enjoyed the closeness of the man she was pretending she hadn't fallen in love with. Heck, the man she'd never fallen *out* of love with. "I already packed an overnight bag," she whispered in return.

She turned her head to his, and the heat that filled his eyes was all she needed.

It might hurt when he left her on Sunday, but she was going to enjoy these next two nights to the fullest.

As she watched him, something over his shoulder caught her attention.

"Oh shit," she muttered.

Instead of following her gaze, Mark went still. "What is it?" he asked.

"Rob."

Mark's eyes closed on a sigh. "What the hell is he doing now?"

Andie casually glanced around, noting the photographer had not seemed to notice Rob standing off in the side hall. Or if he'd noticed, he remained focused on the crowd in the dining room instead.

Mr. Jordan had noticed, though. His gaze was trained on his future son-in-law. And on the bridesmaid he was standing with.

"He's flirting with Wendy again," Andie said through gritted teeth. "He's even leaning into her as they're talking. He has a hand braced on the wall above her head."

It was obvious they were having more than a hey-how-are-you-doing conversation.

"I'm going to say something," Mark told her.

"No." Andie reached out and put a hand to his chest. "Please don't cause a scene," she pleaded. "Michael from *Today's Brides*—"

"I won't." Mark picked up Andie's hand and pressed a kiss to the back of it. "I won't do anything to hurt your business. I'm simply going to suggest—*politely*—that he get back to his bride."

"Oh." Andie nodded. She let out a shaky breath. "Yeah. That will be okay."

She looked back at Phillip Jordan, to find him still watching. The man then glared in her direction, as if Rob's behavior were her fault.

"Phillip is not happy," Andie muttered. "Please get Rob away from that woman."

"Will do, babe."

Mark winked, then leaned in and pressed his lips against her mouth. Calmness engulfed her with the heat of his touch, and she closed her eyes. She could almost pretend they were somewhere else and she didn't have to worry about her company climbing or falling, depending on the outcome of a single event.

Then Mark pulled away, and she opened her eyes and remembered that she was in the middle of a party. And she was the host. She glanced at Phillip again. The man was still glaring.

Terrific. Another public display of affection on her part. She wondered if he would read her the riot act again.

Because if he did, she just might tell him where to shove it. She was pretty much tired of tiptoeing around the man.

Mark headed off to talk to Rob, and Andie caught sight of Rob's grandparents being ushered in by his parents. The elder couple had arrived only that afternoon, and had settled in at the inn to rest before this evening's dinner.

Andie crossed the room to greet them. As she did, she caught sight of Gray heading over to sit with Roni. Roni looked up from the keys of the piano, saw who'd sat down beside her, and gave him a wolfish smile. Andie watched for another minute, wishing she could keep things as simple as the two of them had.

They were just having fun. Gray would leave, Roni would not be hurt, and both of them would move on to their next adventure.

Andie shot a look at Mark.

He would leave, she would be crushed, and she had no idea if she'd ever have another adventure.

After greeting the Mastersons, Andie moved on to the Kavanaughs. The entire clan had come in as she'd been talking with Rob's family, and she couldn't help the huge grin as she approached them.

"Andie." The greeting came from Jonathan's wife. Though the woman was several years older, they'd gotten along like sisters from the moment they'd met. "It's so good to see you. Celeste has done nothing but brag on you for a week."

Hugs were shared all around, and Andie took a few moments to stand with them and reminisce. As they talked, she couldn't help but admire all the Kavanaugh men. Even the father, Wayne. Every one of them was dashing. With their dark hair and tall, broad frames, it would flutter a girl's heart to see this group walking down the street.

Before she could return to her post by the bar, Mark joined her. He casually slipped an arm around her waist as he chatted with his family, and she watched the expressions of his parents and brothers change. Eyebrows went up, his youngest brother, Eddie—though still a year older than Mark—grinned widely, and Celeste quietly studied Andie's face. It made Andie wonder if she thought Mark was pushing her again.

"Mark, this must be your family."

All eyes swiveled from Mark's hand on Andie's waist to the newcomer to the group. It was Penelope.

"Ah," Mark said. He removed his arm from Andie and beckoned Penelope into their circle. "The beaming bride."

Andie caught him toss a quick glance over Penelope's head, his gaze landing on Rob, who was standing with Gray near the head table. He then brought his attention back to Penelope.

"Let me introduce you," he said.

Penelope beamed and smiled prettily with the compliments handed out with each introduction, but when Mark got to Eddie, she reached forward and held out her hand.

"My friends call me Penny," she said.

Andie blinked. That was news. She hadn't heard even one of them call her Penny the whole two weeks. At the blank stares she was getting from both Andie and Mark, Penelope—*Penny*—giggled and blushed. She touched her hand to her cheek.

"I mean, I *wish* they would call me Penny. I've tried for years, but my parents always insist on Penelope, so…" She gave a little shrug, looking embarrassed now. "Everyone else seems to follow."

The moment seemed suspended for several long seconds, and then Eddie cracked the cutest smile as he took the hand Penelope was still holding out in front of him and brought it to his lips.

"Then I will call you Penny," he declared.

All eyes now turned to Eddie.

Wayne coughed into his hand. Ryan, the second oldest Kavanaugh son, locked his gaze on his brother's and Penny's hands still clasped in the space between them, and Jonathan finally elbowed Eddie in the side.

Eddie released Penny, and everyone let out a collective sigh of relief.

Penelope didn't seem to be in a hurry to leave, and since the evening wasn't at all about Andie, she quietly slipped away and returned to stand to the side of the bar, where she could once again observe.

Everyone seemed to be having a great time. With the restaurant filling up, it appeared most of the guests had arrived. Drinks were flowing freely, smiles and good humor were being passed around, and it was looking like the ladies of Seaglass could once again pat themselves on the back.

They had done well.

The main event was tomorrow, and then Andie would collect her bonus and head for the bank.

Seaglass was safe.

After that it would be only a matter of Andie figuring out if she wanted to continue with the position she held or if she preferred to hand off more responsibility to Kayla. Maybe there was another opportunity here on the island waiting for her. She enjoyed the startup more than the day-to-day work. Possibly that's where her talents lay.

She watched Mark laugh with his family, and couldn't help but smile along with them. She'd missed being a part of that group. They were good people.

"Ms. Shayne." Christopher Jordan approached, and Andie flicked her eyes over the solid frame of Penelope's brother. He did make an impression. "My sister tells me you're to blame for all of this."

Andie's eyes widened, but she kept herself from seeking out Rob. Had Penny's brother figured out that something wasn't right with the bride and groom? "Excuse me?" she asked.

Christopher's mouth turned into a crooked slash, and then he laughed, loud and hearty. His blue eyes took on a mischievous spark. Andie laughed along with him—though her laughter came more from nerves.

"I swear," he said. "I meant that in a good way. Penny has done nothing but sing your praises since I got here. I'm Chris. Her brother."

"Oh." Surprise colored Andie's voice at the compliment. "Thank you. She's a treat to work with. And please, call me Andie."

"You should have seen your face." He chuckled a bit more, his gaze teasing her, and then he cranked his smile brighter. She couldn't help but be flattered by the attention.

A large hand appeared between them at the same time another slid possessively across her back.

"Mark Kavanaugh," Mark said in greeting. He shook Chris's hand while keeping a firm grip on Andie. She glanced up at him. He was jealous?

Then she scanned Chris one more time from head to toe. Hell yes, he was jealous. This man was hot. And he'd been hitting on *her.*

The knowledge that it bothered Mark made her warm inside.

"I was just telling Andie here how pleased Penny is with everything."

Andie beamed, unable to keep from smiling just a tad too bright. She'd just discovered that jealousy was an aphrodisiac.

Mr. Jordan stepped beside his son, and all eyes went to him. Andie's growing passion took a nosedive. Mr. Jordan had mostly done nothing but glare at her since last Saturday's boat trip, and he wasn't falling short of that now.

"Can I talk to you privately?" he asked her. The words were polite, but his voice was hard.

No! she silently shouted.

"Sure," she answered instead. She glanced toward Mark, and when she did, her eyes caught on Rob and Penny, now standing in the hall. Rob did *not* have his arm casually propped on the wall above his fiancée as if looking for any excuse to get closer. And Penny did *not* look happy.

Their voices were too low to hear, but it was clear they were arguing.

Mark followed her line of sight and his jaw tightened.

What a few minutes earlier had felt like a successful event suddenly felt like a night snowballing downhill at a rapid pace. She swept her gaze over the crowd to find Michael with his camera trained toward the hallway.

Terrific. She could already imagine an eight-by-ten of a fighting bride and groom showing up in *Today's Brides* instead of photos showcasing Penelope's dazzling wedding dress and the elegant cake they would all have the next day.

"Ms. Shayne." Phillip Jordan's voice grew even colder, so she turned and followed the man, mentally making a face at his back. She was sick of him, too.

Once they stepped inside the kitchen, he stopped.

"What can I do for you, Mister—"

"It's what you can stop doing."

"I don't know—"

"You and your whole family." Rage spewed from the man to the point that she could barely make out his words, but Andie had no idea what had him so upset.

"If you'll explain the problem," she calmly began, "I'm sure we can figure out a solution."

Aunt Ginny chose that minute to walk through the area. She'd apparently arrived during the last half hour but had remained in the back. When she saw Andie and Mr. Jordan, she stopped as if a deer frozen in headlights. Andie could see her mother standing a few feet behind Aunt Ginny in a similar frozen state.

"*She* knows what the problem is," Phillip ground out, pointing to her aunt.

Andie turned to Ginny, at a loss for what to do. Then she watched her aunt's face turn a bright shade of pink.

Behind her, Cassie took on the same hue.

"What is going on?" Andie whispered to her aunt. She still had no idea, but the identical looks of guilt on Ginny's and Cassie's faces had her more than worried.

Mr. Jordan turned to her once again, his face red with fury. "Marilynn and I went out for our morning walk this morning at sunrise, and came upon these two." He glanced at Ginny and Cassie, and then turned a heavy scowl back to Andie. "They were in the water. Naked."

CHAPTER TWENTY-ONE

Mark pulled the rental into the small drive of the bungalow and shifted into park before turning to look at Andie. They'd finished the rehearsal dinner a while ago, most everyone had headed out in limos to continue the party, and Andie had spent the last hour trying to calm the Jordans. Apparently neither of them took kindly to walking up on skinny-dippers before their first cup of coffee of the day.

"I suppose you could look at it as a good thing," he suggested.

She focused a narrowed gaze on him. "How do you figure?"

"Your mother and your aunt seem to have gotten over their issues with one another."

Andie merely shook her head and made a sound of disgust. "What a blessing," she muttered. She shoved open the car door, so he followed on his side.

"Also, he could have brought it up first thing this morning," Mark added. "At least you didn't have to worry about it all day."

"So...what?" She held her hands up in the air as if in question, as she stood on one side of the hood with him on the other. "It's better to spring it on me in the middle of the rehearsal dinner? When I had a photographer there from *Today's Brides...and* Rob and Penelope were each either flirting with someone *else*, or arguing with each other?"

She had a point. It had been a tough night all the way around.

He reached toward her, and she pointed a finger at him. "And what was your brother thinking, flirting with the bride?"

Mark guffawed. "I think you've got that one backwards, sweetheart. 'My friends call me Penny,'" he mimicked. "What in the hell was that about? What was Eddie supposed to do?"

"Not chase after her all night like a dog with a new bone!" Andie just shook her head and began to move. They met in front of the car, and he slipped an arm around her shoulders.

Yeah, he thought. Eddie had done that. Things might have gone somewhat smoother if his brother hadn't become infatuated with the bride. The whole night had been a comedy of errors. Except none of it had been funny. And Mark had yet to be able to help Andie calm down.

"I'm sorry it was such a rough night for you, sunshine," he whispered, pressing a kiss to her ear. "But it's over now. Let's go down to the beach and listen to the ocean."

The water had always calmed her, so it seemed a good plan.

"I can hear the ocean from here," she grumbled. But she let him lead her around the small cabin to where he could make out the start of a path. The night was clear and the moon was almost full, so there was no need for a light.

Once they stood just feet away from the water, he felt her tension begin to drain away. He wrapped his other arm around her and shifted her to face him, then began to move slowly back and forth with her in his arms.

"I've wanted to dance in the moonlight with you since I saw you at Gin's two weeks ago," he whispered.

She pressed her cheek to his chest. "I wanted to kick you in the balls when I saw *you*," she murmured.

He both laughed and cringed. "If I recall correctly, you did."

He couldn't see her face but suspected she smiled. More tension was easing from her with each passing minute, and he suddenly found himself desperate to let her know how he felt. They only had two nights left, and though he had a whole seduction thing he'd played out in his head, he didn't want to wait another minute.

With her still cradled against his chest, he slipped a hand to her chin and caressed her soft skin. They stood there, continuing to sway in the dark until he finally tilted her face up to his. The moonlight glowed on her pale skin. He knew she was what he wanted for the rest of his life. There was no question in his mind.

He brushed his lips against hers and she shuddered in his arms.

"I love you," he whispered.

She stopped moving, and it was as if the ocean ceased movement at the same time. All went silent. He saw her throat rise on a swallow, and he suddenly feared that he'd moved too fast. Or that she didn't love him in return.

A tight knot formed in his stomach. The muscles of his legs became primed, as if ready to flee. All he could do was wait for her response. Finally, she blinked—slowly—and that seemed to release a pent-up breath he held.

"Andie?" he pleaded. "Say something."

She shook her head. "Just kiss me," she whispered. "Will you do that for now? Just kiss me?"

It would have to be enough.

He slid his hands into her hair, and fitted his mouth to hers. Her lips parted and he moaned against her, stroking his tongue along hers. She shook in his hands, giving him hope. He hadn't moved too fast. She just needed a moment to catch up.

When she wrapped her arms around him and flattened herself to his chest, he slid his hands down her back to hold her close. "You feel good against me, babe. I want to make love to you. Out here," he suggested.

Her eyes shone bright for just a second, but then she stepped back and shook her head. "Not out here," she said. "There's been too much 'exposure' today already. Plus," she continued, gesturing with her head toward the cabin, "Wendy's bungalow is on the other side of this one. She's not of a fan of noise from her neighbors. I'm sure she wouldn't appreciate a peep show, either."

Mark glanced in the general vicinity of the bungalow, glad they'd called it a night before the rest of the group. He wanted Andie alone for a bit. Without the prying ears of her family, without a tasteless bridesmaid next door, and without anything else taking up space in her head. He wanted it to be just the two of them in every sense.

So he followed her inside, inhaling the scent of flowers trailing after her.

He wanted her to tell him she loved him.

Once inside she let her purse slip from her shoulder to the floor and turned to him. Heat exploded between them as they kissed, each delving deep inside, intent on uncovering hidden secrets.

When they finally broke apart, he sucked in a steadying breath. "You do things to me, babe. Things that I like."

She gave him a soft smile. She didn't say anything, but he had the thought she was thinking she liked those things, too. Then she pulled her top off over her head and turned toward the hall leading to the bedrooms.

Mark followed her into the master bedroom, and Andie's insides quivered. She hadn't expected him to say he loved her. Not like that. And not with such vulnerability. It had taken everything she had not to say it back.

But until she knew where this was going, she couldn't repeat those words. She had to protect herself. Had to hold on to something that could be her only lifeline. Otherwise, he'd have her on the next plane out of there with him, and she'd forget everything she'd learned over the years.

She faced Mark and dropped her skirt to her ankles. "Make love to me," she urged him, her words soft.

He didn't hesitate. He swept her into his arms and kissed her hard, his hands roaming down her body. Then he held her high against his chest and turned them to the bed. He laid her gently on the queen mattress, and stood staring at her in the light filtering in through the window, and she had no doubts that he loved her. It was so clear on his face.

Needing to protect herself or not, she couldn't let him be there alone.

"I love you, too," she whispered. The sheer pleasure that covered his features was enough for now. To know that she had that effect on him.

She held out her hands and reached for him, hope beginning to leak into her for the first time in four years. She loved him. She wanted to be with him.

She wanted forever.

Mark slipped out of his clothes and covered her with his body. He then lavished attention on every single inch of her. When he had her out of her mind with pleasure, he slipped on a condom and quietly entered her.

They both held still, he with his arms braced on either side of her head, his chest lifted off her as she peered up at him in the darkness. Her heart thundered at the love she saw reflected back, and she gave a little nod. They could figure this out. She loved him. He loved her.

After all these years, it was still there.

Mark moved his hips then, and a naughty smile inched up his face. He rocked hard against her and she sucked in a breath. She would never get enough of him.

"We don't have anyone listening to us tonight, babe," he teased. "I might have to make you scream."

She had a flash of a vision of the two of them trying to quietly make love while small kids slept in another room. Their kids.

Oh, hell.

"Just love me, Mark," she whispered. A tear slipped from the corner of one eye, but she ignored it. Mark saw it, though, and pressed his mouth to the lone track it had made.

"I'm going to love you forever, sunshine."

She closed her eyes with the flood of emotions and felt several more tears slip free.

Mark continued moving against her. Slowly. Reverently. There were no sounds made save for the soft moans that occasionally escaped. His lips and hands left her with zero doubt how he felt, his body connecting with hers in a way she hadn't imagined ever feeling again. And she opened her heart and let in all the hope she'd been afraid to dream of.

They would figure this out.

"I love you," she whispered again.

Mark pushed up off her and stared down into her eyes. He nodded and pressed a soft kiss to her lips. "And I love you."

～

Sometime later the sound of car doors woke her, and Andie blinked her eyes open in the darkness. Mark lay beside her, one arm thrown over her waist and his head tucked in against her neck, and Andie stared up at the ceiling as the fear began to creep back in. Had she given him too much? Was she going to get hurt?

She could hear laughter coming from next door as she closed her eyes. Apparently Wendy had not come back alone.

Good.

Maybe that would keep her off Rob long enough for him to get married.

Mark groaned in his sleep and rolled over onto his back, and Andie could sense when he became alert of his surroundings. The muscles in the arm lying against her tightened slightly, and then he turned his head and looked in her direction.

She did the same. She smiled at him in the dark.

There was enough light coming through the uncovered window that she could make out the planes of his face and the curve of his mouth as he peered back at her.

"I have something for you," he murmured.

He reached across her to the bedside table and opened the drawer. Then he switched on the lamp, and she squinted in the glare.

"Did you have to do that?" she groaned. She'd rather go back to sleep and wait until morning to face the facts. She'd told him she loved him, but nothing about them was different.

Mark pressed a quick kiss to her mouth, and she peeked at him. He looked so happy. It eased a bit of the stress building inside her. Maybe they *could* figure this out.

When he returned to lying on the bed beside her, both of them now on their backs, he held one hand up above them.

And that was when she saw it.

He had his thumb and forefinger pinched together and between the two was a large, emerald-cut ruby flanked by a row of baguette diamonds. She'd pointed that ring out to him once—years ago—and had said that she would love to get married with a ring like that one day.

When they'd gotten engaged, he'd given her his grandmother's ring instead.

Tears filled her eyes. "I don't understand," she said.

Mark turned on his side and propped himself up on his fist. He kissed the corner of her eye. "I want you to marry me, Andie. I never should have let you go before. I messed up."

Wetness streaked from her eyes to her ears. "Why do you have this ring?"

"I'd gotten it for you back then. You wanted it."

"But you wanted me to wear your family ring."

It hadn't been an argument between them, but it had hurt her feelings that he'd thought the ring she wanted wasn't right for their marriage.

"I was wrong," he said. "I knew that. So I bought it for you."

She shook her head as she stared up at him and tried to follow his train of thought. "You never gave it to me."

Shame flitted briefly across his features. "It's why I stopped at our apartment that day. The morning of our wedding."

Oh. She got it now. "You were bringing this to me before the wedding?"

"Yes." He nodded. "I had finally figured out that we couldn't get married with you wearing the wrong ring."

"Your grandmother's ring was beautiful." And it had been. It had also held three times the diamonds this one did, and was very traditional. Not exactly her style.

"But this is the one you loved," Mark told her. "It's the one that suited you. It took me a while, but I finally understood that."

And then, instead of giving it to her, he'd sent Rob to the church to call off their wedding.

Andie sat up, not touching the ring.

She turned to him. "So you just want to give it to me now? And what? Start back up as if we didn't miss a day?"

The accusation was probably unfair, but the moment she'd realized what he held, his mother's words had come back to her. He was pushing her again. They hadn't solved any of the issues between them, and he hadn't bothered to explain his past.

He'd just presented her with the ring and expected her to swoon.

"That's not what I'm saying," he said. Worry began to lace his voice. "I know we can't just go back."

Mark picked up her hand and slid the ring onto her finger.

"I want to go forward." His eyes were blue and solid tonight. And pleading. "I want to marry you, Andie. I want you by my side. Forever."

Andie sat there and stared at the ring he'd put on her finger, and then closed her eyes. She pulled in a slow breath. This was not going right at all. She wanted to marry him. She knew that with all of her heart. But not like this. They still weren't talking, hadn't communicated enough to know anything more than that the chemistry was still burning bright between them.

And he would expect her to pack her bags and simply follow him back to Boston.

Then what? Be the good little wife he'd wanted before?

But she didn't even know what *she* wanted.

She opened her eyes and looked at him, and slowly shook her head.

CHAPTER TWENTY-TWO

Panic exploded inside Mark as he watched Andie shake her head back and forth.

This could not be happening.

He sat up quickly and reached out to stop the movement of her head.

"Babe," he spoke quickly. "We can do this. We can make this work."

"Mark, you haven't even explained anything. We had issues. *You* had issues. You walked away on the most important day of our lives without so much as a good-bye."

She shook her head again, and reached for the ring, but Mark stopped her, clasping his hand around hers. "I'm talking now," he said. "Whatever you want to know, I'm talking. I'm sorry I did it backwards. I screwed up. But I love you. I *want* to be with you forever."

"And I want to know why you have issues with marriage."

He did *not* have issues with marriage! He clenched his jaw.

"Why did Beth leave you?" Andie asked. "What did you do to make that happen?"

He breathed in and out through his nose. Okay, he could start there. Beth was easy. He could explain that.

"I didn't love her the way a man should love a woman he plans to marry," he stated bluntly.

Andie eyed him. "Then why did you get engaged?"

"Because we were good friends. We had been since we were kids. Our families have known each other forever."

"I thought her name sounded familiar," she softly mused. "I probably heard it mentioned at some point. Did you date her when you were younger, then?"

He shook his head and squeezed her hand, terrified to let it go. He liked the look of that ring on her finger.

"We went to a lot of the same functions in our teens and college years," he said. "But then she moved away. She came back a couple years ago. We ran into each other at one of Mom's fund-raisers and started going out."

Andie was silent as she digested his story. She then peeled his hand from hers and stood to begin gathering her clothes.

"Rob said she had the right prestige," she said, not looking at him as she stepped into her underwear.

"She had the last name Rob would have been impressed with," he pointed out. "That had nothing to do with me. Beth and I were friends, neither of us married. And I thought she…" He paused but then plowed ahead. No sense worrying about being sensitive now. "I thought she'd make a good wife and mother."

Andie pulled her underwear up, watching him now, then tossed his to him. "So she didn't work?" she asked.

Mark coughed out a short laugh, knowing the answer would shock her.

"What?" Andie scowled at him. "Don't laugh at me."

"Oh, babe," he murmured. He stood and began dressing. "I would never laugh at you. I'm simply laughing at the situation. Beth is an engineering professor at MIT. She's one of the most intelligent people I know. And no, she was not willing to give that up to stay at home. Nor did I ask her to."

"Then I don't understand," Andie started.

"I never wanted you to quit your job, Andie." He spoke to her across the bed. "I just wanted you to stay home with me on occasion."

"And Beth would have done this?"

"She had professor hours. They were set. She might occasionally get lost in the lab for an evening, but generally speaking she was finished at a regular hour each day." Plus, he hadn't loved her as much. He hadn't worried about her as much.

Andie nodded, digesting the information. Mark could see she was processing his words.

"What would make her such a great mother, then?" she finally asked. She had her skirt and bra on now, and was headed to the living room for her shirt.

He followed, shrugging into his own shirt as he went. "She was an older sister," he said. "Two siblings. I'd been around her a when she was younger, so I knew she was nurturing."

"So you asked her to marry you simply because you wanted a wife and family?"

He gave her an unwavering look. "I want what my parents have. What my brothers have. It feels right."

"Yet you left me at the altar when I was offering that same thing."

He didn't break contact at her statement. Yes, that's exactly what he'd done. Other than what he'd already told her, he had no other excuse. He didn't know what else he could say.

After a minute of silence, Andie asked, "You did something to push her away, right? So the marriage got called off," she said. "She may have dumped you, but it was your fault."

"Yeah." He nodded. "It was my fault. The first problem started when we were supposed to be looking for wedding venues," he admitted.

"What happened? You refused get involved?"

"Not exactly." He was almost embarrassed to admit the truth. "But instead of locations, I started looking up you."

Her eyes widened. "She discovered this, I take it?"

He gave her a tight smile. "Yeah, she discovered it. When I told her I was just wondering. You know, because I'd never talked to you after. She was fine with that. She understood."

"But then you did it again?" Andie asked.

He lifted a shoulder. "Then I did it again. Every time I was supposed to be looking up location venues, I Googled you instead. I wanted to see what you'd been up to. What you were doing. I was floored to find you here instead of at some high-pressure financial job in the corporate world. You'd seemed so sure that kind of world was what you wanted."

"Yeah, well." She walked across the living room, with her back to him. "People change."

"But why did you?" he asked.

She turned to him and answered his question with one of her own. "Do you really think I did? You never thought that job was right for me anyway." She laughed. A dry, brittle sound. "Come to find out, Aunt Ginny didn't, either. So yeah…maybe I didn't change. Maybe I just moved here and figured out that that life wasn't me."

"Is that what happened?"

She shook her head. "Nope," she said. "Takes more than that to get through my thick skull. After I was fired, I moped around for a couple weeks, and then I realized I was thrilled not to have to go back. But I didn't get that it was the job and not the company I was glad to be escaping. I sent out résumés, but nothing stuck." She shrugged and looked away. "So I talked Aunt Ginny into turning the house into a bed-and-breakfast."

Mark opened the refrigerator and pulled out two sodas. He handed one to Andie and drank part of the other while he waited, figuring she had more to say.

"I sent out résumés again six months later," she added. "This time I got a couple interviews. One in Cincinnati. Not far from my mom. I could have proven my worth there, I was certain."

"What happened?"

She barked out another hollow laugh. "I couldn't get a job. No one would hire me."

That had to have stung. Especially since she'd wrapped her self-worth around her career.

"So I came back here and talked Aunt Ginny into doing weddings."

"Seems every 'no' opened another door for you."

"Who knows?" She shrugged and took a sip of the soda. "I bought the bar after a short stint at an insurance company in Columbus a year later. At the end of my three-month trial period, we all agreed to go our separate ways. So I came back here and I haven't left again."

"What happened last year?" he asked.

She met his gaze over the top of her drink. "What do you mean?"

"Didn't you tell me you talked Ginny into the bungalows last year? What happened to make you do that?"

She lowered the can, and her teeth came out to gnaw at her lip.

"Andie?"

She shook her head. "I don't want to tell you."

He had no idea what it possibly could have been, but he tried for a teasing smile. He wanted to hear it. And he wanted to lighten the mood. "It can't be that bad. Come on, I'm telling you my secrets. You tell me yours," he cajoled.

She blinked her eyes several times then shifted her gaze away from him. Her chest rose and fell with a sigh. "I saw your wedding announcement in the paper," she stated flatly.

Oh.

His chest expanded as he realized she'd been thinking about him about the same time he'd been thinking about her.

Fate.

It had to be.

"So what was problem number two?" she asked.

"What?"

"You said, 'first problem, Beth caught you looking me up.' What was problem number two?"

He drained the soda, taking his time to do so. Trying to steel himself to admit the rest. He had to show her how bad he could let someone down.

"Beth knew about what had happened with Tiffany," he finally said. "Because she'd known me back then."

Confusion clouded Andie's face. "Tiffany?"

"The girl Rob mentioned on the boat."

Andie's eyes went wide. "The girl he said you..." She paused as if not wanting to say the word. He didn't want her to say it, either. Finally, she stepped closer and looked him straight in the eyes. "Killed?"

Mark's chest tightened.

"Right." He nodded. The girl he had killed. His mouth grew dry. "Beth had known me back then, and she had the thought that I was letting what happened in my past impact my life. My relationships."

He didn't point out that Beth had said basically the same thing that Andie had. That he had issues with marriage. Neither of them knew what they were talking about. He plunged ahead, not giving Andie time to jump in.

"I'm not," he declared. "I got over the past long ago. It has nothing to do with now. But with that in Beth's mind, along with her seeing that there was an issue still lingering with you"—Mark paused—"she walked. Said she could do better. And hell, she could. She did. She's found someone now, and I couldn't be happier for her. She and I never should have gotten together in the first place."

He'd been settling, but he'd never disgrace Beth by admitting that out loud. She remained a good friend, if nothing more.

Andie carefully lowered herself to the couch and rubbed the spot beside her as if beckoning him across the room. "So what happened?" Her voice was soft and gentle, as if she suspected he needed to be handled with kid gloves. "With Tiffany?"

Mark sat next to her and grabbed hold when she reached for his hand.

"I was seventeen," he started. "Tiffany was sixteen. She was my first 'real' girlfriend. She was..." He paused and pictured Tiff as she'd been then. She'd smiled all the time. "She loved life. She was impulsive, and would try or do anything. I loved being around her. And somehow I talked her into going out with me."

"I've seen pictures of you at that age," Andie said wryly. "I'm sure it wasn't a hardship to go out with someone like you."

"But that's just it. She wasn't *like* me." He was embarrassed to say the next words. "Moneywise," he muttered. "She went to my school on a scholarship, and it embarrassed her that I was interested in her. She always told me she didn't fit into my life." He gave Andie a pointed look. "Like another woman I met years later."

Andie gave him a small, acknowledging smile and then squeezed his hand, silently encouraging him to continue.

"We'd been dating a few months, and I swear, every time I picked her up, her father would get this look on his face." Mark mimicked the stern look the man had worn. "He'd put a hand on my shoulder, and never take his eyes off mine. And he'd tell me, 'She's your responsibility when she's with you, son. You make sure you always bring my little girl home safe and sound.'"

Mark stopped and sucked in a breath before he continued. He hadn't thought about Mr. Avery in a while, but he could still see him in his mind—looking Mark straight in the eye as if he believed that Mark was as responsible as any other grown-up in the world. Mark had believed it, too. Tiffany *had* been his responsibility. He was the man. The protector.

He'd let her down.

He turned loose of Andie and rose. It felt as if he had a sock lodged in his chest. He'd never told anyone this story before. Many people knew it. They'd been around when it had happened. But he'd never said the words out loud.

"I picked her up one night, intending to take her to a party that one of my friends was having. It was summer, so we could stay out later. She didn't want to go. Said she would be uncomfortable there. But I pushed her. I wanted to go. I was certain she'd have a good time."

He paused, his thoughts going back almost fourteen years to that night. He'd been such a fool.

"I drank a few beers and that pissed her off. We argued, and she wanted to leave. So I agreed, but she had to drive. I was in no shape." He crossed to the kitchen and tossed his empty soda can, then got a bottle of water from the fridge. "But I couldn't have her drop me off at home and drive away with my car. My parents would have known I'd been drinking. So I had her take me to a friend's house. He lived in an area she'd never been to before. And it was so dark that night. It had been raining." He shook his head with regret. "I was too drunk to care the way I normally would have."

He stood in the middle of the floor and faced Andie, his gaze meeting hers with shame.

"I didn't find out until the next morning," he said. "After I sobered up and went looking for my car. She never even got out of the neighborhood. She took a curve wrong. Went too fast—probably because she was still mad at me. Hit water and hydroplaned. And wrapped herself around a tree. She died on impact."

∾

Andie stared at Mark, unblinking, her heart aching at the agony written across his face. He'd been carrying such guilt all these years.

Guilt that he didn't deserve.

But guilt she could tell he'd held on to tightly.

No wonder he struggled to take that final step into marriage. How responsible would he feel for a wife? Kids of his own?

Her heart bled for his pain.

"You really believe her death was your fault?" She needed to help him understand that it was an accident. He was not to blame. If she couldn't, they didn't stand a chance.

Dark eyes locked on hers. The grief had lessened, and all that was left was acceptance. "Of course it was my fault. I took her out that night. I was supposed to get her home safely."

"But Mark. You were drunk. You did the *right* thing by not driving her home."

"I shouldn't have been drinking," he stated.

Still, accidents happened all the time. "But—"

"Don't." He set down the bottle of water that he was still holding, untouched. "I didn't tell you so you could try to convince me it wasn't my fault. It was. But I've moved on. It doesn't affect me. It is a part of who I am, though, and I should have told you about it years ago. Before I ever asked you to marry me. If I wanted you to share things with me, I should have done the same."

"That was part of our problem," she whispered. "Neither of us realized we needed to share."

Mark nodded, the line of his mouth grim. "I'd have to agree." He gave her a quick wink, clearly trying to ease the tense moment. "But we know better now. We're going to do it different this time around."

He really thought there was nothing standing in their way. But they couldn't go *anywhere* if he didn't move on from his past.

She took a deep breath, knowing he wasn't going to like what she was about to say. But for his sake, she had to do it. "I'm with Beth on this," she calmly told him.

Mark's chin angled down at her and his eyebrows went up. "How so?"

"I think Tiffany factors into your issues with marriage." She gave him a tight smile, hoping to ease the sting of the words, and stood from the couch. "With your inability to make that final commitment."

A muscle jerked in his jaw. "I don't have an issue with commitment, Andie."

"Yet you walked before for no good reason."

"I think we've both clarified that neither of us was ready then. We both had issues."

She gave him a nod. "Agreed. But mine came from not being sure of who I was. Yours stemmed from the fact that you're afraid to get married. You're afraid to take on the responsibility of a family."

"Like hell I am." He stomped across the room, passing close in front of her.

Andie stayed where she was and silently watched him. They weren't going to be able to get beyond this. She'd known it all along. It was as if she could literally feel her heart rip in two. Her eyelids fluttered closed for a few seconds, but she did not let herself double over in pain.

She was better than what he was offering her, and she was going to prove it. She would prove it to her aunt and to her mother, but more important, she would prove it to herself.

"Why didn't you show up at the church that day, Mark?" she prodded him, wanting him to admit the truth.

"I told you, the phone. I thought you were using me."

"No." She shook her head. "Not good enough. You knew I loved you. Why didn't you show up?"

"Because I heard you—"

"I said no. That answer won't cut it. If that was all there was to it, you would have opened your mouth and asked me what was going on right then. Why didn't you show up?"

He stared at her, furious. His nostrils flared with his breaths.

"Was I not good enough?" she asked.

"That's bullshit, and you know it."

"Did you not want me to have a job?"

"I already told you—"

"Then *why*?" she stressed.

He gritted his teeth as he fought with his emotions, a muscle working back and forth in his jaw. And then he slowly crossed the room to her. He leaned down and got in her face, his breath hot, his tone harsh. "I couldn't take care of you, all right? Is that what you want to hear? I couldn't take care of you. You were out all hours of the night. I never knew when you were coming home. When you would be out on the streets. I couldn't make sure that you were okay. I couldn't let you die like I let Tiffany."

Mark went silent, and so did Andie. They stared at each other.

"And that," she whispered, tears shaking her voice, "is the issue. I don't need taking care of, Mark. I'm a grown woman. And I am not your responsibility."

"I didn't say you were."

"You treated me that way."

"I treated you like I loved you."

"You hurt me," she told him.

His gaze flickered, then relocked on hers.

"When you didn't show up," she told him. "You hurt me. Bad."

He remained silent.

"And you took advantage of me. You thought you were more important. You always did. Your job versus my job. Your family versus my family."

She picked her purse up from the floor, where she'd let it drop when they'd come in. Then she stood straight, her spine stiff, and said the things she should have said to him four years ago.

"Did it ever occur to you that the reason you didn't know much about my family is because you never asked me? I asked all kinds of questions about yours. I wanted to get to know them. I *did* get to know them. You?" She shrugged, implying he couldn't have cared less. "You didn't bother."

She shook her head slightly, forcing the pain to stay inside for a few more minutes. At least until she got out of there. "I deserved so much more from you, and I especially deserved to have you come to that church and tell me you were too chickenshit to get married.

"What I did *not* deserve," she continued, getting heated and letting her voice rise, "was having Rob show up and offer me a 'good time' since you couldn't make it. He said one night with him and I wouldn't cry over you for a second."

Mark opened his mouth as if to speak, but she didn't let him.

"So, no…" Her voice was loud now. If Wendy wasn't passed out asleep next door, she could probably hear every word. "I will *not* toss away my life and head on up to Boston just hoping you'll grow a pair and marry me someday. I have a family, too. Maybe we haven't been as close as yours over the years, but they're mine. And I'm not going to walk away from them when they need me just because you got a whim that you might want me around."

"Andie—"

"I need more from you, Mark," she stated. Her voice was calm again. "Or I need nothing."

She didn't let the tears fall. She would not give him that.

She slipped the ring from her finger and set it in the middle of the kitchen table, then walked quietly out the back door. It wasn't that far of a walk to the house, and with any luck, she'd have all her tears out before she got there.

As she stepped off the deck and her feet touched the sand, movement at the next cabin snagged her attention. The door had opened and light from inside spilled out.

In the frame of light stood Rob and Wendy. Kissing.

When they parted, Rob tucked in his shirt and zipped up his pants, then laid another one on Wendy and headed off the back deck and across the sand.

Son. Of. A. Bitch!

There was no way in hell Andie was letting Penny marry that man. Screw the business.

EPISODE TEN

CHAPTER TWENTY-THREE

Andie sat with her arms folded in her lap, shoulders hunched in, and lowered her head to the granite countertop of the kitchen island. She turned her cheek to the cool hardness and closed her eyes, pretending she was moaning as loud as she was hurting inside. Pain hit her from too many directions.

She'd lost Mark again. For the last time.

She would *never* let herself get caught up in his life again. She couldn't handle the pain. The ache in her chest was suffocating her.

And she had to cancel the wedding.

A two-second groan slipped free before she could stop herself. There was also the matter of the house...and the lack of bonus.

Reality was, Penny could choose to go ahead with the wedding. But Andie didn't believe for a minute that would happen. Not after she told her what she'd witnessed last night. Which she would soon have to go upstairs and do.

The other reality was that she wouldn't lose the house, either. She'd decided overnight to take her mother up on her offer of money. Only, it would be a loan. And *only* until she could sell the bar and pay her back. It had to be done. Because she would not lose Aunt Ginny's house.

She groaned at the thought. It was *her* house.

Well, she wouldn't lose that, either.

But it still felt like Aunt Ginny's house, and Andie suspected it always would.

She peeked her eyes open as daylight slashed through the back windows and landed on her face. The sun had risen outside, and it looked to be a glorious day.

Soon she'd have to go upstairs and start the torture of the day to come.

She wanted to catch Penelope before she had more than the briefest moment to think that this was about to be the best day of her life.

Instead, Andie would help her face reality.

Men were jerks. They either thought only of themselves, or they were cheating bastards—who thought only of themselves.

She let a moan slip free and closed her eyes again. She rolled her head until her forehead rested flush with the countertop.

Everything hurt so much.

A soft swish registered as the side door slid open, but Andie didn't lift her head to see who it was.

Her heart thumped hard as she wondered if it might be Mark, and she squeezed her eyes shut even tighter. Frustration choked her as tears leaked from between her lashes. She'd thought she would be dry inside by now.

She held her breath. Waiting. Hoping whoever it was didn't see her there.

Hoping it was Mark.

He hadn't even followed her outside last night. Hadn't tried to stop her.

Not that doing so would have done any good.

"Andie." The voice was soft, sounding shocked to find her bent over in the kitchen. It wasn't Mark. Thank goodness. "What is it, dear? Are you okay?"

Andie lifted her head—with her swollen eyes—and looked at her mother. Then she cried some more.

"Oh, baby." Her mother rushed to her side and wrapped both arms around her, holding her tight and resting her head against Andie's shoulder. Aunt Ginny stepped into the kitchen behind Cassie. Both women were wearing swimsuits and cotton cover-ups.

"I'll fix you some tea," Aunt Ginny stated matter-of-factly.

"Please tell me you weren't skinny-dipping again," Andie groaned. She did not want another argument with Phillip Jordan loaded onto her plate that morning.

"Oh, pish posh," Aunt Ginny said. She waved a hand in the air, unconcerned. "That man needs to loosen up and try something like that himself. Maybe if he did, his wife wouldn't go around wearing such a pinched expression all the time."

Andie merely stared at her aunt. Oh, geez. They'd done it again.

"And *no*," Aunt Ginny added as she filled a pot with water and pulled down bags of chamomile tea. "We did *not* go skinny-dipping this morning. Not that it should be a problem where we were yesterday anyway. We were as far away from the house and bungalows as we can get on the property. That man just has a stick up his butt."

Yes, he did. But Andie could see not wanting to walk up on two sixty-something-year-old women in their birthday suits first thing in the morning, either.

"As soon as this wedding is over, we're going to get you out there with us," Ginny told her. She turned then, and studied Andie with a concerned look, her voice losing some of its no-nonsense attitude. "We need to loosen you up, too," she added softly.

Meaning, *We need to help you forget.*

Aunt Ginny didn't have to ask, she knew that Mark had broken her heart. She gave Andie a gentle I'm-sorry-but-I-still-love-you smile, and Andie was grateful. Aunt Ginny would always be there for her.

Her mother lifted her head off Andie's shoulder and smoothed Andie's hair back out of her face. "What happened, sweetheart?" she crooned.

Andie looked at her mother. When had Cassie become this person?

"Did Mark do something?" she asked.

Andie couldn't speak. Her throat had closed shut. She simply nodded. Aunt Ginny joined them, and they all three spent the next couple of minutes hugging it out. Andie cried even more.

When the tears finally ended, Aunt Ginny handed Andie a wad of tissue, and Cassie found a cloth and wet it with cold water. She then wiped the tears from her daughter's face and dabbed the cool cloth against Andie's swollen eyes.

Andie felt as if she'd dropped through a rabbit hole. This was not the same woman who'd shown up barely a week ago.

"What are you doing, Mom?" Andie asked in a tired voice. After no sleep, and along with everything else that had happened the night before, she didn't have the energy to work on polite.

Her mother pulled her hand back, a stricken look her face. "I'm just trying to help. Am I doing it wrong?"

Andie's chest filled with pressure. "Oh, God. No, you aren't doing it wrong. It's perfect. But I mean...*what are you doing*? Here? You're changing." Andie shook her head. "I'm just...confused."

Her mother and her aunt's gazes met across the room before Aunt Ginny gave a slight nod to her sister. Ginny pulled the teapot from the stove and poured three cups of steaming water over tea bags, and then the two women sat down on either side of Andie.

Cautiously, Cassie reached out and took one of Andie's hands. "Your aunt and I have talked a lot this week, Andie."

Andie wanted to tell her to hurry it up and get on with it. Instead, she just sat there. She was too tired to speak. And didn't want to come off more impolite than she already had.

"I want to move here," her mother said in a rush. "Permanently."

The world tilted under Andie's seat. She looked at her aunt. "And you're good with this?"

Ginny nodded. "I'd like it very much."

Andie could see that she would. Her aunt was typically a happy woman anyway, but she'd been different this week, too. She looked more content. Pleased with the world. It floored Andie to think that her mother had put that look on someone's face, but she couldn't begin to understand the power of sisterhood.

The other thing that struck her was the realization that she wanted her mother there as well.

Suddenly, there was a bright spot to the day. She may have had her heart crushed to tiny pieces, but she was going to get the chance to build a relationship with her mother. She would work on herself, and she would work on her and her mom.

And she just might get up the nerve to go skinny-dipping.

She gave her mother a hug. "I would like that, too," she whispered.

The look on Cassie's face was priceless. A smile that seemed more relaxed and genuine than any Andie had ever witnessed appeared, and the lines that only a week ago had made her mother seem old were now adding to her look of joy.

Andie couldn't yet imagine the three of them under the same roof day in and day out, but it was an adventure she was willing to take on. One she found she *wanted* to take on.

"So tell us what happened with Mark." Aunt Ginny redirected the conversation back to Andie's heartache. "What did the idiot do this time, and how hard do your mother and I need to kick his butt?"

Cassie dabbed at Andie's swollen eyes once more as if uncertain what else to do. "The way you were getting along, I'd thought you two might figure it out this time."

Andie thought about nodding. She'd thought they might figure it out, too. But deep down, she'd known she shouldn't get involved with him. She'd just wanted so badly to make it work.

And she had this really hard time saying no to him.

She pictured the ring he'd slid on her finger last night. She still couldn't believe he'd bought it back then, or that he'd kept it all this time. He must have gotten it when he'd gone back to Boston earlier in the week.

She spread her hand flat on the counter and looked down at the bare ring finger. "He gave me a ring," she finally told them. "One I wanted four years ago."

Ten seconds ticked off the second-hand of the round-faced clock hanging beside the door. It seemed overloud in the silent room.

With a *hmph*, Ginny muttered, "The jerk."

Andie chuckled lightly, knowing her statement made no sense. She watched her aunt pull the teabags from all of their cups.

"*And*," Andie continued, "he asked me to marry him. How about that? Out of the blue, he gives me the ring I'd once imagined owning, tells me he loves me, and asks me to marry him. But you know what he didn't do?"

She looked from one woman to the other. They both shook their heads from side to side, and she had the vague notion that the more she saw them together, the more she realized how similar they were.

"He didn't bother to explain the past," she told them. "He'd given me a lame excuse when he first showed up here—which granted, I let him get away with—but I'd already made it clear that it wasn't good enough if we were going to go anywhere this time. There were issues back then. Things that kept me from being ready, and things..."

She didn't want to tell them about Tiffany. It seemed wrong to share his secrets. But this was her family. If she couldn't share with her aunt and her mother, who could she share with?

"There were issues with him, too," she whispered. She closed her eyes and filled them in on Tiffany, ending with the fact that Mark completely blamed himself.

Both sisters remained silent throughout the story, and then Andie opened her eyes and stared at the bowl of fruit on the counter in front of her. The bowl she'd made with her own two hands. She thought about how much she enjoyed teaching the basket weaving class at the senior center. How she enjoyed creating projects herself.

Mark didn't even know she had that talent.

"He never brought Tiffany up," she told them. "He never asked what I wanted, or what I could do with my life if I left here and followed him to Boston. Just asked me to marry him and assumed I would smile sweetly and pack a bag. And when I *did* get his past out of him…" Another round of tears slipped freely down her face. Her mother reached out with the cloth to catch them, and Andie smiled her thanks. "When he did talk about it, he refused to admit he had a problem."

She picked up her cup of tea, glancing at the pile of wet tea bags now on a small plate, and took a calming sip.

"All might not be lost," Aunt Ginny began, with more hope in her voice than there should have been. "At least you got him to talk about the past. And he loves you. We could have told you that even if he didn't. I still feel—"

Andie shot her a hard look. "Don't you dare say anything about fate. The only fate going on here is that I'm *not* supposed to be with him. This whole time." She shook her head. "Back then…now, he was thinking only of himself.

About how to fit me into his life without any upheaval for him. Without *facing* his own issues.

"No," Andie continued. "He doesn't see me as a partner. He sees me as a responsibility. But the funny thing is, in the end I don't even think he would take on that responsibility. He has commitment issues. He walked away from me once before, he pushed Beth away last year. And he won't even consider that both times had anything to do with his hangups over Tiffany."

Andie looked at the two most special women in her life, so glad they were both there for her. "I'm somebody, too. I have a family, too. I have a life. And all of that is more important than hanging on to dreams of his he's never going to go after. I deserve so much more than that," she ended on a whisper.

Her mother hugged her again, and Aunt Ginny patted her hand. Both of them were misty eyed.

"I'm so proud of you," her mother told her. "So proud for you standing up for what you believe in. And for all those years of going after what you want. I always have been."

Andie gaped at the woman. "What are you talking about? When have you ever been proud of me?"

"Andie," Aunt Ginny said warningly.

Okay, that was rude, but she couldn't help it. She'd always believed she'd done nothing to remotely make her mother proud. She held up her hand to ward her aunt off.

"I know," she said. "I'm sorry, that was rude. But, Mom? I've believed my whole life that I've let you down because I'm not as driven as you. I chose to live on the beach instead of chasing the American dream."

Cassie laughed, the sound bitter and ugly, then surprised Andie with her next words. "You think corporate world is the

American dream? It's horrible. All those stick-in-the-muds. All that red tape locking things up, keeping any real work from getting done. I hated it. Every single bit of it."

"But you wanted something out of your life. I didn't dream that all these years. You worked hard. You had goals. Aspirations."

"I wanted something, yes," Cassie said. "I wanted to be successful. And I was. But I was never happy. In fact"—she spoke softly—"I have to admit I've been a little jealous of you."

"What are you talking about?" Andie glanced at Ginny to see if any of this made sense to her. Ginny merely lifted both shoulders.

Pink patches covered Cassie's cheeks when Andie turned back to her. "Ever since you started this business," her mother said. "I've loved the idea of it. It feels fun. It feels like the me I once wanted to be."

Andie dropped her head into her hands as she tried to process the information. How had her mother never been happy? And she'd been jealous of Andie?

"There is something I'd like to ask you," her mother said quietly. "Something I believe would make me very happy."

Andie lifted her head and asked with her eyes. She was drained at this point, and she still had to go upstairs and talk to Penelope. She wasn't sure how much more shock she could take.

"I'd like to buy into the business," her mother stated. "I won't get in your way," she added in a rush. "I can be a silent partner if you'd rather. The money can be invested in advertising, or maybe to build a reception hall. However you feel is best. But I want to be a part of it. I want to be a part of you and Ginny. And I'd love to help if you'd let me."

Again the earth shifted.

"Mom…" Andie started. Where did she even begin? "I don't know what to say."

Aunt Ginny leaned in. "Say yes, Andie. And tell your mother she can help. She can do your job."

Andie looked at her aunt. "Are you firing me?"

"No, child. I'm telling you that you have options. You could share the job with your mother. You could go work at Gin's full-time. You could go to Boston," she said gently. "If anything there ever changed. Or you can do something totally different. You have choices. That's all I'm saying. You don't have to be stuck here just because it was your idea."

Andie had not once mentioned to her aunt that she wasn't completely happy with the job she was doing. How did she always know what was going through her mind?

The sound of Mr. and Mrs. Jordan coming in through the back doors from their morning walk brought the conversation to a halt. They listened as the couple crossed the living room and headed for the stairs. As their voices carried away, Andie thought about Penny, and about how she had to go upstairs and break her heart.

She looked at her mother. "Before we decide, there's something I should tell you first. It might change your mind about buying into the business.

"I'm not going to change my mind, Andie."

She hurried on. "Seaglass isn't exactly on solid ground at the moment. We have this loan—"

"Do not tell me Phillip Jordan is refusing to pay that bonus," Aunt Ginny whispered harshly. She stood from her stool, hands on hips. "I'll march right upstairs and give that man a piece of my mind if he thinks he can pull that because he's mad at your mother and me. You and Kayla are putting on a beautiful wedding."

"No." Andie let out a real laugh for the first time that day. She would love to see her aunt go after Mr. Jordan. "That's not it, but I promise if he says anything else, I'll let you have a go at him. I'm kind of tired of his blustering, myself."

She paused and looked from her aunt to her mother, realizing she wasn't as ashamed to admit her shortcomings as she would have been a couple of weeks ago. It didn't seem so much like failure today as it did a decision that had to be made. Losing the money would hurt Seaglass, but standing up for Penelope was the right thing to do.

Caring for others was the important thing. Knowing that she was making a difference. She couldn't turn her back on someone just because she needed the money.

"I'm about to have a very crucial conversation with our bride," she said. "And I suspect that when I get done, the result will be that Penelope will no longer be a bride."

"Oh no," Aunt Ginny murmured. "What's happened?"

"I'll tell them."

All heads turned to the doorway, where Penelope stood.

She looked almost as bad as Andie felt. She wore a thin cotton robe that hung open over a short, light-pink silky gown. Bed head and her own set of puffy eyes completed the ensemble. And immense sadness in her features. The anguish tugged on Andie's heart.

She knew.

Poor thing.

Andie stood and pulled Penelope over, giving her her seat.

"I'm so sorry, Penny," Andie whispered.

Aunt Ginny slid a fresh cup of tea over, and Penny grate-fully accepted it. Instead of lifting it to her lips, though, she simply wrapped long fingers around it. Andie noticed that the engagement ring she'd worn was now missing.

Cassie wet another cloth and began dabbing at Penny's face. Andie almost laughed. Her mother had found some-thing nurturing, and she wasn't letting it go.

"He's cheating on me, isn't he?" Penny asked. She trained her gaze on Andie's. "I've watched him flirting with Wendy the whole time we've been here, but I didn't think he was that stupid. But my maid of honor..." Penny took a sip of tea and closed her eyes. "She followed him last night after the guys got back. He went to Wendy's bungalow. And he didn't show back up at his room until several hours later."

Aunt Ginny and Cassie both looked at Andie for confir-mation. Andie nodded, so sorry to witness this happening to such a sweet person. "I'm sorry, Penny. I saw him last night myself. As I was leaving Mark's cabin. I was just coming up to talk to you."

Penny opened her eyes and took another sip. "I appreci-ate that you would tell me. And I'm sorry you have to cancel everything at the last minute, but I can't marry him."

"Oh, honey." Andie gave her a tight hug. "Of course you can't marry him. If you'd insisted on going through with it, I might have stood up during the ceremony and protested myself."

Penny chuckled, but the sound was broken.

"Have you talked to him yet?" Andie asked.

Penny shook her head. "I don't even want to. I thought of asking my dad to do it. He likes arguing with people. But that would be cowardly. Plus, I want to see if he'll lie to my face."

He probably would, but Andie didn't say it.

"You just let me know what I can do to help," she said instead.

Penny nodded absently, then reached out and took Andie's hand. "At least you got Mark out of this. Rob told me you two had once been engaged."

Andie froze at the mention of Mark. She didn't want to talk about the fact that she *didn't* get Mark out of this, but given that her doing so might make Penny feel better, she opened her mouth and told her anyway.

"Actually," she said, "the reason I was leaving Mark's cabin was because we broke up."

"Oh no," Penny whispered, sounding almost as stricken at that as she was over Rob. "You two seem like such a perfect couple."

"Yeah, well…" Andie shrugged and felt the tears returning. "What can you do? Some things are meant to be, and some things aren't."

She did not acknowledge the lifted brow her aunt gave at Andie's last comment.

She and Mark were not meant to be. Now she simply had to get over a broken heart once and for all.

CHAPTER TWENTY-FOUR

Andie stepped carefully from behind the bar Monday afternoon and crossed the floor of Gin's, her hands steadying the largest margarita glass she'd been able to locate. She stopped at the table where Kayla sat and studied the top of Kayla's head as she sat hunched over documents, perusing several lists.

"Ah-hem," Andie cleared her throat.

"Just a sec." Kayla held up the finger of one hand while the index finger of the other continued scanning down the list. "I'm making sure we haven't missed anything for this weekend's wedd—"

She stopped talking when Andie set the giant drink on top of her papers. Slushy liquid sloshed over the sides.

"Give it a rest, Kayla," Andie told her. "It's celebration time."

"You spilled tequila on my spreadsheets."

"I spilled top-grade tequila on your spreadsheets. If I can handle that, so can you." Andie pulled out a chair and sat. "Drink up—this is a party."

Kayla eyed the giant drink with two straws sticking from it, then looked around the mostly barren room. "I'm not sure how two people constitute a party."

"Happy Days Are Here Again" suddenly began playing from the corner as Roni joined the party. Andie smiled and motioned to the piano.

"It's a happy-promotion party," Andie said.

Kayla leaned back in her chair, her eyebrows disappearing beneath her bangs. "Promotion? We didn't even have a successful wedding."

"Which was neither of our faults," Andie patiently explained. She actually felt good that they hadn't had a wedding.

"That won't stop that photographer," Kayla said wryly. "He's going to roast us in the magazine for the circus we had here this weekend."

And it had definitely been a circus.

Saturday morning Kayla had gone into action, letting all guests at the hotel and in the bungalows know that the wedding was off, while Aunt Ginny and Andie had gingerly handled the family staying at the inn.

It had been interesting keeping Rob and Penny apart. Also interesting had been hearing the lies the jerk had tried out on Penny. She hadn't bought any of them, thankfully, and had been on the first ferry out of there. Last Andie heard, Penny and her maid of honor were sitting somewhere in the Caribbean, enjoying an all-inclusive resort on Rob's dime.

Phillip Jordan had been ready to skin Rob alive, but Rob's parents had stepped in to take him out of the firing zone. They'd gotten him out of the house, though they had wisely *not* boarded the same ferry with Penny.

Then there had been the good-byes among everyone else. All had tried to act pleasant, as if they were neither embarrassed nor angry, and after a very long day of helping hold tempers in check, Andie had turned to find Mark standing in the foyer of the inn.

He'd come to say good-bye. And it had lasted for about ten seconds.

She supposed she should be grateful he hadn't just disappeared as he had the last time, but she'd wished he had. Her nerves had snapped, and she'd had to spend the next thirty minutes in her room getting herself back under control.

When she'd returned, Kayla updated her that a few of the guests were staying for the weekend in the bungalows, most in the hotel were sticking around since they'd already made the trip, but all had vacated the inn.

Which had been great. She'd then had time to herself.

And she'd cried even more.

Yesterday hadn't been much better on the tear front, but today she was good. Today she'd spent the better part of the day working through details of her mother buying into the business, and had actually caved on her plan of selling the bar to pay off the loan.

She'd felt it was her responsibility to do so, but given that her mother was investing more than the payment amount, Andie had finally been convinced that selling wouldn't be wise. They made too much money using the bar for wedding events. Not to mention, she was looking forward to spending more time there, now that her mother would be shouldering a lot of Seaglass business.

Andie waved away Kayla's concerns about the photographer. "I stuck my mother on Michael," she told her. "We'll be covering his cost down for another wedding later in the season, and he won't be writing up anything about the Jordan-Masterson debacle."

"Wow. Your mother is impressive. Must have some negotiation skills to not only get him to remain quiet but to come back and give us another chance." Kayla gingerly pulled her folder and the dripping papers from under the drink and moved them to the side. She blotted the alcohol from her lists then enjoyed a long drink of the frozen margarita. "That's a damned good drink, Ms. Shayne," she said around a moan of pleasure.

"Why thank you, ma'am." Andie nodded in acknowledgment, then returned to the conversation about her mother. "And yes, she is impressive. All those years in the corporate world weren't totally wasted." She held her breath for a pause. "She's also your new minion."

"My what?"

Andie shrugged and smiled. "Minion. She's buying into the company, so I can't very well make you her boss, but you're in charge. She's going to take over my responsibilities. But I need you to be the one to keep things going." She studied Kayla, hoping this was what the other woman wanted. She shared Kayla's new salary with her. "You're good with all this, right? And Mom has lots of ideas, so we might be growing even more. We'll hire additional help when the time comes."

Shock registered first, and then a giant smile blossomed across Kayla's face. She leaned across the table and gave Andie a huge hug. Then she took another long drink and shoved the second straw at Andie. "You didn't have to do that," she said. "But thank you. And yes, I'm great with it. All of it. Even telling your mother what to do."

Andie chuckled. She couldn't wait to see if her mother maintained the new "relaxed" Cassie, or if she was going to turn back into "corporate" Cassie. Either way, Andie had no doubt that Kayla could handle her. And she looked forward to seeing it.

"I needed to make sure no one like Celeste Kavanaugh stole you away from us," she told Kayla. Not that she thought Celeste would try, but someone could—and Seaglass needed Kayla.

"Like Ms. Kavanaugh stood a chance."

They grinned at each other across the table, then both dipped their heads and sucked tequila up through their straws. Andie blinked at the brain freeze and did a little pucker for the tanginess. Then she went back for more. She made a mean frozen margarita.

Kayla swiped salt from the rim of the glass and licked it off her finger. Her grin got a little wider. Good tequila worked fast.

And apparently two people did make a party.

They giggled together as they continued working on the drink, warmth heating Andie with every sip, but a few minutes later the ever-studious Kayla pulled her spreadsheets back in front of her.

"We don't have anyone arriving until Thursday for next weekend's wedding, but they have a lot going on. We haven't worked out which events you'll be handling and which ones I will."

She shoved the page over so Andie could see it, but Andie held her hands aloft. "Talk to my mom. She's not going to learn until she does it."

"Come on, Andie. You can't just drop out that fast. I need you."

The sentence struck Andie as odd. She'd felt for a long time that Kayla was the backbone of the business, but it was nice to know she was needed, too. She nodded. Of course she wouldn't just leave the two of them in the lurch. "I'll help out with whatever Mom's in charge of, but I want you to work out the details with her. You're far better at this than I am. You love it more. After this weekend, though, I'm considering a long vacation. Maybe Australia. I'm thinking snow."

She wanted to get away in hopes of having a minute or two when she *didn't* think about Mark. Of course, sitting alone somewhere would probably only make it worse. But getting away would give her time to think about her life in general.

And Mark.

And how much she missed Mark.

She sighed. "I'm also going to be spending more time working at the bar," she told Kayla.

Though she was still trying to figure out just what she wanted to do with her life, she did know that what she enjoyed most was being around people. And not necessarily high-strung brides and bridesmaids. She'd leave that work to her aunt, her mother, and Kayla. She was going to find other ways to be successful.

Offering more classes at the senior center was another option. Granted, it didn't feel like a big, successful career, but it was needed. And she enjoyed spending time with the older residents.

Maybe she'd get into charity work, too. She was good at coming up with ideas, and putting together the right team of people to make things happen. Possibly Seaglass could eventually expand into handling charity events.

All were good ideas. Even if she did still feel her path was a little "less" than what her mother might expect from her. She'd come to grips with the fact she wasn't her mother. And she'd come to grips with the fact her mother didn't seem to care.

Though it was all still very odd, and still made her pause on occasion.

Now if she would just quit crying herself to sleep every night.

CHAPTER TWENTY-FIVE

At least you haven't lost your touch in the courtroom."
Mark looked up from his open briefcase to find
Gray standing on the other side of the counsel table. They'd
been on opposing sides today, and Gray's team had not
come out the winner.

"I've got what it takes, I guess," Mark muttered. He
returned to shoving folders inside the case, ignoring Gray.
He wasn't in the mood for small talk. Hadn't been all week.

It was Thursday afternoon, and he still had four days'
worth of work to do before the weekend. That's what happened when one took almost two weeks off, he supposed.

Which, of course, made him think of Andie. Again.

She'd pretty much been top of his mind since he'd
walked out of Whitmore Mansion five days ago with little
more than a stilted good-bye.

The wedding had gotten canceled. Kayla had organized
travel plans to get everyone out of there. Some had stayed
for the weekend.

Mark hadn't seen the point.

Andie had told him no. And then she'd walked away.
She didn't want him. She wanted her business more. Just like
always. Only this time she was blaming it on him and some

trumped-up excuse that what had happened with Tiffany played some sort of role in his life.

It continued to piss him off every time he thought about it.

"Want to grab a drink?" Gray asked.

"No."

Mark snapped the locks on his case and grabbed the handle. Everyone had filed out of the courtroom. Only he and Gray remained. He was normally one of the first out, but not lately. Lately he sat around and spent every spare minute thinking about Andie.

Damn it!

He'd gone down to Turtle Island for closure. And he supposed he'd gotten it. He just hadn't expected it to involve having his heart handed to him on a platter.

How could she just say no? He'd given her the ring she'd wanted. He loved her. She loved him. They were great together. He could offer her the world.

What in the hell was the problem?

He started down the aisle, and Gray fell into step beside him. She'd said she wouldn't throw her life away by coming to Boston with him.

"Go away, McTavish," he growled. She *wouldn't* be throwing her life away!

Gray chuckled. "You're a breath of sunshine aren't you?"

The word *sunshine* made Mark think of Andie. He gritted his teeth.

He slammed his palm flat against the wooden door, and it swung open with a crash. "And you're a wiseass."

He supposed he should be grateful Gray wasn't the kind of friend who would make a move on Andie when Mark's back was turned. As Rob had apparently done four years ago when he'd gone to the church to cancel the wedding. What the hell had that been about? He'd offered to give her a "good time"? If Mark had found Rob before they'd whisked him away Saturday, he would have put another fist in his face.

What he should do was catch a flight to Chicago and kick his ass now. Andie didn't deserve being treated that way.

"At least I'm not an idiot," Gray said. His cavalier tone pissed Mark off.

Mark turned, aware they now stood in the hallway of the courthouse where they could easily be overheard by anyone walking by. "I'm sure you'd like to rephrase that," he suggested, his tone clear that his buddy needed to back off.

Gray scratched at the underside of his chin, making a face as if thinking it through. "Nope," he said, shaking his head. "No rephrasing. You're an idiot. What in the hell happened down there?"

"None of your business." Mark walked away.

"She spent all day Sunday crying."

Mark stopped. He silently counted to five, telling himself the whole time he didn't care. It was her own fault she'd had anything to cry over. "How would you know?" He kept his voice low and steady but did not look at Gray.

He'd asked Andie to marry him. He'd darn near *begged* her to. She shouldn't have been the one upset.

"I didn't leave until late Sunday night," Gray said. "Roni filled me in."

The sight of Andie standing in Mark's cabin Friday night, telling him he was afraid to take on the responsibility of a family, flashed through his head like a disco ball spinning in a nightclub. Did she really think he would balk on her again?

He could hear her as if she were standing right there. *"I am not your responsibility."*

"You hurt me." "You took advantage of me." "You thought you were more important."

He hadn't.

He didn't.

Did he?

"I will not toss away my life and head on up to Boston."

"I have a family, too."

"I'm not going to walk away from them when they need me."

Mark shook his head, trying to shake Andie free, then walked back into the empty courtroom. Gray followed.

"How did you just let her walk away, man?" Gray asked when the door closed behind him. His voice changed from smart-ass to concerned friend. "She's the best damned thing to ever happen to you. And you lost her twice."

"I need more from you, Mark."

"Or I need nothing."

What did she want?

He had no idea.

Looking at Gray, Mark wasn't sure what to say, but he felt certain of one thing. "She wants something else."

That's why he hadn't gone after her Friday night. Deep down he knew he could never give her what she wanted.

CHAPTER TWENTY-SIX

Rain threatened the late-afternoon sky as Andie bent her knees and tucked into position, ready to snap the football on Hunter's call.

"Blue forty-two!" the kid yelled.

Andie watched the group of boys and girls across from her waiting to charge. They were local kids, ranging from ages eight to thirteen. All regulars for the Sunday pickup games there on the beach. Andie showed up whenever she could, and Roni and Ginger had even started joining them.

"Blue forty-two!"

She looked to the side where Maggie stood, their lone cheerleader, and winked at the little girl. Maggie giggled and raised a bedraggled blue-and-white pom-pom in the air.

"Hut!"

Sixteen people scrambled as Andie passed the ball between her legs.

She blocked as best she could, then took off down the beach as the football went sailing overhead. It shot toward one of the older kids. Hunter was no idiot. He knew who stood a chance at scoring.

A streak of pink flashed to Andie's right, and she saw Ginger charging on the kid, her hand outstretched so she could grab the flag if she caught him.

"Go! Go! Go!" Maggie jumped up and down, arms and legs flailing. It didn't matter who had the ball—she cheered for everyone. It was one of the most beautiful things about young kids. They were exuberant about everything.

It made Andie wonder when that kind of enjoyment started to fade. When did kids begin to grasp the reality of life and that everything wasn't always happy?

And then she thought of Mark again, and her throat clogged up with tears.

Dang, it had been over a week now. When was it going to stop hurting, even just a little?

She hadn't talked to Mark at all. Nor had she expected to. She'd made herself clear. She couldn't do what he was asking. He couldn't promise forever. She wouldn't put her life on hold to wait and see how things between them turned out.

And anyway, she still didn't know what she wanted to do with herself.

Life had been mostly good this past week. Her mother had moved into her own room in the house, and the two of them and Aunt Ginny had been getting along really well. Andie had even insisted that her mother take the ankle bracelet back. After all, it represented the bond between her and her sister. Cassie had begun wearing it every day, same as Aunt Ginny.

Andie had kept the sea turtle charm Mark had given her, though, and had stupidly put it on a necklace she currently had around her neck. She'd bought a long chain so it hung down between her breasts, hiding from everyone, but she also wore it every day.

Mark may be out of her life, but she wasn't quite ready to let him go.

She would get there. She had to. But she was giving herself permission to take her time.

At least this time she knew why they couldn't work.

"Andie?" Roni jogged up beside her. "Where'd you go?"

Andie looked around and realized everyone had gotten back into position, yet she was standing several yards away, her mind in the clouds. Or more like, in Boston.

She started to return to the game, but suddenly couldn't do it. She didn't want to laugh and enjoy the afternoon. There was nothing inside her that felt joyous anymore. She shook her head as her throat tightened. This had to stop. She had to move on.

Instead of rejoining the game, she headed to the edge of the water. Roni yelled for them to continue without them and then followed along with her.

"You okay?" she asked as they separated from the group.

Andie shook her head again. She wasn't sure she'd ever be okay.

They reached the edge of the water and stopped, letting the waves touch their bare feet. A gray cloud moved overhead, and Andie tilted her head back, watching it, wondering if she would ever have any answers. Was she going to go through her whole life like her mother, living but knowing she was just out of reach of...*something*?

"I'm not happy," she finally admitted to her friend. A sigh leaked from her chest, and she repeated the words, more slowly this time, "I'm not happy."

Roni slipped an arm through hers and lightly squeezed. "I know, hon. Not deep down, you aren't. You haven't been in years."

Andie looked at her friend and thought back over the twenty-one years they'd known each other. They used to have the best times there in the summers. They were twelve when they made the pact that they would all someday live on the island. At the time only Ginger was a permanent resident. Andie smiled. Now they all were. Other than during those innocent early years, she'd never believed it would happen.

"I was happy when we were kids," she confided.

Roni nodded. "You were."

"And during part of my college and graduate years," Andie added. "I loved being in school." She just hadn't loved the thought of getting out of school and having to prove herself to her mother.

"You were always the smart one."

Andie laughed. She'd never thought of herself that way, but that's what she and her two friends had always said as kids. She was the smart one, Roni the musical one, and Ginger the homemaker. From an early age Ginger had wanted a husband and kids. And now she ran her dad's business all by herself, and Andie had never seen her happier.

She studied Roni.

Roni was hiding secrets herself, but Andie hadn't pushed her. Something had happened to send her back here. Yet generally speaking, Roni was happy, too.

It was only Andie who had an issue.

They turned the opposite direction from the football game and began slowly walking along the shore.

"I'm going to start babysitting the wedding kids more,"Andie said. Since she was stepping away from the day-to-day activities of the company, she'd offered to take on more of the responsibility to watch after guests' children. It would save Seaglass money they'd otherwise spend hiring sitters.

Plus, she enjoyed it.

"That's good, sweetie." Roni nestled her head on Andie's shoulder as they walked. "What else?"

"What do you mean?"

"You like to fill your hours when you're searching for answers. What else do you have lined up?"

Andie laughed again. Her friend did know her well. "I signed up to teach another class at the senior center. And I talked to the historical society. I'm thinking maybe Seaglass can partner with them for a fund-raiser."

"That sounds good."

They turned around and splashed back the way they'd come. Andie knew what was going on with the impromptu questions. Roni was helping her work through the madness inside her head.

Roni, Ginger, and Andie had gotten together several times over the past week just to talk. About Mark, about life in general. About her mother and how everything there seemed to be magically falling into place.

But her friends hadn't pushed her. They'd merely let her be. Ready to be there for her when she fell. Because Andie knew she would fall. She might have had a good cry that first weekend, but she hadn't hit rock bottom yet. She couldn't start climbing out of the hole until she hit bottom.

"What do you enjoy doing?" Roni asked.

The question caught Andie off guard. "I like kids. I like volunteering. I like making a difference. I just...I want to take care of people."

Andie grew quiet as a realization began to dawn.

What she wanted to do was take care of people.

Kids.

A husband?

She swallowed against a lump in her throat.

Mark?

A pain the weight of a semi pushed into her chest as she fought for a deep breath. She wanted to take care of kids and a husband.

After all this time, and all those fights, this was what she wanted?

She glanced at Hunter and Maggie, at the other children running around the sand, shouting out to one another, and she smiled. She began to breathe faster and tears started trickling from her eyes. That was what she wanted.

Toss in some volunteer work, maybe help out with a charity or two, and she would be content. She would thrive. She would be happy.

Andie knew it as deeply as she knew she wasn't going to get over Mark.

She'd fought the exact thing she wanted because it had seemed beneath her. She was supposed to be like her mother, supposed to be somebody. Have a career.

Yet that hadn't made her happy.

Heck, it hadn't made her mother happy, either.

Though her mother was already happy here, working with Seaglass. That had become clear the instant she'd started helping last week. She was a force. And she and Kayla would make an exceptional team.

And Andie wanted to be a wife and mother.

She wanted Mark.

She dropped to her knees and let the water roll up over her hips as more tears came.

"Oh, Roni," she whimpered.

Roni dropped beside her. Ginger appeared from nowhere and settled in on Andie's other side.

Soon the three friends were soaking wet, with their arms woven together.

"I love him," Andie admitted.

"I know." Ginger murmured. She stroked Andie's hair and cooed softly.

"You did before he ever showed up here," Roni added.

"But I pushed him away. I turned down his proposal."

"You had a good reason," Ginger reminded her. "He walked away before. He didn't think of you, and he just walked away. And if he doesn't deal with his past…"

Nausea washed over Andie, and she bent at the waist, arms crossed tight over her stomach. The ends of her hair dipped into the salty water. "I didn't try. I should be helping him." She shook her head and squeezed her eyes shut. "I gave up on him."

"Shhh." Roni soothed her. She pulled Andie's hair back behind her head and smoothed a loving hand down her back. "You had to protect yourself, hon. You had to do what you thought was right."

"But I sent him home. I didn't even consider trying to help him."

"And he didn't consider doing anything but exactly what he did before. And that didn't work, right?"

Damn Roni and her common sense. Andie nodded, still bent over, curled into a ball.

"So you did the right thing."

Andie turned her head to Roni. "You're saying I'm supposed to be without him? I'm going to hurt like this forever?"

"No, sweetheart." Roni pulled Andie into her arms and Ginger followed suit. "I'm saying he needed to go home without you. You aren't the only one in love here. I guarantee he's missing you as much as you are him."

"But what if it doesn't matter? What if he can't change?"

"What if it does?" Ginger whispered. "What if he can?"

Andie tilted her head back and rested it against Ginger's arm. With her face to the sky, that dark cloud finally opened up and raindrops started bouncing over Andie's face.

She laughed at the picture the three of them must make. The kids probably all thought they were crazy.

But for the first time in her life, she thought she was fine. Really, truly fine. *Good* even.

"There has to be a way," she whispered, smiling now as she thought about Mark and going to him, forcing him to face his past. "For something that's lasted this long and is this strong, wouldn't there be a way?"

Ginger pressed her cheek to Andie's. "Ginny would call it fate," she said.

Andie laughed freely and let her tears mix in with the rain. Yes, Aunt Ginny would call it fate.

And just as she'd seen Aunt Ginny sometimes twist fate to suit her needs, Andie suddenly knew that she was going to do everything she could to twist it to suit hers.

She didn't want to give up on Mark so easily. She didn't want to give up on them.

If she loved him, shouldn't she be there by his side? Helping him through his past?

So they could figure out how to make *them* last forever?

The rain suddenly stopped and the clouds parted, and there above the three of them was a perfect rainbow stretching to the horizon. It looked like the beginning.

And it looked like forever.

CHAPTER TWENTY-SEVEN

Monday evening brought with it the same thing the previous nine days had brought. Exhaustion, and several more hours of work to take home with him.

Mark grabbed his suit jacket off the back of his chair and headed for the door. First he was going to the pub for dinner and a nice dark stout. Maybe he'd check out a hot girl or two while he was at it.

He snorted. "Check out" was all he would do. What was the point? Andie was still right there, messing with his mind. He didn't get through a single hour without thinking about something she'd said or something she'd done. Or how much he missed her.

And he had those thoughts multiple times each hour.

He was sick of it.

"I'm out of here," he muttered to himself. His brother had headed out earlier, so he stopped at his dad's office and poked his head in to say good-bye. Instead of his father, he found someone else.

"Mom?"

Celeste looked up from the papers she was reading on the desk. "Hi, baby."

"Don't call me baby. I'm thirty-one years old."

"And still my baby." His mother rose, and he noticed she wore a slim-fitting black dress.

"Going to a charity event?" he asked.

She looked down at herself and smiled secretively. "No. Your father is taking me out."

"Nice," he said. "Tell him I'm out of here, will you?"

He turned to go, but his mother stopped him by calling his name. He looked back.

She pointed to one of the chairs on the other side of the desk. "Have a seat," she instructed. She used the voice that meant he couldn't say no.

Feeling like a teenager in trouble, he grumbled but crossed the room and lowered himself to the chair. He'd done a good job avoiding her since they'd been back in Boston, and knowing his mother well, he had a good idea what the topic of this conversation was going to be.

He didn't want to talk about Andie.

"I've convinced your father to hire a replacement for when he retires."

Not what he was expecting to hear. "Excuse me? Seems that would be a conversation Jonathan and I should have been involved in, too."

She nodded. "Jonathan was there."

"Oh." Well, hell. "Why exactly did you leave me out?"

"Because we knew you would resist."

He narrowed his eyes. "What are you up to, Mother?"

She sat back down and crossed her hands on the desk in front of her. The innocent look wasn't cutting it. "I don't want you feeling as if you have to stay here your whole life just because your great-grandfather started the firm. There's a whole world out there."

Irritation snapped inside him. "I like it here."

"Yes, but you might like it somewhere else, too. Civil litigation isn't unique to Boston, you know? Your brother will be fine without you. Another partner—"

"Would be a decision I would be involved with."

She dropped the act and eyed him. "You're a moron, Mark. What did you do to lose Andie this time? Do you not know that she loves you?"

Irritation turned to anger. "Butt out."

He stood.

"Sit *down*."

Blood pounded through his system as he glared at his mother. "It is not your place to do this."

"Someone has to," she said. "Sit down, Mark. Tell me what happened."

He paused, forcibly relaxing his fingers from their tight clench, and quickly came up with an easy explanation.

"It didn't work out," he said. He shrugged one shoulder as if he couldn't care less. "We shouldn't have gotten back together in the first place." Lying sack of shit. He shouldn't have let her walk away from him. "She wants something else."

"She wants *you*," his mother insisted. "What did you offer her?"

"What?" Uncomfortable now just standing there, he returned to his seat. "What do you mean, what did I offer her? Andie isn't something you barter for."

"I mean, did you offer to move there? Did it ever even cross your mind?"

"Of course it didn't. Our firm is here. I live here."

"And she lives there." His mother shook her head at him, a look of disgust on her face. "Did you even consider that? She has a career there. She's making a good life for herself. She can't just pick up and leave because you would rather be here."

"You don't know what you're talking about." He did not want to get into all the problems between him and Andie. "And what makes you think I could just pick up and leave?"

She went quiet and sat back in the chair, pressing her shoulders to the leather. The look she wore was one of pride. "Because you're a Kavanaugh. For the woman you love, you should be willing to pick up and go anywhere. You aren't defined by your job, son, but by what you make of your life."

If only any of it were that simple. "And you would be okay if I left Boston? I thought you liked us here. Aren't you the one I hear complaining that you've already lost two sons to other cities?"

"I also get on a plane and go see them. And they come here."

He shook his head, pain returning to his chest. He needed to move on and forget that he wanted Andie. "It's not that simple for us, Mom. She…" He glanced away, embarrassed to admit that he couldn't keep her. "She wouldn't want me there."

"Of course she would. Go to her, Mark. You can work long distance on the important cases. You can open a firm there. You don't have to stay here for us."

He closed his eyes, exhausted. "I'm telling you, Mother, she doesn't want me there. Let it go."

He knew this without a doubt. Andie didn't trust him to follow through with marriage.

He was beginning to wonder if she had a point.

"That is the most ridiculous thing I've ever heard."

It wasn't as ridiculous as what Andie thought. That his problems stemmed from Tiffany.

An unmistakable sound registered, and he popped his eyes open. His mother had the phone's handset to her ear.

"What are you doing?" he barked out.

"I'm going to call and ask her myself."

"Like hell you are." He reached across the desk and snatched the phone from her hand, slamming it onto the base. "Stay out of it."

"I'm going to fix it."

"You can't fix it, Mother. It's not fixable." Their voices had risen until they were yelling at each other, both of them now on their feet, inches separating their faces.

"Explain why not," she growled out.

"Because I killed Tiffany!" he shouted.

Silence echoed through the room as pain flashed across his mother's face. She dropped back into her seat, and Mark forced himself to return to his, reality hitting him as sharply as a bucket of ice water in the face.

He couldn't protect Andie because he'd killed Tiffany.

Son of a bitch, she was right.

And he was screwed. Any way he looked at it.

Marriage wasn't in the cards for him at all. No wife. No kids. No nothing. Just the damned job. The one his mother was trying to push him out of.

Andie had done the right thing by walking away.

They sat there staring at each other, neither speaking. His breathing the only noise in the room. He didn't know what else to say.

Finally, his mother reached out a hand to him. He ignored it.

Her eyes clouded in pain. "This is what you've always believed?" she asked.

"It's what I've always known." No need to tiptoe around it. "I got drunk, and I put her in a car on wet roads in a place she didn't know. Of course it was my fault. Who else's could it have been?"

She shook her head at him. "It was an accident."

"That shouldn't have happened."

"No accident should happen, yet you see them every day. You go to bat for people on a regular basis, fighting that they weren't the cause of them."

That statement gave him pause. He did do that. And he believed it.

But this was different.

He shook his head and stood. "Not the same."

Mark walked out the door, ignoring her plea for him to return, and headed to his car. When he got behind the wheel, instead of pulling out and heading to the pub, he went the opposite direction. He didn't know where he was going, but after that exchange all he wanted to do was drive.

He'd been surprised, actually, to learn that his mother didn't believe Tiffany's death was his fault. He'd always assumed everyone thought it was.

He knew that if asked, Tiffany's father would say Mark was to blame.

His foot pressed harder on the accelerator, taking the busy streets faster than he should. He didn't slow, sliding back and forth between other cars, as the ache inside him grew.

If only he could go back fourteen years, he'd do it differently. Then, maybe, he could marry Andie. He could make her proud.

And he could make her happy forever.

It occurred to him that he hadn't just thought he wanted to take care of her forever. He did, but only in the way that he wanted her to take care of him. By nurturing what they had. Each of them being there when the other needed someone.

Not protect, as if to keep alive. Which was exactly how he'd always thought of it.

Something had changed. He just wanted to make her happy. He wanted to love her, and see her love for him shining back.

And he wanted babies.

Little redheads. He'd seen pictures of Andie when she'd been younger. Her hair had been as red as Ginny's. He could imagine a miniature Andie, with wild red curls, running around.

Maybe a boy, too. Love swelled inside him at the thought of them as a family. He could make her proud. He knew he could. And she would be a wonderful mother.

He glanced around, realizing he'd driven out of the city and had turned into a neighborhood. And then his breath caught as it occurred to him where he was. He was about three blocks from where Tiffany had died.

At one point, he'd come by here every year on the anniversary of her death.

Oh shit. He pulled out his phone and looked at the date. Today was fourteen years since the wreck.

He gulped. His mouth had gone dry.

His pulse sped up and he took the next left. Then another left.

In the distance he could see the tree standing just outside the curve of the road. The car had damaged the bark but hadn't hurt the tree long-term.

That had always struck him as odd. She'd been wiped out in an instant, but the tree just kept growing.

As he neared the spot, he noticed a red pickup pulled over about twenty yards before the curve. He had the thought that it could be Tiffany's parents, but he didn't see anyone around. He pulled in behind the truck and got out. After he stepped across the guardrail and crossed the ditch, he saw him.

Tiffany's dad was stooped against the tree as if in prayer. He clutched a single pink flower in one hand and rested the other against the misshapen bark where Mark's car had once been wedged into the wood.

Mark turned back. He didn't need to be there.

He didn't need Tiffany's dad to see him.

"Mark," Mr. Avery said behind him.

Mark stopped. He didn't move, terrified to look at the man.

He remembered seeing Tiffany's family at the funeral but had been in no shape to talk to them, and neither had they. Plus, what was he supposed to say? Sorry I killed your daughter?

But he was a grown man now. A civil conversation was possible, surely. And if the man threw a punch, well then, Mark deserved it. He turned back around and headed to the tree.

"Mr. Avery," he said as he approached. He nodded politely.

The man was nearing sixty but looked a good fifteen years older.

"It's good to see you," Mr. Avery said. He held out a hand, motioning for Mark to come closer.

Mark hesitantly headed his way.

"I want to show you something," Mr. Avery said. The man sounded excited.

What could he possibly be excited about?

When Mark stepped beside him, he noticed several bushes of pink flowers matching the one in Mr. Avery's hand. They circled the base of the tree on one side. He remembered seeing them there before.

"They bloomed again," Mr. Avery said. "Every year they've bloomed."

Seemed an odd place for bushes like this to be. Mark nodded. "I noticed them years ago. I'm surprised…" He stopped. Why would he bring up the wreck right off the bat? If felt as if his rib cage was trying to crush his organs.

"What?"

Mark shrugged, not wanting to say it but seeing the man was going to push. "I'm surprised the wreck didn't kill them," he said. "I seem to recall there being a lot of dirt disturbed."

"Oh, Mark." Mr. Avery reached out a hand and patted his shoulder. Mark could feel his own muscles bunching under the touch. "We planted these here the year after Tiffany died. Her mother and I. On the first anniversary. They were her favorite flowers—peonies—and they've bloomed every year."

Ah, geez. He'd never known these flowers were here for her.

"That's pretty amazing," Mark said. Especially considering hers hadn't been the only wreck that had happened in this curve. No one else had been killed that he knew about, but he'd heard of several wrecks over the years.

Finally, the city had installed the guardrail.

Mr. Avery turned back to the tree, and a calmness grew inside Mark as he stood there studying the blooms. They were lovely. He could see these being Tiff's favorite flower. They were big and bushy, and they seemed to be too heavy for their stems. They flopped around in all directions, doing their own thing instead of standing up straight as flowers in a vase would.

They were a little wild. And a lot of fun.

"They remind me of her," Mark said

"Yeah?" Mr. Avery looked at him. He nodded. "I know. Out of control. They were her mother's favorite, too."

He chuckled and Mark couldn't help doing the same. "She was so fun to be around," Mark said.

Mr. Avery nodded. A weathered sadness colored his features, but he smiled. "So full of life. Just like her mom." He glanced at Mark. "I lost her last year, you know? Her mother. She was a good woman."

"Oh, sir. I'm sorry. I didn't realize."

He nodded. "We had a lot of years together. And we managed to hold on after we lost Tiffany. A lot of couples couldn't have done that. But we had a lot of love."

Mark understood. Losing a child had to be the worst thing in the world.

The calmness he'd felt only moments earlier disappeared, replaced by the weight of his guilt. He'd taken this man's daughter from him. After all these years, the least he could do was offer an apology.

Bracing himself for backlash, he cleared his throat. "Sir?" he said. "I'd like to, uhm..." Hell. Sound like a child?

Mr. Avery put a hand on Mark's shoulder again. It felt heavy. "What is it?" Mr. Avery asked.

Mark looked at the grass for a moment and blew out a breath. He then raised his gaze to the older man's. He looked him straight in the eye and could hear Andie telling him to grow a pair. He almost smiled.

"I'd like to apologize, sir. I should never have put Tiff in the position of needing to drive herself home that night. I should have gotten her there myself." He swallowed then pushed ahead. "I apologize for taking your daughter from you. I know it changes nothing, and I should have said it years ago, but…" He shook his head; it wasn't enough. "I'm sorry."

Tears filled the man's eyes and Mark couldn't help it, but tears filled his, too.

"It wasn't your fault, son. Is that what you've always believed?"

Mark stared. What? He nodded. "Of course it was my fault. It had been raining, she didn't know the streets. I should have been driving."

"You had been drinking, had you not?"

"Yes, sir."

"Then no, you should not have been driving."

Mark tilted his head in acknowledgment. "I *shouldn't* have been drinking."

"That's true. But your drinking isn't what killed my daughter."

Mark didn't know what to say. He didn't want to argue with the man about it.

"If you knew anything about Tiffany, you'd know she was a bit impulsive."

Mark did smile then. "That was one of the things I liked so much about her. You never knew what she would do next."

"Right. And that included when she was behind the wheel." Mr. Avery stepped away from the tree, and together to two of them walked side by side toward their vehicles. "She hit this tree doing eighty. Did you know that?"

Mark blinked. He looked down the road the way he'd come. He wouldn't think it was long enough to get a car up to eighty.

Her father let out a dry laugh. "Guess you missed that. She liked to go fast. Just like her mother. I have no idea how she got it up to eighty on this stretch, but the reports show she did. It was all her."

"She was mad at me that night," Mark threw out. "That had to be why she was going so fast."

"You're not hearing me. She already had two speeding tickets in the three months she'd had her license. I helped her get out of them so she didn't lose her right to drive. It made it easier on us if we didn't have to take her back and forth to her job." He wiped a tear from his eye. "I shouldn't have done that. Then she wouldn't have gotten behind a wheel. She needed to learn from her mistakes, and I didn't see to it that she did."

"It wasn't *your* fault," Mark stressed.

"No," Mr. Avery said. "But I didn't help. It was an accident. A bad one. But it was nobody's fault but hers."

"No," Mark began.

"I'm so sorry you've carried this guilt all these years. I didn't realize. Her mother and I were too distraught to think of anything but ourselves or I might have noticed."

Mark chuckled wearily. "Sir, my own mother didn't realize. I doubt you would have."

Mr. Avery looked at him then, from head to toe, and gave him a nod. "You might be right. But I wish I'd paid attention anyway. It wasn't your fault, son. Let it go. No one has ever blamed you."

Except me.

He kept his gaze on Mark as if waiting for a response. Mark had no words to give him. Finally, he simply nodded and Tiffany's father patted him gently on the cheek. He gave Mark a lonely smile and turned to his truck.

After Mr. Avery drove off, Mark stood there on the side of the road, watching the peonies sway in the wind. Then that calmness he'd felt earlier came back. It had never occurred to him Tiffany's death might not have been his fault.

He closed his eyes as he stood there and pictured Tiffany back then. She'd been blonde and beautiful, and she'd liked to paint her fingernails in the brightest colors she could find. She'd laughed as if never concerned of what others would think. And she'd always moved fast, no matter what she was doing.

Whether she was walking down the halls at school or being the one to kiss him before he got up the nerve to kiss her first. Or driving well above the speed limit. She'd done everything fast.

How had he not realized she'd gotten his car up to eighty on this road?

She smiled at him in his mind, and then she was gone.

He opened his eyes. He had to go to Andie before she gave up on him for good.

CHAPTER TWENTY-EIGHT

Come *on*, Kayla," Andie said, pounding her hand on the kitchen counter. "I need to go."

"Just one day more, I swear."

Andie dropped her suitcase to the floor. Frustration had her breathing hard. She'd already waited four days since she'd figured out she should be by Mark's side. She wanted to go now. He needed her.

She hadn't called because she'd wanted to surprise him. Thought it might mean more if she just showed up. But that was when she'd intended to go up on Tuesday.

She'd wrapped up everything she could on Monday; made sure her mother, aunt, and Kayla would be fine on their own; and made arrangements for Ginger to handle her class at the senior center this week. Ginger wasn't the ideal substitute in that she was unable to actually construct a usable basket, but until Andie knew for certain that she would be staying in Boston, she didn't want to look for a permanent replacement.

Then Ginny had gotten sick and spent a full day laid up in bed, and Kayla had had one crisis after another with the week's weddings. Maybe her mother wasn't going to work out if they couldn't get through a couple of days without Andie.

The last straw had been Ginger calling at the last minute that morning to cancel at the center. Andie couldn't just skip the class. Too many people looked forward to it each week.

She ground her teeth together and paced the floor.

"What is it that can't possibly wait?" She'd already moved her flight once that day so she could have the class. She needed to leave for the airport soon or she would miss her flight altogether. And now Kayla wanted her to stay another day?

"There's a last-minute wedding at the bar tonight." Kayla used her pleading voice.

"And what's so important about it that my mother can't help?"

"There's just a lot of people. Some of them are older, and they're going to be on the beach. We need all hands on deck." Kayla twisted her hands in front of her and chewed on her bottom lip. She really seemed distraught.

Andie stared at her normally freakishly well-controlled event director, unable to understand what had her in such a state.

"And if I stay, what's it going to be tomorrow? Because I'll tell you, it's starting to feel as if you're making up excuses to keep me here."

"No." She shook her head vehemently. "I swear. There will be nothing tomorrow. But I've got to have your help tonight."

Andie clenched both hands into fists. She pulled her phone out and seriously considered calling Mark. It had been almost two weeks. She needed to talk to him.

He might begin to think she didn't care.

A little voice reminded her that he hadn't called her, either, but she ignored it. He had stupid pride. She knew that about him. It was something she'd decided she was willing to accept.

But she would not give up on them without putting everything she had into it.

She looked at Kayla. "One more day. That's all."

"I swear." Kayla nodded. "I'll make flight arrangements for you right now."

Kayla disappeared before Andie could say anything else. She forced herself to breathe calmly instead of screaming in frustration, then picked up the suitcase that had been packed for two days, grumbled out a "Fine" to herself, and stomped back upstairs.

"We'll leave right before dusk," Kayla yelled from the other room.

Thirty minutes before Andie had planned to head back downstairs, there was a knock at her door. She pulled it open to find her mother standing there wearing a lovely, pale yellow lace tea-length dress. She was carrying another inside a clear protective cover.

"I bought you a nice dress the other day," her mother said, not waiting to be invited to enter the room. Andie looked down at the straight skirt and top combination that was often her working attire.

"I'm fine as I am," she said. She grabbed her purse. "Let's go."

"Just try this on, will you?"

Her mother held the dress up to Andie and tilted her head at an angle as if imaging what it would look like on her. It was beautiful. A peaches-and-cream color with loads of lace, but it was too dressy for work.

"Your aunt and I decided we'd wear nice dresses tonight. So we bought you one, too."

"Stop it." Andie pushed the dress away. She wasn't in the mood. "I don't want a nice dress. I just want to leave."

She looked at her mom. "And why would you have bought me a dress for tonight? I was supposed to be on a plane to Boston two hours ago."

Instead of answering, Cassie hung the dress on the back of the door and went to work on the buttons of Andie's shirt.

"What are you doing?" She slapped at her mother's hands.

"We have to hurry. Now come on." No-nonsense Mom was back.

Andie sighed. Fine. It wasn't a fight worth having. She'd overdress and make her mother happy. Then maybe everyone would leave her alone and let her go to Mark.

But as she slipped the dress on over her head and turned to the mirror, she let out a small gasp. It was gorgeous. It was just body hugging enough to be sexy but not overtly so. The hemline was shorter in the front than in the back. And there was a swell of a tail from the back of her knees to her ankles, ending in a scooped gathers.

Before she could comment, her mother was pulling the gold chain from around Andie's neck.

"Don't." Andie pressed her fingers to the sea turtle charm against her chest. "I want to wear this."

"It doesn't look right with the cut of this dress." Her mother was relentless in her pursuit, and had the necklace off and was replacing it with another before Andie could do anything about it.

"This is one of mine," her mother said. It was an old-fashioned strand of pearls, and actually looked very nice with the lace. "It was my mother's," Cassie added.

Cassie pushed Andie into the seat in front of her dressing table and began fussing with her hair as Andie stared at herself in the mirror. She was being transformed. As her mother twisted the majority of Andie's hair to the top of her head, leaving a few tendrils hanging, Andie met her gaze in the mirror.

"What's going on?" she asked.

Hairpins appeared in Cassie's hands and were quickly fastened to Andie's hair. "I told you, your aunt and I wanted new dresses for tonight. It might be your last wedding with us, so we thought it would be nice to make it a little special."

The thought that this could be her last wedding was sobering. It very well might be. She couldn't help but wonder if that was the reason behind everything going on this week. Did they not want her to go?

She looked at her mother in the mirror again. "Are you okay with me leaving, Mom? I know we just started getting to know—"

"I'm fine with it, sweetheart." Her mother patted Andie gently on the cheek, and then picked up a makeup brush. "I only want you to be happy."

Andie nodded. She'd discussed her plans with her mother and aunt, but she hadn't been convinced that either thought she was doing the right thing. "You didn't say much about it when we talked Monday," she said.

"Only because I was worried about you then."

"And you aren't now?"

Steady green eyes met hers. "Mothers always worry. I have since you were born. Even though you never knew it. But this time…" She smiled and leaned in, brushing her cheek against Andie's. "This time, I can see that you know what you want. I'll support anything you choose when I can see that look in your eye."

The words meant more than Andie would have thought. "And you'll be okay if Mark and I get married someday and I do nothing but stay home and have his babies?"

It frustrated her that she still worried about upsetting her mother with her decisions.

Cassie pulled Andie to her feet. "I'd be more proud than you could ever imagine," she whispered.

Andie's eyes watered. She believed her mother when she said that. She could see the pride shining in her.

"I want this, Mom," Andie whispered. "I only hope I can help him get over his past so we can have a future. I want kids with him. I want a forever."

Her mother's eyes went glassy. "And I want to come visit you and those babies."

"Oh, Mom."

Andie reached for her mother, and they spent the next minute in a tight embrace. When she pulled back, she asked. "You think I can convince him?"

She was terrified she would fail.

Cassie nodded. "You're my daughter. You can do anything you set your mind to."

Pride swelled in Andie's chest as she slipped on the jeweled flip-flops her mother handed her and brushed gloss over her lips. She followed her mother out the door. She couldn't believe how far they'd come in such a short time, and she hated to step away from it.

But she needed to go to Mark. Plus, she imagined her mother and her aunt needed to make up for lost years themselves.

They would all visit. And life would be good.

As Andie reached the bottom of the stairs, Kayla looked up from where she stood by the front door and gave a little gasp. Andie frowned at her, suddenly remembering that Kayla was the reason she wasn't currently heading to Mark.

"We aren't walking over?" Andie asked. Kayla had car keys in one hand.

"We have things we need to take," Kayla answered. She turned and walked out of the house without another word. Cassie followed.

"Fine," Andie muttered. She slammed the door shut behind her. "Did you get my flight set up for in the morning?"

Kayla nodded. Cassie sniffled.

"What is going on with you two? And where's Aunt Ginny?"

"She's already over there," Kayla informed her.

After only a couple of minutes, the car was pulling into the parking lot of Gin's. Andie looked up at the caricature of her aunt and smiled fondly. She loved this place. Even though she didn't plan to be around too much in the future, she was glad she hadn't sold it. She wanted it in their lives. It represented so much of who she was.

The three of them stepped from the car as the sky was beginning to streak with purples and pinks. Andie could make out a crowd on the beach. And yes, there were a lot of older people. But if they'd needed so much help, why had none of them waited for the three of them to get there?

Plastering on her wedding planner smile, she headed toward the boardwalk.

"Let's go in through the bar," Kayla suggested.

"Why?" Andie motioned toward the crowd. "Looks like no one is waiting for us anyway."

Her mother grabbed Andie's hand without a word and tugged her to the side door of the bar. Andie gave up trying to make sense of anything and simply followed, but she noticed Kayla had headed around the outside of the building to the patio.

When Andie stepped inside and saw Maggie Walker, she got an odd sensation in her stomach. The little girl who'd been Sunday afternoon's cheerleader was wearing a pale orange dress with a shiny sash around the middle. Her hair was a cascade of curls. She was holding a vine basket that looked to be one made in one of Andie's classes, and it was filled with a wild assortment of flowers. The jumble of colors inside the basket looked like a florist had gone crazy. When Maggie spotted Andie, she began to bounce on her toes.

No one else was in the bar except for the bartender. He gave Andie a quick smile and ducked his head.

Andie looked at her mom. "What's going on?"

Her mom offered her arm. "We have a surprise for you."

She took her mom's arm and followed her to the patio doors. When she stepped past the sheer curtains, all she could focus on was the gathering just beyond the patio. Everyone was turned in her direction.

There were small torches circling the perimeter of the crowd, and tiny white lights running along the sand on either side of an aisle. The aisle led to a white wicker arch, where a tall dark-haired man stood solemnly waiting. With three separate groupings of flowers attached to the arch, the colors were a mix of reds, oranges, and yellows. The flowers matched the ones in Maggie's basket, and the hues were definitely not the the typical cream and pale bridal colors. The effect was more like an explosion of happiness.

It was perfect.

It made Andie's heart happy.

Under the arch stood Mark in a tailored black suit.

His jaw was tight, and he seemed nervous. Andie could have helped him out by giving him a smile, but she hadn't yet decided if she liked what appeared to be happening.

She noticed Vanilla Bean and Chester Brownbomb standing together in the crowd. Vanilla beamed at her. Surrounding Vanilla and Chester were Andie's other students from the senior center, and in front of the adults were the kids she made a habit of playing with each week. Several of them waved at her with their whole arms, grins spread across their faces.

Other locals filled in the crowd, and Ginger stood to one side of the arch. She was dressed in an orange similar in color to what Maggie was wearing. She looked gorgeous against the backdrop of the approaching dusk, but Andie wondered why Roni wasn't beside her.

On the other side of the arch stood all three of Mark's brothers. His parents and sisters-in-law lined the front row.

Tears began to well in Andie's eyes.

"Why is Aunt Ginny standing with Mark?" she whispered to her mother. Ginny looked brilliantly amazing in a dress similar to her mother's, only hers was a very pale green.

"She's going to perform the ceremony."

Andie jerked her head around to her mother. "What do you mean?"

"If you want her to." Cassie patted Andie's arm where it still rested against hers. "She spent Tuesday filling out the paperwork to get ordained. Mark called Monday night. He asked if I would walk you down the aisle, and if she would perform the ceremony."

"That was his idea?"

Her mother nodded. She gave Andie a tentative smile.

Maybe Mark had paid a bit of attention to what meant the most to her after all.

"He called and invited all the guests himself. We helped him with names, but he set it all up."

"He called me, too," Maggie chirped. She grinned at the adults, showing two overlarge front teeth.

Andie smiled down at the girl. She was going to miss her a lot.

She peeked back at her mother. "So I'm just supposed to walk down there and marry him? After not talking to him for almost two weeks?"

Her mother lifted a shoulder. "It's kind of romantic."

Yeah, Andie thought. She supposed it was. Especially for someone terrified of marriage.

"Are you sure it'll be official if Aunt Ginny does it?"

Cassie nodded. "Unbreakable."

Would serve him right if she did marry him, then. That way he couldn't get out of it.

And then she really got it. Whatever had happened since he'd left, he was letting her know that she could count on him. He would marry her whenever she wanted.

They would no doubt still have issues arise occasionally, but they had a ton of love for each other. Given that she'd been about to chase him down so she could stick by his side anyway, it suddenly seemed silly to stand there one minute longer.

"He also said to tell you that he doesn't want to push you," her mother said. "If you don't want this yet, we'll simply turn this into a beach party. No one will mind. But he wanted to let you know that he's ready."

Andie looked at her mother, at the love shining from her, and was thankful to have her in her life. "I'm going to miss you, Mom," she whispered.

Her mother kissed her on the cheek. "I will never be far away again," she promised.

A single tear slipped down Andie's cheek.

Kayla appeared from nowhere and held out a document. "Sign here. It's your wedding license."

As Andie signed beside Mark's signature, Kayla wiped the tear from Andie's face and smoothed out her makeup. She applied more gloss to Andie's lips. The bartender stepped onto the patio, and he and Kayla signed the license as witnesses, then Kayla thrust a bouquet of white orchids into Andie's hands and pressed something small into Cassie's.

Andie's heart began to race. She was about to get married.

"One more thing," her mother said. She turned her hand over and opened her fingers. "Your aunt and I bought you an ankle bracelet to match ours."

A thin gold chain lay in the palm of her mother's hand. It held a moon charm, a star charm, and the sea turtle her mother had taken from her neck earlier. It represented all three of them. Several more tears slipped out and Kayla sighed at her side.

She once again fixed Andie's makeup before taking the bracelet and stooping to lock it around Andie's ankle. When she stood, she gave Andie a wavering smile. "Now quit making a mess of yourself and go marry that man," she whispered.

Andie nodded. That was exactly what she was going to do.

She kicked off the flip-flops and leaned down to whisper into Maggie's ear, "Let's go get married, Maggie Moo."

The little girl squealed and turned to the crowd. Andie stood straight. She caught Mark's eye, and then she smiled at him with all the love she held inside her. His entire body relaxed. She suddenly wanted to run as fast as she could to the beach. She took a step forward.

"Hold on," her mother said, tugging against her. "Maggie has flowers she's been looking forward to scattering for two days."

Andie glanced at the girl. Maggie nodded, her brunette curls bouncing.

"Then let's do it," Andie said with a wink.

Maggie grinned and took off skipping toward the sand. Chords from a piano started, and Andie jerked to a stop. She looked around. Below the far corner of the patio, just on the edge of the beach, sat a platform that hadn't been there before. It held an upright piano with Roni sitting behind it, and Andie realized she hadn't even noticed it had been missing inside. Her gaze met her friend's and her heart swelled.

"That was all Mark, too," her mother confirmed.

The gesture was the icing on the cake.

She was going to marry that man, right there, right then.

And she was going to love him for the rest of her life.

~

Mark watched Andie step off the patio and head in his direction.

"*Hmph*," Ginny said at his side. "Looks like you did good."

He nodded. He had done good. He'd figured out what was important, and she was now walking toward him.

"About stinking time," Ginny muttered.

He ignored her, knowing she was just teasing him.

Andie glowed as she headed toward him, and he knew that he'd finally done it right.

She reached the front of the aisle, and the music changed to Roni playing the wedding march. Mark surveyed the crowd. He'd called everyone he could think of who meant something to her, and had begged them to be there that night. He hoped he hadn't missed anyone.

Finally, his gaze fell on Andie's and he smiled at her. He was the luckiest man in the world. He would spend the remainder of his days proving it.

As Andie drew near, her arm linked with her mother's, he couldn't miss the happiness shining from her. It wasn't purely for him, he knew. She'd found her way with her mother these past weeks. He couldn't have been more thrilled.

Mark watched everyone in the crowd, all eyes on Andie, and knew his mother had been right. He wasn't defined by his job but by what he made of his life. And he was going to make his life with Andie.

When she reached him, she kissed her mother on the cheek and then looked up at him, and he couldn't breathe.

"I'm sorry," he whispered.

She nodded. "Me, too." She gently touched his hand. "Are you okay?"

The concern in her eyes was his undoing. All the stress of the last two weeks fell away. She was giving him another chance.

"I am now." He wanted to kiss her but held himself back. "We don't have to do this now if you don't want to," he hurried to say. "I know women like to plan their weddings themselves."

Her mouth curved. "And I am a wedding planner."

He nodded. "I probably got something wrong. We can wait. We'll just party. But I wanted you to know that I'm serious. My guilt over Tiffany was holding me back, but it isn't anymore. Now it's just you and me." He grabbed her hands, the bouquet of flowers between them. "But even if we wait, I'm staying here."

"You're what?" Confusion clouded her face. "For how long?"

"I'm moving in," he told her. "Me, you, Ginny, and Cassie. I'm never leaving you again." He grinned wide, thinking that was a lot of estrogen in one house, but he couldn't wait to do it.

"But your job is in Boston."

"And my life is with you." He couldn't wait any longer. He leaned in and pressed his lips to hers. Ginny cleared her throat. He pulled away but didn't glance at Ginny for fear she'd give him one of her looks. Instead he focused on Andie.

"We're hiring another lawyer for the firm. I'll have to make the occasional trip back, but I'm staying here. Will that work?"

Her smile wobbled. "I was coming to Boston for you," she told him. "They kept me from getting on the plane."

Shock registered. He glanced at Ginny, and she smirked. She'd known all along that he had nothing to worry about, yet she'd let him panic and stress over his plans all week. He narrowed his eyes on her. Oh yeah, living there was going to be a blast.

"We're soundproofing our room," he grumbled.

Andie and Ginny both laughed, and Ginny muttered, "I hope so."

A lovely blush covered Andie's cheeks. "We'll work it out," she told him. "I think I could stand to be away from these two occasionally."

The laughter died, and he and Andie stood there staring at each other.

"I love you," he stated. He was pretty sure at least half the crowd sighed at his words.

She nodded. "And I love you."

"So we're going to make this a party, then?"

"Oh no." She chuckled. "I'm not risking you not showing up again. We're going to make this *official*."

Any remaining nervousness left him. She was his.

"I knew I wanted this the first moment I saw you again," he told her.

She leaned in and kissed him. This time Ginny didn't interrupt.

When they parted, Andie turned to hand her flowers to Ginger but paused as she caught sight of Roni standing beside her as well. She had run from the piano to be by her friend's side. She took the flowers from Andie, and both she and Ginger gave Andie a nod. They'd given their blessing.

Andie faced Mark once again and took both his hands in hers.

"Marry me, Mark," she whispered. "I think it's meant to be."

He rested his forehead against hers. "I know it is, sunshine. It's fate."

ABOUT THE AUTHOR

Kim Law wrote her first story, "The Gigantic Talking Raisin," in elementary school. Although it was never published, it was enough to whet her appetite for a career in writing. First, however, she would try her hand at a few other passions: baton twirling, softball, and music, to name a few. Voted Bookworm and Most Likely to Succeed in high school, she went on to earn a college degree in mathematics. Law spent years working as a computer programmer and raising her son, and she now devotes her time and energy to writing romance novels (none of which feature talking raisins). She is a past winner of the Romance Writers of America's Golden Heart Award and currently serves as president for her local RWA chapter. A native of Kentucky, she lives with her husband in Middle Tennessee.

Kindle *Serials*

This book was originally released in episodes as a Kindle Serial. Kindle Serials launched in 2012 as a new way to experience serialized books. Kindle Serials allow readers to enjoy the story as the author creates it, purchasing once and receiving all existing episodes immediately, followed by future episodes as they are published. To find out more about Kindle Serials and to see the current selection of Serials titles, visit www.amazon.com/kindleserials.